D0437423

NO LONGER
PROPERTY OF PPLD

Also available from
Linda Lael Miller

The Parable series

Big Sky Wedding
Big Sky Summer
Big Sky River
Big Sky Mountain
Big Sky Country

McKettricks of Texas

An Outlaw's Christmas
A Lawman's Christmas
McKettricks of Texas: Austin
McKettricks of Texas: Garrett
McKettricks of Texas: Tate

The Creed Cowboys

The Creed Legacy
Creed's Honor
A Creed in Stone Creek

The Stone Creek series

The Bridegroom
The Rustler
A Wanted Man
The Man from Stone Creek

The McKettricks

A McKettrick Christmas
McKettrick's Heart
McKettrick's Pride
McKettrick's Luck
McKettrick's Choice

The Mojo Sheepshanks series

Deadly Deceptions
Deadly Gamble

The Montana Creeds

A Creed Country Christmas
Montana Creeds: Tyler
Montana Creeds: Dylan
Montana Creeds: Logan

Coming soon

Big Sky Secrets

**Also available from
Lindsay McKenna**

The Loner
High Country Rebel
The Defender
The Wrangler
The Last Cowboy
Deadly Silence
Deadly Identity
Guardian
The Adversary
Reunion
Shadows from the Past
Dangerous Prey
Time Raiders: The Seeker
The Quest
Heart of the Storm
Dark Truth
Beyond the Limit
Unforgiven
Silent Witness
Enemy Mine
Firstborn
Morgan's Honor
Morgan's Legacy
An Honorable Woman

Coming soon

Down Range

LINDA LAEL MILLER

LINDSAY McKENNA

A PROPOSAL FOR
Christmas

HARLEQUIN® HQN™

Recycling programs
for this product may
not exist in your area.

ISBN-13: 978-0-373-77813-3

A PROPOSAL FOR CHRISTMAS

Copyright © 2013 by Harlequin Books S.A.

The publisher acknowledges the copyright holder of the individual works as follows:

STATE SECRETS
Copyright © 1985 by Linda Lael Miller

THE FIVE DAYS OF CHRISTMAS
Copyright © 2001 by Lindsay McKenna

All rights reserved. Except for use in any review, the reproduction or utilization
of this work in whole or in part in any form by any electronic, mechanical or other
means, now known or hereafter invented, including xerography, photocopying and
recording, or in any information storage or retrieval system, is forbidden without
the written permission of the publisher, Harlequin HQN, 225 Duncan Mill Road,
Don Mills, Ontario M3B 3K9, Canada.

This is a work of fiction. Names, characters, places and incidents are either
the product of the author's imagination or are used fictitiously, and any resemblance
to actual persons, living or dead, business establishments, events or locales is
entirely coincidental.

This edition published by arrangement with Harlequin Books S.A.

For questions and comments about the quality of this book, please contact us
at CustomerService@Harlequin.com.

® and TM are trademarks of Harlequin Enterprises Limited or its corporate affiliates.
Trademarks indicated with ® are registered in the United States Patent and
Trademark Office, the Canadian Trade Marks Office and in other countries.

Printed in U.S.A.

CONTENTS

STATE SECRETS

Dear Reader,

The Christmas season is a beautiful time of year—full of family, joy and lots of presents! And as many of us can attest, it's also a time when truths are revealed and the gifts we receive are not always what we expected. Filled with mystery, secrets and the love that surrounds this time of year, I am delighted to bring back *State Secrets*.

Holly Llewellyn is a cookbook author and a distant relative of the president of the United States. As such, being something of an outspoken renegade, Holly represents a security risk. Secret Service agent David Goddard is dispatched to keep an eye on her and make sure she behaves herself.

As with any other assignment, David has a plan of action: he'll get to know Holly casually in order to satisfy the government's curiosity. It's strictly business. But when he unexpectedly finds himself taking personal interest, he's no longer sure he can stick to the rules.

Falling in love isn't one of Holly's goals, nor is it part of David's assignment. Still, love plays by its own rules, doesn't it?

Love,

Paula Bird Miller

1

The tall man ran one hand through his dark hair and shifted uncomfortably in his seat. Despite the heavy woolen overcoat he wore, he was still cold. Swift indigo eyes scanned the first page of the dossier. "So what, Walt?" David Goddard bit out, frowning. "She's the president-elect's third cousin. Since when do third cousins qualify for Secret Service protection?"

Walt Zigman made a contemptuous, impatient sound. Apparently, this assignment wasn't exactly dear to his crusty old heart. "It isn't protection, Goddard," he snarled. "Remember that. This is a surveillance project."

David sat back in his chair, drawing his right ankle up to rest on his left knee. "Surveillance," he muttered, suppressing an unprofessional urge to fling the file on

Holly Llewellyn back into the mess that littered Walt's desk. "That isn't our—"

"I know, Goddard," Walt interrupted, falling into his own chair and reaching into one ink-stained shirt pocket for a match to light the cigar stub that was always in his mouth. "I know. I tried to give this thing to the Bureau. I even tried the CIA. But they both threw it right back in my lap. Anything connected with the president or his family is our bailiwick—according to them."

David breathed a swearword. He was tired and he could still feel the bite of the crisp November wind outside. He wanted to get out of Washington and have Thanksgiving dinner in Arlington with his sister, Chris, and her family. He wanted to spoil her kids and lounge in front of her fireplace. "Okay, Walt. So Ms. Llewellyn is our problem. Why am I the lucky one?"

Walt chortled. "Born under the right star, I guess. Come on, Goddard, how bad can it be? You spend a few weeks—maybe a few months—in Spokane. You get the lady to like you. And you make damned sure she's really what she claims to be, and not a courier for that brother of hers."

David had the beginnings of a headache. He opened the dossier again, skimming the rundown on Holly Llewellyn. Twenty-seven years old. Blond. Blue-eyed.

Five feet, seven inches tall. A one hundred twenty-three pound pain. "What makes you think she's running secrets? It says here she writes cookbooks."

"Middle Eastern cookbooks," David's supervisor imparted with dramatic import.

David's mouth twisted into a wry grin. "That alone should convict her," he mocked.

"Dammit, Goddard, keep your sparkling wit to yourself. Can't you see that we've got the makings of a scandal here that would make Watergate seem insignificant?"

"A scandal?"

"Yes! How would it look if the new president's cousin turned out to be a traitor? Isn't it bad enough that her brother sold out? She could be cut from the same cloth!"

David sighed. "That's unlikely, Walt. It says here that she's written a book about Scandinavian meatballs. Good God, maybe she's spying for the Swedes!"

"Stow it."

"Or the Danes. You've got to watch those Danes, crafty little devils, one and all."

"Goddard!"

"She wrote *Fun With Tacos,* too, I see," David pressed on dryly. "Do you think she's working for the Mexicans? Holy guacamole, Batman—do you suppose they're planning to rush up here and take back Texas?"

Walt was leaning into the desk, his meaty hands braced against the edge, his cigar stub bobbing up and down in outrage. "I'm glad you think this situation is funny, Goddard, but it just so happens that the next president of the United States doesn't agree with you! This little lady happens to have a bona fide, card-carrying traitor for a brother!"

David flipped through the rest of the dossier, not so hastily this time. His headache was worse. "Craig Llewellyn," he muttered.

"You remember him, don't you, Goddard?" Walt gibed, going to stand at the barred window of his dingy little office.

Remember? David remembered, all right—how could he help it? Craig Llewellyn's defection had never made the national news, by some miracle, but every federal agent in the country knew the sordid story. "Being Llewellyn's sister doesn't make the lady a security risk, Walt," he pointed out quietly.

"Maybe not. If she wasn't related to our next president, I wouldn't be worried. If she hadn't just spent two months in Iran, I wouldn't be worried. As it is, I'm *damned* worried."

"You'd think the opposition would have caught on to this before the election…" David speculated, thinking of the outgoing president and the no-holds-barred campaign he had conducted.

"They didn't," Walt broke in. "I'll expect your first report early next week."

"Right." David stood up and stretched. Every muscle in his long frame ached with residual cold. "Is this operation covert, by the way, or do I just knock on Ms. Llewellyn's door and flash my identification?"

Clearly, Walt Zigman had a headache, too. "That was a stupid question, Goddard. You've been on White House Detail too damned long. Spent too much time walking the first lady's dog. Of *course* it's covert!"

David shrugged, feeling weary. Maybe Walt was right; maybe he was getting soft. Instead of thinking about this case on every level, a part of him was anticipating a day at Chris's place. The kids would be watching the Macy's parade on TV. The smell of roasting turkey would be everywhere….

He reached for the dossier. "Can I take this?"

Walt waved impatiently. "Yeah, yeah, that's your copy."

David tucked the file under one arm. He supposed it was the forthcoming holiday that was distracting him, stirring up bittersweet memories and half-formed hopes, making him feel far older than his thirty-four years. He tried to imagine Marleen, his ex-wife, roasting turkey or settling a band of freckle-faced rug rats in front of the tube to watch a Thanksgiving parade and couldn't. "You having dinner here, Walt?" he asked, his hand on the doorknob. "Tomorrow, I mean?"

Zigman grinned around his cigar stub. "Nope. Going to New York to see my daughter. Happy Thanksgiving, Goddard."

David laughed, though he had a bereft feeling inside. He thought of Marleen studying chimpanzees in Borneo and wondered if she remembered that she'd once wanted to raise an entirely different kind of monkey. "I'll call you on Monday."

"Right."

David stepped out into the wide, familiar hallway, with its lighted paintings and expensively shabby carpeting. In front of the Oval Office, two agents guarded the heavy double doors. He nodded and they nodded back, their faces solemn.

Downstairs, David left the White House by a side door, then strode through the snow-dusted parking lot to his car. At one of the high wrought-iron gates, he showed his ID, even though he was going out, not in, even though he knew the young Marines on duty, knew their wives and their kids and their collar sizes.

Again he felt lonely. Even quietly desperate. As the White House gate clanked shut behind him, he turned up the car radio in a belated effort to cover the sound.

Holly Llewellyn placed the elegantly scripted invitation in the center of the kitchen mantelpiece. Hands tucked into the pockets of her cozy blue jogging jacket, she stood back to admire it.

"Imagine," said her friend and secretary, Elaine Bateman, from her chair at the cluttered trestle table. "Being invited to the White House! An Inaugural Ball! Good heavens, Holly, what are you going to wear?"

Holly's bright, aquamarine eyes danced with mischief and she withdrew her hands from her pockets to push her chin-length blond hair atop her head. "Nothing," she crooned, striking a cheesecake pose.

"That ought to cause a sensation!"

Holly made a face and went back to the printer set up on the end of the trestle table. She began printing out the pages of "Ka-bobs for a Crowd," the initial chapter of her new book. "I meant that I'm not going," she pointed out. "After all, Toby is in school and I've got my classes to teach and this book to finish. These recipes all have to be tested and retested, you know. And there's my newspaper column—"

"Excuses!" Elaine cried, ignoring the finished manuscript, *Soups are Super,* that she was supposed to be indexing. "Good Lord, Holly, how many times does a person's cousin get elected president? I can't believe you'd miss a chance like this! Besides, you've got until January."

The rhythmic whining of the printer was giving Holly a headache; she closed her eyes and ran her hands down the sides of her trim-fitting jeans. "I'm not going," she repeated sharply.

Elaine sighed in a way that made Holly regret her tone of voice. "Okay, Holl. No problem. Listen, tomorrow's Thanksgiving—do you mind if I take this home and work on it there? I've got a turkey to stuff and ceramic pilgrims to set out in strategic places."

Holly laughed, able to look at her friend now. "Go," she said. "And leave the manuscript here. It will keep until Monday."

Elaine beamed triumphantly, gathering the stack of blue-penciled pages into a neat pile. "You were always a soft touch for ceramic pilgrims," she grinned. "Are you sure you don't want me to work Friday?"

"Positive."

Elaine looked worried now, her wide green eyes watchful. "You and Toby have somewhere to go for Thanksgiving, don't you? I mean, you're not going to sit here and brood or anything, are you?"

Holly felt a tender sort of exasperation. "We're spending the day with Skyler's parents, worrywart. Hie thyself home, before that husband of yours tries to stuff the gobbler on his own. Remember last year? He cut himself on the giblets."

Elaine laughed. "Roy means well," she said, taking her coat from the antique wall rack beside the back door. Shrugging into it, she tossed her glossy brown hair back over her shoulders. "How was he to know that a partially frozen turkey neck can be lethal?"

"How indeed?" Holly chuckled, wondering why she felt so sad. Skyler's parents were nice people; she and Toby would both have a good time at their house.

"Happy, happy," Elaine sang, opening the door to leave and letting in a rush of frigid November air. "See you Monday."

"Monday," Holly confirmed, smiling hard. But when her friend was gone, she sat down on the long bench beside the trestle table and sighed.

Just then Toby scrambled in from the other direction, still wearing his jacket, earmuffs and mittens. His

"Moon Boots" made puddles on the redbrick floor, and he was waving a multi-colored construction-paper turkey in one hand. "Look what we made, Mom! Look what we made!"

From somewhere in the depths of her, Holly summoned up another smile. "Wow!" she crowed. She didn't bother to correct the little boy, to remind him that she was his aunt and not his mother. She never did that anymore.

The seven-year-old was trying to peel off his winter garb without crumpling his purple, green, pink and black turkey. The cold glowed in his plump cheeks and his china-blue eyes sparkled.

After ruffling his irresistible corn-silk hair with one hand, Holly aided him by taking the bedraggled, paste-crusted turkey while he wrestled out of his jacket.

"I've never seen a turkey quite like this," she remarked.

Toby laughed and Holly felt a pang at the sound; he was so like her brother, Craig. Poor, hunted Craig. "I wanted him to be different, Mom!" For a moment, the child looked sheepish. "Besides, all the brown and gold and orange paper was gone."

Holly walked to the huge side-by-side refrigerator and attached the turkey to its surface with magnets. To make room, she had to take down the previous month's construction-paper pumpkin. "No matter," she said. "I like this bird. He has character. Are you hungry?"

"Starved," the little boy exclaimed, and there was a scuffling sound as he made a place for himself at the paper-and-book-littered table.

Holly plundered the refrigerator for lunch meat, sliced cheese, lettuce and mustard. She thought ruefully that another trip to the supermarket was in order.

Carrying the armload of sandwich supplies over to the counter, Holly set everything down to open the old-fashioned wooden bread box.

"We're still going to Skyler's place tomorrow, right?" Toby asked without looking at her.

Holly was closing the bread sack, tucking it back into its nook. She sighed. "Not exactly. We're going to his parents' house, remember? They live in the country."

"Oh."

"You don't like Skyler very much, do you, Toby?" she ventured, buttering a slice of bread, adding cheese and lunch meat and a lettuce leaf.

"Are you going to marry him?" the child countered, watching Holly with pensive eyes.

It was a fair question, but since Holly didn't know

the answer herself, she could hardly offer one to Toby. "I don't know. I like Skyler."

"A lot?"

Holly thought. "Yeah. I like him a lot."

"Do you love him?"

Holly's knife clattered in the mustard jar. "Well—"

"You're supposed to love somebody if you're going to marry them. The way Elaine loves Roy. She's always kissing him and when he says something, she looks at him like every word is real important."

Holly paused, feeling oddly shaken, and gave her nephew a lopsided grin. "You've been watching Dr. Phil again," she teased.

Toby looked puzzled. "Huh?"

"Never mind. How was school today?"

The little boy sighed. "I didn't get any orange paper."

"I remember," Holly replied, putting the finished sandwich on a plate and carrying it to the table. "How come that happened, anyway? Were you late for art class or something?"

Toby was gathering up the sandwich in eager hands. "I had to talk to the principal."

"Toby Llewellyn! Did you get into trouble?"

"No," Toby said through a mouthful. "He wanted me to talk about the new president next week at assembly."

A jolt of mingled alarm and fury raced through Holly; she had to take a deep breath before she could speak calmly. "What? How did he know—"

Toby shrugged. "Maybe there was something in the paper. Mr. Richardson was pretty disappointed when I told him I didn't know the president."

Holly was pacing the floor, her hands tucked into the hip pockets of her jeans. The celebrity of being a cookbook author was one thing—only a select group of people cared one way or the other, of course—but this shirttail relationship to the future president could get to be a real problem. Suppose reporters started taking an interest? Suppose what Craig had done got talked about? Toby could be hurt or even put in real danger!

"Did you see any newspaper people, Toby? Did anybody ask you questions?"

Toby shook his head. "Can I watch TV?"

Holly nodded somewhat impatiently. "You'll tell me if anyone you don't know tries to talk to you, won't you, Toby?"

"Sure. Is there any lemonade?"

Agitated, Holly forced herself to stop pacing. There was no reason to panic, no reason. After all, she and Craig were only distantly related to the new president.

"Mom?"

"Cocoa. I'll make you a cup of cocoa. It's too cold for lemonade."

"Okay," Toby agreed amiably, on his way out of the kitchen. A moment later, as she searched the cupboard for a saucepan in which to prepare the cocoa, Holly heard the television set in the next room blaring. Her hands trembled as she collected the milk, salt, sugar and chocolate.

Oh, my God, she thought. *Craig, what have you done to us? What have you done to all of us?*

She reflected on her brother's problems as she made the cocoa and carried it into the family room to Toby. The telephone shrilled and Holly jumped, startled out of her skin. She raced back into the kitchen and grabbed up the receiver. "H-hello?"

"Hello, kitten," said the familiar masculine voice on the other end.

Holly sank into the chair at her small desk, her knees wobbly. Skyler. It was only Skyler. She was so glad that she didn't even ask him not to call her by that silly, condescending nickname. "Hi," she said.

Skyler cleared his throat. Skyler always cleared his throat when he was about to suggest something he expected Holly to oppose. "Listen, Holl, I was wondering—why don't you and I and the kid just drive up to my folks' place tonight, instead of waiting until tomorrow? I could close the shop early."

Holly bit her lower lip, considering. She hated the way Skyler always referred to Toby as "the kid," as though he didn't have a name. But confronting him about it had about as much effect as asking him not to call her "kitten." Which was none at all.

"Holly?" Skyler prompted when the silence grew too long. "Are you still there?"

"I was just—I was just thinking."

"Is it that hard to decide?" he snapped, impatient now.

Holly drew a deep breath and let it out slowly before answering. "No, Skyler, of course not. But, well—"

Skyler made an exasperated sound. "I suppose you're afraid I'll want you to sleep with me. In my parents' house, Holly? Give me some credit, will you?"

He was being unusually defensive, Holly thought, but then sex was an issue between them. While Holly was certainly no innocent, she wasn't ready for that kind of intimacy, not with Skyler Hollis at any rate. "Sky."

"Well? That is what you were thinking, isn't it?"

Holly sighed as she rubbed her aching temples with a thumb and forefinger. "Yes. And I refuse to discuss it over the telephone."

Skyler's struggle for equanimity was almost audible.

"Right," he said presently. "Do I pick you up tonight or not, Holly?"

"What time would we leave?"

"I can be ready in about an hour and a half. We could eat dinner on the way if you'd like."

Holly found herself smiling in spite of the odd tension Skyler always managed to inspire in her. "That sounds like a good idea. I really don't feel like cooking."

Skyler chuckled. "Little wonder."

"On the other hand, I've got a freezer full of experimental ka-bobs. Test run from yesterday."

"I'm in no mood to be a guinea pig," Skyler retorted quickly, and there was a disturbing note of conviction in his voice. "I'll see you at—" he paused and Holly could imagine him looking at his thin gold watch "—six-thirty."

"Six-thirty," Holly confirmed, and after a few perfunctory words of parting, they both hung up.

Somebody should have said, "I love you," Holly thought as she left the kitchen.

Skyler stood before the mantelpiece, frowning at the invitation to the Inaugural Ball. He was a tall man with sleek, fair hair, an altar-boy face and elegant, long-fingered hands. The owner of a very successful stereo-

and-television dealership, Skyler was prosperous, and his tailored gray slacks and tasteful cashmere sweater were meant to convey that to even the most casual onlooker.

Holly stood watching him, waiting, her hands in the pockets of her black corduroy skirt. With it she wore high leather boots, a burgundy blouse and her black velvet blazer. Her hair, cut in a layered, easy-care style, glistened, and her makeup was perfect.

"You didn't tell me you knew—" Skyler began, pensively, turning to frown at her.

"I know lots of famous people, Skyler."

"Yes," Skyler mused, one perfect golden eyebrow arched in speculation, "but shaking somebody's hand on *The Today Show* and getting invited to an Inaugural Ball are two different things."

Holly folded her arms and allowed herself a wry smile, though inside she felt shaky. She always did with Skyler; his very presence seemed to evaporate her self-confidence. "Howard is a distant cousin, Skyler. I didn't mention it because I didn't think it mattered."

"Howard! You call the next president of the United States 'Howard'?"

Holly shrugged. "It's his name, Skyler."

"Still—"

Suddenly Holly was impatient. "I'm not going to the

ball anyway," she said, reaching for her purse, which sat on the corner of her desk. "Shall we go? The traffic will be horrendous and it's still snowing."

Skyler nodded distractedly, but even as they left the kitchen, he kept casting his eyes back to the invitation. "Right," he said.

Once Toby and his suitcase, which also contained Holly's things, had been tucked into the tiny back seat of Skyler's sleek, sporty car, and the boy had been carefully buckled in by a seat belt, Holly glanced quickly at her old-fashioned brick house and felt a sweeping, dismal sort of loneliness.

Mentally, she shook herself. Good heavens, she was acting as though she would never see her cozy home again.

The traffic, as Holly had predicted, was terrible. The number of cars leaving the city was equaled only by the number of cars coming in, and the snow swirled and spiraled in front of the windshield, making it almost impossible to see.

"We're in hyperspace!" Toby cried in delight. Out of the corner of her eye, Holly saw Skyler grimace and tighten his grasp on the steering wheel.

She let her head rest against the back of the seat and closed her eyes. Skyler Hollis was what her mother might have called a "catch," with his good looks and his flourishing business, but his antipathy toward Toby, carefully hidden though it was, disturbed Holly. She wondered if he felt that way about all children or just her nephew in particular.

An hour and a half later, when they had eaten at a roadside restaurant and were again on their way, Toby asleep in the back seat, she broached the subject. "Do you want children, Skyler?"

He glanced at her and then turned his attention back to the hazardous road. "Of my own? Most men do, Holly."

Holly sat up a little straighter. "Of my own," he'd said. "In other words, you wouldn't accept Toby?"

Skyler's clean-shaven jaw worked for a moment, and his narrow shoulders grew tense. "Your brother will probably come back for him one day, Holly. You told me that yourself."

Holly sighed and looked out the window at the fierce flurries of snow. She had told Skyler that, it was true. But now she had grave doubts that her brother would ever actually reclaim his son or be in a position to take care of him. After all, Toby's mother was dead, and though few people knew it, Craig was a wanted man, suspected of espionage. It was possible, in fact, that he wasn't even in the country.

"Craig won't come back," she said quietly, after a long silence.

"How could he not come back?" Skyler demanded angrily. "You've got his kid!"

His kid. When Skyler said that, used those simple, everyday words, it always sounded inhumane. "And I want to keep him, Skyler. Craig is in no position to be a real father and besides, I love Toby. I love him very, very much."

There seemed to be nothing to say after that. Skyler shoved a classical CD into the slot on the dashboard and the car was filled with thunderous Beethoven.

Chris's kitchen was a bright, warm, cluttered place. The walls were graced with shining copper utensils and a fire crackled in the huge wood-burning stove in one corner of the room. Two long shelves held the largest collection of cookbooks David had ever seen.

Frowning, he took down a copy of *Fun With Tacos* and studied the colored photograph of the author on the back cover. Tousled, honey-colored hair, enormous blue-green eyes. Holly Llewellyn.

"Taking up the culinary arts?" Chris asked mischievously, standing beside him.

Startled, David thrust the thin volume back into its place on the shelf and shook his head.

Chris, a lovely woman with dark hair and eyes, laughed warmly and hugged her brother. "We live in a new age, you know. Men are actually cooking, among other things."

A new age. David's mind caught on those words—he was uneasy, even jumpy. He had the strangest feeling that he was on the edge of something momentous, something that would change his life forever. He took Holly Llewellyn's cookbook down from the shelf again, turned it over and studied the captivating face on the back.

Llewellyn, he thought, if you turn out to be a fink, I'm not going to be able to take it.

2

Holly looked with a jaundiced eye at the mechanical department-store Santa Claus nodding beside the escalator. Thanksgiving is over, she thought ruefully, so bring on Christmas.

In the toy section to her left, a horde of shoppers were engaged in a good-natured battle of some sort.

Reaching the next floor and the cookware section of the large store, Holly found Elaine already there, her hair pinned to the top of her head, a clipboard in hand.

"What's going on downstairs?" Holly asked irritably. The weekend with Skyler and his parents had been a disaster.

Elaine chuckled but did not look up from the list she was going over. "They got in a shipment of Webkinz."

Shrugging out of her winter coat, Holly assessed the room. The store had done a good job of setting up; there were tables, aprons and even chefs' hats for all the students. In the cooking area, where Holly would demonstrate the fine art of baking fruitcake, an assortment of copper utensils had been set out on the counter.

She peered at Elaine's clipboard. Normally, twelve students were accepted for her popular cooking classes, but this time the list showed thirteen names. "David Goddard? Who the devil is that?"

Elaine gave her friend and employer an understanding, patient look. "There's always room for one more, right?" She grinned. "The guy was so eager...."

Holly was annoyed and tired. All she wanted to do was spend the night at home, in front of the TV or better yet, in a hot bath with a book. Anywhere but in this posh downtown department store, teaching thirteen people how to bake fruitcake. "Elaine," she began stiffly, "this is a popular class. There is a waiting list several months long, in case you've forgotten. So where do you get off letting some bozo walk in and sign up just because he's eager?"

Elaine colored prettily. "Actually, he's better than eager. He's a hunk."

"Great! You let him in because he was good-looking!"

Elaine shrugged. "What can I tell you? I looked up into those navy blue eyes and I could not deny the man ten lessons and a chef's hat."

Holly muttered an expletive and flung down her purse and coat. "I'll be glad to deny him for you," she snapped, washing her hands at the gleaming steel sink that was part of the store's fully equipped kitchen. "Where is he?"

"Downstairs, I think, in the toy department," Elaine replied, unruffled, as she checked the supplies of flour, sugar and assorted other ingredients against another list on her clipboard. "He said something about buying a couple Webkinz for his nieces."

Holly found an apron and put it on over her jeans and cotton shirt. Despite repeated pleas from the store's publicity director, she refused to wear a chef's hat. "I don't know why I agree to do these cooking classes, anyway," she muttered.

"You have a contract with the store," came the blithe reply from her secretary. "And they pay you big bucks."

"Thanks for reminding me."

Elaine looked up from her clipboard and made a face. "Anytime, boss."

Holly couldn't help it; she had to grin. "I don't know how you put up with me. I've been a grouch all day and I'm sorry."

Elaine sighed. "A weekend with Skyler Hollis would do that to anybody. Everything checks out, Holly. Could I go now? Roy and I are going to have dinner out and then do some early shopping."

"Go. Leave me here to tell the hunk that he can't learn to bake fruitcake." Holly paused and assumed a pose of mock despondency. "The help you get these days."

Elaine laughed. "When you see him, you'll let him stay. Believe me, God was in a good mood the day He threw this dude together. Everything is definitely in the right place."

"Elaine Bateman, you are a happily married woman!"

The pretty brunette was pulling on her coat. "Yeah. But I'm not blind," she twinkled, before taking up her purse and starting off toward the escalators.

Holly was alone for about five minutes, and then a heavy, earnest-looking man arrived. She asked his name—it was Alvin Parkins—and checked it off on Elaine's list. One by one, the other students came, some of them bringing copies of Holly's books to be autographed.

And then he showed up. Number Thirteen. The intruder. At the very first sight of him, Holly's stomach did a nervous flip.

He was tall and his hair was very dark, neatly cut, and his eyes were a piercing navy blue, just as Elaine had said. He wore blue jeans, a soft white sweater and a brown leather jacket and under each of his powerful arms, he carried a plush toy.

Holly lifted her chin, squared her shoulders and approached him. "Mr. Goddard?"

He tilted his head slightly, in acknowledgment or greeting or both. His cologne was musky and Holly found herself trying to identify it by name.

Holly glanced at the toys, trying to delay the moment when she must tell this man that there simply wasn't room for him in the fruitcake class. "Mr. Goddard—I—" Holly cleared her throat. "The fact is, Mr. Goddard, that there just isn't…there just isn't room in this class for another person. I'm sorry."

He set the toys down on one of the tables and calmly removed his jacket. He didn't look as though he planned to go anywhere. "I'm sorry, too. That it's a problem, I mean. But your secretary took my money and told me I had a place in good old Fruitcake 101 and I'm staying."

Holly felt the color rising in her face. "You're going to be difficult, aren't you?"

David Goddard smiled and folded his arms, stirring that appealing musky scent and touching something deep inside Holly. "If necessary," came the simple reply.

To hide her annoyance, Holly looked down at her watch. It was time to start the class and all the other students were there, ready to begin. It wouldn't do to make a scene in front of them and besides, Elaine had told the man he could participate. "All right, then," she muttered, "you can stay."

"Thank you," he replied, and the deep warmth in his voice soothed Holly somehow, taking away the anger that had arisen at his stubbornness.

David Goddard proved to be an attentive student, listening closely to every word Holly said, watching every move she made. She could almost feel the steel-trap agility of his mind.

When the class was over and Holly was cleaning up, he stayed behind to help. Without a word he rolled up his sleeves and began running hot water into the sink.

Holly gathered mixing bowls and spatulas and bread pans and brought them to the counter. It was odd, the feeling she had—as though they were old friends instead of strangers, washing dishes together in a homey kitchen instead of a busy department store.

"This is quite a setup," he remarked, up to his elbows in hot, soapy water.

Holly found herself smiling. "I know. I was impressed the first time I saw it, too." And the first time I saw you, Number Thirteen.

"Did they put all this in just for you?"

She shook her head and took a dish towel from a top drawer. "I think it was a demonstration kitchen at first—you know, so people could see how the appliances would look in a home setting. When I started to become well-known, Cookware and Books put their heads together and came up with the idea that I should teach classes here."

David smiled. He had a nice smile, she noted, a smile touched with humor. Full of straight white teeth. But what was that sad detachment in the depths of his ink-blue eyes?

"Doesn't that take up a lot of your time? Teaching, I mean?" he asked.

Holly dried a lacquered copper mixing bowl to a red-gold shine. She liked the way it looked, so bright and cheery. "I guess it does. I travel a little, write my books. And I keep up a weekly newspaper column, too." She paused, then shrugged. "I like teaching, though. I get to meet new people that way."

"You don't meet people when you travel?"

She smiled again, wearily. "Not really. I take classes in other countries, and sometimes I'm the only student. It's precise, exhausting work and I usually don't even get to see the sights, let alone strike up lasting friendships. What do you do for a living, Mr. Goddard?"

"Call me David or I'll never tell," he retorted, and even though his glance was pleasant, Holly had a feeling that he was stalling, for some reason.

"All right. What do you do for a living, David?" she insisted, watching him.

The navy blue eyes were suddenly averted; he was concentrating on scrubbing a baking pan. "I'm in law school at Gonzaga," he finally answered.

The answer seemed incomplete somehow. David Goddard was in his mid-thirties, unless Holly missed her guess. Surely old enough to be through with college, even law school. On the other hand, lots of people changed careers these days. "What kind of lawyer are you planning to be? Corporate? Criminal?"

He took up another baking pan. "Actually, I'm taking review courses. I graduated several years ago, but I haven't been practising. I thought I'd better brush up a little before I tackled the Bar Exam again."

"The Bar Exam? I thought you only had to take that once."

"It varies from state to state. I didn't study in Washington."

He was hedging; Holly was sure of it. But why? "Where did you study?"

David still would not look at her. "Virginia. Do they pay you extra for washing dishes?"

The sudden shift in the conversation unsettled Holly, as did something she sensed in this man. In a flash it occurred to her that he might be a very clever reporter looking for a story. Her cooking career usually didn't generate a lot of interest, but being third cousin to the next president of the United States just might. And what if he knew about Craig?

Holly paled and withdrew a little. "I can finish this myself," she said stiffly. "Why don't you go?"

Now the inky gaze was fixed on her, impaling her, touching that hidden something that did not want to be touched. "Is there a sudden chill in here or am I imagining it?" he countered.

Holly kept her distance. Gone was the feeling of companionship she had enjoyed earlier. There was danger in this man; there was watchfulness. Why hadn't she noticed that before? She fielded his question with one of her own. "Why would a lawyer want to learn to bake fruitcake?" she asked.

David went right on washing, his hands swift and strong at the task. "For the same reasons the other people in this class do, Holly. There was a bookkeeper, if I remember correctly, and a construction worker—"

"Maybe a journalist or two," she put in sharply, glaring at him now.

"A journalist?" He looked honestly puzzled for a moment, and then a light dawned in the blue depths of his eyes. "You think I'm a reporter," he said.

"Are you?"

"No," came the firm and immediate reply. And Holly believed David Goddard, though she couldn't have explained why.

"You really want to bake fruitcake?" Did she sound eager? Lord, she hoped not.

David laughed and touched the tip of her nose with a sudsy index finger. "I really want to bake fruitcake."

They finished cleaning up and David lingered while Holly put on her coat and reached for her purse.

"Was there something else?" she asked, trying to keep

her voice level. For some reason Number Thirteen had a strange effect on her.

"Yes," he answered. "I plan to walk you to your car. It's late and I don't want you to get mugged."

Holly felt warm. Protected. Though she cherished her independence, it was nice to have someone looking out for her that way. "Thank you," she said.

Her car was in a parking tower in the next block, isolated and in shadow. It probably wasn't safe, walking there alone, but she hadn't thought of that in her hurry to get to the store and conduct her class. She was glad David was with her.

He waited beside her sporty blue Toyota until she had found her keys, unlocked the door and slid behind the wheel. Toby's model airplane, a miniature Cessna flown by remote control, was on the seat, and she moved it in order to set down her purse and the small notebook she always carried.

"Is that yours?" David asked with interest, his eyes on the expensive toy.

"Actually—" Holly grinned "—it belongs to my nephew, though I do admit to flying it now and then up at Manito Park."

Again there was an unsettling alertness in David, as

though he was cataloging the information for future reference. But why would he do such a thing?

"I have a plane like that," he said, and Holly ascribed her instant impression that he was lying to weariness and an overactive imagination.

David Goddard was a kind, attractive man, not a reporter or an FBI agent. She was going to have to stop letting her fancy take over at every turn or she would become paranoid. She said goodbye, started the car and backed out of her parking space.

There was a light snow falling and Holly drove up the steep South Hill at a cautious pace, her mind staying behind with David Goddard.

He *could* be a reporter, she thought distractedly as she navigated the slick, slushy streets. He could even be an FBI agent hoping to find Craig.

Holly laughed at herself and shook her head. "You'd better take up writing fiction, Llewellyn," she said aloud. "You've got the imagination for it."

But even as she pulled the car to a stop in her own driveway, even as she turned off the engine and gathered up her purse, her notebook and Toby's airplane from the seat, she couldn't shake the conviction that David Goddard was something more than a second-time law student who liked to cook.

Inside the house, Holly found her housekeeper and favorite babysitter working happily in front of the living room fireplace. Madge Elkins was a middle-aged woman, still trim and attractive, and her consuming passion was entering contests.

Now, she was busily writing her name and address on one plain white 3-by-5-inch piece of paper after another.

"What are you going to win this time, Madge?" Holly asked pleasantly, putting down the things she carried and getting out of her snow-dampened coat.

"A computer system," Madge replied, tucking a paper into an envelope and sealing it with a flourish. "Printer, software, monitor, the whole shebang."

Another person might have laughed, but Holly had known Madge for several years and in that time had seen her win more than one impressive prize in contests. A car, for instance, and a mink coat. "Is Toby sleeping?"

"Like the proverbial log," Madge answered, gathering a stack of envelopes, all addressed and stamped, into a stack. "You had a couple of phone calls—one from Skyler and one from a man who wouldn't leave his name."

Again Holly felt uneasy. "What did he say? The man who wouldn't give you his name, I mean?"

Madge shrugged, fussing with her contest paraphernalia. "Just that he'd call back. Skyler wants you to call him."

Holly was suddenly testy. If Skyler wanted to talk to her, he could darned well call back. She saw Madge to the door and then headed off toward the kitchen, planning to take one of her experiments out of the freezer and zap it in the microwave. She'd been running late before cooking class and hadn't had a chance to eat dinner.

Just as the bell on the microwave chimed, so did the telephone. Muttering, Holly dived for the receiver, afraid that the ringing of the upstairs extension would awaken Toby.

"Hello?" she demanded impatiently.

The voice on the other end of the line was haunted, shaky. "Sis?"

Holly's knees gave out and she sank into the chair at the desk. "Craig! Where are you? What—"

Her brother laughed nervously and the sound was broken and humorless, painful to hear. "Never mind where I am. You know I can't tell you that. Your phone might be bugged or something."

"Craig, don't be paranoid. Where are you?"

"Let's just say that this call isn't long-distance from Kabul. How's Toby?"

Holly deliberately calmed herself, measuring her

tones. She was desperate not to panic Craig and cause him to hang up. "Toby is fine, Craig. How about you?"

"I'm all right. A little tired. More than a little broke."

Holly closed her eyes. So that was the reason for his call. Money. Why was she always surprised by that? "And you need a few bucks."

"You can spare it, can't you?" Craig sounded petulant, far younger than his thirty-six years. "You're a rich lady, sis. Didn't I see you on *Ellen* a few months ago?"

"Craig, come home. Please?"

He made a bitter, contemptuous sound. "And do what? Turn myself in, Holly? Give me a break—I'll be in prison for the rest of my life!"

"Maybe not. Craig, you're not well. You need help. And I promise that I'll stand by you."

"If you want to stand by me, little sister, just send a cashier's check to the usual place. And do it tomorrow if you don't want me to lose weight."

"Craig, listen to me—"

"Just send the money," he barked, and then the line went dead. Holly sat for five minutes, letting her kabob get cold in the microwave, holding the telephone receiver in her hand and just staring into space.

Finally she hung up, forced herself out of the chair, and took the ka-bob from the microwave. Although she ate, she tasted nothing at all. The ka-bobs she had taken such pride in making might as well have been filled with sawdust.

David Goddard locked the two Webkinz into the trunk of his rented car, shaking his head as he remembered the way he'd had to scramble for them. He sighed, then grinned. The kids would like them, so it had been worth a few scars.

On his way back to the parking garage's lonely elevator, he passed the place where Holly's Toyota had been. Instantly, his mind and all his senses brimmed with the scent and image of her.

He reached the elevator and punched the button with an annoyed motion of his right hand. Walt Zigman was full of sheep-dip if he thought that woman was capable of espionage. Holly Llewellyn was harried and she was haunted, but she was nobody's flunky.

The elevator ground to a stop; the doors swished open. David stepped inside and punched another button. He smiled to himself, thinking of the first fruitcake he'd ever put together in his life. It was a good thing no one had bothered to taste it; his cover would have been blown then and there. He'd been too lost in Holly Llewellyn's aquamarine eyes to concentrate on baking.

Baking. He rolled his eyes. For this I went to law school, he thought. For this I walked the first lady's dog.

He reached the first floor of the parking garage, where there was a wine shop and an old-fashioned ice-cream parlor. Ice cream, in this weather? David shivered and lifted his collar before stepping back outside, onto the street.

At the corner, he paused. Gung ho Christmas shoppers surged past him when the light changed, carrying him along. He went back into the department store where Holly had taught her class and again braved the toy department. This time he bought an airplane, a model that would fly by means of a small hand-control unit. Manito Park, she'd said.

Half an hour later David entered his apartment, acquired only two days before, with mingled relief and reluctance. It was a small place, furnished in tacky plaids. The carpet was thin and the last tenant had owned a dog, judging by the oval stains by the door and in front of the fold-out sofa bed. At least he had a telephone. David went to it and, with perverse pleasure, punched out Walt Zigman's home number.

It was after one in the morning on the East Coast and Walt's voice was a groggy rumble. "Who the——"

"Goddard," David said crisply, grinning. "I said I'd report Monday. This is my report."

Zigman swore fiercely. "Goddard, did anybody ever tell you that you're a son of a—"

"I met her."

"Holly Llewellyn?" Walt's interest was immediate. Clearly, he was now wide-awake. "How did you manage that so fast?"

"Simple. I bought yesterday's paper and read the food section. There was a write-up about her new class."

"Her new class in what?"

David closed his eyes. There was no way out of this one. "Fruitcake," he answered reluctantly.

Zigman laughed. "Fitting," came his rapid-fire reply, just as David had expected.

"You're getting corny in your old age, Walt."

"Did you find out anything?"

David unzipped his jacket and flung it down on the couch. It covered the toys and the model airplane in its colorful box—he'd be up half the night assembling that sucker. "Sure," he snapped. "She fed me grapes and poured out the whole sordid story of her life in the underworld."

"Don't be a smart—"

"I met her. That's all. But I can tell you this much, Walt—she's no traitor. I'm wasting my time here."

"You're getting paid for it. Keep your eye on the ball, Goddard. When it's time for you to come back to D.C. and follow the new first lady around, I'll let you know."

This time it was David who swore. "Tell me, Walt," he began dryly, "does she have a dog?"

"Three of them," said Walt with obnoxious satisfaction. "By the time the new first family takes up residence, you'll be back on good old Pennsylvania Avenue, passing out poochie treats."

"You're funny as hell, you know that? In fact, why don't you take your goddamned job and—"

"Goddard, Goddard," Walt reprimanded in his favorite fatherly tone. "Calm down, I was just kidding you, that's all. You're a damned good agent."

Agent. If he hadn't felt like screaming swearwords, David would have laughed. "I didn't work my way through law school so that I could walk dogs, Walt."

"You really are unhappy, aren't you?"

"In a word, yes."

"We've been through this before."

"Yeah. Good night, Walt."

"Goddard!"

David hung up.

After a few minutes he hoisted himself up off the foldout couch, dug the stuffed animals out from under his coat and set them on the scarred counter that separated his living room–bedroom from the cubicle the landlady called a kitchen.

Thinking of his nieces and how they were going to enjoy the Webkinz, he began to feel better.

Presently, David took a TV dinner out of the tiny freezer above his refrigerator and shoved it into the doll-sized oven. While it was cooking, he stripped off his clothes, went into the bathroom and wedged himself into a shower designed for a midget. After drying off with one of the three scratchy towels the landlady had seen fit to lend him, he went back to the living room and dug his robe out of a suitcase. Someday, he promised himself, he was going to write a book about the glamorous life of a Secret Service agent.

After consuming the TV dinner, he set about putting the model airplane together. It was after midnight when he finally gave up, washed the glue from his fingers, folded out the sofa bed and collapsed, falling into an instant sleep.

3

It was very bad luck that, after a quick visit to her bank that bleak Tuesday morning, Holly encountered David in the neighborhood branch of the post office. Or was it luck?

Holly looked at the carefully wrapped parcel in his arms and decided he was only mailing the Webkinz he'd bought the night before to his nieces. No doubt he lived nearby and it made sense that he would be here.

"Don't you have classes today?" she asked as they waited in line, stiff pleasantries already exchanged.

David smiled wanly. "One o'clock," he answered. He hadn't looked at the address on the envelope Holly carried, as far as she could tell, but she held it against her coat all the same.

Soon enough, it was Holly's turn at the window; she laid the envelope addressed to Craig's go-between girlfriend on the counter and asked that it be registered. While she filled out the form and paid the small fee, David had ample opportunity to study the address, but there was no helping that. She couldn't very well turn around and say, "Please don't look at this envelope. I'm sending money to my brother, who is a fugitive, you see, and there is a chance that you might be a reporter or even an FBI agent." So she said nothing.

"See you tonight?" David asked in a deep quiet voice as she turned away from the window to leave.

Holly hadn't even thought about the classes; she'd been too intent on getting that cashier's check sent off to Craig. "Tonight," she confirmed, but her mind was on the letter she had just mailed. It would reach its destination, Los Angeles, within a day or so. Had she done the wrong thing by making it easier for Craig to keep on running? She knew she had.

She would have left then, but David caught her arm in one hand and stayed her. "Are you all right?" he asked, ignoring the impatient post-office clerk, who was waiting to weigh and stamp the package he still held.

Holly nodded quickly and then fled. In her car, she let her forehead rest against the steering wheel for a moment before starting the engine and driving away. As she pulled into a supermarket parking lot a few minutes later, she was still trembling. She loved Craig; he was her brother. But she almost wished the FBI would catch him. That way there wouldn't be any more lying, any more hiding, any more guilt.

She got out of the car, locking it behind her, and went into the supermarket. Think about the couscous you've got to test today, she told herself. Think about the spices you'll need. Don't think about Craig and especially don't think about David Goddard. It was a coincidence that he was in the post office just when you were. It was a coincidence!

That seemed unlikely, but by the time she had chosen a cart and gotten out her shopping list, Holly had convinced herself that she was being fanciful again. Paranoid, like Craig.

He was wearing a navy blue football jersey with white numbers, jeans and polished leather boots. Holly, exhausted from a day of making couscous over and over again, gave herself a mental shake. What did she care what David Goddard wore, for heaven's sake?

Her beautiful aquamarine eyes looked hollow and smudges of fatigue and worry darkened the flawless skin beneath. David ached for her. Things were going to get worse, maybe a lot worse, for Holly Llewellyn before they got better.

If they ever got better.

Again he lingered, quietly helping her with the mess left behind by thirteen people struggling with a complicated German recipe. I'll have to go through this eight more times, Holly thought dismally. All the rest of this week. All of next week.

"Coffee?" David asked, drying his hands on one of the pristine towels provided by the store.

Holly found the idea oddly appealing, considering that, on at least one level, she was afraid of David Goddard. "I don't know, I…"

"Please?"

She felt the pull of his blatant masculinity and tried to field it with words. "You didn't take your fruit-cake home last night," she said. "The janitor must have thrown it away."

David folded his arms and arched one eyebrow. He saw through what she was doing; she just knew it. "I threw it away myself," he replied, watching her. "I was afraid you might taste it and flunk me on the spot. Now, are we going for coffee or not?"

Holly couldn't help the nervous, weary chuckle that

escaped her. "I'll make you a cup at my place." Now what made her say that? She never brought men to her house; only Skyler came there and he usually invited himself.

"Great," agreed the alarming David Goddard before she could take back the offer. "I'll follow you in my car."

Holly put on her coat, thinking that the kitchen table at home was still littered with reference books and parts of the manuscript Elaine had been indexing all day. The remains of that day's couscous experiments probably covered the counters, since Madge wasn't supposed to clean until the next morning; tonight she was only babysitting.

Reaching the parking garage, Holly was jarred to find that David's car was next to her own. Not for the first time, she had the unsettling feeling that he always knew where she was and what she was doing. But that was silly. He was a gentleman, that was all. A rare enough animal these days.

"You wanted to make sure I didn't get mugged," she guessed distractedly as he unlocked the door of a small, ordinary brown sedan.

David executed a teasing salute, but Holly was looking at his other hand. The car keys he held were affixed to a chain bearing the insignia of a nationally known rental agency. He rented his car? That seemed odd, just as the vehicle itself was odd, unsuited to him in a myriad of vague ways.

Puzzled, Holly got into her own car, started the ignition and, doubts notwithstanding, led the way to her sizable "cottage" on Spokane's quietly elegant South Hill.

"You rent your car," she said the moment they were in her living room. Not "welcome to my house," not "take off your coat," but "you rent your car." Holly felt stupid.

"Yes," David confessed readily. "Mine is in the shop."

Of course, Holly thought, but she was still bothered on a subliminal, barely discernible level. She drew a deep breath and forced herself to smile. "About that coffee I offered. This way to the kitchen."

David followed her across the shadowy living room, lit only by the dying fire in the hearth, and even though he was walking behind her, she was aware that he was taking in a tremendous amount of information just by looking around.

"Be prepared for a mess," she chimed, to cover her uneasiness. "My assistant and I spent the day making couscous."

They entered the kitchen and Holly stopped so swiftly that David nearly collided with her from behind; she felt the hard wall of his body touch her and glance quickly away.

Madge was at the sink, just finishing an impromptu cleaning detail, but her presence wasn't what caught Holly so off guard. Skyler was sitting at the table, sipping coffee. Why hadn't she noticed his car outside?

He looked up and there was a challenge in his brown eyes as they assessed David Goddard. "I don't believe we've met," he said coldly, rising from the bench at Holly's table to glare at David.

Skyler was acting like a jealous husband and it infuriated Holly, but before she could say anything at all David crossed the room and extended his hand to Skyler.

"David Goddard," he said in crisp introduction.

Madge took in the scene with bright, interested eyes, but did not say anything. Neither did Holly, who was too taken aback by the intangible storm that was suddenly raging in her quiet, cozy kitchen.

"Skyler Hollis," came the grudging response.

David took in Skyler's sleek blond hair, elegant green sweater and custom-made slacks in one swift, indigo sweep. "Did you ever appear in *GQ* magazine?" he asked.

Madge made a chortling sound and turned back to the sink. Holly rolled her eyes heavenward and then stomped over to the counter, where the coffeemaker waited.

"I own a stereo store," Skyler announced, either missing the reference to his wholesome good looks or choosing to ignore it. "What do you do, Goddard?"

David, Holly saw in a quick glance over one shoulder, gave a slow smile. "I'm learning to make fruitcake."

"Fruitcake," Skyler huffed, scowling. "I meant, what do you do for a living?"

"I'm a door-to-door salesman," was the icy and totally false reply. "I sell air fresheners. You know, those little bowls with the flowers in them—"

"Here's your coffee," Holly broke in archly, setting David's cup down on the just-cleared trestle table with a resounding thump. "Skyler, do you need a refill?"

Skyler shot her a look and carried his cup to the sink, where he thrust it into the hands of a sedately amused Madge Elkins. "No!" he barked.

"Am I breaking up a meaningful relationship?" David asked, lifting his cup in an unsuccessful attempt to hide a grin.

Skyler's look darkened; he leaned back against the counter and stubbornly folded his arms.

Holly was embarrassed and exasperated. "Skyler Hollis, will you just sit down, please? David is—"

"I know what David is," Skyler snapped before he stomped out of the kitchen. Seconds later, the front door slammed.

"I'm sorry," David said.

"I could swear I saw smoke coming out of that man's ears," Madge put in, receiving a swift look from Holly for her trouble.

The housekeeper smiled and shrugged, then took her leave without waiting for an introduction to David Goddard.

They were alone. Holly sighed heavily and fixed her gaze on her own cup of coffee.

"Are you in love with Skyler—what's his name? Hollis?"

The directness of the question brought Holly's gaze shooting up from the dark brew in her cup to David's face. "In love with him?" she echoed stupidly.

"You do realize, I hope, that if you marry that guy your name will be Holly Hollis?"

Holly burst out laughing. "You know, I never thought of that. I guess I'd just have to go on calling myself Llewellyn."

David's impossibly blue eyes were filled with gentle humor. "I really am sorry if I caused any trouble, Holly. If you want me to apologize to Hollis, I will."

"No," Holly said quickly. Perhaps too quickly. "Skyler had no right to act that way," she added moments later, in more carefully measured tones. "He has no claim on me and if I want to bring a friend home for coffee…"

"Is that what I am, Holly? Your friend?"

Holly clasped her hands together in her lap. She was twenty-seven years old, an adult, but she suddenly felt like a fifteen-year-old on her first date. "I hope so," she said softly.

Graciously, David changed the subject. The muscles in his forearms worked as he reached for the sugar bowl and added a spoonful to his coffee. "You aren't even thirty yet, unless I miss my guess," he said. "How did you happen to accomplish so much by such a tender age?"

Holly was comfortable with the subject of her career, at least. She pushed aside the strange suspicions she had about this man who sat across the table from her and allowed herself to forget, for a little while, her worries about Craig and her impossible relationship with Skyler Hollis. "I was lucky. My grandmother wrote cookbooks, you know, and she taught me a lot. And I worked hard."

"You must have spent a lot of time with your grandmother," David remarked, watching her.

"My brother and I lived with her, along with our mother. Our father was killed in an accident when I was seven," Holly blurted out in a rush. There, she thought. If he asks about Craig, I'll know something is wrong.

She held her breath.

"Your mother and grandmother are both gone now?" David asked gently.

Holly was unaccountably relieved, though her throat tightened when she answered. "Grandmother passed away, yes. Mother married a missionary doctor and we don't see her very often."

David's rugged face seemed to grow taut for a moment. "You've never been married?"

Holly shook her head. "I almost was, once." Strange. She could think of Ben now, without hurting. "What about you?"

David laughed, but there was no amusement in the sound or in the ink-blue flash of his eyes. Holly knew before he spoke that he'd once been hurt, and very badly. "I got married during my second year of law school," he said. "Marleen was a graduate student in Animal Sciences."

There was anger as well as pain in his voice. Holly deduced that Marleen had not died, as Ben had. "And?" she prompted.

"And she's now in Borneo studying chimps. She finds them endlessly fascinating and far less demanding, I would imagine, than a husband."

The bitterness in his tone stung Holly profoundly. David still loved Marleen despite his anger; she was sure of it. And for some reason, that hurt. "I'm sorry," she said, getting up hastily to go to the coffeemaker and bring the decanter back to the table, where she refilled her own cup and then David's.

"Don't be," David replied succinctly. "Marleen is happy."

But what about you? Holly wanted to ask, though, of course, she didn't dare. She put sugar into her coffee— something she never did—and kept her eyes averted.

"You said you were almost married once. What happened, Holly?"

Holly's throat constricted again. "My fiancé was killed," she managed to say. "He was working on a construction project in Alaska and...and he fell."

"You loved him a lot, didn't you?"

Holly nodded. "I wanted to die, too, at the time. And I was so angry."

There was a short, companionable silence. The coffeemaker made gurgling sounds and the fire crackled on the kitchen hearth. David's hand came, strong and warm, across the tabletop, to shelter Holly's hand.

It was then that Toby shuffled into the kitchen, looking sleepy and rumpled in his cherished Spider-Man pajamas. "Is it time to go to school, Mom?" he asked, befuddled.

Holly's eyes darted involuntarily to David's face, then shifted to her nephew. "No, sweetheart, it's still night. Go back to bed."

Toby gave David a curious look. "Who's that?" he demanded.

"This is Mr. Goddard, Toby. He's a friend of mine, a student in my cooking class."

Toby assessed David again. "You cook?" he wanted to know.

David laughed and the odd tension Holly had felt was broken. "Not very well, slugger," he retorted kindly, "but I'm learning."

"I'm not going to learn," Toby said firmly, drawing just a bit nearer to David, sensing, as Holly did, that this was a man who liked children.

"Oh, yeah? Why not?" David asked. And he sounded truly interested, not patronizing. "Don't you think men should cook?"

Toby shrugged, not exactly sure what he thought.

"Mom cooks enough stuff. Do you think men should cook?"

David thought. "Yeah," he answered presently.

"Why?"

"Because they get hungry."

Toby grinned. "Wanna see my airplane?"

David looked to Holly for her permission; she liked him for doing that. She nodded.

"Sounds interesting," the man said to the boy, and then they were off to Toby's room to inspect the radio-controlled Cessna. The sound of their retreating voices gave Holly an odd feeling of well-being. Which was immediately spoiled by the ringing of the telephone.

She answered with a brisk and biting, "Yes?"

"Who is that Goddard guy?" Skyler demanded without preamble.

Holly drew a deep breath, then let it out again. Control, she must maintain her control. "David is a friend of mine, Skyler." Sugary acid slipped past her resolve, dripping from every word. "I am allowed to have friends, aren't I?"

"Not men!"

"Good night, Skyler," Holly sang, and then she set the receiver firmly back in its cradle.

Seconds later, the telephone rang again.

"Hello?" Holly said sweetly.

"Don't you ever hang up on me again, Holly Llewellyn!" Skyler shouted.

Of course, Holly had no choice but to do exactly that. She then adjusted her answering machine to pick up on the first ring. If Skyler chose to call again, he would be cordially invited to leave his name, number and message. If he felt called upon to deliver a lecture, he would get only an electronic whirring sound in reply.

Holly was at the sink when David returned to the kitchen; though she didn't hear him, not consciously at least, she was aware of him in every sense. She stiffened as he came toward her, his boots making a melodic sound on the hard brick floor.

"Holly?"

She turned to face him. She couldn't keep her fingers from clenching the counter behind her.

David stopped, looking stricken. "You're afraid of me."

"Y-yes."

"Why?"

How could she explain, when she didn't understand it herself? She was afraid of David Goddard, and yet his nearness was causing every nerve ending in her body to jump and crackle like naked electrical wire. Not even

Ben—tender, laughing, lost Ben—had ever affected her in quite that way.

"Holly?" he prompted.

Holly felt very silly and not a little old-maidish. She blushed and gave a nervous, shaky laugh. "It's not as though I think you're...I mean...I know you're not—"

He was closer now. Holly could feel the heat and the strength of him. He was not yet touching her, but God help her, she wanted him to. She wanted him to hold her and kiss her and— He did. He kissed her. He cupped his gentle, strong hands, one on each side of her flushed face, bent his head, and kissed her. His lips were soft and cautious, making no demands.

A strange warmth filled Holly, stabbing her in some places, soothing her in others. She trembled when his tongue persuaded her lips to part for him and she moaned at his thorough, masterful yet entirely tender conquering.

And his body was warm and hard against Holly's, pressing, igniting licking flames of unfamiliar, unexpected passion. It hadn't been like this with Ben, she reflected frantically. Not even when they actually made love.

David drew back suddenly, with an obvious effort.

"I'd better leave," he said in a hoarse voice, his eyes not quite linking with Holly's.

She was wounded and still breathless. "David—"

At last he looked at her, and she saw anguish in the depths of his eyes, along with a cold, self-directed anger. "I'm sorry," he rasped, reaching for his jacket.

Holly wanted to cry. She wanted to laugh. She didn't know what she wanted to do, except make love to David Goddard and have him make love to her. And that wasn't possible, of course, because they'd only known each other for a day and because Toby was sleeping upstairs. "Don't be sorry. You didn't do anything wrong."

"Didn't I?" he asked, speaking more to himself, it seemed, than to Holly.

Holly couldn't believe the crazy things that were going on inside her, the aching, melting sensations. The howling hunger. And her breasts. Her breasts quivered with a need to be fondled, their tips still at eager attention. What was happening to her?

"Will you come and have dinner with Toby and me tomorrow night, David?" she heard herself ask.

A log fell in the fireplace, sparks snapping. The silence was terrible and so was Holly's suspense. Which would be worse: his refusal or his acceptance?

"Yes," he said finally, and with some reluctance. "I know better, but I'll do it."

"Seven?" Holly asked with a calmness that amazed her. "We could go on to class afterward."

David wasn't looking at her; it seemed that he couldn't. The telephone jangled but the answering machine picked up instantly. The silence was heavy, pulsing.

"Seven," he said hoarsely, and then he was leaving, striding away from Holly with determined motions.

After she'd heard the front door close and the engine of his car start up with a fierce, revving sound, she could move again. She locked the house and turned out the few lights that still burned, then made her way upstairs.

Her bed looked as it always had—the same Pennsylvania Dutch quilt covered the practical flannel sheets beneath. The same brass headboard glistened in the light from the lamp on her dresser. The same two pillows waited, neither having ever borne the weight of a man's head. Not Skyler's certainly. Not even Ben's.

The bed was unchanged, but Holly's feelings about sharing it were vastly different. Tonight it looked lonely and cold rather than spacious.

Shaking her head, she went into the small bathroom adjoining her room, washed her face, brushed her teeth, stripped off the black slacks and red sweater she had worn that night, and finally the wispy panties and bra underneath.

Holly stood naked before the full-length mirror on the back of her bedroom door. She saw a well-proportioned if unremarkable body, curved in some places, hollowed in others.

She permitted herself to remember that long-ago summer, between high school and college, when she and Ben had given in to the dizzying, constant demands of their youthful bodies. She had not soared, as books and movies had led her to believe she would, but she had not been traumatized, either. Ben's lovemaking had been gentle and pleasant, if not truly fulfilling.

But now, as the result of one brief kiss, Holly knew that, with David Goddard, her body would respond with abandon. It would sing. It would quiver.

The prospect was completely alarming.

With flouncing motions, Holly stormed over to her dresser, wrenched open a drawer and pulled out a long T-shirt-style gown. She quickly put the garment on, as though that would dispel the crazy hungers, the yearnings, that had lain dormant until one particular man had kissed her.

Determinedly, she got into bed and settled into the

warmth of the soft flannel sheets. Unable to sleep, she tossed this way and that, plumping her pillows, lying down and sitting back up again.

After almost twenty minutes of this, Holly faced a very disturbing fact. Sure as the sun would rise in the morning, sure as the December snows would fall, David Goddard was going to make love to her. It was inevitable; it was inescapable. The self-control she needed in order to feel strong and safe would desert her.

Tears burned in Holly's eyes and flowed down her cheeks. She would be changed forever and then she would be left because David was not what he seemed to be, not what he claimed to be.

All her instincts warned that this was true and yet she could feel herself sliding toward him, careening down some steep psychological hill. And there was nothing to grasp, nothing to break her fall.

She rolled over and sniffled, tucking both hands under her face the way she had as a little girl. Skyler. She would think of Skyler and everything would be all right.

What did Skyler look like? She couldn't remember. After dating the man for months, she couldn't remember!

"Oh, damn!" Holly cried into the quilt edge that was

bunched in her hands. Again she tried to summon Skyler's face to her mind but it wouldn't come; instead, she saw David's dark hair, David's strong jawline, David's ferociously blue eyes.

"Who are you, David Goddard?" Holly wailed inwardly, her mind full of shimmering tangles of fear and joy, happiness and dread. Who are you?

Except for the wild, thunderous beating of her own heart, there was no answer.

4

David bent and tapped the side of the glass fishbowl with an impatient index finger. The two goldfish floated, one above the other, just staring at him, their shimmering fan-shaped tails barely moving.

"You guys are really boring, you know that?" he complained in an undertone. "I bought you to give this place some color and flash and what do you do? You just sit there, watching the world go by. Swim, dammit!"

The fish regarded him implacably, still hovering midway between the surface of the water and the bottom, with its blue rocks and shifting plastic fern and dimestore diver.

"No class," David grumbled, turning away and

wrenching the damp sweatband from his forehead in one irritated movement.

Still breathing hard from his customary morning run, he stumbled into the bathroom and took a quick shower. Later, as he dried himself and dressed—in the living room, for God's sake—he wondered how the hell he was ever going to impress Holly Llewellyn with a place like this.

Draping a towel over his shoulders because his hair was still dripping wet, he took in the goldfish, the un-made sofa bed, the spots on the carpet. No class. Like those seventy-nine-cent goldfish, the place had no class.

The telephone rang and David, who had been indulging in a fanciful nostalgia for his real apartment in far-away Georgetown, was startled. He put images of good art, the hot tub in his bathroom and the ivory fireplace out of his mind as he lunged for the instrument.

"Goddard," he answered, and the long-distance buzz coming over the wire told him that he'd been right. This was his call from Washington.

"Zigman here," Walt replied. "The Bureau staked out the address in L.A., Goddard, but they must have muffed it somehow, because Llewellyn didn't bite."

David had a headache. He had hoped the FBI would be able to collar Llewellyn immediately; like a child about to have a sliver pulled, he'd wanted the whole thing to be over with. "He was an agent himself once. He probably knows the signs."

"Yeah."

"Does this mean I can drop the case and come back to Washington?" Part of David hoped it did, while another part wanted to watch Holly Llewellyn forever.

"Hell, no. The little lady sent him a letter, didn't she? You saw it with your own eyes, Goddard. That means she's in fairly regular contact with our boy, doesn't it?"

David resented the "little lady" reference. Holly was so much more and the phrase seemed to demean her. "Holly is a woman, Walt. With a brain."

Zigman's laugh traveled three thousand miles to annoy David as instantly as if he'd been in the same room. "Goddard, you are going soft. Don't get to liking this broad too much. She's in line for an indictment herself, you know."

"For what?" David snapped.

"Christ," Zigman swore impatiently. "For aiding and abetting a fugitive. Are you going to wake the hell up, Goddard, or do I have to send somebody else out there to handle this thing?"

David bit back all the fury that surged like bile into his throat. He'd never been pulled from a detail in all the time he'd worked for the service, and he wasn't about to start now. Besides, he couldn't be sure how another agent would manage the situation. And it was delicate. Holly's emotional state was delicate. "I can handle it," he said.

"Wouldn't have sent you if I didn't think you could," Walt replied in smug tones. His cigar stub was probably bobbing up and down in his mouth, and David wished he could be there to squash it into the man's teeth. "Keep a sharp eye out, Goddard. Llewellyn could turn up there. If he does, I want him busted. On the spot."

The thought made David half-sick, and he closed his eyes. His wet hair was dripping cold trails down his neck and he began drying it with one end of the towel. He could imagine the look on Holly's face if he casually wrestled Llewellyn to the floor in her living room. "Yeah."

"Can you handle him by yourself or do you want a detail? The Bureau has an office in Spokane—"

"You keep the Bureau the hell out of this, Walt! I mean it!" The outburst was too sudden, too emotional. David drew a deep breath and stopped toweling his hair to sigh. "Llewellyn is a former agent," he reiterated a moment later, when he could speak more moderately. "If he sees a bunch of three-piece suits and crew cuts watching his sister's house, how do you think he'll react?"

"He'll split, just like he did in L.A."

"Right." David sighed again, running one hand through his hair. "Let me handle this, will you, Walt? If I need the Bureau, I can always call them in."

"All right," Walt agreed in his gruff, wry way. "But you remember why you're there. It isn't to make fruitcake, Goddard. Or time."

David's headache was infinitely worse. "Yeah," he agreed after a long, long time. "I'll remember."

"Good," came the brisk reply. "When do you see the broad again?"

Enough was enough. He'd let that word pass once; he couldn't do it again. "Don't call her that again, Walt. If you do, your nose will be where your right ear is now. I'll see to it."

Zigman swore and rang off.

David held the receiver in his hand for a long time, doing some swearing of his own. Craig Llewellyn was going to show up in Spokane, he could feel it in his bones. It was only a matter of time. Holly was going to be destroyed by the inevitable arrest, by David's deception.

Why the hell had he accepted the dinner invitation,

dammit? Suppose there was a replay of that episode when he'd kissed her, in the kitchen? What then? David had spent most of the night reliving that ill-guided indulgence and imagining all the sweet pleasures that could have come after it.

He shook his head, trying to dislodge the thought, but his body recollected perfectly. Heatedly. He'd had his share of women, of course, but none had ever made him feel quite the way Holly did. She could reach past the hard finish painted over him by his Secret Service training. She could so easily reach past it.

Maybe Walt Zigman was right; maybe he was losing his ability to be objective. Maybe he was getting soft.

David allowed himself one rueful, humorless chuckle. *Soft* was definitely not the word. Not where Holly Llewellyn was concerned.

The day was a full and busy one, but it took forever to pass, all the same. Instead of thinking about her newspaper column, as she should have been, every turn of Holly's mind seemed to lead to David Goddard.

Elaine was gathering together the leaves of the manuscript she had been working on, preparing to leave. "What time is the hunk coming over?" she asked.

Color leaped into Holly's cheeks and pounded there.

"What hunk?" she asked tightly, a little annoyed that Elaine could read her preoccupation so easily.

"Don't give me that. I'm talking about your date with David Goddard and you know it. What are you serving? What are you wearing? Do you want me to take Toby home with me for the evening?"

"Once your questions start coming, there's no stopping them, is there?" Holly countered, still flushed. She took the disk containing her pitiful effort at a cooking column from the computer and shut off the machine with an angry flourish.

Elaine was not intimidated, but she did back off just a little. "I could take Toby home," she offered again. "Roy and I enjoy him so much, and—"

"Toby is staying right here!"

"Why? Do you need him as a buffer, Holly?"

Holly had been halfway out of her chair; now she sagged back into it. "I wouldn't use Toby that way, Elaine," she said, but the doubt in her voice bothered her.

"It's all right, you know, to want time alone with an attractive man. It's not going to scar Toby's psyche or anything."

In spite of herself, Holly chuckled. Elaine did have a

way of lightening a situation. "Last night," she confessed after a few moments of reflection, "David kissed me."

"So?"

"So it was weird, Elaine. The earth moved. Bells chimed. All the corny stuff you see in movies and read about in books—it all happened."

Elaine beamed. "That's great!"

"It is not," Holly insisted, her face set and serious again. "It's terrible. That man is dangerous, Elaine."

"Dangerous? Why?"

Now Holly felt foolish and she couldn't quite bring herself to meet her friend's eyes. "He's not like Skyler. He's—"

"Thank God for small favors."

Holly was putting her computer disk into its paper folder, turning off the printer, clearing her desk. Anything to keep from looking directly at Elaine. "You don't like Skyler, do you? I can understand why Toby doesn't, but you should."

"He's all right," Elaine conceded with a heavy and somewhat dramatic sigh. "It's just that he's so, well, you know, safe. Boring."

"He's reliable, that's what he is," defended Holly. "I might marry him."

"If you do, you're crazy. You don't love Skyler, Holly."

"How do you know?" Holly demanded. But she wished with all her heart that she could love Skyler, truly want him. Even need him. It made her mad that she couldn't.

"If you loved him, ninny-brain, you wouldn't be all hot and bothered because David Goddard is coming to dinner. You haven't thought straight all day."

Holly slumped. "I'm not 'hot and bothered'!" she lied in a plaintive wail.

Elaine only laughed. "Let me take Toby home with me. Please? I promise to give him the most nutritionally balanced TV dinner in the freezer, and I'll bring him home after your class lets out."

Holly hadn't even thought about the class. Dear Lord, that was one more thing to add to the worries she already had, like what she was going to serve David Goddard for dinner and what she was going to wear. She wanted to look attractive, but not predatory....

It was as though, by their long and friendly association, Elaine had learned to look right inside Holly's brain and read her every thought. "Wear something sexy. Leopard skin, maybe."

Holly laughed. "Leopard skin? This is a quiet, casual dinner, not a movie about barbarians! And I have no desire to look 'sexy.'"

"Pity," Elaine said, looking entirely serious. "A woman ought to wear something sort of Frederick's-of-Hollywoodish once in a while."

Holly only shook her head, amazed. She wanted to ask if Elaine herself ever wore such garments but didn't quite dare.

"Hey, Tobe!" Elaine yelled, shaking off the look of deep thought, beaming again. "Come on! You're coming home with me tonight!"

The TV, blaring in the family room, went silent. The next sound, in fact, was a little boy's whoop of delight. Toby bounded into the room, already struggling into his jacket, his face shining. "Do you think Uncle Roy will play Donkey Kong with me?"

Elaine gave the child a conspiratorial smile. "Yes. But you must promise to let him beat you at least once."

Toby squared his small shoulders manfully and looked charitably reluctant. "Oh, all right. But just once."

There was a whoosh of goodbyes, Toby planting a quick, wet kiss on Holly's cheek, and then a swirl of cold air when the back door was opened. And they were gone.

Holly sighed, and as an aching sense of loneliness grasped her, she took herself firmly in hand. "Frederick's of Hollywood!" she muttered irritably as she went to the freezer to take out falafel and couscous experiments from last week's chapter of her new cookbook.

She slammed the foil-wrapped packages down on the countertop, near the sink. If David Goddard didn't like eating experiments, the heck with him. What did he think this place was, a restaurant? Why, if he said one single word, she would...she would...

Holly sighed. Who was she kidding? She put the foil packages back into the freezer and took out the special beef stroganoff she'd been saving in case Skyler's parents decided to come to Spokane on one of their infrequent visits.

After straightening the kitchen and throwing together a green salad, she raced upstairs to take a shower and exchange her jeans and madras shirt for something more— more what? Sexy?

Still dripping from her shower, wrapped only in a bright pink bath sheet, Holly shoved the white cashmere suit back into the closet. It was too clingy, that was all. Entirely too clingy.

She brought out a flowing blue dress, interwoven with tiny silver threads, that she'd picked up in Iran only the month before. Even then she'd had no idea where she would wear such a thing, but she hadn't been able to resist the gown's quiet elegance.

She returned that garment to the closet, too. After all, it had that deep neckline and it was too formal. Whatever she chose would have to do for the cooking class she had to teach after dinner, she reminded herself.

Finally, Holly settled for tailored black slacks and a soft mulberry sweater. Not exactly suited to making Belgian fruitcake, she thought, but at least she would look halfway decent when David arrived and she could always push up the sleeves later, when it was time to conduct her class.

Hurriedly, she brushed her hair, applied her makeup and brushed her hair again. She allowed herself one cool misting of the expensive perfume she'd once bought on a dash through the Paris airport.

When the rites of womanhood had all been performed, she stood back from the mirror to look at herself. Her lipstick was crooked, and she wiped it off and reapplied it, this time using a lip liner. "Color inside the lines, now," she mocked herself.

David arrived promptly at seven o'clock, just as they'd agreed. Not a moment before and not a moment after. Something about this small precision bothered Holly, but she pushed the feeling aside.

There was a fire crackling in the living room fireplace and the table in the rarely used dining room had been set with pretty china and her grandmother's silver. David looked impossibly handsome in his gray slacks, creamy white sweater, and navy blue jacket. No indeed, this was no time for silly doubts.

"Come in," she said, stepping back.

David smiled, but the look in his eyes was weary. Perhaps he'd had a hard day at law school. He extended a bottle of wine and then took off his coat. "Where's Toby?" he asked, and the expression in his indigo-blue eyes was suddenly expectant.

Holly was a bit embarrassed. Now she was going to have to say that Toby was spending the evening at Elaine and Roy's, and it would look as though she'd been setting the scene for a steamy seduction. Why, oh, why had she lighted the fire and set the table so carefully? "He had a previous engagement," she said.

"Good," David replied smoothly.

"Good?" Holly echoed, confused.

David laughed. "A man's got to have a social life," he answered, and Holly remained off-balance because she didn't know whether he meant that Toby needed a social life or he did.

They ate in the dining room, with the candles lit— Holly had been too shy to light them, so David had done it—with the wine and the good china and the glint of the aged silver flatware. Holly hadn't entertained a man in this particular way in as long as she could remember, and she was uncomfortable and distracted, not knowing what to do or how to act. The fact that she silently flogged herself for being silly didn't help; she still felt like a fifteen-year-old about to go to her first prom.

"Do we have time to sit by the fire for a while," David asked easily, setting his wineglass aside, "or are we off to tackle the mysteries of Belgian rum sauce?"

Holly laughed, even though the thought of sitting in front of a romantic winter fire with a man—with *this* man—patently made her nervous. "We have a few minutes."

He stood up, but instead of coming around to pull back Holly's chair, as Skyler would have done, he started gathering up dirty dishes. Holly was disappointed for a moment, but then she decided that one act was as considerate as the other and began to help.

Holly waited, every nerve screaming, for him to kiss her. He didn't do it while they were clearing the table, of course, and in the kitchen he kept the dishwasher door between them as they put the china and silverware inside. Was he shy or something?

Holly's cheeks stung with color. Elaine was right, she castigated herself angrily, you're hot and bothered!

Once the dishwasher was churning away, David caught Holly's hand casually in his and led her back to the living room as though it were his house. As though they had all the time in the world.

"Maybe we shouldn't—" she sputtered, lifting his hand so that she could peer at the watch on her own wrist. "It's getting late—"

David sat down on one of the soft Indian pillows facing the fireplace and pulled Holly after him. She tumbled against him, and her heart lurched into her throat at even that small contact, driving the breath out of her lungs and causing a curious ringing sound in her ears.

She settled herself primly on the other pillow, careful not to look at him. She knew that she would see the familiar, quiet amusement shining in his navy blue eyes.

"Holly."

She swallowed, knotting her hands together in her lap. "What?"

"Look at me."

She looked at him because doing otherwise would have been foolish and petulant. Even infantile. "So, I'm looking already," she said.

He laughed and that was at variance with the look in his eyes which, instead of humor, betrayed a reluctance of some kind. A hurtful reluctance.

Holly was stung. David wanted to resist her as badly as she wanted to resist him! Wasn't she attractive? Did he find her— David bent his head and kissed her, and an almost inaudible groan rumbled up through his chest and brushed against her lips. He was only nibbling at her mouth, tasting it as though it were a delicacy to be savored. He muttered something, and to a dazed Holly, it sounded as though he'd said, "Why?"

She couldn't think of that now. She couldn't think of anything except the havoc that reluctant kiss was causing inside her. She shivered and placed her hands on his strong shoulders, where they moved of their own accord to caress his neck.

He kissed her in earnest then, his tongue exploring the sweet depths of her mouth, enlisting her own to respond in quick, fevered parries. His hand moving gently up and down the length of her thigh caused the flesh hidden beneath to quiver.

Holly wanted to die and she wanted to live forever. She wanted to stop and she drew him nearer, allowing him to shift her body and his own so that they were both prone before the crackling fire.

His hand left her thigh to move up over her hip, underneath her soft mulberry sweater, over the flesh at her waist, over her rib cage. He freed her from his sorcerer's kiss to nibble gently, provocatively, at her ear-lobe and her neck.

"I want you, Holly," he said in that forthright way of his, his voice a gruff caress against the base of her neck.

Holly shivered, even though there was a heat pulsing inside her that made her long to fling off her clothes. "David, I...we..."

"I know," he chuckled, and his hand had found the catch at the front of her bra. There was a feeling of sweet, wanton freedom as her breasts were released, and then his fingers were soothing her, searching out a nipple that already awaited them at strictest attention. "Tell me to stop."

If Holly hadn't been so bedazzled, she would have slapped him. "I can't..." she admitted, her words falling away to a groan as he found that arching nipple and rolled it gently between his fingers.

He drew her sweater slowly upward, his hand cupping the captured breast, shaping it for conquering. When he bent his head to lave the throbbing peak softly with his tongue, Holly gasped with pleasure and arched her back in reflexive surrender.

"We...can't do this..." he managed to say as his mouth blazed a path from the conquered breast to the one that awaited sweet defeat. "We can't..."

"I know," Holly agreed. But when his tongue touched the untended nipple, she knotted her hands in David's rich, mink-soft hair and held him close.

Holly Llewellyn was to wonder many times, sometimes with regret and sometimes with relief, what would have happened if the telephone hadn't rung when it did. Its cold, jarring jangle made David thrust himself away from her as if in fury.

Stung and shaken and still needing, Holly hastily fixed her bra and stumbled off at a half jog to answer.

"Hello!" she gasped, winded and embarrassed. She could see David from where she stood and he was just staring into the fire, his broad back rigid.

"Sis?"

Holly wanted to cry. Not now, she thought frantically. Oh, God, not now! She lowered her voice. "Hello, Craig."

"'Hello, Craig'? Is that all you've got to say?"

Holly stiffened, very conscious of the man sitting before the fireplace. Her breasts were still heavy and warm with passion, their peaks moist. She tried to breathe properly. "What should I say, Craig?" she asked petulantly, forgetting this time to keep her tone at whisper level.

"I tried to pick up the money," Craig rushed on angrily, frantically. "Guess what? There were crew cuts all around Cindy's place!"

Holly trembled, then drew a deep breath. "Crew cuts?" she repeated, confused. David's back stiffened almost imperceptibly, or was that a trick of the firelight? He didn't appear to be making the slightest effort to hear what was being said, but appearances could be deceiving.

"FBI agents. Holly, they were everywhere! Did you turn me in?"

"Of course I didn't!" At this outburst, David turned his head, assessing Holly with a look she could read all too well: it was full of stark, angry pity.

"Just listen," Craig rasped. God in heaven, how desperate, how hunted, he sounded. "I'm going to need money, Holly, and if I have to come there and get it, I will!"

"You can't do that! Toby would be—"

"Toby. Always Toby. Don't you ever think about anybody besides that kid, Holly? What about me? I'm your brother, remember?" Craig stopped to draw a harsh breath and then began to cough. It was a frightening sound.

"You're sick!" Holly exclaimed, watching David. He had turned his eyes from her again and was now gazing into the fire, one knee drawn up under his chin. "Craig, please—turn yourself in. They won't hurt you, I swear it!"

"I'll call again tomorrow!" Craig roared impatiently, and then he slammed the receiver down so hard that Holly flinched. She was on the verge of tears when she placed her own receiver in its cradle.

The silence in the living room was complete, except for the snapping merriment of the fire. David looked at Holly but did not rise from his seat near the hearth. Holly closed her eyes momentarily, in a vain effort to shut out the reality of Craig and his problems, then drew a deep breath to steady herself.

"Y-you're a lawyer," she began, speaking as casually as she could. "If someone is wanted by the law, and another person…a person close to them…knows where they are and sometimes gives them money…"

David rose slowly to his feet with the grace of a predatory animal, but he kept his distance. And it was more than a physical distance. "Then that person is guilty of aiding and abetting a fugitive," he said evenly. "They could, under some circumstances, be imprisoned."

Holly trembled and bit her lower lip. When she closed her eyes against the possibility, her already precarious balance was affected and she swayed. David was instantly clasping her shoulders, holding her upright. And while there was a gentleness in his touch, there was little sympathy.

"I can help you, Holly," he said hoarsely. "If you'll just allow yourself to trust me, I swear I can help you."

Holly longed to pour out the whole ugly story, to tell him how scared and confused Craig was, to explain that he hadn't meant to do all those awful things. But she didn't dare. The fact that she had almost given herself to David moments before, making a joyous offering of something she held dear, changed nothing.

David Goddard was still a stranger.

5

The rest of that week was dismal for Holly. She couldn't concentrate on her work and she was short not only with Elaine but with Toby. When Skyler called, offering an innocent-sounding invitation to lunch, she all but bit his head off.

In the evenings, of course, she taught her cooking class, and David was always there, always attentive—and never friendly. He might have been a total stranger, answering what casual questions Holly could contrive to ask with flat, clipped banalities. Not once did he stay to help with the cleanup, as he had those first two nights, and he certainly made no effort to contact her outside of class.

Holly was devastated and she was scared, too. Craig

had nearly been caught in Los Angeles. How could the FBI have known where he would be if not for David's seeing the address on that letter she'd mailed? And that night, that shattering night when they had almost made love, David had said, *"I can help you, Holly. If you'll just allow yourself to trust me. I swear I can help you."*

He knew; she was sure he knew. And as far as Holly was concerned, that was reason enough not to see him again. Ever.

Except that she needed him, wanted him. Perhaps, though she couldn't often bring herself to examine the possibility rationally, she was even beginning to love David Goddard.

On Friday night, Skyler called to ask her out for dinner and a movie. Holly refused, pleading a headache, and went to bed early, setting the answering machine because Skyler had a tendency to be persistent. The telephone rang twice during the night, and a sleepless Holly timed the calls at eleven thirty-five and twelve-ten.

The next morning was one of those springlike days that sometimes creep into winter. Though there were still ragged patches of snow on the ground, the sun was bright and the sky was a painfully keen shade of blue.

The weather did much to bring Holly out of her doldrums, and to make up for some of the stresses of the past week, she suggested to a rather wan and distraught Toby that they take his airplane to Manito Park and fly it.

"I'm going to the Ice Capades this afternoon," Toby reminded his aunt, running his spoon glumly through the dish of oatmeal before him. "My whole class is going."

"I remember," Holly said softly. It hurt, this restraint between herself and Toby. It was a sad, pulsing ache. "You'll be back in plenty of time, I promise."

Toby brightened. "Okay," he chirped. "Let's hurry up with breakfast and go!"

His ebullience made Holly laugh, easing the bereft feeling inside her. "Let's do that. Be sure to wear your mittens because it's cold."

Toby nodded. As he passed Holly's desk, his oatmeal gleefully abandoned on the trestle table, he stopped. "Mom, there's messages on the machine. The light is flashing."

Holly glanced uneasily toward the telephone. Between Craig and Skyler, it was getting so that she didn't like to answer the thing at all. It wasn't likely that David had left those messages, she told herself, and she was in no mood to hear a lecture from Skyler or a lot of pathos from Craig. "I'll listen later. Right now, I'm in the mood to fly your Cessna."

"Me, too!" Toby agreed, and he was off again, in search of the warmer clothes he would need for a morning in the park.

Perhaps too conscientious for her own good, Holly went to the answering machine and frowned down at the little red light blinking so industriously, her finger poised over the "play" button. What if the calls had been from Craig and he was in terrible trouble? What if—

She stopped herself, sighed and drew back her hand. It could wait. Whatever it was, it could just wait. Any kind of hassle at this moment would be too much.

The park was sunny, and in places patches of green-brown grass dappled the grubby snow. There were lots of children around, their laughter ringing in the ice-cold air, and a goodly number of parents, too.

"I wish I'd brought my sled," Toby said wistfully, watching as some of the children pushed and pulled each other on Flyers and plastic saucers.

Something twisted inside Holly as she watched her nephew; despite all his friends at school, he was a lonely child, often feeling separate from the others. Alone. While Holly's own childhood had been far from ideal, she had had Craig. Toby had no one near his own age.

The little boy squinted up at her, a grin forming on his face, and the toy Cessna seemed huge in his small hands. "You thinkin' about my dad?" he asked directly.

Holly was stunned. Lately it seemed as though she went around with all her thoughts written on her forehead, so clearly did people read them. "How did you know that?"

Small shoulders, hidden beneath the weight of a down-filled snowsuit, moved in a shrug. "You get a sad look on your face when you think about Dad."

"We were very close once," Holly admitted distractedly, having to look away for a moment because of the tears that stung her eyes.

"Dad's a bad man, isn't he?" Toby probed seriously, his mittened hands working awkwardly with the airplane.

Holly shook her head so suddenly and so hard that her neck ached—as did her heart. "No, Toby. Your dad isn't really a bad man, though he has done some bad things. He's sick, Toby, and pretty confused."

"He doesn't want me."

Holly knelt in the snow, which crackled beneath the worn knees of her oldest jeans, and clasped Toby by the shoulders. "It isn't that way at all, Toby. Your dad loves you. But when people have the kind of troubles he does, they just don't seem to have room in their lives for other things and other people."

Toby's face was scrunched up in the battle against unmanly emotion. "I liked Mr. Goddard a lot. How come he didn't come back? Does he have problems, too, like Dad?"

Holly closed her eyes for a moment and drew a deep breath. "No, Toby. I don't think he has the kind of problems that your dad has. As for why he didn't come back—"

"He was a fool," put in a deep, masculine voice.

Holly and Toby looked up simultaneously, squinting against the dazzling winter sun, to see David standing over them. He wore a dark blue ski jacket and jeans, a contrite expression on his face and held his own model airplane in his hands.

"Hi!" Toby whooped, overjoyed.

While Holly was glad enough to see David herself, glad enough to shout, in fact, she was a little injured by Toby's enthusiasm toward the man. It was as though a hopeless day had just been saved at the last, cliff-hanging second. And there were all her misgivings, too…

"Truce," he said gruffly, extending one hand to Holly, the plane tucked under his opposite elbow now. "Please?"

Holly swallowed. It was sheer, foolhardy madness to get further involved with this man and she knew it, but she couldn't quite bring herself to refuse what she knew he was offering. "Truce," she croaked out, after what seemed like a long time.

Eyes of an impossibly dark blue swept over her so swiftly that she could almost believe it hadn't happened, and then they shifted to Toby. "Hi, slugger. Ready to fly?"

Toby was literally beaming. Again Holly found his obvious fondness for David Goddard unsettling. What would happen when David went away? What if he did something that would hurt Craig and thus Toby, too?

"I'm ready!" came the exuberant answer.

David proved to be a lousy pilot, always dropping his hand controls or sending his somewhat odd-looking model airplane plunging into bushes, but Holly was too amused to chalk this up as another reason to be suspicious of him. After all, he'd only said he owned a model plane, not that he was proficient at flying one.

In any case, David's ineptitude only seemed to endear him further to Toby, who patiently demonstrated again and again how to handle the craft properly. Holly stood back and watched, full of mingled dread and tender inclinations. She was glad, even relieved, when Toby offered her a turn with his airplane, for that gave her something to think about besides David Goddard and all the wonderful, terrible things that could come of allowing him into her life.

As the small airplane glided and dipped and roared overhead in a perfect circle, following the commands Holly gave it with her handset, Toby and David both applauded. Privately, she was surprised that she hadn't sent the thing crashing into a tree; her fingers wouldn't stop shaking.

Finally the morning ended; it was time to take Toby home, give him lunch and let him have a few quiet minutes before driving him to the Coliseum, where he would join his classmates for the afternoon performance of the Ice Capades.

Leading Toby toward her car, she glanced uncertainly at David. What would happen now? Did he want to talk? Would he just leave, or would there be a renewal of the dangerous attraction that seemed to be sweeping them together?

Holly felt stiff, almost formal. Walk away and don't look back! screamed her mind. This man is dangerous! But her heart said something entirely different. "We enjoyed seeing you again," she ventured aloud.

David's lips curved into a half grin, one that said he

understood her feelings because they so closely paralleled his own, but his blue eyes were sad. "Toby will be busy this afternoon?" he asked evenly.

"I'm going to the Ice Capades!" the little boy crowed before Holly could assemble a polite answer.

David's indigo gaze touched the child with real affection, then sliced back to Holly's face. "I need to talk with you, Holly," he said quietly. "To be with you. Will you have lunch with me?"

"Sure she will!" Toby announced with loud confidence, scrambling into the back seat of Holly's car, setting his airplane and handset on the seat and buckling himself into the seat belt.

David laughed, but that quiet ache was still visible in his eyes. "Please," he said.

Holly swallowed hard and nodded. "Shall I meet you somewhere?"

"I'll pick you up at your place in an hour or so, if that's all right."

Holly nodded again and got into her car, busying herself with the fastening of her seat belt and the turning of the ignition key. Anything so that she didn't have to look back and see David getting into that rented car of his, that car that didn't suit him. She couldn't bear the strain of wondering about him anymore, of weighing his motives all the time. No, just for this one day she was going to enjoy what she felt, without letting doubt spoil it.

While Toby consumed soup and a sandwich, his appetite made sharp by a morning of fresh air and exercise, Holly exchanged her Saturday jeans for a pair of fitted gray slacks, her T-shirt and poncho for a classic navy blue blouse with a tie at the throat and a charcoal velvet blazer. She brushed her hair carefully and put on makeup, too, telling herself all the while that she wasn't trying to be attractive for David, not at all. It was just that as something of a local celebrity, she had an image to maintain.

Why she hadn't been concerned with that image earlier in the day, when she'd gone to a public park in her oldest clothes, wearing no makeup, was a question she didn't bother to examine.

When she returned from dropping Toby off at the Coliseum, David was waiting in front of her house. And he was driving a different car.

Holly parked her own Toyota in the driveway, locked it and went toward him, taking in the sleek lines of the red Camaro sitting at the curb. David got out, looking devastatingly handsome in jeans and a cream-colored bulky-knit sweater, and came around to open the car door for her.

"What happened to the rented one?" she asked. "The brown sedan?"

David shook his head, but he went back around the car and got in on his own side before answering. "I told you my car was being fixed, Holly. This is it."

Again, Holly was unsettled. This car looked and smelled so new, how could anything have been wrong with it?

"Don't weigh everything I say, Holly," David said watching her. "I'm a man, not a mystery to solve."

Holly said nothing. She couldn't deny that he was a man, but the part about his not being a mystery was certainly open to debate.

Lunch, eaten in a plant-filled restaurant overlooking Riverfront Park, the site of a world's fair and Spokane's coveted antique carousel, was a stilted affair.

Holly was as annoyed as she was self-conscious. Hadn't David said he wanted to talk to her? No, in fact, he'd said he *needed* to talk to her. So why didn't he?

His glass of white wine seemed to fascinate him; he turned it in one strong, sun-browned hand, watching the ebb and flow. The silence lengthened.

"I thought you said we were going to talk!" Holly

blurted out impatiently. What was it about this man that undid her so? She felt sure that it was more than her rising attraction to him, more even than her doubts about his motives for spending time with her.

He chuckled and the sound was hollow and humorless. "You're in a lot of trouble, aren't you, Holly? Or, I should say, someone very close to you is. Why won't you let me help you?"

Holly bit her lower lip. She wasn't about to make any admissions about Craig and her involvement in his many troubles, but she wanted to. She wanted to let everything pour out. "I don't need any help and I'm not in trouble," she said stubbornly when David's indigo eyes impaled her with an unspoken challenge. "What gave you that idea?"

He made an exasperated sound. "I'm not an idiot, Holly. I was there when this person called, whoever they are."

If Holly felt alarm, she also felt a paradoxical sort of comfort. Could it be that, for all her imaginings, David really didn't know that her caller was Craig? "I think we should leave," she said stiffly.

"Fine," David replied, setting his wineglass down with a jarring thump and rising from his chair to draw back Holly's.

The flesh on the back of her neck tingled as it was brushed briefly by the hard wall of his midsection. Even that small contact stirred the melting warmth deep in Holly's middle and made her heart beat at a faster pace.

She was still shivering when they reached his car.

"Take me home, please," she said, struggling not to fling herself into his arms like some helpless bit of fluff and sob out all the things that were tormenting her.

"Don't worry," he replied in a terse whisper.

But, at the house, he lingered. Against her better judgment, Holly invited him inside for coffee. Just passing through the living room, where they had so nearly made love the night Craig called and ruined everything, made Holly's face burn.

She was grateful to reach the cookbook-cluttered, sensible kitchen. What could happen here?

Too late, Holly remembered the first soul-jarring kiss. That was what could happen here.

She busied herself with the coffeemaker, filling the decanter with cold water, putting a new filter and fresh grounds into the basket. She was so very much on guard that her shoulders ached.

"Holly."

She stiffened as she felt David approach, but could not bring herself to turn around and face him. His hands closed over her shoulders and began gently working the taut muscles there.

"Scary, isn't it?" he asked in a low voice, his breath brushing Holly's ear and part of her cheek.

"Wh-what?" Holly hedged. She knew she should break out of David's hold, but she didn't have the spirit to do that. Besides, the massage he was giving her felt so good.

"The way we need each other."

Holly lifted her chin, barely able to keep from letting her head roll as the muscles in her shoulders were forced to relax. "I don't want to need anybody," she managed to say.

"Neither do I," came the prompt, gruff reply. "But there it is."

He was close, the length of his body comfortingly hard and strong against Holly. Suddenly his hands stopped working her shoulders to cup her breasts with a bold gentleness that caused her to draw in a swift, audible breath.

"D-David—"

His thumbs were stroking her nipples through the thin fabric of her blouse and the gossamer bra beneath. "Let me make love to you, Holly," he said hoarsely, his lips now touching the outer rim of her ear and making every part of her leap with a stinging desire. "If we don't, I'm going to go crazy."

Holly trembled, her head falling backward to press into David's broad shoulder, her eyes closed. "At least you're still sane," she admitted, breathless. "I'm already over the edge. I must be, to do this…"

The delicious torment of her breasts stopped; he turned her swiftly to face him. And new torments, even sweeter than those that had gone before, took over as he kissed her. Holly's knees quivered, threatening to give out, and David supported her by pressing closer, fairly pinning her to the counter's edge.

When he drew back, he searched her face with that same broken, needing look in his eyes. "Holly?"

Flushed, Holly nodded, and that was answer enough for David. He lifted her up into his arms and, at her direction, mumbled into his neck, carried her upstairs and into the bedroom. There, he dropped her summarily onto the rumpled covers, and she had cause to be embarrassed again because she had forgotten to make the bed.

To hide that, she tried to make a joke. "You boldly go where no man has gone before, I'll say that for you."

The indigo gaze impaled her. "Are you saying that you've never…"

Hastily, coloring again, Holly shook her head. "No. My...my fiancé—"

He sat down on the bed beside her, his fingers woven together, hands dangling between his knees. "It's all right, Holly. Just tell me one thing: is this really what you want? If it isn't, I'll leave right now and we'll pretend that none of it ever happened."

Holly did not want David to go. She wanted him to hold her, kiss her, love her. But she couldn't say any of those things because her throat was constricted.

David must have read her need in her eyes and in the flush on her cheekbones, for he kicked off his polished boots and stretched out on the bed beside Holly, wrapping one arm around her, holding her close. She loved the clean scent of his hair and skin, the tender threat of his powerful body.

Eventually he kissed her again, tentatively at first, as though he expected her to push him away. When she didn't, the kiss deepened and with his free hand he began to caress her, cupping his other hand at the back of her head. After a very long time, she felt crooned in sleepy surrender, arching her back just slightly in acquiescence.

When the blouse had been opened completely and laid aside, David unfastened her bra. Her breasts moved with voluptuous freedom, the peaks tightening in response to the fate that awaited them and the coolness of the air.

David continued to caress her, brushing the wanton nipples with his fingertips, charting the rows of her ribs, circling her naval. And all the while, he kissed her, seeking every depth and secret, consuming even as he cherished.

After a time, he kissed the line of her jaw, sampled her earlobe, traced a path of fire down the white length of her neck. When he found her breast and took the nipple full in his mouth to suckle, Holly arched her back again, electrified, and gasped out a senseless cry of welcome.

Meanwhile, his hand undid the tricky buckle on her belt, the button of her slacks and the zipper. Holly felt the fabric of both the slacks and her panties sliding downward and gloried in the sensation.

David left the sensuous warmth of her breasts to brush his lips down the length of her rib cage, first on one side and then on the other. He drew her slacks and panties down and away and kissed the hollows of her hips, making lazy, white-hot circles with the tip of his tongue.

Holly moaned with her need of him, so dazed she could barely see. When he shifted away from her and off the bed, she was stricken, until she realized that David was only removing his own clothing, that he would come back to her.

"Are you sure, Holly?" he asked softly as he stretched out beside her again, part of his lean, powerful body covering and making promises to hers.

"Yes," she managed to say.

He kissed her again, deeply and desperately, and their tongues engaged in a savage, fevered battle. His knee prodded her legs gently apart and then he was poised above her, bracing himself with his hands.

"God in heaven, Holly," he muttered hoarsely, "how I've wanted you…from the first…"

Holly's hands were moving up and down the sleek, rippled expanse of his back. She wanted to say something poetic, something memorable, but her arousal was such that she could do no more than gasp his name.

David groaned and entered the sweet sanctum of her body, carefully and with a tenderness that deepened the love Holly already felt for him. He moved slowly at first, rhythmically, sheathing and unsheathing, reacquainting her with the long-forgotten feel of a man's possession.

Holly's few experiences with her fiancé long ago had done nothing, nothing whatsoever, to prepare her for this. This was a glorious, blinding joy, one that centered all of her heart and all of her soul on the singular joining of this man's body with her own. She moved in time with him, making a soft, unselfconscious sound in her throat, a crooning, needing sound.

David's lips were everywhere, brushing her eyelids, tracing the line of her jaw, tasting her mouth. His tongue circled her lips in a way that was somehow territorial and fiercely arousing, and the pace he had set for her body increased by degrees until they both seemed to be hurling themselves at each other, frantic for a oneness that would consume them both.

When that moment came, David growled, his eyes closed, and shuddered upon Holly while she cried out and thrust her hips upward to enclose him as completely as she could.

They both sank into a sleeplike state for a time, their breathing ragged, eyes closed. David's fingers, tangled in Holly's hair, moved soothingly against her scalp. Then, suddenly and with devastating determination, he thrust himself free of her, cursing under his breath as he wrenched on his clothes.

Holly, shameless only moments before, now felt tawdry. She clasped the edge of the quilt covering her bed and pulled it over herself.

"David, what is it?" she finally dared to ask, watching wide-eyed as he completed the angry rite by jerking his boots back onto his feet.

He might have stormed out without saying anything at all if Holly hadn't spoken when she did, but then he froze, his back turned to her, rigid and impassive. "It was a mistake," he muttered at length.

"It was your idea!" Holly cried, wounded.

David lowered his head but did not turn around to face her. "Yes. It was my idea," he conceded raggedly.

"You feel guilty, don't you, David?"

Now he turned and met her eyes. "I'm sorry, Holly. I wanted you so badly I lost my head."

"You lost your head?" Holly was suddenly energized, electrified. But this time it was fury, not passion, that surged through her. Heedless of her nakedness, she flung back the quilt and bounded off the bed. "I beg your pardon?" she screamed.

David silenced her by laying three fingers gently, ever so gently, over her mouth. His eyes were dark with some pain that Holly couldn't understand and couldn't share. But whatever it was, she would gladly have traded her own confused, hurt feelings for it.

"Believe me when I tell you, Holly, that I've never wanted or needed a woman the way I needed you just now. Never. But it was a mistake. We can't let it happen again."

It would have hurt less, Holly was certain, if he'd slapped her. "What do you mean, it was a mistake? It was…it was…"

David kissed her forehead, wiped away the tears gathering at the corners of her eyes with practiced thumbs, then turned to walk away. He closed the door quietly behind him, but Holly waited until she was sure he was out of the house before flinging herself facedown on the bed to cry.

6

The telephone rang. Sitting up on the bed, brushing her tangled hair back from her face, Holly reached out for the receiver, overriding the answering machine downstairs. Please, God, she prayed, let it be David.

"I left you two messages last night!" Craig blurted out the moment she said hello. "Don't you return your calls anymore, or is it something I said?"

Craig. Holly settled back on the pillows, which still bore the scent of David, and sighed. "I'm sorry, Craig. I was busy and—"

"You were *busy?* Good God, Holly! Remember me? I'm your brother, the man who is in trouble?"

Holly's throat was thick with despair, and her head

ached. "We all have problems, Craig," she reminded him quietly, thinking of David Goddard.

"Sure, Holl. I know you're probably all torn up about whether to pay your Keogh Plan before the end of the year and what color to paint your toenails."

The sarcasm, following the scene with David as it did, was too much. "Listen, Craig. I care about you and you know it. I do everything I can to help you. But you're the one who got yourself into this mess—kindly remember that!"

He subsided. "I know. Holly, I'm so scared."

Tears smarted in Holly's eyes, sudden and hot. It was a surprise because she had been certain that there were none left to cry. Images of another Craig, bright and fit and funny, rose in her mind. Dear God, what had happened to change him this way? During the troubled years after their father's death, when their mother had been so confused and distracted, he had been Holly's strength, her lifeline.

"I know, Craig, I know. I beg of you, give yourself up."

"I can't, Holly. I just can't. You don't know how these guys treat a fink—"

"Craig, they're not going to hurt you. I'll have a

lawyer present. You're still a citizen and you still have rights."

"Not anymore, I don't," he muttered. "I've had dealings with al-Qaeda, Holly, and they know it."

"Why, Craig? Why did you turn to…to those people? Why did you do it?"

He made a strange sound and Holly was shattered to realize that he was crying. "I have a habit, Holly," he finally said.

Dread electrified Holly, and she bolted upright. "What kind of habit?" she whispered, her eyes wide and burning. "Dammit, Craig, *what kind of habit?*"

"Cocaine," he said.

"Oh, God," Holly groaned.

"Listen, I need money. Cindy managed to bring me what you sent, but that's gone now."

"No."

"What did you say?" Craig sniffled, and his voice sounded angry again.

"I said no, Craig. I'm not giving you money to buy poison! I absolutely will not!"

"Holly, I need—"

"You need help and I haven't been giving it to you! Oh, God, how could I have been so stupid—"

"Get the money, Holly. Send it to this address—" He

rattled off a post-office-box number in a small Oregon town. "I mean it, Holly. If you don't, I'll be home for Christmas. And not to turn myself in."

"What are you saying?"

"I'm saying, sister dear," he answered with tart patience, "that if you don't help me I'll take Toby on the road with me. That's what I'm saying."

"No! I won't let you! I won't let you expose him to that, drag him around the country—"

"You won't be able to stop me, Holly. I know where he goes to school, and I know where you live. And remember I'm a former federal agent—I'll find the kid no matter where you try to hide him."

"Craig!"

"Send the money," he said. He repeated the address once more and then hung up.

Slowly, her hand trembling so hard that she had to make several attempts before she could manage the task, Holly replaced the receiver in its cradle.

She sat there on the bed, cross-legged, her head in her hands, until she heard Toby downstairs. "Mom!" he yelled exuberantly, probably still excited from his afternoon at the Ice Capades, "I'm home!"

Holly quickly leaped off the bed, found herself a robe and went down the stairs.

Toby was waiting at the bottom, his beloved face alight. "Geez, Mom," he said, barely able to stand still, "the ice show was great! They had the Flintstones and—" He stopped, taking in Holly's bathrobe and mussed hair with concern. "Are you sick, Mom?"

"No, darling, I'm not sick," Holly answered swiftly, forcing a smile to her face. "How did you get home, by the way? I thought I was supposed to pick you up."

"David brought me!" Toby sang, spreading his mittened hands for emphasis.

Holly swayed backward, just slightly, stunned. How could she have missed seeing David, when he was standing only a few feet away? Why hadn't she sensed that he was near?

"I hope you don't mind," David said quietly, but there was much, much more that his eyes were saying. They looked haunted, hollow.

Holly's temper flared, fanned by her fear, and she shifted her eyes to Toby's trusting, upturned face. "Don't you ever, ever get into anyone's car but mine, young man!" she hissed.

Toby retreated a step, looking as though she'd struck him. "But, Mom, David—"

David laid a quieting hand on the child's shoulder. "No, Tobe. She's right. We made a mistake, you and I."

Toby was not appeased. He darted one furious look at his trembling aunt and dashed off into another part of the house, probably to take solace in the late-afternoon cartoons he loved to watch on television.

"What are you doing here?" Holly half whispered, watching David, loving him even though her every instinct commanded her to tear out his hair.

"I couldn't stay away. Bringing Toby back from the ice show seemed the perfect excuse, so I did it. I'm sorry, Holly. I didn't mean to undermine your authority."

Holly held her chin high, but inwardly she was all too conscious of her appearance. "You are very, very good at finding excuses to keep tabs on me, aren't you, David?"

There was a thunderous silence, and David averted his eyes for a moment before meeting Holly's glare directly. "I love you, Holly."

Nothing he could have said would have surprised Holly more; she came a step nearer and her hand tightened on the banister until her knuckles ached. "What did you say?"

"Don't make me say it again, Holly. I already feel like enough of a fool as it is."

"Thanks a lot!"

"Just get dressed, will you? We need to talk, you and I. Not fight, not make love. Talk."

Holly stared at him for a few minutes and then, too confused to deal with anything, turned and dashed up the stairs. Safe in the shower stall, with hot water pouring down over her head and her newly awakened body, she rested her face against the tiled wall and tried to catch her breath.

David made himself at home in the kitchen, conscious of the glum little boy sitting slumped at the trestle table. "Your mom didn't mean to yell at you, Tobe," he said, finding the coffee and the filters before pouring cold water into the top of the coffeemaker.

"She's sure grouchy lately! And it's almost Christmas, too!"

David smiled somewhat sadly, and then turned to look directly at Toby, leaning back against the counter, the coffeemaker chortling behind him. "Sure enough, it is almost Christmas. Time to get a tree."

Toby brightened a little, but he was still miffed. "Yeah, I guess." His eyes strayed to Holly's desk, to the answering machine there, its light blinking frantically. "She never listens to her calls, neither."

For the first time since high school, David Goddard blushed. David Goddard, who had guarded presidents. "She's been sort of busy."

The child bounded off the bench, a study in impatience, and stomped over to the machine. Before David could intercede, he had pushed two buttons on the machine. There were two brief messages from Holly's brother, followed by a long conversation that told David more than he really wanted to know.

Craig had a cocaine habit. He needed money. And he was in a town in Oregon, watching a certain post-office box. When he began to talk about taking Toby from Holly, David strode across the room and turned off the machine abruptly.

Toby's eyes were brimming with tears, and his color, high from the cold weather outside and his time at the ice show, drained away. "I want my mom!" he blurted out, fleeing the room.

David swore and cast one despairing look at the ceiling before leaving the house. Five minutes later, from a phone booth outside a supermarket, he called the FBI.

Skyler, arriving unannounced, frowned at Holly. "My God," he muttered, "you look terrible!"

On this dismal Sunday morning, a soft snow was falling; a fire was crackling on the kitchen hearth. "Thanks, Sky," Holly said, stepping back to admit him to her kitchen. "A compliment always gives a day that little extra something."

"Don't be difficult," Skyler chided, taking off his stylish muffler and shaking it, a look of disapproval on his face. "I bring great tidings and all that."

Holly could have used some great tidings to offset the problems she was having with Craig and the confusion she felt over David's disappearance the day before. He'd seemed so eager to talk, but when she had finished her shower, dressed and gone downstairs, he had already left the house. After a quick search, she'd found Toby in his room, sobbing into his pillow, and the little boy had refused to tell her what was wrong.

Finally, he had fallen asleep. When he woke up later, Holly had offered him dinner, but he had refused. He was still silent this morning, and his mood added to Holly's growing collection of worries.

"So, what glad tidings do you bring?" she asked, going to the coffeemaker and helping herself to her third cup since getting out of bed an hour earlier. After pouring a cup for Skyler, she sat down at the trestle table and nodded for him to do the same.

He took in her drawn face and the smudges under her eyes with puzzled concern. "Holly, what's wrong? You look—"

Holly held up one hand to stop him. "I know. Terrible."

"You're still in your bathrobe!" he marveled, shocked. Skyler didn't believe in looking less than one's best at any time of the day or night.

"Toby had bad dreams last night," she said, as though that were an explanation. She didn't add that she had been tormented by nightmares, too—when she had been able to sleep at all.

Skyler shrugged, looking helpless and a little annoyed. "What you need, what you both need, is a day in the country. Holly, let's drive out to my folks' farm and cut down a Christmas tree."

Holly knew that she shouldn't go, that she would be encouraging Skyler's affections if she went. Even though her involvement with David Goddard was an unholy mess, she didn't want to do that.

On the other hand, a drive in the wintry countryside would certainly be a pleasant distraction.

"Skyler, I—"

He sighed, and his fondness for Holly was naked in his eyes. "I know, Holly. You've been seeing someone else. Surely it isn't so serious that you can't spend a day with me?"

Holly's heart twisted slightly. The truth was, her entanglement with David was so serious that she *had* to spend a day with Skyler. If she stayed around the house, waiting for David or for another of Craig's devastating phone calls, she would surely go insane. And Toby needed the outing just as desperately as she did.

Gently, she reached across the table and closed her hand over Skyler's. She was surprised to find that he was trembling just a little. And she was saddened by what that probably meant. "I have been seeing David regularly, Sky. And I do care about him a great deal."

"I'd guessed that by the way you kept turning me down whenever I asked you out, Holly."

"I'm sorry," Holly replied softly, and she truly was. She had never wanted to hurt Skyler or anyone else, but she clearly had done just that.

"Say you'll come with me today, Holly. We'll find a couple of Christmas trees and Mom has a great dinner planned."

Skyler looked so hopeful that Holly wanted to cry. "Okay," she said. "Just give me a few minutes to get dressed and throw some breakfast together."

Skyler wasn't looking at her but into the depths of his coffee cup. "Don't bother with breakfast, Holly. We'll stop and eat on the way out of town."

Holly left the table, but she paused in the doorway of

the kitchen, looking back at Skyler. Her throat ached and her answer came out sounding hoarse and raspy. "You're a good friend, Skyler Hollis. Do you know that?"

Skyler said nothing at all. After watching him for a silent, painful moment and wishing that things could be different, she hurried upstairs to get dressed.

"I'd like it better if David was taking us," Toby grumbled when Holly stopped by his room to ask him to get ready to go and find a Christmas tree.

So would I, Holly thought sadly, but she said, in a voice that quivered just the slightest bit, "Please don't be difficult, Toby. We need a dose of fresh air, you and I, and we're going to have it. Get ready, please. Skyler is treating us to breakfast."

Glumly, Toby went about obeying. Just as glumly, Holly went on to the bathroom to take her shower.

The day with Skyler was, for Holly, a bittersweet experience. They were two people who knew that their relationship was going nowhere, and were trying to be cheerful despite it. All the same, it was a pleasant day, at least for Holly, giving her the time she needed to paste herself back together and think.

During breakfast she pondered Craig's cocaine problem and his threat to take Toby away. While she was frightened by the things her brother had said, she began to suspect that the part about stealing his son was just hysteria. Deluded though he was, Craig couldn't possibly believe that he would be capable, under the circumstances, of taking care of a child.

As for the cocaine, well, while it was certainly a horrible shock, it did explain a lot about Craig's treason. And that's what it was; Holly forced herself to accept the fact. It was treason.

After that, she was unable to finish her hearty breakfast, no matter how much a subdued Skyler might urge her. But what she had already eaten helped Holly considerably. She felt stronger, better able to cope.

Toby, too, was coming out of his curious mood, however reluctantly. He enjoyed eating in restaurants even when it involved spending time with Skyler.

When they left the restaurant, snow falling all around them and with an easy day ahead, Holly was able to put most of her problems out of her mind and chat with Skyler. Toby sat in the back seat, armed with a pocket trivia game, shouting out an occasional question.

Skyler, in Holly's view, was uncommonly patient. "The Lone Ranger's uncle!" he called out once, in exuberant answer.

"Wrong," said Toby smugly, in the often-insensitive way of children. "It was Pinky Lee!"

Skyler rolled his eyes and tossed Holly a beleaguered look. She laughed because if she hadn't, she would have cried.

After an hour and a half of trivia, they reached the dairy farm owned by Skyler's parents. The Hollises were friendly people, and they greeted both Holly and Toby with comforting warmth. Hanging behind them, though, on the porch that stretched all the way around that carefully painted, solid old Victorian house, stood a young woman Holly had never seen before.

"Hello, Mary Ann," Skyler greeted the guest somewhat self-consciously. "How are you?"

A fetching blush rose in Mary Ann's pretty cheeks. "I'm all right. You?"

Skyler risked one broken glance at Holly and cleared his throat. "I'll get by," he answered gruffly.

Holly looked at Mary Ann again and hoped devoutly that Skyler would fall in love with her, here and now. It was obvious that the dark-haired, blue-eyed woman adored him—perhaps she and Skyler had grown up together and perhaps Mary Ann had always cared for him....

She brought herself up short. Fantasies. She was just

weaving fantasies in hopes of making it easier to end her own relationship with Skyler.

"Mary Ann and I found some real good trees," Skyler's father announced cheerfully, and a glance at his leathery, good-natured face told Holly that he knew more about his son's relationship with the city lady than he was letting on.

Again Holly felt guilty. It was going to be so hard, telling Skyler she didn't want to see him anymore, even though he must certainly have guessed it from their conversation that morning.

After a round of coffee in the huge, high-ceilinged farmhouse kitchen—Toby, of course, had hot chocolate—everyone except Mrs. Hollis set out for the woods.

It was a bracingly cold day, and here in the country the snow was cleaner and, alas, deeper, making the jaunt to the woods rather hard going for Holly. Flinging back an occasional polite look, Mary Ann kept to the lead with Skyler and Toby.

Wearing high rubber boots and a heavy, plaid woolen coat that smelled pleasantly of tobacco smoke and hay, Mr. Hollis stayed beside the lagging Holly. Something in his manner inspired confidence, and Holly, feeling an innate need to talk with someone older and wiser, ventured, "Mary Ann and Skyler must have known each other for a long time."

Mr. Hollis smiled. "Since kindergarten," he replied, keeping his voice low, as Holly had, so that no one else would overhear. "I'm afraid it's pretty obvious that Mary Ann has her cap set for him. 'Bout broke her heart when he went away to the city to start that store of his. Mine and Mother's cracked a bit, too, as it happens."

Holly was saddened. Skyler was the Hollises' only son, though he did have one sister. Probably, his parents had hoped that he would want to take over the family farm someday. "I'm sorry," she said.

"Ain't your fault," came the quick reply, and a smile lighted the older man's eyes as Mary Ann picked up a handful of snow and flung it at Skyler, who shouted in good-natured protest and then returned the volley.

Toby, never one to stand on the sidelines, gathered up ammunition of his own and joined the battle.

"Mother was real pleased with that cookbook you sent up, the one with your autograph in it. She shows it to all her friends."

Holly didn't know what to say to that, beyond "thank you"; she wedged her hands into the pockets of her old coat and sighed, slogging grimly along in the wake of the escalating snow war up ahead. Skyler's, Mary Ann's and Toby's laughter mingled, a bright song in the chilly, snow-flecked air.

"That's a fine boy you have there," Mr. Hollis persisted. Perhaps he sensed her need to talk and her paradoxical difficulty in doing so.

"Thank you. Toby is actually my brother's son, but I forget that most of the time, he seems like my own."

"Reckon if you take care of him and love him, then he is your own. It's the day-to-day of it that matters, you know."

"Yes," Holly agreed, thinking of Craig, remembering when he had been a fine father to Toby. But that had been several years ago, before Craig's wife, Allison, had died. Before his habit had driven him to sell out his own country.

"You don't say much, do you?"

Holly laughed. They were almost out of the pasture and into the stand of pine trees and Douglas firs that was their destination. "I'm usually more sociable," she said. "I'm sorry."

"No need to be sorry." He paused and caught her elbow in his strong, work-worn hand. His eyes were kind as they touched Holly's face. "A person's got to follow their heart, Miss Llewellyn. And sometimes it don't lead where they'd like it to, but they gotta go after it anyway."

So he did know that the relationship between her and Skyler was over. If it had ever really existed at all.

"I'm hoping that Skyler will find someone else soon," she said, her voice trembling a little. Cool snowflakes collected on her eyelashes and chilled her cheeks, and Holly glanced ahead at the laughing Mary Ann. "Maybe…"

Mr. Hollis looked pleased, and he gave a guffaw of laughter. "Maybe so," he agreed.

As if to lend the theory credence, Skyler lunged at a gleefully shrieking Mary Ann and threw her down into the snow, rubbing a handful in her face. She came up sputtering and laughing, making exuberant threats. Toby, having watched all this with mingled delight and uncertainty, hurled a questioning look back at Holly.

It's all right, she told him with her smile, and his face was again alight with the joys of the day.

There was a bewildering array of trees to choose from, but Holly, her jeans snow-sodden to her knees, was not inclined to be persnickety. Skyler shook out a fragrant fir that stood about seven feet tall and appeared to be symmetrical, and she nodded in answer to the question in his eyes.

Mr. Hollis handed over the small hatchet he carried, saying he was "too derned old" for such carryings-on, and Skyler chopped down the tree.

With Toby frolicking at his heels like a puppy—for this was proof that Christmas, that most elusive of childhood days, was truly coming—Skyler began dragging the tree back toward the house.

"Don't you want a tree for yourself?" Holly asked him, ignoring the territorial looks from Mary Ann. These, she supposed, were her just due for falling into step beside Skyler.

"I'll get one another time," he said softly.

Holly knew then that he had contrived the whole idea of tracking down a Christmas tree for her benefit; after all, it was still three full weeks until the holiday. He had seen how upset she was, sensed that she was frazzled and overwrought, and tried to help.

A feeling like love but sadly different twisted in her throat. "Thank you, Sky," she said gently.

Skyler only shrugged, but when he shifted his attention to Mary Ann and started teasing her his voice was a determinedly cheerful boom.

Mary Ann gloried in the attention, though she pretended to be outraged, and Toby jumped and leaped in the scratchy snow trail left in the wake of the fallen tree, his cheeks pink, his china-blue eyes shining. How mercifully innocent he was just now, Holly thought, how unaware he still was of the complications that lay ahead in the process of growing up.

They ate a sumptuous dinner of fried chicken, mashed potatoes and country gravy, biscuits, and green beans that Mrs. Hollis had put up herself. She and Mary Ann talked so easily about farm things; the prices they could get for cream and eggs, the patterns they would use for sewing their Christmas dresses, whether to plant peas on St. Valentine's Day or later on, in March.

Holly listened with interest and a sort of weary nostalgia, and when the meal was over, she volunteered to do the dishes. Mrs. Hollis, having worked in the kitchen all day, was obviously tired.

Skyler and Mr. Hollis and Toby went outside to tie the Christmas tree to the roof of Skyler's car, and Mrs. Hollis retired to the living room to "put her feet up for a spell." Mary Ann, her eyes looking everywhere but at Holly, stayed to help with the dishes.

Holly felt a need to put Skyler's friend at ease. After all, Mary Ann belonged here, fitting in better than Holly herself ever could.

"You and Sky have been friends for a long time," she

said quietly, taking up a flour-sack dish towel when Mary Ann had elbowed her away from the sink.

Now Mary Ann's dark, beautiful eyes swung to Holly's face, confused, but wary and full of challenge. "I love Skyler," she said in a low, earnest voice.

Holly smiled. "I know," she answered. "Toby and I won't be back here anymore after today."

There was a silence while Mary Ann absorbed that statement and dealt with it in her own way. Finally, she turned a bright smile on Holly. "It was good to meet you all the same," she said.

Holly laughed, and after that, the two women worked in swift accord, putting the kitchen right again in no time at all.

7

Toby's eyes were round and sleepy as he looked up at Holly, and he yawned. "Let's decorate the Christmas tree," he suggested, valiant in the face of his fatigue.

Holly laughed and rumpled his hair. "Tomorrow, sweetheart. After school."

With an acquiescent shrug, he turned and scampered up the stairs, stopping midway to look at Skyler and say, "Thanks for taking us to the country. It was real neat."

Skyler shoved his hands into the pockets of his jacket, looking ill at ease and shy. He didn't truly belong in this house any longer, and that saddened Holly even though she knew it was for the best. "You're welcome, kid," he said.

Holly suppressed a tired smile. Some things didn't change. "Will you stay for coffee, Skyler?" she asked.

He shook his immaculately groomed head. "I don't think that would be a good idea." Toby was gone by then, busy getting ready for bed. "It's over, isn't it, Holly?" he added in a sad voice.

"Yes," she said quietly. "I'm sorry."

There was a painful silence, and then Skyler sighed and shrugged his shoulders. When he met Holly's eyes again, he was smiling with an obvious effort. "I'd better bring in the tree before I go. Where do you want it, Holly?"

Holly gestured vaguely toward the living room, and Skyler cleared his throat as though he might say something more. Then he ran one hand through his neatly styled hair, something Holly had never seen him do, and turned away without speaking at all.

The tree stood in the corner of the dimly lit living room, leaning, lushly green and fragrant, into the corner. There were no decorations on its boughs just yet, and to Holly, all alone now that Toby was asleep and Skyler had gone home, it was a forlorn sight.

She sighed, knowing that for all the exercise and fresh air of the day just ending, sleep would elude her.

She turned off the living room lights and went into the kitchen, where she poured a cup of coffee and sat down at the trestle table.

"Coffee," she mocked herself, lifting the cup. "Just what your average insomniac needs before bed."

It was then that the flashing light on the answering machine caught Holly's eye. Resigned—one couldn't shut out the world forever—she stood up and crossed the room to her desk, pressing the button marked Play.

The first voice on the recording was Elaine's, saying that she had the flu and might not make it to work the next day. The second belonged to Holly's housekeeper, promising to come in to clean on Tuesday.

Holly frowned. This was strange. What had happened to those two brief messages from Craig? He'd said he'd called twice.

A third voice came on, jolting her out of her reflections. David's voice.

"Holly, call me, will you please? My number is 555-6782. It's important, so don't worry about the time."

Holly stood frozen in that lonely kitchen, such a busy place in the daytime but so echoingly empty now. Why should she call David after the way he'd treated her? Hadn't he made love to her and then said they'd made a mistake and left her alone with her confusion and her conscience? And then he'd come back, saying that he loved her, saying that they needed to talk—and disappeared before they could!

Something besides the two vanished calls from Craig niggled at the back of her mind but she couldn't quite grasp what it was.

David answered on the first ring, not with a hello but with his name. And that bothered Holly, too.

To cover her uneasiness, she blurted out, "David, if this is a game, I don't want to play! You said we needed to talk before, and then you just left!"

His sigh came, a raspy sound, over the wire that linked them together so tenuously. "Something came up, Holly, and I had to leave. I'm sorry."

Holly sank into her desk chair, turning the telephone cord in the fingers of one hand. "Toby was very upset, David. Do you know why?"

David hesitated and finally said, "No."

He was lying. Holly knew he was lying. But why? Whatever doubts she might have about David Goddard, she was absolutely certain that he would never do or say anything to put Toby in such a state. "You said you wanted to talk," she prompted coldly.

"I do. But not over a wire. Holly, could I come over? Please?"

Holly sighed and glanced ruefully at the Seth Thomas clock on the kitchen mantelpiece. "It's late, David—after eleven."

"Do you think you'll sleep tonight if we don't talk?" he asked.

Holly felt her face flushing. "That's all we're going to do—provided I agree to your visit, that is. Toby's home and—"

"I didn't ask you to go to bed with me, Holly," came the patient reply. "I really do want to talk with you. In person."

Holly's face grew hotter still, and she closed her eyes as memories of David's lovemaking washed over her in a heated, crushing wave. Perhaps that was what gave her the courage to refuse—if it was courage. "We can talk tomorrow, David. I've had a long day, and I'm tired."

"Holly—"

"Tomorrow," she said firmly.

"Tomorrow," he sighed, and then the line went dead. Holly hung up the telephone, frowned at the answering machine for just a moment and then went upstairs to bed.

Surprisingly, she slept soundly that night, without the dreams that had been troubling her so much.

Getting Toby off to school in the morning was a

madness of lost textbooks and half-eaten oatmeal, as usual. Elaine called to say that she was still sick and definitely wouldn't be over.

Once she was alone, Holly eyed the work waiting on her desk with trepidation. Her newspaper column was due in two days and needed to be extensively rewritten, but she couldn't work up the self-discipline necessary to do the job.

It was almost a relief when David knocked at the glass panes in the kitchen door and then let himself in at Holly's somber nod. By that time, she had lugged the huge boxes of Christmas tree decorations down from the attic and was going through the newspaper-wrapped contents in search of the red-and-green stand.

"I'm sorry about last Saturday, Holly," he said quietly.

Holly's face heated again, and then chilled. There was a guilty, reluctant look about David, as though he had something important to say, something that he dreaded saying.

"That's okay," Holly lied, turning her attention back to the ornaments and the pieces of the large crèche left her by her grandmother. "Have some coffee."

"Where were you yesterday?" David asked, finding the cups and rattling the coffeemaker's glass decanter against the mug when he tried to fill it.

It gave Holly a perverse sort of pleasure to answer, "Skyler took Toby and me up to his parents' farm to look for a Christmas tree."

David was silent for so long that Holly finally had to turn around and look at him. Still wearing his brown leather jacket, he was watching her with unreadable indigo eyes, leaning back against the counter as he sipped the too-hot coffee.

"Are you in love with him, Holly?"

Holly sighed, unwrapping one of the three wise men and turning the large porcelain figure in her hands. "No. In fact, I told Skyler last night that we shouldn't see each other anymore."

There was another silence, broken at long last by David's noncommittal, "I see."

And suddenly Holly was furious. She whirled, the wise man still in her hands, and cried, "Dammit, David, you said you wanted to talk! It was your idea, remember?"

A half smile curved his lips. "Isn't that what we're doing? Talking?"

"No, damn you, it isn't! We're…we're shadowboxing!"

David sighed, set his steaming mug of coffee aside and shrugged out of his jacket, laying it over the back of a kitchen chair without particular concern. Holly had a feeling that he was used to expensive things, which the jacket obviously was.

"You're right," he said. "We are sparring. Holly, I meant it when I told you that I love you."

Holly's hands were trembling; she set down the endangered wise man. "So you did," she finally croaked out, keeping her head averted because there were sudden, inexplicable tears in her eyes and she couldn't bear for him to see them. "But something is terribly wrong between us, David. I know it. I sense it. You're keeping something from me."

He came to her then and clasped her shoulders in his hands. His throat worked fruitlessly for a moment, as though it were difficult for him to speak. "Whatever happens, Holly, remember that I love you. When we made love the other day—"

Holly pulled away from him, both drawn to him and frightened. "When we made love, you said it was a mistake," she reminded him, wounded by the memory.

The Christmas-tree stand was uncovered, and she pulled it out of the box. David took it from her hands and put it aside.

"Look at me, Holly."

Holly didn't want to obey, but she did. She had to.

"I thought I loved Marleen," he said slowly, his hands on Holly's shoulders again, firm and strong. "When she left, I hurt for a long, long time. And then it got so that I didn't feel anything, didn't want to feel anything. I had a lot of affairs, Holly—I'm not denying that—but until I met you I didn't think it was possible for me to really care about another woman."

One tear sneaked down Holly's face and she brought one hand up between David's arms to wipe it away. "Still something is wrong...I..."

He bent and kissed her briefly, tenderly. "Just trust me, Holly. I know that's a lot to ask, but I'm asking you."

"Something awful is going to happen!" Holly cried, frantic.

"Maybe. Sometimes things happen that are very painful at the time, but they're still for the best. And I'll be on the other side, waiting for you."

He was being so damned cryptic! Holly wanted to pound his chest with her fists, to claw out his eyes. Unfortunately, another part of her wanted to take David by the hand and lead him upstairs to that bed where they had made such sweet love, where she had been transformed, if only temporarily, into a woman with no problems, no doubts, no pain.

David caught her chin in his hand and lifted her face so that she had to look directly into his eyes. "I love you," he repeated slowly. "Whatever happens, I don't want you to forget that, Holly. Promise me that much."

She swallowed hard. "Tell me what you know, David. Who you are. What do you want—"

"I want you."

"You are being deliberately obtuse!"

He smiled, but it was a sad smile, and something vital lay broken in his eyes. He released Holly and took up the Christmas-tree stand, turning it slowly in his hands. "I'll set the tree up for you, if you want."

Holly bit her lower lip and then nodded. It was obvious that she wasn't going to get any more information out of David, but God help her, she didn't want him to go. Not yet.

"Thank you," she managed to say.

Setting the tree in its stand proved to be just what David and Holly needed to lighten the impossible weight of the situation. By the time Holly was finally willing to admit that the tree was as straight as it could possibly be, they were both laughing.

While David was washing the pitch from his hands, Holly impulsively lighted a fire in the living room hearth and put on instrumental Christmas music. As if to accommodate her oddly festive mood, a soft snow began to drift past the windows.

I'm crazy, Holly thought. I'm definitely certifiable. Half an hour ago, I was crying and now, just because David and I put up the Christmas tree, I'm lighting fires and playing music and setting the stage for something that shouldn't happen.

David returned, a cautious smile on his face. Without saying a word, he caught Holly's hand in his, sat down on the couch and pulled her gently into his lap. He smelled deliciously of fresh air and pine, and his blue eyes, often so disturbing, were as warm as the snapping fire on the hearth.

"I love you, David," Holly blurted out without stopping to think. How could she think when he was holding her that way, his hands making tender circles on her shoulder blades?

He laughed. "At last you admit it."

Holly was honestly surprised that she hadn't said the words before. God knew, the truth of them had been as much a part of her as her breath and her heartbeat, almost from the first. "David—"

He turned her on his lap and kissed her. "Shh. It's Christmas."

Holly was gasping by the time the kiss ended. She

knew that her hair was probably mussed and her cheeks flushed. "It is *not* Christmas—"

David's face was buried in her neck, his lips making tantalizing forays along its pulsing length. "Woman," he groaned, and the word was at once a reprimand and the most flagrant praise. "You argue about everything."

The buttons on Holly's blouse were opening, one by one, and his mouth was following the ever-deepening vee of bared flesh intrepidly. Heat so intense that it bordered on pain surged through Holly as he explored the rounded side of one breast and nuzzled that side of her bra down far enough to bare what he sought.

"Ooooh," she groaned as he took brazen nips at the aching nipple and then suckled it. And all her doubts fled before the flames of her passion and his.

As David undressed her, never really ceasing his tender assault on her throbbing senses, all memory fled. By the time he had subjected her to the scandalously delicious release meant to prepare her for final conquering, Holly couldn't have recited her own name.

He did not enter her gently this time, but with a thrust that was fiercely pleasurable for Holly. Her hands moved wildly over the muscle-ridged expanse of his bare back, pleading, urging.

There was something sweetly wicked about making

love on the living room couch, and Holly's passion was heightened by it, as, she sensed, was David's.

When the moment of scalding release came, it enfolded them both. David was kissing Holly as they moved together, and his moans of tender defeat echoed inside her mouth, mingling with her own fevered cries.

They lay entwined for some time afterward, their breathing ragged, their hearts pounding as though to break past flesh and bone and be bonded together.

This time, to Holly's enormous relief, there was no talk about their lovemaking being a mistake. And this time David did not leave her.

No, they showered together, laughing and flinging soapsuds at each other at first, later slipping into passion again. They made love a second time, their bodies still slick with water, on Holly's bed. After that, they dressed and made a tongue-in-cheek agreement to behave themselves.

When Toby got home from school, he found them in the living room, sorting the lights that would set the freshly cut Christmas tree aglow. His greeting to David was a whoop of delight and a hurling of his small, solid body into the man's arms. David laughed and pretended to be falling under the weight, and Holly, watching them both, was more certain of her love for this enigmatic man than ever before.

They worked, the three of them, until dinnertime, transforming the fragrant tree into a thing of glory. By the time the last glass ball was hung and the last strand of tinsel had been draped from just the right bough, it was dark outside.

"You can fix dinner now, Mom!" Toby announced magnanimously, his eyes on the shimmering wonder of the Christmas tree. "Us men are starved."

David laughed and shook his head. "Us men," he corrected Toby with mock sternness, "are going for take-out chicken. Your mom has done enough for one day."

Holly's eyes linked with David's and she blushed. That "enough" didn't bear recounting. "You don't have to go out. We've got lots of food in the freezer."

"Yuk," Toby complained. "I'm tired of ka-bobs. I want to go with David to get chicken."

Both of her men stood watching her, waiting for her approval. "Okay," she relented, smiling even though she tried to look insulted. "But you stay with David, Toby Llewellyn. Don't go wandering off and don't ask for two desserts. Or for pop."

Toby flung David a beleaguered look. "I'm not allowed to eat much sugar," he complained.

David chuckled and rumpled Toby's corn-silk hair. "You're so abused. Tell me your sad story in the car, will you?"

And after David had kissed Holly soundly but briefly, they were off.

Holly sat alone in the living room with the lamps turned off, admiring the lights of the Christmas tree. "When it comes to glow, Tree," she said aloud, "you've got nothing on me."

David liked being with Toby, and he had certainly enjoyed the day. Still, Craig Llewellyn was much in his thoughts as he navigated the snow-slicked roads in the Camaro he had rented after returning the brown sedan.

The little boy, fastened firmly into the seat belt on the passenger side, chattered on and on about the Christmas tree, the day they'd flown model airplanes in the park and the trip to Skyler Hollis's family's farm. David listened patiently, though in actuality he was going over the facts Walt Zigman had given him during their last telephone conversation.

Craig Llewellyn had managed to elude the FBI in that little Oregon town, just as he had in L.A. He was smart, Llewellyn was, and slippery. But he wasn't smart enough.

David knew that he would appear in Spokane very soon. And he was worried about Llewellyn's threat, overheard the day Toby had impulsively turned on Holly's answering machine and replayed her conversation with her brother. She obviously didn't know that David had heard the recording; maybe she didn't even realize that the machine had been on when she'd picked up the telephone.

He glanced at Craig's son and wondered how cocaine could have been bigger than such a treasure of a child. God, if this boy were his own...

David stopped himself. Once this thing with Craig actually broke, there would probably be little left of what he and Holly shared. She would hate him and so would the boy. It was a grim irony that he'd chosen her of all people, to fall in love with.

David seemed subdued when he and Toby returned with the take-out chicken. His eyes dodged Holly's and his contributions to the conversation were few and far between.

"What's wrong?" she asked, when a grumbling Toby had been settled at the trestle table to do his homework, and they were alone again beside the Christmas tree.

"I guess I'm tired," he said.

Holly was on the verge of tears. Was he going to spoil the day, after all they'd shared? Was he going to start talking "mistake" again?

"I guess you're shutting me out," Holly argued evenly. "And I don't understand it, David. Not after today. You can't make love to me and then treat me as though I'm some bad habit you wish you could break."

The word "habit" hung between them, or so it seemed to Holly. But David couldn't know about Craig's confessions to her concerning cocaine; there was no way he could know that.

"I can't do this problem!" Toby wailed from the kitchen. "Somebody help me!"

"I'll do it," David volunteered, his eyes still averted. And a moment later, he was turning his back on Holly and striding off toward the kitchen. He remained there until Toby's homework was done and it was bedtime.

While Holly appreciated the help David gave Toby—math was her secret nemesis—she felt a bit put out, too. How had things changed so completely, just in the time it took David to go and buy the take-out chicken?

When she came downstairs, having tucked Toby into bed and heard his prayers, David was sitting in front of the living room fire, staring ponderously into the flames as though some drama were being played out there.

Holly needed a moment to think, to collect herself; where this man was concerned, she had a way of plunging over emotional precipices, of saying and doing all the wrong things. Turning into the kitchen, she suddenly halted, stunned.

Craig was standing there, leaning casually against the counter, a cup of hot coffee in his hand. He looked so ragged and thin, with a fevered light in his eyes that made Holly despair.

"Craig," she whispered.

He toasted her sardonically with a lift of his coffee cup. "You didn't send the money," he said.

Holly could barely breathe, so great was her shock at seeing this wasted parody of the man who had been her brother. His filthy army fatigue jacket seemed two sizes too large and his eyes were sunken and haunted. "Craig, I couldn't," she said, keeping her voice low for fear that David would hear. "I didn't have a chance. You only called on Saturday…"

Craig's eyes swept the room, as though he might be assessing the value of things he saw there. "That guy helping Toby with his homework. Who is he?"

"Keep your voice down! He's still here!"

Craig's thin shoulders lifted in an impertinent shrug. "What's his name and where did you meet him?"

Holly sighed, half-sick with surprise and confusion, afraid that David would hear Craig and, conversely, afraid that he wouldn't. "His name is David Goddard and I met him in a class I'm teaching."

"I thought so. I remember him from the good old days."

"You—you what?"

"I remember him. He's a Secret Service agent, Holly. Or didn't he tell you that? I'll bet he asks a lot of questions about your misguided big brother, doesn't he?"

The room swayed around Holly, rising and falling, tilting at stomach-clenching angles.

"You mean you didn't even suspect?" Craig taunted in leisurely tones. "He must be pretty good."

Holly had suspected; she *had*. So why was it such a brutal surprise? She groped for the trestle table's sturdy edge, collapsing onto the bench. "Oh, my God. My God."

"The Secret Service doesn't usually handle this sort of thing," Craig speculated idly. "Must be connected to our dear cousin Howard, the never and future king."

It happened then; David came through the doorway. Holly heard him, felt him there, but could not look at him. Or at Craig.

"Llewellyn," he said, and Holly supposed it was an

offhand greeting, though David had given the name no tone at all.

"Goddard," Craig replied calmly.

Holly looked up then, afraid. Suppose Craig had a gun? Suppose—

"Would you leave us alone, please?" Craig asked her companionably. "We're old friends."

Holly hadn't the strength to rise from that bench at the trestle table, and even if she had, she still would have stayed.

She darted a look from one expressionless man to the other, praying that there would be no violence, praying that Toby wouldn't stumble in.

David didn't so much as glance in her direction, and when he spoke again, he addressed Craig. "This can be easy, Llewellyn, or it can be difficult. The choice is yours."

Craig laughed and then horrified his stunned sister by pulling a pistol from beneath his tattered army coat and laying it on the table. "I'll take it easy," he said. "Besides, the bushes outside are probably crawling with crew cuts by now. I'm not so far gone that I don't know you guys have been watching this place."

David took up the pistol deftly and unloaded the chamber, slipping the bullets into his pocket. His gaze slid to Holly just for a moment, and there was nothing in it to indicate that they had ever laughed together, ever been lovers.

When he went to the door to admit the inevitable agents, Holly sagged against the table's edge and covered her face with both hands.

8

By morning, the news of Craig Llewellyn's "dramatic" capture was all over the newspapers. It was on television; it was on the radio. And it was in Elaine's face when she returned to work, largely recovered from her flu and wide-eyed with concern.

Holly sat blindly at the trestle table, a newspaper spread out before her.

Elaine took off her coat and sat down on the bench across from Holly. Being a true friend, she didn't ask why she had never heard anything about Craig before. "Are you going to let Toby go to school today?"

Holly sighed. "I don't know. Oh, Elaine, I don't know anything."

"It must have been awful."

Images of FBI agents surging into her kitchen throbbed in Holly's mind. Images of David, so cold, so quiet, so determined. "At least Toby slept through it all," she managed to say.

Elaine's hand came across the table to squeeze Holly's. "David Goddard—"

"Don't mention that man's name in this house, Elaine! Not ever again!" Holly flared, her eyes filling with tears of betrayal and fury.

"You were in love with him," Elaine said flatly. "I thought so."

"He wasn't in love with me!" Holly wailed. "Oh, Elaine, it was all an act from the first! I should have known—I *did* know but I wouldn't listen to my own instincts."

"That's very hard to do sometimes," Elaine comforted quietly. "Did David tell you that he cared for you?"

"Yes! But he lied—he only wanted to find Craig!"

"Maybe he didn't lie, Holly. Maybe he meant what he said."

"He lied. He wanted my brother." Holly was calmer now, though her heart was still thick with despair and raw sobs lurked beneath her carefully modulated words. "He lied."

"Well," Elaine said, "one thing is for certain—we're

not going to get any work done today. And I don't think
Toby should go to school until things quiet down a bit,
do you?"

Holly shook her head. Eventually, the little boy was
going to have to face the things his father had done,
but she wanted him to hear the truth directly from her,
and not on the school grounds. "C-could you take him
home with you, just for the day? I'm afraid there will
be reporters…"

"You know I'll do anything I can to help. What
about your class tonight, Holly? Are you going to go
ahead with that, or shall I call everyone and tell them
the course has been canceled?"

Again Holly shook her head. "I'll go crazy if I don't
keep on working."

"What if David comes to class?" Elaine asked softly.

"I don't think even he would have that kind of gall.
But if he does show up, I have a few things I want to
say to him, you can bet on that!"

"It might be better to listen to what he has to say,
Holly. I can't believe he—"

"Believe it. I was just something above and beyond
the call of duty to him, Elaine. A means to an end."

Elaine looked as though she might want to say more,
but she held her tongue. The telephone began to ring

and she leaped up to answer it, her voice crisp and in charge.

"Do you want to talk to the press, Holly?" she asked after a few words with the caller, her hand over the mouthpiece.

"No!" Holly cried.

"I'm sorry," Elaine said into the receiver, "Ms. Llewellyn has no comment." With that, she hung up and turned on the answering machine to record a similar message for any future callers, setting it to pick up automatically.

And it was then, of all times, that Holly remembered what it was that had eluded her before, concerning the answering machine. After leaving those two vanished messages, Craig had called her again and the machine had been on. It would have recorded both sides of the conversation between her and her brother.

David Goddard had listened to that conversation, and he had erased it from the machine! He would have heard Craig mention the town in Oregon, the cocaine habit. And when the FBI had failed to find her brother there, he had no doubt deduced that Craig was desperate enough to come to Holly.

Which explained, of course, why he had spent the day there. Putting up the Christmas tree. Making love to Holly, going out for fast food so she wouldn't have to cook. And, finally, helping Toby with his homework. All very neat and professional.

In that moment of realization, if David had been standing before her, Holly was certain she could have killed him without hesitation.

Elaine had gone upstairs to fetch Toby, and the back door burst open and snapped closed again so forcibly that Holly was startled out of her grisly reflections.

Madge Elkins, the housekeeper, was turning the lock and getting out of her coat at the same time. "Good Lord, there must be a hundred reporters and TV people out there, Holly. They chased me up the driveway!"

Like an automaton, Holly got up from the bench and went to the window over the sink. Sure enough, the backyard was full of paparazzi. So, probably, was the sidewalk out front.

If they step on my tulips, Holly thought ferociously, stomping through the house. And there they were, dozens of them, with cameras of every sort in their hands and avid looks on their faces.

Holly flung open a window in the living room and yelled, "Get out of my flower beds!" Before so much as one question could be asked, she slammed the window shut again, so that their sudden burst of words only bounced off the glass, a dull, babbling sound.

In the kitchen, Elaine and Toby were getting ready to make a break for it. Holly knelt in front of her nephew and held his small shoulders in her hands, hurting for the confusion and fear in his face.

"Tobe, everything is going to be okay," she said in a voice that didn't sound the least bit like her own. "It really is."

"Why are all those people out there? What did we do?"

"We didn't do anything. Toby, your dad was arrested last night and they want to ask us about him. You don't have to say anything at all to them—just stay close to Elaine."

Toby's eyes were wide and frightened. "Dad was arrested? Why?"

There was no choice but to be honest. Now, at this late date, Holly wished she had told Toby about Craig to prepare him for this inevitable disaster. "Your dad has a lot of problems, Tobe. Remember that day in the park, when I told you that he does bad things sometimes?"

"They put bad people in jail!" Toby protested, his lower lip jutting out.

"The police are not our enemies, Toby. It might not

seem so right now, but being arrested was the best thing that could have happened to your dad. Now he'll get the help he needs."

Toby was clearly still confused, but he was calmer. Madge, on the other hand, was fidgety, standing at the kitchen window and peering out.

"I don't know if you should try to get past them, Elaine," she fretted. "It might be better to stay here."

This particular dilemma had been gnawing at Holly, too. She kissed Toby's forehead and stood up again, wondering what to do. It was then that David appeared at the back door, his breath a white fog in the winter air, his face set and determined. Holly would certainly not have admitted him, but Elaine did just that, before she could protest.

He barely glanced in Holly's direction, speaking instead to Elaine as he distractedly ruffled Toby's hair and then drew the child against him. Not knowing of David's part in this debacle, the little boy held on to the man as if for dear life. "What's the plan?"

Holly simmered, too furious to speak, but Elaine answered David's question as though he had every right to be there, every right to ask such a thing.

"I want to take Toby over to my place, but we're not sure about shuffling him through that crowd."

David, still not sparing so much as a look for Holly, nodded crisply and reached down with one arm, lifting Toby to ride on his hip. He smiled, actually smiled, into the child's trusting face. "Tell you what, slugger. I'll take you to Elaine's car. You just pretend those people aren't even there, okay?"

"Do they want to hurt me?" Toby asked in a tone that twisted Holly's heart.

"No way," David said confidently. "They want to ask you questions, just like your teachers do at school. But we don't have time to talk, do we?"

"No," grinned Toby, wrapping his arms around David's neck. "We don't want to talk."

David's eyes shifted to Holly's then, meeting her gaze squarely. And the expression in those fathomless indigo depths said that he was not apologizing for Craig's capture.

Holly would not have expected him to do that. Craig was a sick man and his arrest, as she had told Toby in other words, was, though painful, the end of a long nightmare. No, it was the way David had used her that hurt. The way he had insinuated himself into her life, caused her to care for him and lied again and again, both by word and by action, about his own feelings.

Now, though he hadn't said a word, he was asking

her permission before plunging into the crowd of TV and newspaper people. Seeing the trust in Toby's face, knowing it would be better if he spent the day away from the house, she was forced to give that permission. She nodded, letting her eyes tell David Goddard that despite this concession, the distance between them could never be bridged.

With Elaine at his heels and Toby perched on his hip, David opened the kitchen door and went out. Madge fretted and fussed at the window; she was braver than Holly, who could not bear to look.

"They made it!" the housekeeper crowed after a few seconds of terrible suspense.

"D-David isn't on his way back in here, is he?" Holly ventured to ask, wringing her hands.

"No," Madge replied, apparently innocent of the intrigue that had just taken place between her employer and the man in question. "His car must be out front, because he went the other way. Maybe he's going to follow Elaine and Toby to make sure they aren't bothered en route."

The possibility that some of the reporters might trail after Elaine had not occurred to Holly until then, and she was jarred by it. "You don't suppose they will, do you? You don't suppose these…these people will bother Elaine and Toby?"

"They'll stay here," Madge said confidently, her face still pressed to the window. One of her hands waved in an annoyed gesture. "Get out of there!" she shouted to someone outside. "You'll crush the lilac bush! You! Yes, you! Leave that birdbath alone!"

Despite everything, Holly had to laugh at the ludicrous comedy of it all. She poured herself a cup of coffee and went to her desk in the corner of the room, as though this were any ordinary day. The way the answering machine kept picking up on phone calls proved, of course, that it wasn't, as did the horde Madge had ordered away from the birdbath and the lilac bushes. Until Elaine called to say that they had arrived at Roy's mother's house out in the Spokane Valley, she left the machine's volume up so that she could hear each caller.

Grasping the receiver quickly, she spoke with Elaine and, for a few moments, with a gleefully excited Toby. It seemed that the whole matter had become an adventure to him, which was a relief to his aunt. After glorying in the fact that he didn't have to go to school that day, he hung up, and Holly pushed the volume button on the machine to its lowest setting before starting to work on her column.

Toward midmorning the media people got tired of standing around in the cold weather and began to straggle away, a few at a time, until the yard and driveway were empty again.

One would almost have thought that nothing abnormal had happened at all, Holly reflected as she worked on her cooking column and Madge dusted and vacuumed in another part of the house.

The answering machine was a reminder, of course; the moment one message had been left, another caller would try to get through.

But when Holly finished her column, which was surprisingly good, she thought, under the circumstances, she began to think about David again, and how he had betrayed her. How he had seduced her.

She didn't quite dare to go outside, but if she didn't work off some of her anger, and soon, she knew she was going to be tearing her hair. Staunchly, Holly went upstairs and exchanged her jeans and sweater for her workout clothes. She pinned up her hair, drew a deep breath and made her way to the family room just off the kitchen, where the mini-trampoline was kept.

Rolling it out of a closet, she set it on its sturdy legs. She switched on the TV to a cable channel devoted exclusively to old movies and bounced furiously on the trampoline while watching Claudette Colbert win Fred MacMurray's heart.

Holly ran, she did jumping jacks and then she just bounced again. Up and down, higher and higher she went, but she couldn't escape the fact that she loved David Goddard, no matter how hard she tried to distract herself.

The housekeeper, like Elaine, seemed kindly disposed toward David. Or, at least, she let him into the house when he knocked tentatively at the kitchen door.

"Where is she?" he asked.

The woman went back to the table, where she had been eating lunch and following the details of Craig Llewellyn's arrest on the screen of a TV roughly the size of a postcard. "In there," she gestured toward the inner doorway, "trying to bounce herself through the family room ceiling."

David frowned and wedged his hands nervously into his pockets before going to the doorway to investigate. Holly's soft blond hair was pinned up haphazardly, her breathing audible even over the television set she was watching.

Her back was turned to David and she didn't hear his approach, for she kept right on bouncing. Bouncing. A shimmering film of perspiration shone from beneath the loose tendrils of honey-colored hair at the nape of her neck. "Don't you trust him, Claudette," she sputtered out. "All men are rat finks."

David felt a lot of things at that moment: sympathy, regret and, most of all, a desire to wrench Holly Llewellyn off that damned jogger-thing and make love to her on the family room floor.

He rounded Holly and stood before her, inwardly bracing himself for what he knew was coming.

Her beautiful aquamarine eyes, somewhat swollen and red, widened at the sight of him. He felt like Benedict Arnold crashing a party at George and Martha's place. At least she'd stopped that damned bouncing.

"Get the hell out of my house!" she hissed, her perfect cheekbones flaring to the color of her pink pants, her hands clenched into fists at her sides.

"No. I'm not going anywhere until you get down off that thing and talk to me."

"I'll call the police!"

"I don't think so. Besides, I probably have more sway with them than you do." He turned, admired Claudette Colbert's unique face for one steadying moment and then switched off the TV. "Get down, Holly," he ordered, facing her again.

She bit her lower lip, flashed him a look of beleaguered hatred and began to bounce again. Slowly. Defiantly.

It was giving David motion sickness. With a muttered curse, he grasped her and wrenched her down. She stumbled and fell against him—every day had its high point, he thought wryly—and then she righted herself, bunching up her fists and using them to thrust away from his chest.

"I was telling the truth when I said I loved you, Holly," he said, allowing her to keep the small distance she apparently needed, "so stop flaring your nostrils and clenching your fists and listen to me."

"You go straight to hell, Mr. Goddard!" she gasped out. "Or is it 'God' for short?"

David's jawline tightened painfully. "Dammit, Holly," he bit out, "can't you see that I was caught in this trap as much as you were? I came here to find out if you were helping Craig in any way and—"

"You mean you were spying on me, too? That you weren't just waiting for my brother to stumble into your net?" Right then he wanted to turn her over his knee and blister her delightful rear end. That was unthinkable, of course, but he did take some comfort in the fantasy.

"The president-elect was afraid you might be helping Craig sell secrets, Holly," he said evenly.

"Howard thought I was some kind of female James Bond?" She was seething now, showing her teeth. God, even though she was mad as hell and sweating, she was magnificent. "I don't believe it!"

"Believe it," David said.

"You lied to me the whole time!"

"Not the whole time. I meant it when I said I love you."

"Get out of my house!"

David stood stock-still. "Don't you want to know what's going to happen to Craig now that he's been taken into custody?"

That stopped her. She stood stiffly, attentively, her eyes searching his face. "Yes," she said in a whisper. "David, will they hurt him?"

"You've been watching too many espionage movies. They'll debrief him—" He paused, holding up both hands to stay the frantic questions he saw brewing in her green-blue eyes. "That only means that they'll find out what he knows and what he's told al-Qaeda, among other people he might have been dealing with. And then, because of the cocaine problem, they'll hospitalize him for a while. Whether or not he actually goes to prison will depend on a lot of factors that can't be determined right now."

"He was so afraid of being caught!"

David ached for Holly, wished that he dared take her into his arms and hold her. "Holly, being stopped was the best thing that could have happened to Craig. The cocaine alone would have killed him. And what was the situation doing to you? To Toby?"

She was gnawing at her lip again, her eyes bright with unshed tears. "I'm glad that Craig won't have to run anymore. I—I didn't realize how sick he was until he told me about the drugs."

"I know," David said softly.

Holly stiffened, and her eyes flashed again. "I was going to turn him in myself, you know. I didn't need you to come here and pretend you loved me. I could have handled the situation."

"Could you, Holly? Do you have any idea how insidious cocaine addiction can be, what it can make a person do?"

He saw her tremble and knew she was bracing herself against him, against all he represented. In that instant, he accepted the fact that he'd lost her.

"Get out," she said. "And don't come back, David. Don't call and don't come to my classes."

"Your classes? Surely you're not going to teach this week—the press will be lying in wait for you, Holly. They'll eat you alive!"

"I can take care of myself," she said. And then she turned away and David didn't have the heart to turn her around to him again.

"I love you," he said gruffly. Then he drew a deep breath, struggled to control the burning in his eyes and left her. She switched the TV back on and climbed back onto the trampoline, bouncing with a vengeance.

As David passed through the kitchen, the housekeeper gave him a sympathetic look. He shrugged and without speaking opened Holly's back door to step out into a world that was never going to be quite the same again.

The moment David was gone, Holly sank to her knees on the trampoline, covered her face with both hands and let the sobs that had been scalding her throat have free reign. Claudette Colbert laughed merrily on the television screen, and Madge spoke softly from the doorway.

"Go after him, Holly. If you love that man, don't you let him get away. You'll be sorry all your life if you do."

Holly stopped crying and drew a deep breath. She would be sorry all her life that she'd *met* David Goddard, maybe, but she would never be sorry for sending him away. Damn his sneaky hide anyway. Let him go and use some other unsuspecting woman.

"I will not have that traitor mentioned under this roof again, Madge," she said, rising to her feet and dashing away her tears with the cuff of her jogging jacket. "If he calls or comes to the door, he is to be turned away. Do I make myself clear?"

There was a brief, tense silence. "Yes," Madge said finally, with resignation. "Clear enough."

Sorry that she'd had to speak so harshly to Madge, who had always been as good a friend as she was a housekeeper, Holly nevertheless left the room without apologizing. She went upstairs, stripped and showered.

At seven o'clock, she got into her car and drove downtown to teach her fruitcake class. The reporters were there, just as David had warned they would be, but so were the students. By sheer force of will, Holly taught the class as usual, the only deviation being that she didn't stay to gather up and clean the baking pans and mixing bowls.

Later, at home, Holly steeled herself and played back the messages her machine had been recording all day. With one startling exception, the calls were from news reporters. As if in a daze, Holly sat down to listen to the surprisingly ordinary voice of the next president of the United States.

"Hello, Holly. This is Howard. I'm sorry about Craig and all the fuss the press is probably stirring up. Maggie and I just wanted you to know that we hope you'll come to Washington for the shindig next month." Having said his piece, Howard hung up without another word and there were no more messages after that.

This is Howard...sorry about Craig...hope you'll come to Washington... The phrases echoed in Holly's overwrought mind and her broken heart. Maybe, just maybe, she would go to Washington. Maybe she would attend the balls and the parties and the swearing-in. Maybe she would tell Howard to his open and trust-worthy face that she was just as loyal an American as the next person. "Do you solemnly swear," she imagined the Speaker of the House asking dear Howard, "that you will monitor the activities of your third cousin, the cookbook author, lest she undermine the security of this great country of ours?"

Howard, of course, would so swear.

Just then, Elaine arrived with Toby and, to Holly, she looked just a bit sheepish. Toby was carrying a dime-store fishbowl as though it were gold, frankincense or myrrh, and two goldfish hovered inside, staring stupidly.

"David gave me these," the little boy spouted before Holly could make any kind of comment at all. "He said I could take care of them for him, but I'm not s'posed to worry if they buy the farm 'cause they only cost seventy-nine cents a piece and they're spendable."

Expendable. Of course. The way Holly was expendable. The way Toby, though he hadn't made that painful discovery yet, was expendable. "Take the fish to your room, Toby," she said evenly.

When Toby was gone, she attacked an uncomfortable Elaine with, "You let David see Toby, didn't you? Why did you do that, Elaine, when you knew—"

"He only wanted to say goodbye!" Elaine broke in defensively. She looked pale and tired and a little harried, and Holly realized belatedly how hard this day had been for her friend.

"I'm sorry, Elaine. I shouldn't have jumped all over you that way."

Elaine managed a shaky smile. "We're all on edge, I suppose. I can't tell you how much I'm looking forward to putting on my old chenille bathrobe and curling up with Roy and a good book!"

Holly felt a touch of envy, somewhere in the deepest, darkest corner of her heart. Was she ever going to have anybody she could wear a chenille bathrobe in front of and "curl up" with?

It didn't seem very likely because she knew that she was never going to love a man the way she'd loved David Goddard. Never ever again.

"You can take the rest of the week off if you'd like," Holly offered in an unsteady voice.

"Not me," Elaine said, squaring her shoulders and trying to look intrepid. "I'm made of better stuff than that and so are you."

Holly smiled, even though tears were dangerously near the surface. "So you are. Thank you, Elaine, for everything."

Elaine hugged Holly briefly and patted her shoulder. "Anything for the boss," she said, and then she was leaving again, on her way home to Roy and the chenille bathrobe and a good book.

If Holly hadn't liked her friend so much, she would have hated her for being so lucky.

9

Walt Zigman had seen that look before; it was a look that meant an agent had lost his spirit and maybe his grip. Damned shame it had to happen to a man like Goddard. He sat back in his desk chair and maneuvered his cigar stub from one side of his mouth to the other.

Goddard sat in the chair Walt knew the agents called the "hot seat," his long frame lank with an effort to hide tremendous pressure. "I told you she was clean," he said after a long, uneasy silence.

"Maybe you read palms or tea leaves, Goddard, but I don't. We had to know."

Goddard darted Walt a look meant to slice deep, and to Walt's surprise, it did. "Holly Llewellyn wasn't guilty of any crime. As far as I'm concerned, she's been harassed."

"Horsechips. She aided and abetted a suspected felon, Goddard. She's lucky we didn't bring her in, too."

Goddard was glaring now; his hands, gripping the arms of his chair, whitened at the knuckles. Though he hid the fact, Walt was pleased by the reaction; maybe this agent would be all right after all.

"Here." Goddard slapped a thin file folder down in the middle of a stack of memos and notes. Walt's whole life was one big memo these days, what with the transition from one administration to another and the inaugural festivities coming up in January. Security problems were everywhere and Walt Zigman didn't need another hassle.

"What's this?"

Goddard averted his eyes and shifted in his chair, but then he met Walt's gaze squarely. "My letter of resignation," he answered.

If there was regret in his voice, Walt didn't catch it. He wanted to swear. "You sure about this, Goddard? You're a good agent."

"I'm sure."

"What the hell are you going to do with your time, for Christ's sake? Walk dogs?"

Goddard made a visible attempt to keep his temper. "I'm qualified to practice law, in case you've forgotten."

"That little—that Llewellyn woman really got under your skin, didn't she?" Walt paused, sighed, lit the cigar stub and puffed industriously for a few moments. "Dammit, Goddard, we're swapping administrations here. We got an inaugural coming up in a little better than a month! I need every experienced agent I've got right now!"

Goddard was waving away the cigar smoke with one hand and Walt ground the stub out in an ashtray. "For what? Standing around in Saks while the new first lady tries on six hundred pairs of shoes?"

"You'll be assigned to the president himself, Goddard."

Goddard pointed one index finger toward the ceiling and spun it round and round in a contemptuous circle.

"Well, what the hell do you want?" Walt snapped, annoyed and a little insulted.

"I want out of the Service," David replied flatly. "I'll stay until after inauguration week is over, but I want the presidential assignments—no walking dogs. No strolls in the Rose Garden. It's strictly Oval Office and Air Force One, Walt, or I'm out of here."

"All right, all right, you're on presidential detail."

Walt took up the folder Goddard had laid on his desk and extended it. "You keep this."

"You keep it," Goddard argued, standing up. "I meant it when I said I wanted out."

"What the devil do you plan to do after January?"

Goddard shrugged. "I told you, Walt. I intend to practice law."

Walt muttered a swearword and picked up the remains of his cigar again. "Take over for Erickson, then. He's got a root canal scheduled for this morning."

Goddard winced sympathetically. "Where?"

"In his mouth, dammit," Walt grumbled, tossing the folder containing his best agent's resignation letter into a deep drawer.

"I was asking where to find the president, Walt," came the strained and humorless response.

Walt didn't look up. "Oval Office," he bit out.

Holly was just getting through her days and nights, operating on automatic pilot, so to speak. She tried to see Craig, but he refused any contact with her or with her lawyer. Soon after that, he was transported to Washington, D.C., for the debriefing David had told her about.

It hurt, having to hear that on the evening news along with the rest of the world.

Christmas was fast approaching, though, and for Toby's sake, Holly tried her best to get into the spirit of things. She shopped, she baked, she decorated the house and put a wreath on the front door. But every time she so much as looked at the Christmas tree, she was filled with memories that brought tears to her eyes and a painful catch to her throat. David was gone, really gone. She knew because she had looked up his address in Elaine's records of the last cooking class and driven to his apartment.

Two college girls were living there now, and they couldn't tell Holly anything about David Goddard except that he must have had a dog because there were these "grungy" stains on the rug. Holly had turned away and gone blindly back to her car, sitting there in the parking lot for a full fifteen minutes with her forehead resting despondently against the steering wheel. She had already known that David had returned to his old life in Washington, D.C., so why was it such a crushing blow to find that strangers were living in his apartment? What would she have said to him if he had been there?

Holly hadn't known the answer to either question and now, kneeling on the floor of her own living room, struggling to wrap a last-minute gift for Toby, she still hadn't worked it all out.

The doorbell rang, and Holly sniffled and dashed a stray tear from her cheek. Who could that be? After all, it was Christmas Eve, and nearly eleven o'clock at that.

She opened the door to find Skyler Hollis standing on the porch, looking uneasy and snow-dappled and rather earnest. For the space of a second, Holly had allowed herself the fantasy that David would be there in the glow of the porch light, and she hoped her disappointment didn't show.

"Sky," she said. "Come in."

"I hope you don't mind my coming by, Holly. I know it's late—"

Cautious because Skyler could be damnably persistent at times and because she didn't want to give him the wrong idea, Holly stepped back to admit him without saying anything.

He was carrying two beautifully wrapped packages in his arms. "I did my Christmas shopping last July," he explained. "I couldn't very well give Toby's to Mary Ann, so—"

Holly smiled because it was just like Skyler to do his Christmas shopping in July. He had probably addressed his cards then, too, though she hadn't received one. "Come in, Sky, and sit down. I think there might be some eggnog left."

He entered the living room ahead of her, put the two packages beneath the tree, then went to the hearth, ostensibly to examine Toby's as-yet-unfilled stocking, and confessed, "I've been worried about you, Holly, since that thing with your brother broke." He let the stocking fall back into place and turned to face her with the eyes of a concerned friend. "Are you all right?"

Holly shrugged and averted her gaze so that he wouldn't see the tears that had gathered there. "I'm all right," she lied.

"Toby?"

Toby was resilient. In fact, he was rather enjoying the notoriety of having a "spy" for a father. "Toby is okay, too, Sky. How have you been?"

A smile broke across his face, warm and, to Holly, very reassuring. "I'm dating Mary Ann," he said.

Holly was pleased and she hugged Skyler impulsively. "That's wonderful."

Skyler was still grinning. "I'm opening another store, too—up in Colville. I've been wanting to spend more time there."

Colville was a good-sized town and very near the farm. Holly smiled, starting to ladle out a cup of eggnog from the crystal bowl in the middle of the coffee table. Earlier, Roy and Elaine and Madge had all been by, and Holly had done her best to present them with some sort of celebration. "Your parents must be happy about that."

"Oh, none of that for me," Skyler said quickly, referring to the eggnog. "That stuff is fattening, you know."

Holly chuckled and took a sip from the cup herself. Lord knew, she spent so much time running on the mini-trampoline that she didn't have to worry about calories.

"You really ought to get away from Spokane for a while," Skyler said, watching her with a sort of gentle disapproval that implied she wasn't her usual self. "Hawaii, maybe, or—"

Holly laughed. "I can't go away, Skyler, much as I would like to. Toby is in school."

"All the same—"

She went to him, standing on tiptoe to plant a sisterly kiss on his cool, clean-shaven cheek. "Don't worry about me, Skyler. Please. I'm going to be just fine. You just concentrate on Mary Ann."

He returned her kiss, though her forehead was the target. "That guy is gone, isn't he?"

Holly's throat felt thick and sore again; she could only nod.

"He's a real fool," Skyler said. There was a long silence and then he started toward the door again, still wearing his coat. "I guess I'd better go," he said gruffly, his hand on the knob. "I've got a long drive to make."

"Be careful," Holly managed to say.

Skyler cleared his throat and nodded. When he met Holly's eyes, his gaze was full of something she had been getting too much of lately—sympathy. "I will. Merry Christmas, Holly."

Holly swallowed hard. "Merry Christmas, Skyler."

When he was gone, Holly walked back to the living room. The fire was burning low, the lights on the tree were glimmering and a Christmas carol was coming softly from the stereo. Holly swallowed again, squared her shoulders and methodically filled Toby's stocking until it bulged. For the first time in her entire life, she cried on Christmas Eve.

It seemed to Chris that her brother's smile was a little sad as he filled the girls' Christmas stockings and returned them to the hooks on the mantelpiece. He was looking at the two stockings that remained: his own and Chris's.

"I didn't know you still had these," he said gruffly.

Chris ached for him; though he hadn't said much about the disaster in Spokane, she knew David well enough to guess that he'd fallen for someone out there— probably Holly Llewellyn herself—and lost her. Her own painful divorce was two years in the past, but enough of the hurt lingered for her to sympathize.

"Holidays are the worst, aren't they?" she prompted softly, perching on the arm of the sofa and watching her brother.

David was tracing the letters of his name, awkwardly written in glitter across the top of the old red corduroy stocking. "Remember the year Mom made these, Chris? She was so proud of them."

Chris closed her eyes momentarily, scrounging up a smile. "You were Joseph in the church play," she recalled aloud. "Mom made your robe from an old sheet with Batman all over it."

David laughed gruffly. "Yeah. You were an angel that year. Talk about miscasting." He fell silent, then turned to face his sister, his dark blue eyes full of pain. "Do you miss Dennis?"

The truth was that Chris rarely thought of her ex-husband. She was too busy with her girls, the house, the cover designs she painted for romance novels. "At

Christmas I get a little sentimental. Most of the time, I revel in how much he and Mona deserve each other."

David laughed again, and the pain in his eyes faded a little. "I think the same thing about Marleen and her monkeys," he confessed.

"Something is hurting you," Chris prompted gently, folding her arms.

"Being a two-time loser, I guess," came the hoarse admission.

"Holly Llewellyn?"

David lowered his handsome head. "Not much gets by you, does it, Chris? You ought to be an FBI agent or something."

"Walt's daughter tells me you're resigning."

David cursed, but with less spirit than Chris would have liked. "Zigman has a big mouth."

Boldly, Chris went to her desk, picked up the telephone in both hands and thrust it toward her brother. "Call Holly and wish her Merry Christmas," she said.

"It's too late—"

Chris glanced at the clock on the mantelpiece. "It's only eleven out there. I'll bet she's still up."

David considered the telephone for a moment, as though it were some complicated equation, then turned resolutely away. "Shall I bring the girls' presents in from the garage?"

Chris sighed. From long experience she knew how stubborn her brother could be. She set the phone back in its place. "Let me check and see if they're asleep yet. Sometimes they pretend."

"How do you know if they're pretending?" David asked, so guilelessly that Chris had to laugh.

"Men! You tickle them, of course. If they giggle, they're playing possum."

David shook his head, grinning. Because his eyes had strayed to the telephone, Chris turned quickly and hurried up the stairs and into her daughters' room. She remained there, in the darkness, long after discovering that they were both asleep.

The telephone was ringing. Holly stared at it over her shoulder, parts of the Lego village she was trying to assemble still in her hands. She dropped a plastic palm tree and lunged for the receiver, telling herself that she mustn't let Toby be awakened by the noise.

"Hello?" she whispered, breathless with the foolish hope she couldn't seem to let go of.

Long-distance. The special ring had betrayed the call as long-distance. Holly's weary heart leaped within her.

LINDA LAEL MILLER

"Hello?" she said again, because her caller seemed stumped for words.

"This is David," came the gruff, belated greeting.

Holly sagged onto the couch, dizzy with relief and with pain. "Oh," she said woodenly.

"Did I wake you?"

"N-no—I was putting out the Santa Claus things for Toby," Holly answered. Damn you, you should be here helping me, she added in her mind. For the moment, the fact that she had sent David away herself escaped her.

"How is Toby?"

God, the man was a conversational genius. Maybe that came from standing silent guard over presidents, ever-alert for any sort of danger. "He's doing okay," Holly replied. "He still has the fish."

"I hope their personalities have improved. They were definitely lackluster company when I had them."

Tears were streaming down Holly's face now, but they weren't audible, she hoped, in her voice. "What do you want from two goldfish? The old soft-shoe?"

David laughed. It was good to hear that sound, even if it was distant. "A medley of Elton John's greatest hits would have been nice."

"I'll buy them a little piano."

David's chuckle seemed to reach across the three

188

thousand miles that separated them and caress Holly. "Have you forgiven me yet?"

"Quite honestly, no." It was sad to feel the anger again, the hurt. "Why concern yourself, David? You got your man and all that."

"It's my woman I'm concerned with."

Holly thrust out her chin, determined not to let him touch her with his voice. But she reddened to remember being his woman on that very couch and her body responded with a keen, embarrassing ache in her middle and a warm swelling in her breasts. "There are two college girls living in your old apartment," she said, and then hated herself for revealing that she'd gone there.

David must have sensed her discomfort, for he mercifully allowed the faux pas to pass. "Did they get the stains out of the rug?" he quipped.

Despite herself Holly laughed. "No. As a matter of fact, they didn't. They asked me if you had a dog."

There was a short, uncomfortable silence. "Holly," David finally ventured, "are you coming to Washington for the inauguration?"

Holly was winding and unwinding the phone cord around her finger. "I hadn't thought about it," she lied. The truth was that she had thought of little else; she'd been wondering if David would be at any one of the round of parties that were scheduled.

"Think about it."

"Why?"

"Dammit, you know why! Because I'll be in the president's hip pocket the whole time and I want to see you, that's why."

"Some Secret Service agent you are," challenged Holly hotly, flustered because he'd touched a nerve. "Do you always flirt with women while you're supposed to be protecting the chief executive?"

David sighed and it was a sound heavy with exasperation and strained patience. "I'll make time for you, don't worry."

"You're not going to make any kind of time, mister, so don't *you* worry!"

"Damn it all to hell, Holly, will you pull in your righteous indignation for one minute and listen to me?"

"No!" hissed Holly, remembering the lies, the pretense, the humiliation of finding out that she had been used. "You treated me like a...like a bimbo!"

He laughed. He actually had the gall, the temerity, to laugh!

"Merry Christmas!" Holly shouted and then she slammed the receiver back into its cradle.

After a few minutes spent wailing into a sofa pillow, Holly got hold of herself. She dried her tears and then stood up and went back to the Lego village, putting it together carefully. When it was done, she made sure that the red wagon was at just the right angle beneath the tree and that the football was displayed to proper advantage.

Then she burrowed on her hands and knees through the scratchy, fragrant branches, to unplug the tree lights and plunge a conscientious finger into the base of the stand to make sure there was enough water.

Later, upstairs, she put on a nightgown, brushed her teeth, washed her face and stumbled off to bed. Regrettably, no sugarplums danced in her head—only memories of David trying to fly his funny-looking model airplane in the park, David mixing fruitcake batter in the department-store class, David ushering Elaine and Toby through a pressing crowd of reporters and cameramen. David making love to her.

"Nerd!" she whispered, pounding one fist into the pillow. "Get out of my mind!"

David remained in Holly's mind until she slept; then he haunted her dreams. It seemed she had barely closed her eyes before Toby was bouncing gleefully on her bed, his tightly filled Christmas stocking in hand.

"Look, Mom!" he crowed, holding up the evidence. "Santa Claus came!"

Holly widened her eyes in feigned wonder; it was a game they played every Christmas morning. In truth, Toby had already added Santa to his list of fictional characters, along with the Hardy Boys, Superman and the Tooth Fairy. He was still undecided about the Easter Bunny.

Toby upended the stocking and the booty spilled out over the quilt—an orange, a bottle of bubbles, a deck of trick cards, a candy cane and at least a dozen other things. His delight uplifted Holly as nothing else could have.

"Can we go downstairs and open the presents?" the child demanded once the stocking goodies had all been inspected and mentally categorized in order of usefulness.

Holly pretended to be surprised. "I think we should eat breakfast first," she said.

Toby caught her hand in his and literally dragged her out of bed, giving her only a second to scramble for her robe and slippers before proceeding out into the hall and down the stairs.

The next half hour was happily absorbed in ripping away paper and ribbons. Toby received a model car and a Scrabble game from Elaine and Roy, along with gifts from Holly herself, from Madge, from some of his friends at school. Skyler had given him a radio with— he was a true friend, that Skyler—earphones.

"Aren't you going to open any of your stuff?" he asked, surrounded by loot of every type. The eagerness in his eyes made her choose the package he and Elaine had wrapped in secret and put under the tree with a converse sort of ceremony.

"This one has been driving me crazy," she confessed, taking sidelong notes of the little boy's quick, delighted grin. She opened the parcel to find a book she had been longing to read tucked inside. And her pleasure was real.

After that, Holly uncovered a frying pan from Skyler—that made her smile—and a bottle of her favorite cologne from Elaine and Roy. There were other things, too, sent by her mother and faraway friends, but nothing, she assured the little boy, was quite as wonderful as the book he had chosen for her.

Toby was frowning, peering into the depths of the tree. "What's those things?" he asked.

"What things?" Holly asked, honestly puzzled.

"In there. There's two presents in there, in the branches!"

Holly smiled, thinking that Elaine must have hidden away an extra surprise or two for Toby. She liked to do things like that. "Guess you'd better investigate," she said.

Toby drew out a sizable box—Holly couldn't imagine how she had missed seeing it—and then a smaller one. Both were wrapped in gold foil.

"The big one's mine!" Toby crowed after reading the tag. He was already tearing at the wrapping as he extended the other present to a confused Holly.

She looked down at the tag on her own gift and her heart stopped, then started again with an aching lurch. "Love, David," was written upon it in a typically firm hand.

Trembling just a little, Holly did not open her gift but, instead, watched Toby rip away a second layer of paper to reveal a plain box. Inside was a small robot, complete with hand controls and a set of batteries.

Toby lifted round, shining eyes to Holly's face. "Who's this from?" he whispered, awed. It was obvious that he was considering shifting Santa Claus from the fiction list to the one peopled by Holly and his teachers and everyone else he could see and touch.

"From David, I think," Holly said, and thank heaven, Toby was too enthralled with the gift to notice the tremor in his aunt's voice.

"Wow," he said, dragging the word out for that emphasis peculiar to seven-year-old boys.

Holly's eyes were stinging a bit, and she averted her face for a moment before opening her own present with numb, awkward fingers. Inside was a small, elegant velvet box, and inside that was the most beautiful diamond engagement ring she had ever seen. Still trembling, Holly opened the note that had been rolled up and slipped through the ring itself. *"Marry me or I'll jump off the Washington Monument. Subtly, David."*

Holly couldn't help it. She laughed. She bit her lower lip to stop herself and that didn't help so she laughed again. Tears were streaking down her cheeks and Toby was looking at her in total confusion.

"What's-a-matter, Mom?" he asked, flushed with concern.

Holly closed the ring box firmly. "Nothing," she said. "Nothing is the matter."

"Was it a joke present?" Toby wanted to know, and his manner said that he wouldn't consider that untoward.

"Yes," Holly managed to say, taking the gift, box, wrapping paper and all, to the mantelpiece, where she tucked it behind a picture of her grandmother. Out of sight, out of mind, she told herself without much conviction.

All through that hectic day, all through the hurried breakfast, all through the drive to Elaine and Roy's apartment, all through Christmas dinner and the rousing trivia game that followed, Holly's mind and heart kept straying back to that ring and all it meant.

Of course, she couldn't marry David Goddard, as intriguing as the possibility was—not after what he had done. But she would take a certain pleasure in throwing that diamond in his face when she went to Washington next month to attend Howard's inauguration.

10

Elaine was fairly dancing with excitement, her eyes bright and wide. She hugged Holly unreservedly, as other passengers pressed past them to board the airplane, and enjoined, "You have the best time anybody has ever had at an inauguration, Holly Llewellyn!"

Holly felt rueful and wary—perhaps it was a mistake to go to Washington after all—but she did return Elaine's hug. "Take care of Toby," she said.

"You know I will," Elaine scolded good-naturedly.

Holly wished she could back out at this late date but resigned herself to the fact that she couldn't. She squared her shoulders, drew a deep breath and entered the covered passageway leading to the airplane. She looked back once, wavering, but Elaine made a little shooing motion with her hands and winked encouragingly.

The flight was uneventful. Holly had a brief stopover in Denver, and then it was on to Washington, where a car and driver were waiting to take her to the White House—was this really happening to her? As a relative of Howard's—good heavens, she barely remembered him—Holly was to be accommodated in style at 1600 Pennsylvania Avenue.

Escorted by a grim-looking Secret Service agent who would obviously rather not have been bothered, Holly was quickly shuffled into a limo with tinted windows and driven to the most august address in the United States.

On the way, she tried to make conversation with the agent who sat in the back with her. A little chitchat, she thought, might ease her nervousness about what was to come. "Jimmy Carter came to Spokane once," she ventured, "to speak at Riverfront Park. He rode past in a car like this one, with darkened windows, and I think he smiled at me because I saw a flash of teeth."

The chauffeur chuckled to himself, though his eyes were fixed on the crazy Washington traffic. But the Secret Service man only reacted with a look that questioned her sanity. She supposed that Jimmy Carter and his teeth were old news to this guy, but he could have been a little friendlier all the same. Holly resisted an urge to tap on his forehead with her knuckles and ask if there was anybody in there.

They entered the White House grounds through a back gate, snow crunching beneath the limo's tires as it came to a stop at a rear door. Holly drew in her breath and let it out as a long, Toby-like, "Wow."

The Secret Service agent cleared his throat, got out of the car and extended a hand to Holly. Reluctantly, she accepted it. This character had no personality at all, it seemed. He was certainly nothing like David.

Holly left the limo with as much dignity as she could summon. Perhaps David would behave in just this manner when he was on duty; for better or worse, she was about to find out.

In a small anteroom—Holly had no way of knowing what part of this fabled mansion they were in—another agent appeared. Like the first one, he wore a trim three-piece suit, a no-nonsense expression and a very small earphone that probably connected him to all sorts of small in-house intrigues.

Holly was more nervous than ever, and that made her chatter again. "George Washington actually slept here," she muttered, wide-eyed.

The agents exchanged a long-suffering look, probably thinking how unfortunate it was that the president-to-be had to have such a bumpkin for a cousin. "This way, Madam," one of them said, and Holly found herself being propelled through a series of rooms and up a rear staircase.

"Do you know David Goddard?" Holly tried again. Maybe these guys were at least semi-human.

The agents traded another look. Apparently the answer to that question was a state secret, for neither of them bothered to respond.

They were now on the floor where the first family resided. Holly decided charitably that that accounted for the reticence of the two men escorting her. She was deposited in a lovely room decorated all in blue. To her amazement, her baggage had already been brought up, and a small, plump woman in a maid's uniform was busy taking Holly's new evening gowns from the garment bag and hanging them carefully in the closet.

Here, perhaps, was a human being, though after the Secret Service agents, Holly didn't want to make any rash judgment.

"Hello," she ventured.

The maid, an elderly woman with a look of long service about her, smiled warmly. "Hello, Ms. Llewellyn. And welcome to Washington."

"Thank you," Holly said with a sigh of relief.

"I'm Mrs. Tallington, and I'll be helping you while you're with us. The first lady asked me to tell you that she will be in to greet you shortly."

So, Holly thought, Howard's Maggie is already referred to by that lofty title, even though the swearing-in isn't until tomorrow. "Have you worked here for a long time?" she asked as Mrs. Tallington examined Holly's blue chiffon, made a cluck-clucking sound and shook her gray head.

"Since JFK and Jackie," came the brisk answer. "They come and they go. Some are happier to leave than to arrive, I might add. This gown will need pressing."

Holly chuckled and relaxed enough to set her purse on a mahogany dresser and remove her winter coat. "I was afraid everyone here would be like those men who brought me upstairs."

A mischievous light twinkled in Mrs. Tallington's bright blue eyes. Her snow-white hair made a little knot on the top of her head, just visible through the gauzy fabric of her cap. "Don't speak ill of those who are probably standing right outside your door," she warned good-naturedly.

Drawing in a quick breath, Holly went to the door, opened it a crack and peered out. The two agents looked back at her impassively, and she closed the door again with a resolute click.

Mrs. Tallington was chuckling. "A little unnerving, isn't it? But they're there to guard you; they mean you no harm. Just make yourself comfortable and pretend they're not around."

Holly had never been "guarded" before, and she was nonplussed. Once again she had misgivings about the wisdom of coming here, to this place where she didn't belong, where everything was so formal and intimidating.

"I'd like to see the room where Mr. Lincoln slept," she said to distract herself.

Mrs. Tallington nodded, her eyes twinkling again, toward a huge painting of the Great Emancipator himself. "You're in it," she replied matter-of-factly. "Some say they've seen Abe sitting on the edge of that very bed, taking off his shoes."

Holly shuddered despite her pleasant surprise at finding herself in a room once occupied by one of the greatest men in history. She certainly hoped that Mr. Lincoln would not deign to sit upon the side of the bed while she was in it—that would be most disconcerting.

There was a slight ballyhoo outside and then a knock at the door. Before Holly could issue any sort of invitation, Maggie swept into the room, all campaign-trail smiles, her glistening blond hair artfully coiffed, her dress a designer original.

"Holly, dear! How marvelous to see you!"

Holly stiffened, then worked up a smile. After all, this was Lincoln's bedroom and this was the first lady of the land. Such things had to be accorded due respect. "Hello, Maggie," she said.

Maggie bypassed Holly's cheek with a distant-cousin-by-marriage kiss. "Howard and I are so pleased that you could come!"

Mrs. Tallington, the wrinkled blue chiffon evening gown draped over one capable arm, ducked out of the room without a word. Holly watched her go, using the time to overcome her secret ire over what Howard and his suspicions had put her through.

The first lady drew back her guest's attention with a trilling, musical laugh. "Howard will apologize himself, of course," she said, "but I did want to tell you that we're both very sorry over what happened to poor Craig."

Holly was momentarily annoyed. They were very sorry. Did they think their third cousin from Spokane had come down in the last snowstorm? They had believed, actually believed, that Holly could turn on her own country. "Thank you," she forced herself to say.

Maggie dragged discerning eyes over Holly's rumpled woolen suit. "You'll want to change before meeting with the president, of course."

Which president? Holly wanted to ask, but she bit the perverse inclination back. The outgoing administration was probably out-gone anyway. "Of course," she answered.

Maggie smiled her blinding, trust-my-husband smile. "Wonderful. When you're ready, just tap at the door and the men stationed outside will see you to the Oval Office."

The Oval Office. Holly's knees weakened and she hoped she didn't sway visibly. Me? she thought. In the Oval Office?

Maggie noted with a glossy smile that her guest was properly overwhelmed by the magnitude of it all. With a cheery word of farewell, she swept out.

Holly wobbled her way into the bathroom that must have been added on sometime after Mr. Lincoln's demise, undressed and ran a hot bath. Half an hour later, she was presentable again, her hair neatly brushed, her makeup fresh. Wearing an expensive suit of beige and emerald, she drew a deep breath and tapped at the door, as instructed.

It opened to give Holly Llewellyn the shock of her life. David Goddard was smiling down into her face. "That outfit makes you look like a Midwestern schoolmarm," he muttered out of one side of his mouth.

Holly grappled inwardly for composure, then lifted her chin and retorted, "If it was good enough for *The Today Show,* buddy, it's good enough for Howard."

For a moment, before the intangible veil of officialdom fell over his eyes, making them expressionless, David allowed them to transmit a welcome that made Holly pinken slightly.

She was led to the Oval Office itself. There were Marines guarding the double doors, and beyond that point, there was a spacious outer office, populated by secretaries and advisors of various stations. One of them pressed a button on an intercom and said, "Mr. President, Ms. Llewellyn has arrived."

It was unsettling, the way everyone around there seemed to know Holly's name without her telling them. Did they know how much she owed on her charge cards and what kind of hairspray she used and whether or not her library books were overdue, too?

She flung one scathing, sidelong look at David, remembering just how personal a presidentially ordered investigation could get. "Rat," she whispered, and one side of David's firm mouth twitched almost imperceptibly.

"Send her in, send her in!" boomed Howard's jovial voice over the intercom.

Holly was escorted right to the doors—what did they think she was going to do? Bolt and run? Make a stirring speech in favor of Osama bin Laden?

"Let go of me!" she hissed.

Both agents immediately released their hold on her elbows. Though his face was completely expressionless, David's mouth twitched again and something danced in the blue depths of his eyes. "Give 'em hell, Llewellyn," he said, to the other agent's obvious distress.

And then Holly was inside that office of offices, alone except for Howard, and she couldn't hide her reaction to it all. After all, this was a place where dramatic decisions had been made. John F. Kennedy had discussed the Cuban missile crisis with Bobby. FDR had planned the New Deal. Abe Lincoln had listened to the ominous beat of Confederate drums from just across the Potomac....

"Wow," she said.

Howard, a genteel-looking, gray-haired man with a

powerful build and a winning smile, stood up in gentlemanly deference. "My sentiments exactly," he said. "Actually, I'm just getting the feel of the place myself. This isn't my office yet."

Holly liked Howard for saying that. "Your predecessor—?"

"He's around somewhere," Howard said. "We both want the transition to go as smoothly as possible and the president has been decent about this whole thing."

Howard gestured toward a long, comfortable-looking sofa, only one of several in the massive, overwhelmingly significant room, and Holly sat down gratefully with a smile.

But her smile faded as she considered the tremendous burdens that were about to be placed on this man's sturdy shoulders.

Howard had apparently guessed what she was thinking. "I'll do my best," he promised quietly and with conviction.

Holly's respect for the man deepened. "Waking up every morning, being responsible for much of the free world—I don't think I could do that."

The future president chuckled. "I can't make a decent wonton, so I guess we're even." He paused and cleared his throat in an I'm-about-to-say-something-momentous way. "Holly, Maggie and I are both very sorry about that investigation and the trouble it must have caused you."

Maggie's apology had been somewhat varnished and breezy, in Holly's opinion, but Howard's came across as the real thing. "You certainly had reason to doubt Craig," she admitted with dignity, "and I suppose you had no way of knowing that I would never take part in such a thing."

Howard watched her with kindly, rather tired eyes. "Thank you, Holly."

Holly bolted to her feet, conscious of the drains on this man's time and energy. She didn't want to be one of them; he had important things to do. "I'd better go and let you get back to your work. Do you think I could look around a bit?" She paused and chuckled nervously. "It isn't every day that a cookbook author from Spokane finds herself in the White House, you know."

"Nor a lawyer from Oregon," quipped Howard, referring, of course, to himself.

Holly cocked her head toward the sturdy double doors and lowered her voice to a conspiratorial whisper. "Do those two goons have to be on my heels the whole time?" It felt good to refer to David Goddard as a "goon," unsuitable as the word might be for such a smooth operator.

Howard laughed his loud, ingenuous laugh. "I'm afraid so, Holly. They go with the territory."

"You mean, the whole time I'm in Washington—"

"The whole time you're in Washington," confirmed Howard with resignation.

Holly shook her head in irritated wonder and laid her hand on a knob touched by some of the greatest—but she wasn't going to ride that mental train again. Presidents, as had just been brought home to her, were as human as anybody else. Still, it was exhilarating to venture among such illustrious ghosts.

David was waiting, sans his partner, just beyond the doors. "I'd like a tour, please," she said, delighting in the brief flicker of irritation that moved in his eyes and tightened his splendid jawline a little.

They spent the rest of the morning visiting various parts of the White House, some accessible to tourists, some private. David might have been a stranger, so clipped were his explanations of this painting and that chair, and Holly told herself that it was just as well. After what he had done to her, who wanted intimate conversation?

She did. But she did a commendable job of hiding her disappointment at David's formal, distant manner.

It wasn't until he brought her back to Mr. Lincoln's bedroom that he said anything unagentlike, and even that was brief because the two men assigned to stand outside Holly's door and look intimidating were already zeroing in.

"I'm off duty at seven," he intoned. "Meet me outside the tourists' entrance."

"I will not—"

David was turning away. Damn, but he looked magnificent in his navy blue, don't-mess-with-me-I-guard-presidents suit. "Be there," he tossed back in parting.

Holly dodged inside her room and closed the door, impotently furious. The thing that made her maddest of all was knowing that even if it meant missing dinner with Maggie and Howard, she would be at the tourists' entrance at seven sharp.

David was pacing. He stopped occasionally to glare at his watch. Holly so enjoyed his discomfiture that had it not been for the two suits walking within lunging distance of each of her elbows, she would have hidden behind a statue and watched for a while.

"You're relieved," he said bluntly, his eyes darting from one impassive Secret Service face to the other.

"You got clearance for this, Goddard?" dared the taller one.

"Call upstairs and ask if you don't believe me," was David's response to the challenge.

If this was a bluff, the "goons" were calling it. One of them muttered something into the little device in his sleeve, his eyes never leaving David's face. Good heavens, Holly reflected, they don't even trust each other!

There was a buzzing sound, the response being discernible only if you happened to be wearing one of those communication contraptions, which, of course, Holly wasn't.

"You're clear, Goddard."

David's jawline tensed, then relaxed again. Was it possible that he found all this cloak-and-dagger stuff just as tiresome as Holly did? "Gee, thanks, Ranford," he bit out. And then as he pulled Holly into the protective curve of one arm, he added, "Don't wait up for us."

Holly found herself being ushered outside into the icy, snow-laced Washington wind and across a slippery parking lot. "Will they?" she asked, glancing back over one shoulder.

David opened the passenger door of a small green

sports car and hustled her into the seat. "Will they what?"

Holly waited until he was behind the wheel before replying impatiently, "Will they wait up for us?"

David laughed. "No. They'll follow us. They'll sit across the street from my apartment building until we come out and then they'll tail us back to Pennsylvania Avenue. At which time they will collect you at the rear entrance and muscle you upstairs to your room. Neither of them will draw a calm breath until you're tucked in, safe and sound."

"I don't want to go to your apartment—"

David's perfect teeth flashed in the relative darkness. "Too bad," he replied.

"A lot of damned good it does to have bodyguards!" Holly spouted, unnerved but tingly at the prospect of being alone with David Goddard. Distinctly tingly.

David only laughed. At the gate, he stopped to show his ID and the guard peered in, taking a long, level look at Holly.

"Do they always make such a big fuss about every little move a person makes?" Holly demanded, looking back as a limo followed them out, the gate slamming shut behind.

"Yes," David sighed. And he sounded tired and exasperated.

As they drove through the dark, snow-dusted streets of Washington and into an area Holly recognized as Georgetown, she glanced back at their one-car entourage and sighed, "Nobody will ever accuse those guys of being subtle. How do you stand it, David?"

"Stand it? I've done it myself a thousand times."

"Followed people? Who?"

"People who were taking a president's daughter out on a date, for one example."

He maneuvered the car into an underground parking area beneath one of the historic, renovated houses Holly had heard and read so much about. To hide her sudden case of jangly nerves, she sat up very straight in the seat and said, "This is quite an expensive car. It's good to know that civil servants are so well compensated for their work."

David grinned at her sarcasm, apparently unaffected by it. "Wait until you see my apartment," he baited her.

Holly was scowling as he parked the car and came around to collect her. As they hurried toward an elevator, she could hear the rhythmic click-click of the agents' shoes behind them. "They're not making any effort to be quiet, are they?"

"Why should they? They know that we know they're there."

"I thought you said they would sit outside, in the car," fretted Holly, looking back over one shoulder.

David thrust her into the elevator the moment the doors opened and took obvious delight in the fact that his colleagues were summarily shut out. "They'll stand outside my door for a while just to make sure we're not up to anything—" he paused, winking in a way that made Holly flush with quiet outrage "—un-American."

Holly gave him an arch look. "Why don't you just tell them that you've already checked me out, Agent Goddard?"

The man was impossible. Instead of getting mad, he laughed and said, "I've missed you, you tart-tongued little wench."

Holly bristled. "Tart-tongued little what?"

They had reached David's floor, the elevator doors whisking open to reveal an expensively carpeted hallway. He avoided answering by catching her hand in his and pulling her up to a door marked 17B.

It turned out to be a place that would raise the hackles of any taxpayer. The carpets were lush, the furniture was sturdy and obviously antique, and the lighted paintings on the walls had not come from the housewares department at K-Mart. One of them, unless Holly was mistaken, looked like a Picasso.

A lulling, bubbling sound came from everywhere and Holly saw that there were no less than four sizable aquariums in the living room, every one of them populated by expensive tropical fish. The effect was quietly exotic.

Holly turned to David, desperately stalling, wondering why she had allowed him to bring her here at all. "You are overpaid, Mr. Goddard," she accused.

He laughed and touched her nose with a winter-chilled index finger. "Before you lodge an official complaint, may I say in my defense that my grandfather owned a large farm in Nebraska, and furthermore, that when it was sold at his death, I inherited half the money?"

Holly sagged a bit, tired and at a loss, but then rallied with a challenging, "Who got the other half?"

David's eyes danced and he grinned. "My sister, Chris. Are you disappointed?"

"Why would I be?"

He was easing her coat from her shoulders, and as ordinary as that gesture was, it seemed strangely sensual then. "I think you were hoping to add philandering to my other crimes. Be honest, Holly—for just a moment, you thought I was married, didn't you?"

The thought had crossed her mind. After all, if David would lie about his occupation and his feelings for her, he might have lied about his marital status, too. "I considered it. Then I realized that no woman in her right mind would ever put up with you."

Having laid her coat aside, David went to a beautifully carved bar and began rattling bottles and glasses about with a decorum suited to his surroundings. "Would you like something to drink?"

A drink might steady her nerves, Holly thought. Then again, it might lead her to make a fool of herself. "White wine, please," she said primly, seated now on a plush sofa.

He brought the wine, holding a mixed drink of some sort in his other hand, and sat down, not on the couch beside Holly, but on a matching hassock nearby. Introspectively, David studied the amber depths of his glass.

"What did you think of your Christmas present?" he asked gruffly, still avoiding her eyes.

Reminded, Holly opened her purse and brought out the present in question, settling the small velvet box on the coffee table. "I think you shouldn't have given it to me," she replied coolly.

She ached at seeing his strong shoulders stoop just slightly. "My timing was less than perfect, I guess," he reflected, at length.

"Considerably less," Holly said softly, hurting because it was obvious that David did. "But Toby liked his robot."

Indigo eyes searched her face. "Holly, give me one more chance. Just one."

Holly tightened both hands around her wineglass, as though it could anchor her, enable her to ride out the emotional storm that was coming. "I didn't come to Washington so I could see you again, David," she said. And it was only after the words were out of her mouth that Holly realized she was lying.

11

"Are you hungry?" David's question broke the uncomfortable silence.

Holly had eaten aboard the airplane but that, of course, had been some hours before. "A little."

David laughed, but it was a ragged sound, humorless and painful to hear. "God knows who you might have rubbed elbows with tonight if you hadn't come with me. The least I can do is take you to the best restaurant in town."

"No," Holly said quickly, glancing apprehensively at the door. "I don't want those men watching every lift of my fork." Or following me to and from the restroom, she added to herself.

David stood up to remove his suit coat. Nestled ominously against his broad chest was a holstered pistol. "Sorry," he said hoarsely, catching Holly's look of horrified surprise.

She looked away, reminded once again of all the things that stood between them, then heard the brisk click of a drawer and what she thought was the turning of a key.

"I make a mean omelette," David offered in a low voice.

Holly forced her eyes back to him, and to her abject relief, the gun was gone. She managed a shaky smile. "I hope it's better than your fruitcake," she ventured, and this time, David's responding chuckle was warm and real.

He executed a sweeping bow, reminiscent of a continental waiter. "This way, Madam," he said.

Against her better judgment, Holly rose from the sofa and followed him through a small, formal dining room and into the kitchen. There was a butcher-block table in the center of the room, and copper kettles hung from a black wrought-iron rack above that. The stove and sink were both within easy reach.

"Pretty nice," Holly approved, since she knew kitchens if she knew anything at all.

"Don't be too impressed," David warned with a half

smile as he rolled up the sleeves of his white shirt and then went to the sink to wash his hands. "I wouldn't know an egg timer from hollandaise sauce. I only bought all this stuff to please my housekeeper."

"Is there anything I can do to help?" Holly asked, torn between attaching herself to this man like a barnacle and bolting out of the apartment on a dead run. The depths of her feelings for him were truly frightening; she had to remind herself that a relationship between them could never work.

"Yes," David responded, bringing an armload of ingredients from the fancy refrigerator, which had a sliding, opaque door. "Sit down at the table and relax."

Instead Holly claimed one of three high stools at the luncheon bar. There were louvered doors beyond them, opening into the dining room. She fixed her attention on the elegant refrigerator and tried to imagine it covered with memos and samples of a little boy's artwork. She couldn't, and that saddened her.

David's hands were busy chopping scallops crisp enough to appear in a *Bon Appetit* layout, but his eyes scanned Holly's face with a sort of weary tenderness. "You look as though you might just fall asleep in my culinary triumph," he observed.

Holly had no intention of falling asleep anywhere but

in Mr. Lincoln's bedroom. "I'm all right," she said but an involuntary yawn belied her words.

David grinned and shook his head, moving on from the scallops to a mound of mushrooms. "Whatever you say," he replied.

Holly felt a blush rise in her face; it revived her a little, stinging the way it did. "I'm wide-awake," she insisted.

He stopped slicing mushrooms, bracing himself against the block table with his hands. "What do you think I'm going to do, Holly? Pounce on you if you so much as close your eyes?"

That made Holly laugh, however reluctantly. That was exactly what she'd thought, she realized. And it was a ridiculous notion. "I'm sorry," she said.

David went back to the project at hand, grinning mysteriously to himself. Holly would have given her Cordon Bleu diploma to know what he was thinking, but she was wise enough not to ask. Instead she just watched, yawning periodically, as David whisked eggs into a foamy froth, browned the scallops in butter, added the mushrooms and eggs at just the right moment.

They ate in the dining room, by candlelight, saying little. And good as the food was, Holly nearly disgraced herself by nodding off over her plate.

Exactly how it happened, and this was a very momentous "it," all things considered, was something that would always elude Holly. All her jet lag, all the rigors of the past couple of months, suddenly caught up with her. The room seemed to darken and the candlelight undulated and then David's arms were beneath her, strong and secure.

Holly yawned and made some senseless remark and David laid her gently down on a bed. "I can't...this isn't... Howard and Maggie..."

"Hush," he said, laying his fingers to her mouth and covering her with a satiny comforter.

"But—"

"Just sleep. As the president's cousin, you have a big day tomorrow. I'll make sure you're at the Capitol Building in plenty of time."

It was madness, but Holly believed him. And she was simply too tired to rally herself and get up. "It must have been...the wine..."

David chuckled and his lips touched her forehead, just briefly. "That and enough emotional trauma to devastate Jack Bauer. Sleep, sweetheart."

And Holly slept. She awakened a couple of hours later, confused and disoriented. When she remembered that she was in David Goddard's apartment, that the two agents assigned to her were probably still outside and coming to all sorts of scandalous conclusions, she sat bolt upright and gasped aloud.

It was a moment before she realized that David was not in the bed with her; when she made the discovery, Holly was both relieved and disappointed. "David?" she whispered, swinging her legs over the side of the bed. She was still completely dressed except for her shoes. "David?"

When there was no answer, she rose, not bothering to turn on a lamp, and groped her way out of the room. The living room beyond was dimly lit, but empty.

"David?" she ventured again. A small, cherrywood grandfather clock chimed three times. Good Lord, how was she going to explain this to the Secret Service, to Howard and Maggie? "David!" she yelled.

He materialized, a man made of shadows, at the end of the hallway. His hair was rumpled, his eyes were glass and his chest was bare. Holly didn't dare look any lower. "What?" he yawned.

"Take me back to the White House this minute! My God, what those men must be thinking—"

"'Those men' were called off hours ago. Go back to bed, Holly."

Go back to bed? Was the man insane? "May I point

out that it is three o'clock in the morning? My reputation is at stake here!"

David yawned again and stretched his arms above his head and the play of the all too masculine muscles in his shoulders and naked torso unsettled Holly all the more. "Right. Three o'clock. Your reputation," he mumbled.

Holly glared at him for a moment. "The agents really left?"

"Yes."

"How did you manage that, may I ask?"

"I told them you and I were going to spend the night making love."

Holly flushed. "You didn't!"

"Oh, yes I did. And what they don't know won't hurt them. You're not the only one with a reputation to maintain."

"Very funny! Take me home this instant."

"I'm going back to bed. I would recommend, Ms. Llewellyn, that you do the same. If you don't, I may forget my good manners and—"

A jolt went through Holly's just-awakened system, and it wasn't an unpleasant one. "And what?"

"Don't ask." He turned to leave her, there in the middle of his living room.

"I'll take a cab!" she threatened in a high-pitched voice. "I mean it, David Goddard..."

Her announcement trailed off when he suddenly whirled on his heels and came toward her, an evil, teasing look in his eyes. "That's it," he said. "I warned you."

Holly trembled as he lifted her effortlessly into his arms. She should struggle. She should walk out. She should go down to the street and hail a cab. But she could do none of those things. She couldn't even speak.

David carried her back into the room where she had been sleeping only minutes before, stood her on her unsteady feet and began to undress her. "Maybe there is one way, lady, to convince you that I love you."

He removed the prim blouse and skirt she had changed into to meet him earlier, tossing each garment casually aside. Holly stood speechless before him in her camisole and her tap pants, overcome by the feelings she had been struggling against ever since Craig's arrest.

Her head fell back as David bared her breasts and caressed them, his thumbs chafing the nipples until they stood out in eager surrender. Simultaneously, she trembled and sighed.

Presently David removed the camisole entirely, as he had her other clothes, flinging it aside. And then her tap pants were sliding down over her quivering hips and thighs and they were gone, too.

"David," she choked in sweet desperation as he continued to caress her, more freely now, and with a boldness that made Holly ache to submit.

Finally he kissed her and if Holly Llewellyn had not been lost before, she was lost then.

David drew back from her mouth with obvious reluctance and muttered, "I must be the world's biggest fool—"

"Second biggest," Holly struggled to say as he placed her upon the bed and joined her there. Then he began doing the most delicious, wicked things to her.

He drew sweet nectar from her breasts, he touched and stroked her, mastering her in ways that exalted, ways that soothed. And he brought her to a soaring preliminary release that left her quivering like a string, unable to see and nearly unable to breathe.

David entered her gently, with a low groan and an urgency as old as the stars. In the ensuing minutes, Holly quite literally lost her mind, groping for it as explosions of shattering joy shook her, finding it in her own cries of release and in David's.

Holly's face was hot, but she kept her eyes straight ahead as her personal Secret Service contingent escorted her through the rear part of the White House and right to the door of Mr. Lincoln's bedroom.

Inside, she rested her back against the heavy, carved wooden panels and struggled to catch her breath and cool her flaming cheeks with hands still icy from the frigid weather outside.

Mr. Lincoln observed her pensively from within his costly frame.

"I couldn't help it, Abe! I'm crazy about the man!" Holly hissed defensively as she stomped into the bathroom, peeled off yesterday's clothes and ran herself a deep, hot bath.

By inauguration time, Holly was dressed again, her hair and makeup done to perfection. Nothing of the abandon of the night before showed in her face—she hoped.

Holly rode to the Capitol Building in a limo, as a part of a long motorcade.

"Sure is a cold day for standing outside," observed the chauffeur.

Holly was grateful for his attempt at conversation, for she needed something else to think about besides the way she had tossed and writhed in David Goddard's bed the night before. It didn't help that he'd drawn that damned veil down over his eyes the moment he had deposited her in the waiting hands of her bodyguards. That had been so impersonal, so cold, and Holly's pride was still stinging. "I'll be glad when it's over," she sighed. "Isn't that terrible? I mean, this is a historic occasion and everything."

"It is that, Ma'am," replied the driver kindly. "A historical day and all that, I mean. But that don't change the fact that it's cold as the devil's heart out there."

The Secret Service agents sitting on either side of Holly were a different set than she'd had the day before, but they were just as dour and silent. Thank God the driver wasn't intimidated by their presence.

"No," said Holly. "It don't."

That deliberate slip of grammar brought a look from one of the agents, anyway. Holly thought she saw a grin peer out from behind the rim of his retina, though it disappeared, of course, in less than a moment.

Reaching the crowded Capitol Building, Holly and her escorts left the car. A microphone had been set up at the top of the fabled steps, along with a canopy of sorts and a number of folding chairs. Maggie and Howard were nowhere in sight, though there were hundreds of guests milling about in the chill of that day, Secret Service agents moving among them. They were easy to spot, not only because of their conservative suits and their earpieces, but because their eyes moved constantly, searching every face, noting the rise of any arm.

When Howard and Maggie arrived, closely followed by the majority leader, they were surrounded by a bevy of agents, David among them. Like the others, he scanned the crowd incessantly, and Holly shivered, not because of the biting cold but because she knew in that instant that he would lay down his life for the president without hesitation. Just as promptly, he would take the life of anyone who was so foolish as to attempt an attack.

Holly barely heard the swearing-in itself; she was too busy watching David and trying to solve the mysteries he personified. She had every respect for his dedication to his job, of course, but it was very difficult to reconcile this cold-eyed man with the one who had made such thorough, gentle love to her the night before.

Tears of hopelessness began to burn behind Holly's eyes and ache in her sinuses. Like a fool, despite everything, she had entertained a fantasy or two concerning David Goddard and the future they might have together. Now, standing in the brutal wind, she had reality to deal with; David was always going to be the man who had come into her life as a liar, a pretender, an imposter. He was a man who wore a gun under his jacket, a man who would kill if he deemed it necessary.

Holly shivered again and clapped with numb hands as the new president lowered his right hand and turned to say a few words to the crowd. She didn't hear a word he said, so intent was she on David's immobile, watchful face. How could she have considered living with him, loving him for the rest of her life? Even if all the other problems could have been solved, there was still the ominous fact that he could be killed or crippled at any time. His work was dangerous.

"I'd like to leave now," Holly said to the agent standing at her right side. Without making any verbal response, he took her elbow in a firm hand and ushered her back to one of a dozen waiting limousines.

Safe in her room again some twenty minutes later, after declining an offhand, rushed invitation from Maggie to attend a state luncheon, Holly collapsed onto her bed with a pulsing headache.

Presently, Mrs. Tallington appeared with a tray and a look of sympathy. "Do you need a doctor, Madam?" she inquired.

Holly closed her eyes. She had taken two aspirin before lying down and she hoped they would be sufficient. "No, thank you," she said. "I'll be fine if I just rest a while."

"Eating a little something might help," imparted the veteran, and then she was gone.

When Holly could sit up without feeling queasy, she inspected the contents of her tray. Beneath aged, mellow silver covers were generous servings of creamed crab, mixed vegetables and warm, crusty bread.

Knowing the wisdom of what Mrs. Tallington had said, she forced herself to eat, though most of the portions were larger than she could have handled even if she'd felt her best.

She slept—her dreams were damnably erotic replays of the night before—and when she awakened there were lengthy shadows in the room and the tray had been taken away. Her blue chiffon, pressed to meet Mrs. Tallington's impeccable standards, hung from a peg on the closet door.

Holly wished she had the nerve to thrust that gown and all her other clothes into her suitcases and make a dash for the airport. That would be so much easier than facing David again!

But she couldn't bring herself to do it. The biggest of all the inaugural balls was to be held that evening, and Holly was enough of an adventuress to really want to attend. After all, she would probably never have a chance to do anything like that again.

Holly took another long, leisurely, scented bath, washed and dried her hair, carefully painted her nails. She was wearing only a towel when the telephone at her bedside jangled, startling her so much that she jumped and had to clasp the towel in place again.

"Hello?"

"Holly, this is Howard. The staff tells me that you're a little under the weather."

Holly sighed, feeling troublesome and out of place. "I'm fine, Mr. President. Honestly. I think I was just a little tired."

"'Mr. President', is it?" Howard chuckled. "Well now, Holly, I like the sound of that, but I'm still just Howard to you."

Still just Howard. Grinning, Holly shook her head in wonder but said nothing, waiting for her illustrious caller to go on.

"I've arranged for you to meet with Craig first thing tomorrow morning, Holly. He's ready to talk with you now."

Holly's knees went weak and she sank to the edge of the bed. "C–Craig? He's here?"

"He's at Walter Reed for the time being. Do you want to see him, Holly?"

Her throat tightened, memories of another Craig

swirling in her mind: a laughing, responsible, healthy Craig. A devoted big brother. "Oh, yes," she said softly. "Yes, I want to see him."

"Good. We'll send you over there in a car, bright and early. In the meantime, young lady, you put on your dancing shoes and prepare to have yourself a good time at the shindig tonight."

Holly chuckled, though there were tears swimming in her eyes. "Being in the White House, going to an inaugural ball—I think I should wear glass slippers instead of dancing shoes."

"Can't dance in glass slippers," Howard retorted immediately. "You save a waltz for your old third cousin from Oregon, now."

"I will," Holly promised, and Howard rang off in his politely abrupt way.

Slowly, she set the receiver back in its cradle, drew a deep breath and went to the closet to find the special, strappy shoes she bought to wear with the blue chiffon. Turning one in her hand, Holly reminded herself that she was not Cinderella and that Howard was certainly not Prince Charming.

No, if Prince Charming attended the ball at all, he would be wearing an earpiece and a look fit to freeze-dry coffee beans.

★ ★ ★

The ballroom glittered with crystal chandeliers and silver punch bowls and guests one couldn't hope to encounter even on *The Today Show.* Holly spotted David almost immediately and spent the next fifteen minutes trying to ignore him.

The orchestra played and Holly danced with a pudgy, wheezing man a head shorter than she was. An emissary from some country Holly had never heard of, he spoke immaculate English.

Following that, she was waltzed around the enormous room by a man wearing a bright gold cummerbund and a dazzling array of medals. He was an ambassador from one of the Slavic countries.

When Howard and Maggie deigned to make their appearance, there was a hush and all eyes were upon them. Maggie looked every inch the first lady, and despite the unspoken strain between them, Holly was proud of her.

The president and first lady danced together then, the crowd moving back for them, the Secret Service agents looking on as alertly and unemotionally as ever, ready to pounce upon anyone foolish enough to make a wrong move.

Looking at David, Holly despaired. This was not the

man who had loved her with such sweet ferocity the night before. This was a stranger, an automaton.

Some minutes later, Holly had her dance with the president of the United States, his last before retiring with Maggie from the festivities. "No glass slippers, I see," he teased as they waltzed, flashbulbs bursting all around.

Holly laughed. "No. I ordered a pair from Saks, but they didn't have my size."

Howard responded with a laugh of his own, but he looked tired. Holly thought of how the next four years would age him and felt sad.

"When you see your brother tomorrow morning, Holly, you tell him I'll do all I can to see he gets the help he needs."

"Thank you," Holly replied softly. "For both of us."

Howard nodded somberly. "I'm just sorry it had to come to this," he said. "You'll be with us a few more days, won't you?" he added a moment later, deliberately changing the subject.

Holly shook her head. "I've got to get home to my nephew and my work, I'm afraid. If I possibly can, I want to leave tomorrow, after I see Craig."

Howard responded politely, then the dance was over. A few minutes later he left the ballroom with Maggie and their Secret Service entourage, David included. Holly remained at the party for another half hour and then departed, leaving no glass slipper behind.

It was late and David was exhausted. Like several of the other agents assigned directly to the president, he had worn a tuxedo, and he was eager to hurl the thing into the depths of his closet and forget it existed.

Walt Zigman sat at his desk, as always, oblivious to the late hour. A widower, his children grown and gone, he had nothing better to do, David guessed. He hoped to God his own life would never come down to that.

He laid his identification card and the earpiece down on the desk.

"You told me you'd stay until inauguration week was over!" Walt blustered, his jowls quivering, his cigar bobbing between his teeth.

"I lied. I'm out, Zigman. Gone."

Zigman swore. "I knew it. I damned knew it."

David sighed and stuffed his hands into the pockets of his trousers. "I suppose Ranford gave you a full report on last night," he said, his eyes linked with Walt's.

"We didn't get it on tape, if that's what you're talking about, Goddard. Tell me something, though. What is it about this Lewellyn woman that makes her different from all the others?"

David had a headache; he rubbed his temples with a thumb and forefinger. "If I knew that, Walt, I might be able to put two sane thoughts together."

"She feel the same way you do?" Walt was apparently in a fatherly mood. His eyes were averted, though, and he was cleaning his fingernails with an unbent paper clip.

David had been struggling with that question all day. It had distracted him, making it hard as hell to keep his mind on the president and the endless crowds at the swearing-in and at the ball he'd just left. Holly had certainly responded in bed the night before, but come the rueful morning, her aquamarine eyes had been full of doubts. Misgivings. And a grudge that just might last a lifetime.

"It will be a long time before she trusts me completely, if she ever does."

There was a short, reflective silence.

"I'm sorry about this whole thing, Goddard, for what it's worth. I should have sent someone else."

"You didn't know I was going to fall in love with Holly," David said, his jaw growing taut of its own accord and then relaxing again. "I didn't either."

Walt reached out and collected the earpiece and the

identification badge. "You keep in touch, Goddard. If things don't work out out there in Podunk, Washington, you come back here."

David had no answer for that. If things didn't work out in Spokane, he didn't know where he would go or what he would do. The only thing he could be certain of was that he was never going to come back to this job.

Leaving Walt's office, he squared his shoulders. Things would work out with Holly, dammit. He was going to *make* them work out.

12

Holly was delivered to Walter Reed Hospital first thing the next morning, as promised. She was, of course, flanked by the usual Secret Service set of two, but at least they stayed outside of Craig's room, exchanging toneless rhetoric with the FBI man who guarded the door.

Craig sat alone in the room, wearing a striped bathrobe that was too big for him, his gaze fixed on the panoramic view offered by a huge window.

Holly lifted her chin and gave herself a silent order not to cry. Her brother looked so broken, so small and in so much trouble. "Craig?"

He turned, his eyes sunken and circled. His face, stubbled with a new beard, looked gaunt; he might have been a hundred instead of just thirty-six. "Hello, Holly," he said, and his voice was as hollow as his eyes.

"Are they treating you well?" she asked, and the words sounded stiff, stilted. Talking to this wasted remnant of a man was not the same as talking to her brother.

Craig shuddered and executed a rueful parody of a smile. "They're not shining lights in my face and telling me they have ways of making me talk, if that's what you mean."

Holly had no plans to ask about the cocaine habit that had brought him to this pass; the ravages of his withdrawal, which would probably go on for some time, were clearly visible in his face.

She forced herself to go to him, to lay one hand on his thin shoulder. Touching him seemed to work some magic—he became Craig again. Tears stung in her eyes and ached in her throat as she bent to kiss the top of his head.

"Oh, Craig, how did this happen?"

His shoulder stiffened beneath her hand. "The way it always happens, Holly," he said brokenly. "You try cocaine and you're on top of the world. You can do no wrong. You're Superman, you're James Bond. And then one day you find out that you've gotta have the stuff and there aren't any choices anymore."

Holly swallowed hard and reached up with one hand to surreptitiously wipe away her tears. Her falling apart was not going to do Craig any good; she had to be strong now. "Is there anything I can do?" she whispered. "Special doctors, anything like that?"

Craig shook his head. "Forget I was ever born," he said hoarsely, looking at the view again. "That's the best thing you can do for yourself and for Toby."

There was nothing to say to that. If and when Craig overcame his cocaine problem, he might still be faced with a long prison term.

"You're still all tangled up with Goddard, aren't you?" Craig's question was so direct and so unexpected that Holly gaped at him for a moment, unable to answer. "He's bad news, Holly. For your own sake, walk away."

"That's going to hurt," she managed to say, at length.

Craig gave a humorless chuckle. "Lots of things hurt in this life, Holly. Too many things hurt. But Goddard used you and I don't want you to forget that. He'd use his own mother, if the Service asked him to. Believe me, I know."

Holly wound a finger in one of Craig's lank curls—once they had been so springy that she had teased him about them—and waited for him to go on.

"Find yourself a flesh-and-blood man, Holly," he

complied after some time. "Goddard is a robot, like me. Like all the rest of them. He's nothing more than a hit man on the right side of the law."

Holly shivered. David wasn't a hit man! He wasn't!

"Lift your hand or a camera or a comb in the same room with the president or his lady sometime, Holly, if you don't believe me. You'll find yourself facedown on the floor with your hands cuffed before you catch your breath."

"There is a reason for that, Craig!"

He looked up at her. "Yes. But can you live with it, Holly? Can you live with guns and subterfuge and international intrigues that would curl your fingernails? Believe me, he knows things that he can't share with you, but they'll make him hell to live with all the same."

I love David, screamed some forlorn part of Holly's heart, I love him! "You needn't worry," she said aloud. "Anything that David and I might have had was over the moment I found out that it was you he wanted, not me."

They were silent again for a while, lost in their own thoughts, their own griefs and regrets.

"I'd better go," Holly said finally. "I've got a plane to catch."

"Right."

She came around to look into his face. "Is there anything I can send you, Craig? Books? Magazines? Anything?"

"Books," he said, and for a moment there was a hint of the old Craig, an inveterate reader, in his eyes. He even chuckled. "Nothing about spies, though, okay?"

Near tears again, Holly bent to kiss his forehead. "No spies," she promised, and then she hurried out lest she break down in front of him.

It was a relief to board the airplane, to leave the White House and the Secret Service and everything else behind. Everything except David.

Holly buckled her seat belt and pretended to listen as a flight attendant explained the mysteries of oxygen masks and No Smoking signs. She wondered if she should have called David and said goodbye. Said *something*.

Vigorously, she shook her head in answer to her own questions. It was better this way, better to make a clean break and forget all about Agent Goddard and his novel investigating techniques.

The plane was barreling down the runway; Holly closed her eyes and braced herself for the lurching leap it would take when it left the ground. She hated that part of flying, along with the full reverse thrust of the engines upon landing; it always made her feel as though the craft would go tumbling end over end.

A hand closed over her fingers, which were clutching the armrest with painful force. She opened her eyes just as the plane lunged into the air and the landing gear ground into place.

David. David was sitting in the seat beside hers, big as life.

Holly blinked her eyes, certain that she was hallucinating, but he was still there when she looked again. Wearing tan corduroy slacks, a brown cashmere turtleneck and a cocoa-colored leather jacket.

"It's me, all right," he said calmly.

"What are you doing here?"

He peeled her fingers from the armrest and soothed them between his own, lifting her hand and inspecting her nail polish with a slight frown, as though he didn't quite approve of the shade. "Take a wild guess," he said.

Holly finally gathered the presence of mind to wrench her hand free. "Just go and sit in some other part of the plane. Or better yet, why don't you jump out over Kansas?"

David chuckled and settled into the seat with a comfortable sigh. "I've never liked Kansas. Besides, we won't be there for a while yet. We're probably over Maryland."

"Maryland would do just as well, I'm sure," Holly snapped, turning her head and looking out over the wing and a floor of cumulus clouds trimmed in pink and gold.

"Give me until Kansas to win you over." There was a wry, injured sort of humor in David's tone.

She swung her eyes around, giving him a look that sliced deep. "Watch my lips," she said coldly. "We could fly to Hong Kong. We could fly to the moon. We could fly to *hell*, Mr. Goddard, and you couldn't win me over!"

The captain gave some garbled message over the speakers and the No Smoking and Fasten Seat Belt signs blinked out, making chiming sounds. The flight attendants reappeared with their smiles and their rattling service cart.

"You weren't even going to say goodbye?" David asked, and this time there was no hint of humor in his tone. He sounded hurt and more than a little bewildered.

For just a moment, Holly's impractical heart clogged her throat. She knew there were tears glistening in her eyes when she looked at him, but she couldn't help either the tears or the looking. "I didn't see any point," she managed to say.

His jaw tightened and he paled a little beneath his winter tan. Probably, Holly thought, it was a health-club tan, as artificial as the feelings he had claimed to have for her.

"I'm getting tired of playing the heavy. The investigation and Craig's arrest are both in the past—can't we go on from here?"

How Holly wished they could, but that would be asking too much. She might love this man—she *did* love this man with all her heart and all her soul—but what good was that without trust? And she was never, ever going to trust him.

"Maybe they're in the past for you," she said stiffly, shaking her head when a flight attendant stopped to offer liquid refreshments. After David had ordered and paid for a scotch and water, and the attendant had moved on, she finished, "I'm always going to remember, David. I'm going to remember your lies. I'm going to remember watching you handcuff my only brother in my kitchen."

"How about the way we made love, Holly? Are you going to remember that? Are you going to remember the things we said and did when our passion was so great that we couldn't bear it?"

Holly closed her eyes tight. "Don't!"

"Someone has to, Holly. What we had—what we

have—is too rare and too precious to let go of without a fight. I've accepted that fact even if you haven't."

Holly snatched away his drink and took a gulp of it before handing it back, and David laughed.

"Face it, baby," he teased in an Edward G. Robinson voice, "you're stuck with a G-man!"

"I've already had to deal with all the 'G-men' I care to in this lifetime, thank you very much."

"We must be nearing Kansas. Do you still want me to jump?"

"More than anything," Holly sighed, unable to look at him now. If she did, she would tumble witlessly into those indigo eyes and the fall would be much deadlier than the one to Kansas. "What are you doing here, anyway? Don't you have to guard Howard or some visiting potentate?"

He hesitated and Holly sensed that he was hiding something—a possibility that infuriated her. "I've got some time off," he finally answered.

"I hope you're not going to Spokane," she replied in all honesty.

"I'm going wherever you go."

Holly sighed, sinking back into her seat. But when a flight attendant came by, she sat up straight again and announced in a clear voice, "Miss, this man is bothering me."

David laughed and the flight attendant looked him over in appreciative confusion, obviously wondering how a man like that could "bother" any woman in the unpleasant sense of the word.

"Is...is this true, sir?" asked the pretty attendant, not certain what to do.

"Oh, it's true all right," David confessed benevolently, rising from his seat and stepping into the aisle. He handed what remained of his drink to the stewardess and braced his hands against the back of the seat and the one just ahead. "And I'll go right on bothering you, Holly Llewellyn, because I love you. Because I need you."

Holly flushed with furious frustration and a need that rivaled the one he professed to feel. "You go to hell, Mr. Goddard," she replied, and then she fixed her eyes on the back of the seat in front of her and stared at the grubby tweed until it began to shift and undulate. When she dared to look, David was gone.

Holly felt a bereft sort of triumph. He meant to haunt her, he'd as much as said that straight out. He meant to follow her and pursue her until she gave in to him. And Holly was afraid she might do just that.

The airplane landed in Denver, where Holly was to catch her connecting flight to Spokane. Even before she looked back to confirm her suspicions, she knew that David was following her, she could feel him there, like a spectre.

She visited the restroom and the gift shop, trying to kill the hour layover, becoming more and more tense with every passing moment. Finally Holly whirled on David and hissed, "This is harassment! Leave me alone!"

He stepped closer, oblivious to the stream of people flowing around them on all sides, his eyes gentle. "Tell me you don't love me, Holly," he said quietly. "If you can truthfully say that, I'll go away."

Holly swallowed. That wasn't so hard, was it? Four little words, only four. I don't love you. She tried to say them and they would not pass her throat.

David waited patiently.

Holly tried again, failed again and turned away with a stifled sob, one hand to her face. David took her elbow in a firm grasp and escorted her into the nearest lounge. There, he settled her at a shadowy corner table, holding both her hands in his. At his request, a waitress in jeans and a Western shirt brought two cups of coffee.

Holly freed one hand to lift her cup to her lips; some of the steaming brew inside sloshed over to burn her hand and stain the tablecloth. David deftly removed the cup and set it aside to cool.

"I want one chance with you, Holly. Just one chance. Can you give me that?"

"Wh-what if I say no?"

"Then I'll get on the next plane to Washington."

"What about that speech you made on the airplane? What about the way you've been following me ever since we landed?"

David sighed raggedly and looked away for a moment. "I'm sorry. The last thing you need is pressure, I know that. But I was desperate."

"Why?" Holly whispered, and the word sounded pained.

"Because I love you—as, I believe, I have already mentioned on several occasions."

Holly was weary, her head full of dizzying, unrelented images—herself, dancing with the president; Craig, looking so lost and broken; David, carrying her to his bed, making love to her in a way that could still heat her blood. "I'm so confused," she muttered.

He squeezed her hand. "I know," he said softly. "Let me prove to you that I really do care, Holly. That's all I'm asking."

"How do you propose to do that, David?" Holly

asked with a desperation that was more revealing than she could ever have guessed. "You'll always be the man who arrested Craig, the man who lied—"

"I'll always be the man who loves you," he reminded her.

And the man who carried Toby through a frightening crowd of reporters the day after Craig was arrested, Holly thought with disjointed hope. The man who set up the Christmas tree, the man who went out for chicken, the man who was hopelessly inept at flying model airplanes....

She gave herself a mental shake. "I don't think—"

"We'll date, that's all. We'll talk, get to know each other. And this time, it will all be on the level, Holly."

Her coffee had cooled; she took a steadying sip. Maybe David was right. Maybe there was a chance, if they could just approach the situation rationally and take their time. "No lovemaking," she ventured. "We have to start all over again, from square one. Agreed?"

David sighed. "Agreed," he replied with comic reluctance.

Their flight number was called and they left the table, David pausing to pay the check. Holly was settled into her seat on the airplane, pretending to read a magazine, when he caught up with her.

"Very cute," he muttered wryly, falling into his seat on the aisle.

Holly peered at him over the rims of her reading glasses, which she was certain he had never seen before. "Have we been introduced?" she asked primly.

David laughed and rolled his eyes.

The condominium David selected as his new home was in a round building, three floors from the top, and every outer wall was a window. The view was phenomenal, including Riverfront Park, the Spokane River itself and the old brick railroad tower. Division Street was a double strand of diamonds glimmering in the first shadows of twilight.

He sat down on the lushly carpeted floor, drew his knees up and wondered whether he was doing the right thing, uprooting himself like this. Maybe he hadn't liked his job, per se, but he was going to miss the excitement of living in Washington. He was going to miss Chris and his nieces. And his friends.

He stood up again, taking in the spacious, as-yet-unfurnished living room. Holly was here; that was the important thing. Chris and the girls could visit as soon as school let out. And he would make new friends.

The telephone sat on the floor, looking forlorn in

the empty vastness of the room. David moved toward it, then held himself back. He'd promised to go slowly with Holly, promised not to pressure her. And he had to abide by those promises.

He went into the kitchen and opened the refrigerator, which contained a quart of buttermilk and a red-and-white bucket with one chicken wing in the bottom. David gnawed at that as he wandered from one elegant room to another, pondering the lengths he'd gone to just to be near Holly and regretting none of them.

The telephone rang, echoing in the emptiness, and David ambled toward the nearest one, expecting to hear from the real-estate agency or maybe the law school, where he was registered for review classes.

"David?" The familiar shrill of that voice almost made him choke on the chicken he'd been munching. "God, if you knew what I've been through, trying to track you down! I practically had to bribe Chris—"

"Marleen," David said woodenly. "Marleen?"

"I'm on leave," she chimed in bright response, as though she had never walked out when he'd needed her. As though she had never torn his guts out and stomped on them.

"What does that have to do with me?" he managed to ask, hoping that he didn't sound as hollow as he felt.

"We were married!" she sang. "Doesn't that entitle me to call up and say hello, David?"

"I find it hard to believe that you called just to say hello. What do you want? Money?"

There was a silence. "David!" Marleen wailed in injured good humor. "What an awful thing to say! We loved each other once."

"How are your monkeys?"

"Well, if you're going to be that way—"

David closed his eyes and the old pain was a sickness within him. He wished that Holly were there. "Wait," he said. "I was just surprised, that's all."

"Good." Marleen sounded pleased and perhaps a little relieved, which worried David. "Listen, sweetheart, I'm in L.A. right now, visiting the folks and all that." She paused, lowering her voice, presumably so the "folks" wouldn't overhear. "It's just a deadly bore, David, so I was wondering, well, since Spokane is a fairly short flight from here—"

"No," David broke in.

"No?"

David sat down on the floor, his head throbbing. He tossed the denuded chicken wing, because if he hadn't, he'd have tossed the telephone instead. "I mean, I'm just getting settled in here. And I'm flying back to Washington to sublet my place there and make arrangements for my furniture to be shipped. I really don't have time—"

"David, I was your wife!"

"You were the greatest single mistake of my life, Marleen," he said, thinking aloud.

He could almost see her pouting, see the tears welling in her enormous brown eyes.

"I guess I should have known I was going to get this kind of reception," she said. "Chris was positively cold when I called her."

David's head was pounding. "Look, Marleen, if you want money for some research project, apply for a grant. I really don't want to talk to you. And I sure as hell don't want to see you."

She sounded coy now, and just a little predatory. "Maybe you're scared, David. Scared that I might make you care again."

"If that's what you have in mind, don't waste your time. I'm in love with somebody else."

The moment that last sentence was out of his mouth, David knew it had been a terrible mistake. Marleen enjoyed a challenge, and saying that had been as good as flinging down a glove.

Having said too damned much already, David calmly and abruptly hung up the telephone. It rang again moments later; he lifted the receiver and dropped it into place.

The next morning, at twenty-five minutes after seven, he crawled, grumbling, out of the sleeping bag he had spread out in his future bedroom. The door-bell buzzed repeatedly as he groped into his jeans and stumbled, cursing under his breath, to open the door.

Marleen stood in the hallway, her big teeth bared in a smile that brought the jungles of Borneo to mind, her light brown, chin-length hair artfully rumpled.

"Mountain," she said, "meet Mohammed."

David groaned and rubbed his eyes. Maybe this was a bad dream. Maybe he was hallucinating.

"Aren't you going to ask me in?" Marleen wanted to know. "I could really use a cup of coffee and a hot shower."

"There are hotels all over town," David said, barring her way. "Check into one."

"I don't have the money to do that. I spent it all to fly home from Borneo and then come up here."

David cursed, making no effort to keep his voice down, but Marleen only laughed and shouldered her way past him, a suitcase in each hand, her eyes sweep-ing the empty condominium.

"I'll pay for your hotel," he offered lamely. It was

too late and he knew it; short of throwing Marleen out bodily, which he considered doing, his choices were limited.

"Oh, David, stop being so tiresome. I'm not here to cause you any trouble."

"Then why?"

"For old time's sake, that's all. And maybe for a slight—" she winced appealingly "—contribution."

"Anything for your monkeys, Marleen," David said with biting grandeur, his arms sweeping out from his sides.

"Stop calling them 'monkeys,'" came the controlled response. "They're chimpanzees and they are an important link to the past."

"Are they? As far as I'm concerned, they're small, noisy, furry beasts that pick bugs off each other's hides for a snack."

Marleen set down her suitcases, her eyes flashing even though she was still smiling determinedly. "I didn't expect you to be so bitter after all this time, David. I really didn't."

"Bitter? Me?" David retorted acidly. "Why would I be bitter, Marleen? Why the goddamned hell would I be *bitter*?"

She subsided a little, her chocolate-colored eyes wide and suspiciously moist. "I'm sorry that I hurt you."

"Oh, thank you. That makes everything all right. I can feel my ulcers and residual neuroses healing right now!"

Marleen sat down on one of her battered suitcases, a forlorn, elfin creature in a rumpled raincoat, her face in her hands. "Oh, David, don't do this to me," she whispered. "Please—"

David stormed away from her into his bedroom. He'd packed for the flight to Washington the day before, and he was going to leave early. Pale with rage, he showered, then dressed in slacks, a white sweater and a sports jacket.

When he reached the living room, his own suitcase in hand, the hopes he'd had that Marleen would just go away went up in smoke. Her baggage was still sitting there, and he could hear her humming in the kitchen, the sound blending in with the chortling of the coffeepot.

"Damn," he rasped, wondering what to do, how to get Marleen out of his house, out of his life. The answer was a four-figure drop in his bank balance; he wrote out a check with violent strokes of his pen, laid the payoff beneath the handle of one of her suitcases and walked out, slamming the door behind him.

Downstairs, he got into one of the cabs that were almost always on hand, muttering to himself. He would be gone for a couple of weeks, he supposed, making arrangements for his furniture to be moved, saying various goodbyes, giving away several hundred tropical fish.

Surely, by the time he'd driven his car across country—he needed the distance and monotony of the task to think—Marleen would have gone back to Borneo and her monkeys.

13

The circular building towered over Riverfront Park. Holding Toby's model Cessna in both hands, Holly gazed up at it.

"Are we going to visit David?" Toby demanded eagerly, tugging at the sleeve of her pink Windbreaker. "Are we, Mom?"

The bright, springlike shine of that late January day caused a painful catch in Holly's heart, as did Toby's question. It had been a full week since she and David had parted at the airport, agreeing to start over again. He had called just once in that time, and that had only been to pass on his new telephone number and address; he hadn't suggested they get together. Holly's feelings about that were mixed.

Toby tugged at her sleeve again, more forcefully this time. "Mom?" he prompted. "Couldn't we? Please?"

She looked down at the little boy and smiled. "Okay. We'll ask if he wants to come down here and fly the plane with us."

"And ride the carousel!" Toby beamed. "Don't forget, you promised that we could ride the carousel!"

They walked across the rolling, snow-patched lawns of the park, Toby straining to rush ahead, Holly holding back a little, wondering if it was wise to approach David. After all, they had an agreement, and she still had contradictory feelings toward him, stemming from the way they'd met.

"Toby, maybe we shouldn't..." She hesitated when they reached the main door of the exclusive building. There was a doorman on duty, perhaps he wouldn't even let them pass.

"Come on, Mom," Toby insisted, dragging her up to the entrance.

As the doorman looked her over, Holly was painfully conscious of her battered blue jeans, her T-shirt and Windbreaker, her breeze-tumbled hair.

"May I help you?" asked the sentinel, his deep, rumbling voice ringing with genteel authority.

"My name is Holly Llewellyn and this is—"

The doorman's round face broke into a smile. "Go right up, Ms. Llewellyn. I can't say whether or not Mr. Goddard is at home, but I have orders to admit you at any time."

Holly was relieved; inwardly, she realized, she had been expecting to be turned away. Things were shaky between her and David, and there was always the possibility that he had decided their relationship wasn't worth the trouble.

She and Toby crossed the sumptuous, plant-filled lobby. There were two sets of elevators.

"What floor does David live on?" Toby queried when they were inside one of the elevators, his hand poised to punch the proper button.

"Seven," Holly answered immediately, then bit her lower lip. Her eagerness was showing, and she had to get it under control. Letting David Goddard see how easily he could sway her would be foolish.

They arrived on the seventh floor in a whisk and stepped out into a spacious entryway, decorated, like the lobby, with plants.

David's condominium apparently took up the entire floor, for there was only one door in sight. Holly's hand trembled a little as she reached out to ring the bell. She drew a deep breath and summoned up a brave smile just as the door swung open.

A lovely woman wearing a colorful robe answered the door. "Yes?"

Holly was speechless, her imagination running away from her. Toby, on the other hand, had the presence of mind to ask ingenuously, "Is this where David Goddard lives?"

Wide brown eyes swept over Holly's Saturday-in-the-park clothes. "Yes, it is. I'm afraid David isn't home right now, though."

Holly, having surrendered the airplane to Toby, wedged her hands into the pockets of her Windbreaker. A woman—good God, *a woman.* She tried not to panic or jump to conclusions, but her emotions were so raw where David was concerned that she had almost no control over them. "Are you his sister?" she dared to ask.

The woman laughed, running one hand through her soft brown hair. "Good heavens, no. I'm his wife."

"His wife?" Toby echoed, confused.

Holly was outwardly calm. She squared her shoulders, caught Toby's free hand in her own and turned back toward the elevator. Over one shoulder, she said, "I'm sorry we bothered you."

"No problem," Mrs. David Goddard responded

lightly, with a shrug of her silk-clad shoulders. "Shall I tell David you were here?"

Holly debated with herself for a moment, gnawing at her lower lip. "No," she said finally. "Don't tell him anything."

The concern in Toby's upturned face wrenched at Holly's heart. He was too young to understand this sort of betrayal, and she wondered how she would explain it all to him.

"I didn't get your names!" sang out the remarkably calm wife of the man Holly loved as the doors were closing.

"Toby and Holly!" the little boy shouted just before the doors swept shut.

Holly let go of her nephew's hand and sagged against the elevator wall, her hands gripping the polished brass railing, her eyes squeezed closed against tears of rage and hurt.

"What's-a-matter, Mom?" Toby wanted to know.

Holly dragged in a steadying breath and lifted her chin. "Nothing, Tobe. Nothing at all. Let's go back to the park and fly your plane, okay?"

"Okay," Toby agreed somewhat sadly. "But I wanted David to be with us."

"So did I," Holly replied with despairing dignity.

"But sometimes things just don't turn out the way we hope they will."

Somehow, Holly got through the rest of that day, watching Toby's plane buzz in wide circles against a hurtfully blue sky, riding the fabled antique carousel, even choking down a hot dog. It was much later, when Toby had reluctantly taken his bath and tumbled into bed, that she sank into the chair at her desk in the kitchen, lowered her head to her arms and wept.

Being fooled once was bad enough; being fooled twice was devastating. Holly vowed that this was the last time, the very last time, that she would ever cry over David Goddard and his lies.

The trip across country had been a grueling one, and David was tired as he unlocked the door of his new condominium. He asked only one thing of the mysterious forces guiding the lives of mere mortals: that Marleen's failure to answer his telephone for the last week and a half meant that she was gone.

The movers had arrived ahead of him, and the furniture and crates they'd delivered looked ghostly in the dim light straying in through the open drapes. He paused a moment before flipping on the lights.

"Marleen?"

No answer. David shrugged out of his rumpled overcoat and flung aside the one suitcase he'd bothered to take with him. *There is a God,* he thought.

He checked the bedroom, which was full of boxes containing clothes and books, bed linens and towels. The bed had been set up, and he was grateful for that— now he wouldn't have to sleep on the floor or the couch.

"Marleen?" he ventured again. And that was when he saw the note affixed to the headboard of his bed with a piece of tape.

He snatched it into one hand, a peculiar sort of dread niggling in the pit of his stomach. "Darling," Marleen had written in a hand that resembled the efforts of one of her beloved apes. "I've gone back to my work. Thanks for the check and your backhanded hospitality. By the way, Holly came by. Is she your new love? I think she was surprised to find me here, and she said not to tell you that she stopped in. Ciao, Marleen."

David crumpled the note into a ball and flung it away on the strength of a growled curse. What Holly must have thought, encountering Marleen, of all people, was all too obvious.

He picked up the trail of the phone cord and followed it until he found the telephone beneath a pile of rumpled bath towels. Marleen had always been a slob. Holly's number leaped to his mind, but his finger hesitated over the buttons. It was late and this debacle called for more delicate handling than a midnight telephone call. Flowers, at the least, and some very fast talking.

David stiffened as he drew his hand back from the telephone. Dammit, why was he ready to grovel and beg when he hadn't done anything wrong? Whatever impression Marleen might have given—and he suspected that she had played the moment for every possible ounce of drama—the fact remained that he wasn't involved with her and hadn't been in years. Holly was a rational person and she would understand. She had to understand.

Too exhausted to think about the situation further, David staggered into the bathroom and took a long, hot shower, before making his way back to the bed. Marleen hadn't bothered to make it up again before she left, but he didn't care. He flung back the comforter and collapsed, falling asleep within seconds.

The next day was Saturday, and he awakened late. Standing at the windowed wall of his kitchen, he looked out over Riverfront Park, a cup of coffee in his hand, pondering the best way to approach Holly.

The weather was cold and sunny and there were a number of inveterate outdoor people in the park. He could see the carousel turning, a colorful blur inside its glass walls, and the sight uplifted him.

Momentarily, his eyes were drawn back to a small figure dashing in mad circles on the grass. David squinted and bent forward, trying to see. He couldn't so he opened a sliding door and went out onto the balcony surrounding his condo on all sides, resting his arms against the wrought-iron railing.

With the small person was a slightly larger one. One with golden honey hair that shimmered in the sunshine of a false spring.

David grinned, went back inside, shutting the door behind him, and set his coffee cup aside with a resolute thump. He rummaged through boxes in the recreation room until he found his own model airplane, then put on a dark blue Windbreaker and went out.

He sprinted across the park until he was close enough to hear the buzz of Toby's plane, close enough to see them both. Toby was watching, his face upturned and bright with delight, while Holly skillfully executed swoops and dips and sharp turns with the radio-controlled toy.

Holly became aware of his presence by some sixth sense and turned to confirm the dizzying fact with her eyes. David was standing not twenty yards away, holding his airplane in his hands, watching her and Toby.

He looked fantastic in his jeans, navy blue pullover and Windbreaker, but Holly wasn't going to let things like that sidetrack her. Not this time. Gritting her teeth, she worked the handset, guiding her airplane in his direction in a wide sweep. "Bombs away," she whispered with evil relish as she plunged the Lilliputian craft into a dive directed straight at his head. "Mom!" Toby bellowed, appalled.

David crouched, just barely escaping the airplane; it buzzed into another turn and came back toward him.

"Mom, don't!" Toby shrieked. "Don't! You'll hurt him."

"I want to hurt him," Holly replied grimly as David fell facedown in the snow-laced ground to avoid having a miniature Cessna embedded in his back. "Oh, boy, do I want to hurt him."

"Will you stop it!" David roared. Holly noted with satisfaction that the man had no sense of humor. "You're going to kill me!"

Holly brought the plane down again, letting it pass within inches of David's head. Toby, his face flushed with righteous indignation—he'd had lecture after lecture on how to operate that airplane safely—wrenched the controls out of her hands and guided the plane in for a smooth landing.

David sprang to his feet, his eyes snapping, a white line of annoyance edging his jaw. "If you're not happy to see me," he hissed, "just say so!"

Toby was looking frantically from one adult to the other, tears shimmering in his eyes, the handset shaking in his hands. "That was a crazy thing to do, Mom!" he shouted.

Looking down at him, Holly softened.

"You're damned right it was!" yelled David.

Holly shifted her gaze from Toby to David, piercing him with it. And then she turned on her heel and stomped away, toward the carousel, Toby scrambling along beside her like a puppy.

David halted her progress from behind, catching her elbow in his grasp and handing his airplane to Toby in one simultaneous motion. "If this wasn't a public place, lady, I would turn you over my knee," he said through his teeth.

Holly wrenched her arm free. "Stay away from me, you creep!"

"Mom!" Toby wailed, mortified.

She plunged one hand into the pocket of her jacket, pulling out a string of tickets. "Here!" she said to her nephew, with uncommon impatience. "Go and ride the carousel!"

Toby looked uncertain, his china-blue eyes again darting from Holly's face to David's.

"Go ahead, slugger," David urged in a gruff undertone, taking both toy planes from the little boy's arms. "Everything is going to be all right."

After one more glance at Holly, one so wary and concerned that it made her wince inwardly, Toby bounded off to enter the round building housing the carousel. The music of the calliope seemed ludicrous, in light of the situation.

His jaw still working with suppressed outrage, David set the planes aside and lifted his hands to his hips, watching Holly, his gaze burning into her face and finally forcing her to lift furious, tear-blurred eyes.

"What did Marleen tell you?" he asked when he had her full attention.

Holly shrugged, though she was on the verge of flinging herself at David Goddard kicking and scratching and hissing like a she-cat. Her whole body quivered with the need to attack, to hurt. "Only that she is your wife," she said, marveling at the calmness of her voice. She had expected the words to come out as a shriek.

"And you immediately decided that I had lied to you

again," David muttered. Damn him, he didn't look the least bit apologetic; instead, he appeared angry enough to forget that this was a public place and make good on the threat he had issued earlier.

Some of Holly's indignation faded away, driving a slow, pink blush up over her cheeks. "When presented with the evidence, I naturally—"

"You naturally found me guilty!"

Holly retreated a step. "She said—"

"I can imagine what she said! The truth is that we've been divorced for years, just like I told you before!"

People were beginning to stare and the calliope music went merrily on. Holly was getting a headache. "She had on a bathrobe. She was in your apartment—"

"And I was on my way to Washington," David broke in again, more calmly this time, though his tone sliced deep.

Holly was about to start believing him again and she'd sworn she would never do that. She whirled away, stomped into the carousel building and bought herself a ticket. When the ride stopped, she climbed onto a ferocious-looking tiger, spotting Toby ahead on a white horse.

The carousel began to turn, going faster and faster. Holly was dizzy and ill all of a sudden, and she clasped the pole in front of her with both hands. When she opened her squeezed-shut eyes, David was perched, side-saddle, on the black panther beside her, his chin propped in his hands.

Holly held on tighter, feeling the color drain from her face. "I don't think I…feel very well…" she managed to say.

David's face gentled, his eyes scanning her face. She could barely hear him over the shrill piping of the calliope. "Do you want me to tell them to stop this thing?"

Holly shook her head, then rested it against the pole she was still holding with a death grip. What was wrong with her? She had ridden this carousel a thousand and one times. Though it moved rapidly, it was not the sort of ride that could bring her breakfast burning up into her throat.

Finally, mercifully, the carousel stopped turning. Holly was trembling as David pried her hands loose from the pole and lifted her down. She might have stumbled, but he held her firmly, prepared to lift her into his arms and carry her, if necessary. She didn't dare let that happen.

Outside, she drew in fresh air in greedy gasps, praying that she wouldn't disgrace Toby by throwing up in public.

David ushered her to a brightly painted bench, sat her down and went off, returning within moments with a glass of water from a concession wagon several yards away.

"What's wrong?" he asked, bracing one foot against the bench and watching her as she sipped the water, his arms folded across his chest.

"I don't...know," Holly confessed quite honestly. "I must have the flu or something."

"Or something," David muttered, and he sounded so wistful that Holly's eyes shot to his face.

Toby, evidently worried about Holly, had gotten off the carousel and gone to fetch the airplanes and their handsets. He stood a little way apart, watching with large, saucerlike eyes.

"Are you sick again, Mom?" he asked.

"Again?" David demanded, leaning forward slightly.

Toby came a few steps closer, still a bit wary of these two strange adults. "Mom's been getting sick a lot lately. I want her to go to the doctor."

"So do I," David said quietly. "Can you walk now, Holly, or shall I carry you?"

Holly stood up determinedly and nearly sank to the bench again, she was so dizzy. Her stomach was doing leaps inside her. How on earth was she going to drive home in this condition?

David smiled reassuringly at Toby, ruffling his hair, and then casually lifted Holly off her feet, holding her against his chest like a child. She was too queasy to resist.

"My car is…over there…" she offered.

"You're in no shape to drive," David said flatly, looking down at Toby. "Can you manage the planes, slugger?"

Toby swelled with confidence, reassured by David's calm manner. "Sure I can. Can you manage Mom?"

David threw back his head and laughed and Holly was soothed by the scent of his hair and skin, and by the strength of him. "I don't think anybody can manage your mom," he answered presently, "but I mean to try."

"Put me down," Holly said.

"No way," came the implacable answer. "You're going to my place and you'll take it easy until you feel better."

"I can walk!"

"I know, but I like carrying you."

"David, you are making a scene! Now, put me down this minute!"

David was striding off toward the condominiums, his hold on Holly as firm as ever. "You know something, woman?" he teased, his breath whispering through her hair. "You're getting completely out of line here. You need someone to take a firm hand—"

Holly stiffened again and made a strangled sound of furious protest. "I don't need anything of the sort!" she blustered. "I'm a grown woman, perfectly capable—"

David lowered his voice, even though Toby was already bounding ahead, out of earshot, eager to see the place where his hero lived. "We both know what you need, don't we?"

The queasiness had passed and Holly was not only able to walk on her own, she was desperate for it. "Damn you, David," she hissed in a scathing undertone, "you promised!"

He sighed and set her on her feet. "So I did," he said. Knowing that she wasn't going to bolt without Toby, he slowed his strides to stay in step with her. "Holly, could you be pregnant?"

Pregnant! Holly simmered, clenching her fists at her sides. This man was just full of heartening suggestions! But as she walked, she did some mental counting and subsequently felt the warmth seeping out of her face to pool in a hot puddle in the pit of her stomach.

"Oh, my God," she moaned, stopping cold.

David caught her arm and pulled her into motion

again, propeling her into the building, through the lobby and into the elevator Toby was holding for them. Soon enough, they were inside David's lush, if cluttered, digs.

"I didn't think spies made this much money," Toby observed with the innocence of someone about to turn eight.

David and Holly both laughed. For Holly, it was involuntary. David, on the other hand, seemed relaxed, even happy.

He pressed Holly into a seat on the navy blue sofa she remembered from his apartment in Washington, D.C., and then abandoned her to take Toby on a guided tour of the new place.

Pardon me, Holly wanted to call out after him, *but I think I'm pregnant here. Aren't we even going to discuss it?*

She sank back against the sofa cushions, her heart in her throat, one tear slipping down her cheek. *Your chickens, Holly Llewellyn,* she thought with a bittersweet sort of joy, *have just come home to roost. You danced and now you're going to have to pay the piper. Your jig is up.*

Having run through all her favorite clichés, Holly

wiped away the tear and sniffled, then sat up very straight.

"Stay off the balcony," she heard David telling Toby, in another room. "And don't fill up the hot tub."

"Right," Toby sang, eager to be obedient. Not for the first time, Holly resented his desire to please David; it wasn't an emotion she was proud of, but she seized it to keep from thinking about the baby that might, even now, be growing inside her. David's baby.

David came to her and sat down on the sofa beside her, drawing one booted foot up to rest on the opposite knee. "We can talk about this now," he said reasonably, "or we can wait until Toby isn't around. The choice is yours."

Holly swallowed hard. "Are all the choices mine?" she ventured softly.

David met her eyes directly. "Actually, no. If you are pregnant, the child is mine, too."

At least he didn't question that. Holly sighed and knotted her hands together in her lap.

He pried one free and held it tightly. "I'm sorry, Holly," he said in a voice so low that Holly had to strain to hear him. "I wanted you so badly that I didn't stop to ask if you were protected."

Again Holly sighed. She couldn't help being struck by

his willingness to take responsibility so readily. "I wasn't taking the pill. I...I wasn't sleeping with anyone and—"

"It's all right, Holly."

"It isn't all right!" she argued sharply. Then, regretting her outburst, she struggled to take control of her emotions again, to lower her voice. "I'm single, David! And as much as I love Toby, raising him alone isn't easy! How will I manage two children?"

His thumb stroked the length of her fingers. "You would have the baby, then?"

She stared at him, her eyes wide. "Of course I would," she whispered.

"Thank God," he muttered, looking away again. Holly saw a touching struggle for composure going on in his face and loved him desperately for it.

"I'm scared, David," Holly confessed after a long, painful silence.

He pulled her close and held her against the hard curve of his shoulder. "Me, too," he said hoarsely. "Me, too."

The marriage proposal that Holly both hoped for and dreaded was evidently not forthcoming. David got up off the couch as Toby came in, blurting out, "Geez, David, your place in fantastic!"

I would have had to say no anyway, Holly said to

herself, searching for comfort within. It's a good thing he didn't ask me again. It's a good thing.

But if it was such a good thing, another part of Holly wondered, why was it that she had to turn her face away to hide a new crop of despairing tears?

I can't panic here, David thought as he pulled a plate of cold pizza from the refrigerator and slid it into the microwave oven. I've got to remain calm.

Toby sat at the table, looking up at him with trust and liking shining in his face. For the millionth time, David thought how much he would like to raise this kid, fly model airplanes with him and root for him at Little League ball games.

And the other child, the child that might be born—

He couldn't think about that child, he didn't dare. If it turned out that Holly wasn't pregnant after all, it was going to be the worst disappointment of his life. No, whatever he did, he had to keep his head and go slowly and patiently.

Patience, hell, David decided. He was going to walk into that living room, get down on his knees and beg Holly Llewellyn to marry him.

STATE SECRETS

When he got there, she was gone. After a moment of alarm, he heard her in the bathroom, throwing up. And he had never loved her more.

14

There was no way Holly could wait until Monday to find out whether or not she was going to have a baby, but she couldn't quite bring herself to put in an appearance at a hospital emergency room, either. Was there such a thing as an emergency pregnancy?

Holly's hands tightened on the steering wheel of the car. Beside her, the seat belt drawn across his small body, Toby slept peacefully. He'd fallen asleep at David's, and David had wanted them both to stay…

Holly pulled the car to a stop in front of an all-night drugstore and looked back at the huge cylindrical building towering against the night sky. The lights of David's condo burned like sweet beacons, pulling at her.

God, how she'd wanted to stay. How she'd wanted to fall into David's arms, David's bed.

She let her forehead rest against the steering wheel. Even now, it was all she could do not to go back, carrying Toby in her arms as David had carried him down to her car, and ask if he might not have room in his life for two—perhaps two and a half—more people.

But Holly couldn't do that, of course. Not until she knew what she truly felt and what she truly wanted. A baby might be the world's oldest reason for getting married; it was also the world's worst. And besides, David had not mentioned marriage again.

Grimly, Holly got out of her car and locked it, then hurried into the drugstore. There, she bought a home pregnancy test.

At home, she awakened Toby and half ushered, half carried him inside. "We should have stayed at David's," he yawned out as he groped his way up the stairs.

"Right," Holly said, smiling even though she was ready to cry. The paper bag containing her pregnancy test rattled a little in her hand.

"He has a hot tub," Toby argued sleepily. "Right in his bedroom."

"That clinches it," Holly teased. "A man with a hot tub in his bedroom is a person to be reckoned with."

A hot tub in his bedroom, she reflected as she went into the kitchen to check the answering machine and have one last cup of coffee. Or was it to put off taking that drugstore test and finding out whether or not she really was pregnant?

She poured a cup of cold coffee and put it in the microwave to heat. There was one message on the machine, from Elaine, if it could be called a message. Her friend sounded cryptic and excited and hesitant, all at once, but she hadn't really said anything.

With a sigh, Holly took her coffee from the microwave, was instantly nauseated by the smell of it and poured it down the sink. Then, resolutely, she snatched up the innocuous little bag that seemed to contain her, Toby's and David's fate, and she marched up the stairs.

"The test was positive," Elaine echoed with a sigh, her hands clenched tight around her coffee cup. "Well, Holly, clue me in—is that awful news or are we talking balloons and noisemakers here?"

Throughout the long, lonely Sunday just past, Holly had agonized over that very question. And she hadn't been able to come up with a clear answer. "I feel panic-stricken," she confessed. "I also feel like shouting for joy."

"Have you told David?"

Holly had reached for the telephone a thousand times on Sunday, for her car keys a thousand more. But in the end, she had not been able to face David. She was too afraid of leaning on him, too afraid of needing him for the wrong reasons. And too afraid, when she could bring herself to face it, that he would either reject her outright or offer to marry her for the sake of the baby.

"No," she said finally.

"I won't give you the he-has-a-right-to-know speech, Holly," Elaine replied, her voice gentle. "I don't think you need that right now."

"I've given it to myself a hundred times." She paused and assessed her friend. "You have something to tell me, don't you?" she prompted, remembering the brief, disjointed message Elaine had left on the machine over the weekend.

Elaine's pretty face seemed a little drawn. "This is a lousy time to bring it up, but yes, I do have something to tell you. I've been offered a fantastic job, Holly—an editorial position with a regional magazine."

Holly knew what was coming then, and though she would hate losing Elaine, she couldn't help being happy for her. It was the kind of job her friend had always wanted, the kind of job she had been trained for. "That's wonderful, Elaine," she said softly.

Elaine's wide green eyes lifted to Holly's face. "You're not angry?"

"You were the best assistant anybody could have hoped to have, Elaine. But you've outgrown this job. It's time for a change."

"I'll stay until the new book is indexed," Elaine offered, and though she was smiling, there were tears shimmering in her eyes.

"No need. I can do that myself. You just go out there and set local publishing on its ear!"

Elaine laughed and sniffled, both at the same time. "To think I dreaded this so much. Poor Roy—I cried and fretted all weekend, I was so sure you would be upset. That offer couldn't have come at a worse time."

Holly sighed. "I'm not sure I agree, Elaine. The truth is, I think it might be time for my life to take on a new direction, too."

Elaine's eyes widened. "What are you saying, Holly?"

"I seem to be making the decision even as we talk, but thinking about it, I realize that I've wanted to make several changes for a very long time. I hate traveling so much, for one thing, having to leave Toby behind, and, well, cookbooks aren't much of a challenge anymore.

I'd like to find out if I can write something different, Elaine. Something completely different."

"Such as?" Elaine prodded with a genuine interest that touched Holly and gave her courage.

"Maybe a novel," she blurted out bravely.

"Wow!" Elaine beamed. "And I thought you were going to resign yourself to motherhood!"

"Motherhood is wonderful, Toby has already proven that beyond any shadow of a doubt. But I know I need something more. Is that terrible?"

"Of course it isn't terrible. But," Elaine paused, turning her coffee mug in an idle circle, "I'm still old-fashioned enough to think that kids need a father as well as a mother. Holly, are you going to marry David?"

An awkward silence fell. "You know that he gave me a ring at Christmas, I suppose," Holly ventured after a time.

Elaine all but smirked. "I guessed as much. After all, I was the one who hid his packages in the tree so you wouldn't fly mad and send them back in the next mail." She paused, then frowned, her eyes on Holly's left hand. "But I don't see a diamond."

"I gave it back," Holly confessed brokenly. "I was so angry with him, so hurt over that whole deception. And then Craig's arrest—"

"You've dealt with all that now?"

Holly sighed. "I thought I had. I love David so much, Elaine. I think I have from the first. And the more I saw him, the less those things seemed to matter."

"So what's the problem now?"

"There are several problems, actually. I don't know whether David even wants to marry me now. And I'm wondering how much of my—my caring for him is really caring and how much is panic at the idea of having a baby all by myself."

Elaine looked exasperated. "The solution is simple, Holly. You need time to think, time to get your head together, as the kids say. I mean, with all that's happened to you in the past few months, how can you expect to have a handle on everything?"

Holly tangled her fingers in her hair as if to pull it out by the roots. "Think! How can I think, Elaine? That man sends me into fits of confusion every time I see him."

"Then don't see him for a while," Elaine said flatly. "Call a time-out. Give yourself a chance to catch your breath."

"That might be easier said than done," Holly fretted, lifting her own coffee cup to her mouth. She felt her stomach leap at the smell and set the cup back down without taking a sip.

Her grimace made Elaine grin. "Everything is easier said than done," she agreed, patting Holly's hand. "But what the hell?"

"Yeah," Holly replied with a wry arch of one eyebrow. "What the hell?"

The two women spent the rest of that day determining what had to be done to wrap up Holly's lucrative career as a cookbook author. There was one more set of classes to teach at the department store and the manuscript on Middle Eastern cooking had to be edited and then indexed. The newspaper column could be stopped with a month's notice.

Elaine had already gone home, taking a copy of the new manuscript with her, when the telephone rang. Holly drew a deep breath and answered it with a hello meant to sound cheerful. Except it came out a little hollow.

"Did you see your doctor?" David demanded without preamble, his voice gentle but gruff with weariness.

Holly closed her eyes a moment, stung by David's tone. He was hoping that she would say she wasn't pregnant, that he would be let off the hook. "Not yet," she said. "I have an appointment tomorrow morning."

"You're certainly casual about this, I'll say that for you!" David snapped. "I've been sweating blood ever since Saturday and you say you 'have an appointment tomorrow'!"

A tear slid down Holly's cheek. So much for never crying over David Goddard again. "I'm not being 'casual,' David, believe me," she managed to say. "I bought one of those home tests."

"And?"

"And—" Holly drew a deep breath to steady herself "—and it was positive."

There was a shattering silence at the other end of the line. "Are those things conclusive?" David finally asked, and there was no anger in his tone, but there was no happiness, either.

"I don't know," Holly admitted wearily. "I've never used one before."

"Very funny," came the ragged response.

"I wasn't joking, David."

He sighed; in her mind, Holly could see him leaning back in his chair, his thumb and forefinger to his temples. "I'd like to go with you tomorrow," he said finally, and still there was nothing in his voice to tell Holly what he was thinking.

She thought she knew that all too well. He was probably castigating himself for getting involved with a woman who didn't have enough sense to use birth control. "That won't be necessary, David," she said coldly, hanging up in his ear.

The telephone immediately rang again.

"Don't hang up on me, Holly," David warned. "I hate it."

Holly didn't hang up, but she did begin to cry, helplessly and with all the attendant noise. "Please, David… don't insist on going to the doctor's office with me…I couldn't bear it…"

"Holly." The word was a reprimand, but it was unbelievably gentle.

"I mean it, David!" Holly wailed. "I can't think clearly when you're around…I…"

He spoiled the intangible comfort he had just offered by swearing in a brutal undertone and then snapping, "Neither of us was thinking clearly from the beginning! Why start now, Holly?"

"David!"

"You should have stayed here the other night, Holly," he went on, quietly cruel. "What the hell? We could have made love until dawn. After all, the damage has been done!"

Damage. The word sliced through Holly like a knife.

How could he call their baby, their precious child "damage"? "I hate you, David Goddard," she hissed into the receiver, keeping her voice down only because Toby might be near enough to hear. "Do you hear me? I hate you and I never want to see you again!"

The silence was charged. Holly braced herself for David's answer, but in the end, he gave none. There was a soft click and the line went dead.

In the morning, Holly kept her appointment with her doctor and was told for a certainty that she was pregnant. The baby would be born, she was blithely informed, in late September or early October.

Holly stumbled out of her doctor's office, vitamin prescriptions in hand, stricken by a combination of joy and despair. David was waiting beside the elevator doors.

"Well?" he asked simply, his voice hoarse. Holly was too distracted to even attempt to read the expression in his navy blue eyes. She nodded, her throat too thick to permit speech.

"When?" he prompted, not unkindly.

"Fall," she croaked.

The elevator arrived and David ushered Holly inside. But she didn't look at him, and as far as she could tell, he didn't look at her, either. How could this be? They had made this baby together, in passion so intense that

Holly ached to remember it, and now they had nothing to say to each other. Nothing at all.

Out on the busy streets, people were rushing by, it seemed to Holly, in a colorful, threatening blur. Where had she left her car? Had she even brought the car?

No. She'd taken the bus. She remembered now. She had definitely taken the bus.

She tried in vain to recall which stop to wait at for another. Considering that she had lived in Spokane all her life and taken buses into virtually every part of it since the age of eleven, it was annoying to forget the routes and schedules now.

David's hand was strong on her elbow. "Come on," he said gruffly.

Holly looked at him with dazed, tear-blurred eyes. "Where are we going?"

"My place."

That snapped her out of it. She wrenched her arm free and went rigid. "Why, David? To do more 'damage'?"

Pain moved deep in his eyes, but was overcome so quickly that she thought she'd imagined it. "To talk," he said firmly, and his hand again closed around her arm.

"I don't want to talk to you, David. I don't want to talk to anybody. I just want to lie on my bed and cry."

The statement seemed to wound him; he looked

away, scanning cloud-dappled blue skies for a moment. "All right," he said after a long time. "All right. But, please, let me get you a cab."

It seemed the least he could do, after fathering a baby he didn't want. "Thank you," Holly replied woodenly.

But when she reached her house, high on the South Hill, she did not lie down on her bed and cry. Elaine was there, working on the manuscript, and Madge was cleaning furiously. Both of them were trying so hard to be subtle that Holly forgot her misery for the time being and burst out laughing.

"Yes!" she yelled, spreading her hands wide of a body that would soon swell to pearlike proportions. "I'm pregnant!"

Faced with the certainty, her friends did not seem to know whether to celebrate or commiserate. Thinking it enough that she wasn't flying apart in pieces, Holly gave them no clue. She simply sat down at her desk and turned on her computer and began working on the last of the cooking columns she was required, by contract with the local newspaper, to write.

For the next two weeks, Holly lived in a frenetic kind of limbo, working day and night, praying that David wouldn't call or come by and leaping every time the telephone or doorbell rang.

David didn't call, though. And he didn't come by. Holly was resigned to the fact that, despite his earlier claims to love and want her, she was going to have this baby alone. And raise it alone.

The fates seemed to respect her secret grief, however, and even to aid her in holding up the front she maintained for Elaine and Madge and Toby. Everything went well; Holly's agent accepted her decision to switch from sure-thing cookbooks to novels that might or might not sell, the newspaper was gracious, though they said their readers would miss her columns, and the department-store people didn't give her any flak, either, beyond reminding her that her contract called for one more set of lessons to be taught.

Yes, everything was fine. Until the night Toby ran away.

David was developing a hatred for coffee. He scowled at his empty cup and set it in the sink, looking out over the lights of the city and despairing. Why was he beating the books, night after night, like some college kid? For what?

He sighed raggedly and ran one hand through his hair. For his sanity, that was for what, he admitted to himself. If he didn't bury himself in classes by day and law books by night, he would go crazy. Perversely, he wondered what Holly was doing at that moment. What she was thinking and feeling.

Love for her clenched within David in a spasm so painful that it nearly bent him double. He had to leave her alone; he had to, no matter what the cost. A long talk with Holly's assistant, Elaine Bateman, had convinced him of that. And yet it was the hardest thing he had ever had to do—his every instinct ran counter to this endless, agonizing waiting.

The doorbell rang and David's heart lunged to the pit of his stomach and then swelled into his throat. Let it be her, he thought desperately as he strode to the door and reached for the knob.

Forcibly, David stopped just short of opening it, drew a deep breath and tried to compose himself. It was crucial to say the right thing, to do the right thing— The bell rang again, insistently, and David grinned as he turned the knob and pulled the door open.

Toby was standing before him, head down, jacket askew, his toy Cessna in one hand and the robot David had sent at Christmas in the other.

David scanned the hallway, puzzled, but saw no sign of Holly. Then, hiding the alarm he felt, he crouched to look into the little boy's averted face. It was tear-stained and pink from the cold outside.

Toby looked at him then and David ached at the despair he saw in that small face; it seemed to crumple before his very eyes.

"Don't you want to marry Mom and me?" the child wailed, flinging his arms around David's neck, the plane and the robot thumping to the floor.

David held him and rose to his feet, too overcome to respond immediately. After a time, though, he cleared his throat and asked, "Does your mom know where you are, slugger?"

The small head shook against his shoulder.

David had already guessed the answer to that question, of course, but it made an opening. "I think we'd better call her and tell her you're safe. Right now."

"Okay," sniffled Toby.

His shirt sodden with Toby's tears, David ruffled the little boy's hair and set him gently down on the sofa. This would be the first call he'd made to Holly in weeks, but his fingers didn't hesitate over the buttons as they usually did.

She answered, frantic, on the first ring. "Toby?"

"He's here with me," David said gently. "And he's all right."

"Thank God!" Holly wept. "Oh, thank God! I thought—"

David had to close his eyes for a moment. For some damned, inexplicable reason, he felt like crying himself. He didn't speak because he didn't dare.

"When did he get there?" Holly demanded, sniffling. "What did he say?"

The little boy's words echoed in David's heart. *Don't you want to marry Mom and me?*

"He hasn't said anything much," David lied gruffly, for Holly's sake as well as his own. "How the devil do you suppose he got all the way down here by himself?"

Holly sighed; David could see her in his mind, her wonderful aquamarine eyes puffy, her hair tangled from repeated, nervous ruffling. "I shudder to think," she said.

"Shall I bring him home or do you want to come and get him?" Either way, David despaired in silence, how am I going to be able to bear seeing you? Can that possibly be worse than *not* seeing you?

Holly's answer surprised him. "C-could you keep him, just for tonight?"

David glanced back at Toby, who was watching him from the sofa, his lower lip jutting out in some kind of little-kid defiance. "Keep him?" he echoed, and Toby's eyes widened.

"Evidently it was important to him to see you, David. Maybe you can find out what made him do this."

"I'll try," David promised hoarsely, and then he said goodbye to Holly and turned back toward the child, folding his arms across his chest.

"Okay, slugger. What's the deal? How did you get down here alone?"

Toby was scrambling out of his jacket, ready to stay for the duration, but there was a challenge in his eyes. "Everybody thinks I'm too little to do anything," he complained. "Just like that dumb baby."

Bingo, thought David, but he didn't smile. He didn't want Toby to think that running away in the middle of the night was clever.

"What dumb baby is this?" he asked.

"The one Mom's going to have. She won't want me anymore, that's for sure."

"Oh? And on what do you base that conclusion, counselor?"

Toby squared his shoulders. At least he'd had supper before setting out on the crosstown journey—half of it was still on his striped T-shirt. "I'm not really hers, you know," he said.

"Mmmm."

"She's really my aunt."

"Right. You just call her 'Mom' to make her feel good, huh?"

Toby considered and seemed to find the idea magnanimous enough to claim. "Yeah."

"She loves you, Toby. And no matter how many babies she has, that is never going to change."

The uncertainty in Toby's face was painful to see. "You really think so?"

"I really think so. Now, how did you get here?"

"You won't believe it."

"Indulge me," David replied.

"I walked."

"All the way from the South Hill?" David was horrified, though he did a creditable job of hiding it.

"All the way from the South Hill," Toby confirmed proudly. But his grin faded away. "If Mom loves me so much, how come she said you could keep me?"

"She just meant for tonight, slugger. She's a smart lady—she figured that if you wanted to see me badly enough to run away, well, then she should let you see me."

"Oh. Are you going to marry us? Mom and me and the baby?"

David reeled inwardly but again managed to recover. "I'd like that a lot, Toby, but sometimes things don't go the way we want them to, no matter how hard we try. And right now, you'd better be thankful that I'm *not* married to your mom."

"Why?" demanded Toby, a study in disbelief.

"Because I'd give you the worst spanking you've ever had in your whole life, that's why. Running away is an ultra-dumb thing to do."

Toby pondered this carefully, his face working as he weighed getting spanked against having David for a father. "I guess al-Qaeda could have got me," he said after due consideration.

"What do you know about al-Qaeda?"

"I know they were after my dad."

David went to the sofa and sat down beside Toby, making a big deal of stretching his legs and crossing his booted feet on the glass top of the coffee table. "They're not going to bother you, Tobe," he said after a long time.

Toby looked relieved. "Good. I thought they might think my dad told me a secret or something."

David put one arm around the little boy and held him close. He could understand the depths of Holly's feelings for this child, for he already loved Toby as if he were his own.

"Would you really have spanked me if I'd been your kid?" Toby asked when the silence grew too long for comfort.

"You'd better believe it," David replied honestly. "There are certain things a guy just doesn't do, and running away is one of them."

Blue eyes the size of Frisbees looked up into David's face. "I think I'd still like to be your kid anyway," he said.

David laughed because if he hadn't, he'd have cried.

"You'll probably like the baby better'n me, just like Mom."

"Neither of us will like the baby better than you, Toby."

Toby snuggled close, beneath David's arm. "Babies can't fly Cessnas or nothin'," he said derisively. And then he fell asleep.

David removed Toby's shoes, slipped a pillow beneath his head and covered him with a down-filled quilt from one of the extra bedrooms. He tried to go back to his books—the Bar Exam was only weeks away—but try as he might, he couldn't concentrate.

He kept losing himself in dreams that would probably never come true.

15

Elaine had been right in saying that what was needed was time, Holly reflected as she stepped onto the department-store escalator. She was munching on caramel-covered popcorn and peanuts—her third box that day—and she frowned as she emptied the last of it into the palm of one hand. The minute the morning sickness had passed away, the strange cravings had begun. And caramel corn wasn't the only thing she felt compelled to gorge on, unfortunately. Sometimes she wanted smoked oysters rolled in peanut butter....

Holly made a face and then thumped the box against her hand so that the prize would fall out. It was in a white packet, whatever it was, and she tore the paper away as she strolled toward Cookware, where she would teach her last class.

It was an omen! The prize turned out to be an enormous ring with a plastic solitaire. Grinning, Holly tucked it into her pocket.

Tonight's project was shawarma, and the members of her class were at their tables, sleeves rolled up. She scanned their faces as she did every night, hoping to see David among them and, paradoxically, hoping not to.

David had not called her or put in an appearance at her house since the morning he had brought Toby home. Even then, he'd only said that the little boy was worried about being shunted aside when the baby came. And the word *baby* had been like a barrier between them, impossible to surmount.

Holly was saddened as she dropped her caramel-corn box surreptitiously into a wastebasket and shrugged out of her coat. Determinedly, she smiled at her students. "Looks like everyone is ready to start."

There were nods, grins and expressions of nervousness all around. And then they began.

It was just as the class was ending that David appeared, his hands wedged into the pockets of a Windbreaker emblazoned with the Gonzaga University logo, his eyes carefully avoiding Holly's gaze.

She felt a shivering sort of exhilaration, followed by plunging doubts. Just because David was there, well, that didn't mean that he was ready to make any sort of declaration or renew their relationship. He might even have come to say goodbye, having decided to return to Washington....

This was a considerate class. Each and every student cleaned up his or her own mess, leaving nothing for Holly to do but sneak the occasional glance at David, who was leaning against a refrigerator door, his arms folded, his navy blue eyes touching upon everything except Holly herself.

She smiled as the last goodbyes were said and her students departed, certificates in hand. And then she was alone. With David.

"Time to take the bull by the horns, kid," she told herself, drawing on all her courage as she plunged a hand into her coat pocket. Win, lose or draw, there could be no more guesswork and no more emotional sparring. If David Goddard wasn't going to declare himself, then Holly would state her own case and see what happened.

"Hello," she said, walking over to him and stopping within touching distance.

David gave her a wry look. Obviously he wasn't going to make this easy.

"Thank you for taking such good care of Toby that night," she said hoarsely. She was clenching her fingers so tightly that the small object she held dug into her palm.

"You're welcome," he said.

Holly sighed and rolled her eyes. Now or never, she thought, drawing a deep breath that dizzied her. And then she extended her hand, the plastic ring lying in her palm.

"Will you marry me, David?" she choked out.

He looked as though she had flung a shawarma on him. His face contorted for a moment and he no longer leaned so indolently against the door of that display-floor refrigerator. No, David stood erect now, Secret-Service alert. His throat worked, but he said nothing.

Holly wanted to die. "You haven't mentioned getting married lately, so I thought I'd bring it up," she said lamely.

Suddenly, so suddenly that Holly jumped, David pulled her against his hard chest, that chest she had so missed the scent and feel and strength of, and he laughed. His hands touched her shoulders briefly and then entwined themselves in her hair, mussing it.

"God, Holly, how I love you," he muttered.

"Does that mean you're going to accept my proposal?" she asked softly, searching his face with wide, cautious eyes.

"How could I refuse?" he asked gruffly, his breath warm against her face, his eyes meeting hers with a direct sort of tenderness that made her shiver with the love of him, the need of him. "Holly, are you sure? Have you thought about this?"

"Yes. To the detriment, I might add, of everything I was supposed to be thinking about instead."

"What made you decide?"

"I didn't need to decide because I already knew. I just needed to *know* I knew."

David rolled his eyes—they were shining with laughter—and then he kissed her. Salespeople and customers were probably looking on, but Holly didn't care. She kissed him back.

She was breathless, moments later, as she caught his hand in hers and tried to wedge the caramel-corn diamond onto his finger. It didn't fit, of course, but David accommodatingly wore it on his pinkie.

"I wonder if accepting an expensive gift like this," David teased, "obligates me to submit to lewd and improper demands."

Holly laughed. "You bet it does," she answered. "Your place or mine, handsome?"

"What about Toby?" he asked, so seriously that Holly's already fathomless love deepened with a painful jolt.

"Toby is spending the night with a friend."

A grin broke over David's wonderful, magnificent face. "You planned this!"

Holly laughed. "Do you really have a hot tub in your bedroom?" she asked. "Rumor has it that you do."

His hand fitted itself to the small of her back and Holly found herself being propelled through Cookware and onto the down escalator. "Rumor is entirely correct," he answered. "All the same, I think you should confirm it with your own eyes."

The hot tub made a lulling, bubbling sound in the semi-darkness, filling the room with a tropical sort of heat. Holly luxuriated in contentment as David's hands slowly divested her of her clothes, pausing now and then to stroke and caress whatever prize he had just uncovered.

"I love you," he said, bending his head to one breast and circling the instantly responsive nipple with the tip of his tongue.

Holly groaned and then, somehow, found the strength to push him away. "Oh, no, you don't, fella. You're not going to stand there in all your clothes and make me crazy."

A compliant sort, David was soon standing there without his clothes. And making her crazy.

She went to stand beside the hot tub, looking down into its churning depths. Then David was behind her, drawing her back against him, running his hands from her waist to her breasts. He seemed to be weighing them in his palms, and Holly moaned and let her head fall back against his shoulder as his thumbs coaxed her nipples to a new level of response.

When Holly thought she could bear no more of that, when she was sure she would have to turn to him and demand that he take her, he retraced his path, lingering at her hips for a delicious moment and then knitting his fingers together over her abdomen.

His teeth caught at her earlobe and she quivered against the sinewy length of him, the hair on his chest tickling her naked back. "I want this to last forever," he breathed and again she trembled. "Cold?" he queried as an afterthought.

"Hardly," Holly managed to say.

All the same, David lowered her gently into the hot tub. The warm, moving water seemed to intensify the raging need in her senses to an almost unbearable degree, but Holly hadn't the strength to lift herself out.

Kneeling behind her, David took her hands in his and positioned them so that they were cupped behind her head. And then he began, idly, to toy with her breasts again, now bathing them with warm water, now caressing them, now plying the nipples between skilled fingers. Holly moaned and her own fingers uncurled, but she did not try to lower her arms.

"David," she finally managed to say, "oh, David—make love to me—now—"

He drew her up out of the water and placed her on the tiled edge. Even in the half darkness, she could see the glittering hunger in his eyes, a hunger he appeased at her breasts until Holly was writhing with need, her body still slick and warm from the brief episode in the hot tub.

"I—"

"David," Holly tangled her hands in his thick, dark, rumpled hair. "Now."

"I might hurt you—the baby—"

The concern in his voice caused Holly to free her hands and capture his muscle-corded thighs instead, urging him toward her. "I need you, David. I love you. And we've already waited long enough."

With a moan, he lowered himself to her and sought her solace with his manhood. His welcome was such that, with a rasped exclamation, he surged inside her, deeply but gently. Holly drew her knees up and felt his powerful hips moving slowly against her inner thighs.

She watched him until she could no longer bear the shadowy beauty of him and then closed her eyes. Patches of golden light exploded behind her lids as new feelings blossomed within her like flowers.

David, in turn, was nearly incoherent. "I thought this—would never—happen again—oh, God, Holly— how I need you—"

Holly muttered some wicked sweetness and her reward was a breathtaking increase in the pace of their lovemaking. Their bodies rose and fell in fierce unison, fever after fever raging within Holly and then breaking, each one making her wilder. Her fingernails raked David's back, as his possession and her own became one and the same and they both cried out as the tender anguish bonded them, fusing them into one being with its heat.

David collapsed beside her, his body trembling, his breath a primitive, tearing sound. "Good Lord, woman," he managed after some time, "I'm not sure I can bear up under a lifetime of that."

Holly stretched languidly, an evil wanton in the warm, lush darkness. "You'll 'bear up' just fine," she said, winding a finger in the moist down curling upon his chest.

He laughed, turned her onto her side and gave her bottom a playful swat. "Vamp," he said. "Just for that, I think I'll carry you to my bed and prove your theory."

"You couldn't carry me if you had to," challenged Holly in a sensuous, stretching purr. "Your knees are too weak."

"Is that so?" he asked in a rumbling whisper. And then, as Holly had hoped, he rolled to his feet, pulled her after him and lifted her into his arms. Feigning a dark passion, he dropped her from shoulder height onto the bed.

"Ummm," Holly crooned, stretching her arms upward. David came to her and never let her go throughout that long, glorious night.

EPILOGUE

Holly Goddard glared at her computer screen, muttering. This book had started out as a mystery, and her agent had liked what she had seen of it, but now it seemed to be taking an unexpected direction.

"It's Saturday," Holly grumbled to herself. "In some religions, Saturday is a day of rest."

"Did you say something?" David asked from the doorway of the study they shared. He was wearing blue jeans, a maroon sweatshirt, a denim jacket—and a baby girl in the carrier on his back.

Born in late September, Miss Autumn Goddard was already spending most Saturdays in the park with David and Toby. Her cheeks were pink and her round, indigo eyes sleepy as they peered out of the tiny snowsuit she wore.

Holly was filled with such tenderness that she ached. She forgot the problems she was having with her novel and went to plant a kiss on Autumn's plump cheek before lifting her out of the carrier to cuddle her for a moment.

"Where's Toby?" she asked.

David grinned, sliding back the hood of Autumn's snowsuit, revealing a head of curly, Holly-gold hair. He kissed the baby's forehead briefly before answering, "Downstairs, doing his homework with Marcus."

Marcus was Toby's newest and "bestest" friend; since he and Holly had moved into David's condo, the very day of the wedding, the two little boys had been a package deal. If you wanted one, you had to accept the other.

"Don't you have any homework to do, counselor?" Holly teased as she carried Autumn into the bedroom that adjoined her own and David's. "You have a big case coming up this week, if I remember correctly."

David dodged the question by disappearing into the kitchen, but he was back soon enough, Autumn's naptime bottle in hand.

Holly had already undressed their daughter, changed her diaper and bundled her into a cuddly pink sleeper. Autumn extended her tiny hands at the sight of the offered bottle and was asleep after a few gurgling swallows.

"About your case," Holly prodded, in the living room. Dammit, if she had to work on Saturday, then David was going to be right there in the study with her, plugging away at *Snider vs McCulley.*

Showing not the slightest sign of industry, David sat down on the raised hearth of the fireplace and stared indolently down at his right sneaker, his chin resting on one knee. "I've got that case down pat and you know it."

"Is that so?"

"Yes," David replied flatly, his eyes sparkling as they met hers. "You have to work so you want me to suffer right along beside you—misery loves company and all that."

"I'll be misery and you be company," Holly grumbled, assessing the situation. Toby was downstairs, visiting Marcus. Autumn was asleep. She blushed at the course her thoughts were taking.

David grinned. "And you'll love me?" he leered.

"Anytime I get the chance," Holly admitted.

He assumed his best attorney manner, frowning pensively, standing up to pace back and forth along the hearth as though it were a jury box. "What about your book, Mrs. Goddard?" he demanded soberly. "How do you intend to meet your deadline if you don't write?"

Holly shrugged, her legs curled beneath her on the

navy blue sofa. "I made up the deadline myself. There's no reason to be picky, here."

"Picky?" David boomed, looking suitably shocked, even horrified. He shook his head as he continued to pace, his hands locked behind his back. "Have you no dedication, Mrs. Goddard? No ambition? No—"

Holly giggled at the picture he made. "Don't tease me, David," she wailed. "My plot is so hopelessly snarled that I'll never get it undone and my characters won't do anything I tell them to!"

David stopped, bending slightly to peer into Holly's face. "Exactly what kind of scene are you trying to write, anyway?" he demanded in that same ponderous, lawyerlike tone.

Holly gave him a once-over from beneath coyly lowered eyelashes. "A love scene, of course," she purred.

"Aha!" he cried, pointing one index finger into the air. "In that case, Madam, we are able to ascertain the exact nature of your problem!"

Holly pretended to peer around him. "We?" she echoed.

"Speaking as the prosecution, of course," he admitted.

"Of course. And what, pray tell, is the 'exact nature of my problem,' counselor?"

"Research, of course. A pitiable, contemptible lack of research."

"I see," Holly said, assuming a look of deep chagrin.

"No, Madam," David went on sternly, "I don't think you do see. This is a matter of the gravest importance."

Holly giggled again. "You don't really say things like that in the courtroom, do you?"

"No," David confessed. "I saw it in an old Henry Fonda movie. Now, exactly how do you plead? Guilty or not guilty?"

Holly deliberately batted her eyelashes. "Of what am I accused, sir?"

He sank to his knees before her with a comical thump, his eyes gleaming. "Neglecting your research," he replied.

Thinking of the weeks after Autumn's birth when there had been no lovemaking at all, and the hesitant quality in David's touch even now, Holly's playful mood was dampened. "Or perhaps of neglecting my husband?" she prompted softly.

He bent forward and kissed her. "Never that," he whispered.

"I know it was hard for you—"

David laid an index finger to her lips. "Having a baby was no piece of cake, either, I'll wager. Still, Autumn is almost two months old. Time is passing us by. Maybe we should start another baby right away."

Holly laughed and wrapped her arms around his neck. "I love you, you maniac."

"And I love you. But, as a writer, that doesn't excuse you from doing proper research." He stood up, drawing Holly with him, pulling her against the appealing, granitelike length of him. His face was serious, though, despite his earlier teasing. "Tell me the truth. Does it… does it hurt when I make love to you?"

She stood up on tiptoe to kiss his chin. "No. It feels glorious."

"Really?"

"Would I lie about something as important as research?" She slid her arms around his waist and felt him tremble as their bodies touched, her soft curves a temptation to his hard lines and angles.

"I certainly hope not," he gasped, gazing deep into her eyes, finding things she might have hidden once but was willing to share now. His hands came tentatively to burrow into her silky hair. "Oh, Holly," he breathed. "Holly. Every day, I wake up and I think I can't possibly love you any more than I already do. And every day, you prove me wrong."

Holly's eyes misted with happy tears. "Do you love

me enough to help me with my research?" she whispered.

David laughed and swatted her firm, round bottom with both hands. "Oh, at least that much. I'm in the mood to be magnanimous here."

Holly gave him a long look. "Then what's holding you back? Carry me off to your bed and slake your savage passion at my heaving breasts."

David grinned and feigned a beleaguered look. "God, I hope that isn't a direct quote from your manuscript, woman," he teased. "If it is, you'd better go back to writing about crumpets and tacos."

Holly wriggled against him in reply, and he groaned, lifting her into his arms. "If we're going to research savage passion, I guess we'd better get started."

Their passion was not savage, but tender, mounting with every kiss, every caress, every surrender of a garment. Though they had made love several times since Autumn's birth, David was still afraid of hurting her.

As Holly lay beneath him, her blouse and bra gone, her breasts proudly bared to him, David bent his head and kissed each impudent peak. "Allow me, Madam," he taunted in a rumbling voice, "to slake my savage something or other."

The kisses felt so good that Holly stretched, crooning and thrusting herself upward for more. "Please, do," she said and she whimpered with pleasure as he began to lose his restraint and enjoy her freely, now nibbling, now suckling with the fierce hunger Holly craved.

Finally, leaving breasts moistened and tuned to passion by his lips and his tongue, David traced a path of kisses over her collarbone and up her neck to the sensitive hollows beneath her ears.

"Are you taking notes?" he demanded, working his way back down to a breast, attending to it briefly, and then moving on to the heaving ridges of her rib cage.

"C-copious notes," Holly choked as he circled her navel with a leisure that was positively torturous. She moaned with sweet despondency as his kisses continued. "Th-that isn't at all p-pertinent to my wo-work, sir."

He chuckled, the sound far away and yet so near as to be a part of Holly. "Want to bet?" he asked, his hand stroking her inner thigh, pressing her legs to part.

Research was the furthest thing from Holly's mind then—moments later, she didn't even have a mind, for she had been driven out of it. Only later, after a series of shattering releases, after David had finally given in to her pleading and entered her, his body at once taming and exalting hers, was she free to grope her way back toward sanity.

He lay beside her afterward, his head pillowed on her breasts, his legs still entangled with hers. Smiling to herself, Holly wound a lock of his hair around her finger and speculated, "I think I've got it. I know what I was doing wrong now."

"Believe me," David rasped, still too weak, apparently, to rise from her breast, "you didn't do anything wrong."

Holly laughed. "I was talking about my book, silly."

David growled with pretended outrage and rolled onto his back, hauling Holly up to sit astride him. It was so good, this easiness between them, this lack of restraint or caution. Tears of sheer joy blurred Holly's vision.

David frowned and caught them on his thumbs when they fell. "What is it, love?"

Holly was anxious to reassure him, and she gave a sniffling laugh. "I'm afraid I've used you shamelessly," she confessed.

"How so?"

"I'm not writing a romance; I'm writing a mystery. The love scene I was talking about consists of one kiss, nothing more."

David glared at her, pretending outraged honor. "Wench," he said in gravelly tones, "you'll have to pay for that."

"I will?" Holly questioned, the picture of innocence. "How?"

He shifted slightly and then entered her with an authority that made her gasp with pleasure. His hands rose with brazen idleness to cup her breasts. And that was answer enough.

Holly began to move upon him, slowly, sweetly, a creature of fire and instinct. "You are completely—oh, God—without conscience—"

David matched her pace and then began to set one of his own. "Completely," he agreed, pressing his head back into the pillows and closing his eyes. Several glorious, heated minutes passed, and then they were both crying out for each other, even though they were already joined, seeking each other with desperate hands and hoarse, tender words.

The finding was sweet indeed.

Turkeys. David's fancy refrigerator, with its sliding opaque door, was covered with construction-paper turkeys. Holding a fussy Autumn against her hip with one arm, Holly opened the appliance's door with the other and reached inside for milk.

The draperies had not been drawn, and as Holly sat at the table, rocking her hungry daughter in her arms while the bottle heated, she looked out over the sparkling lights of the city, thinking.

Impatient for her midnight feeding, Autumn flung back her gossamer-tufted head and wailed.

"Shhh," Holly whispered against a tiny neck scented of talcum powder and baby lotion. "You'll wake up Daddy and Toby."

Autumn was unimpressed with that possibility. Her wail intensified to a series of piercing shrieks. Chuckling softly, Holly took the bottle from its warmer and did the gyrations required to hold a furious baby and test the heat of the milk at the same time.

"This looks like a job for Super-lawyer," yawned David, clad in a velour bathrobe, as he took both baby and bottle from Holly and plopped down in a chair. A moment later, Autumn was imbibing greedily.

"Fine thing," Holly scoffed with mock indignation. "I do all the work and you get the credit."

David only grinned, watching his daughter with such adoration in his eyes that Holly wasn't sure she could bear it. Or the feelings inspired in her.

"There was a letter from Craig today," she said quietly, leaning back against the counter, her arms folded. She felt like a housewifely bundle of chenille and love.

David's eyes darted to her face, wary. "Oh? How is he?"

"He's getting better," Holly answered gently. "They haven't decided yet exactly what to try him for. It might be a long time before they do."

There was a silence; obviously David didn't know what to say. And Holly didn't want Craig or anyone else to stand between them.

She went to David and made a place for herself on his knee, unsettling the ravenous Autumn only slightly. Wrapping one arm around David's neck, Holly intoned, "Kiss me, you fool!"

He laughed and responded accordingly.

★ ★ ★ ★ ★

THE FIVE DAYS OF CHRISTMAS

Dear Reader,

It was a thrill to create this wonderful Christmas story involving Morgan Trayhern and his family! Just as they are to you, Morgan and the people who work for the black ops company Perseus are like extended family to me. This story was a joy to write.

Many of you have asked about Morgan and Laura's children and if they will have their own book after they grow up (along with Noah Trayhern and Aly Trayhern's children). Indeed they will! Some of their stories will be found in my Black Jaguar Squadron series (Harlequin Romantic Suspense) and my forthcoming black ops Shadow Warriors series (Harlequin HQN and Harlequin Romantic Suspense). Of course, the real mover and shaker at work behind the scenes of this novella is Laura Trayhern, who created the Five Days of Christmas celebration for the employees of Perseus—and is doing a little matchmaking this holiday!

In this story we get to meet a very tired black ops mercenary, Colt Hamlin, who has simply seen too much on his last mission to Kosovo. He's resting up—actually, hiding out—in Montana. Until Laura Trayhern coaxes him out of hiding by matchmaking him with her son's high school teacher, Abbie Clemens. Abbie had lost her black ops husband a year earlier, so in another way she's emotionally hiding, too. But Laura has a sixth sense about the two of them and makes sure they meet and have to work together during the Five Days of Christmas celebration.

Sit back, relax, prop up your feet and enjoy their story, and say hello once again to Morgan, Laura and their family. I hope you enjoy reading this story as much as I did penning it.

Warmly,

Lindsay McKenna

To Chief Michael Jaco, U.S. Navy SEAL (retired),
Seal Team 6, Red Man Squadron.
Thank you for your twenty-four years of service to our country.
Thank you for helping me with all things SEAL
in my forthcoming Shadow Warriors series.
I appreciate your expertise and help.
You are a true hero in every sense of the word.

1

December 20

"**M**organ, you can't say no," Laura pleaded as she stood in her husband's large office at Perseus headquarters, hidden deep in the Rocky Mountains of Montana. Though his office, which was next to the war room, where so many mercenary and military missions were launched, was officially closed for the holidays, Laura had come to talk to her husband as he wrapped things up. The Five Days of Christmas celebration she ran every year was at the top of her agenda. But there was one important detail she felt had to be taken care of first.

Now, as she watched him scowl and rummage through several top-secret military reports on his desk, love for him welled up in her heart. With silver flecking the temples of his black, short hair, Morgan was getting even more handsome with age.

He lifted his head, and his blue eyes softened as he looked at his wife—at her blond hair in tempting disarray around her slim shoulders, her arms crossed and those soft lips of hers set in a petulant pout. She wore a bright red, cowl neck mohair sweater, dark green slacks and simple oxfords. A piece of green holly with red berries was fastened in her hair. Sighing, he ran his hand across his chin. "Listen, I've tried everything to get Colt out of our safe-house condo. He's hurting, Laura."

Uncrossing her arms, she perched her hip on the side of Morgan's desk and gave him a beseeching look. "I know his mission over in Kosovo was successful. So why is he holed up?"

"It was successful," Morgan agreed, leaning back in his leather chair. Just gazing into Laura's tender eyes made him feel better. She was his anchor. She always had been. And even now, after carrying four beautiful children in that petite but oh-so-strong body of hers, she looked just as young and vibrant as when he'd met her so many years ago. "Colt's suffering from mild PTSD—

post-traumatic stress disorder—according to Dr. Jennifer Ramirez, our staff physician." .

"Well, if that's so, then all the more reason to get him out of there and back with normal people and society." She stretched out her hand. "Morgan, you know what PTSD is. You've suffered from it for years because of your experience over in Vietnam and later, after you were kidnapped. The last thing you needed was to be alone at times like that. Colt Hamlin has worked for you for seven years now and I agree that he needs downtime. But with people." With a mischievous grin, Laura said, "He can help me with the Five Days of Christmas celebration."

Groaning, Morgan sat up, folded his hands on his desk and raised one eyebrow. "You've got that look in your eye, sweetheart. You're making me nervous."

With a lilting laugh, Laura reached out and covered his massive, hairy hand with her own much smaller one. "Now, darling…"

"Now I know I'm in trouble."

"Colt is, actually," she replied playfully. Patting his hand one last time, Laura eased off the desk. "I have a plan, Morgan. One that I think can help Colt and help me."

"Uh-oh..."

"Don't be such a fussbudget about this. Hear me out, will you?"

One corner of his mouth crooked. "That look in your eyes is still there. You have a plan. I feel like I should already be waving a white flag of surrender...."

Chuckling, Laura said, "Listen, you know Abbie Clemens, the biology teacher over at the high school? The teacher that Jason loved so much?"

Morgan nodded. "Sure I do. She's helping you with the Christmas celebration, right?"

Laura's smile deepened. "Yes, she is. What I want to do is lure Colt out of hiding and ask him to help Abbie. She takes care of all the decorations for these five days, and I've got my hands full with all I've got to do."

"You're matchmaking—again...." Morgan gave his wife a warm look. He couldn't stop the smile from edging his mouth. Laura stood there, her shoulders back, her smile effusive and her eyes glimmering with happiness.

"Well..." she murmured coyly, "I just feel it's time Abbie got back into the mainstream of life. Her husband died two years ago in the line of duty while working with Perseus. It's the least we can do to help her, Morgan. She's ready to let go of her past."

"And you think bringing snarling, grouchy Colt Hamlin into her life is a *good* thing? Are you a sadist?"

Laughing at his good-natured jab, Laura moved around the room. "I know he's grumpy right now. I just happen to feel Abbie will be like a healing ointment to his emotional wounds. And if she can handle petulant, hormone-driven eleventh-graders, I'm sure she can deal with Colt." Laura pirouetted, taking in his office as she spun around. There were maps of the world on the walls, photographs of their four children, whom Morgan doted upon, and a pair of crossed Marine Corps ceremonial swords to attest to his time spent in that branch of the service.

Morgan watched his wife move with grace around the windowless room. His office was in the basement of the Perseus complex, hidden beneath a Victorian home. Because of the nature of his super-secret work, Morgan did not want to be found by his enemies…and he'd made many over the last fifteen years. He also wished to protect his growing family. Once, several years before, Laura, their oldest son, Jason, and Morgan himself had been captured by drug dealers who wanted to get even after Morgan's mercenaries destroyed their trade in several key regions of South America.

Frowning, Morgan recalled that horrible experience. Laura had suffered badly at the hands of her captors. His son Jason, although very young when it happened, had been scarred, it seemed, for life. Before the kidnapping, Jason had been an outgoing young boy. Afterward, he'd become withdrawn, a loner, angry and rebellious...even to this day. If it hadn't been for Abbie Clemens, who was like a second mother to Jason, Morgan doubted that his son would have gained an appointment to the U.S. Naval Academy to follow in the Trayhern family's two-hundred-year-old tradition of military service.

Guilt ate at Morgan. His family had suffered needlessly because of his own arrogance, his confidence in Perseus and its ability to protect his family...and the families of people who worked for him around the world. It had been a lesson he never wanted to repeat, so he'd gone underground—literally disappeared—so that no terrorists, no drug dealers, however powerful, could hunt Perseus down and take out their rage and revenge. Moving to the very small town of Philipsburg, Montana, deep in the heart of the Rocky Mountains, had been a brilliant tactical decision. Here, Perseus staff were relatively safe, although none of them let down their guard completely.

As Laura turned and smiled winningly at him, Morgan knew his goose was cooked. He could never say no to her. He loved her too much to deny her anything. Besides, what she was asking was more than reasonable. She was right: Colt needed to be pried out of hiding. Being with people would help him heal.

"Well? What do you think? Can you phone Colt? Tell him you need him, Morgan? Fib a little and tell him you're overwhelmed with work and that you usually do this running around for me in preparation for the Five Days of Christmas celebration, but you can't this time. Colt will understand that. And he'll help if you ask him."

Giving her a wry look and then gesturing to the mission plans on his desk, Morgan growled, "I don't think I'll have to fib one iota about being overwhelmed with work."

Laura came over, slid her arms around his massive shoulders and placed a warm, lingering kiss on his crooked mouth. In response, he lifted her and settled her on his lap. With a sigh, she placed her brow against his and whispered, "I love you, Morgan Trayhern."

"You love me because you can wheedle anything you want out of me, whenever you want it," he chuckled as he lifted his chin and placed a kiss on the tip of her nose.

Drowning in her warm gaze, he added, "But I know you love me for other reasons, too."

"You're such a teddy bear, darling. My teddy bear—big and gruff. But underneath," she continued, sliding her hand against his chest, "you've got a heart of gold. I know you care what happens to Colt. And I can see you're worried about him, though there's nothing you can do about it personally. Maybe my plan won't work fully, but Abbie's lonely and so is Colt. Why not bring two lonely people together? Maybe the Five Days of Christmas celebration will help them."

Catching her sparkling gaze, Morgan placed his hand over his wife's as she pressed against his white silk shirt and red tie. "Okay, I'll give him a call. But no promises, all right?"

When the phone rang, Colt Hamlin nearly leaped out of the chair he was sitting in. A bottle of whiskey, one third of the contents gone from his drinking bout the night before, sat next to the red phone. The phone rang again. Irritated, he snatched it up.

"Yeah?"

"Colt? This is Morgan."

Instantly, Colt sat up. Scowling, he changed his tone.

"Sorry, boss. I wasn't expecting any calls," he said contritely.

Morgan accepted his apology for the snarling start to their conversation. "Don't worry about it. Listen, I need your help. I'm plowed under here with work. Laura needs my help in setting up things for our Five Days of Christmas celebration, but I can't make it, Colt. I was wondering if you felt well enough to take my place. All it means is a lot of running around, pulling things together, working behind the scenes."

Colt rubbed his bloodshot eyes. He'd barely slept last night. And drinking whiskey probably hadn't helped. He felt fractured. Raw. "I don't do parties, Morgan."

"I understand. I'm not asking that of you, Colt. I am asking for your time, and maybe some driving here and there. Maybe helping some of the women set up decorations at our home. That's all."

Rubbing his chin, which had a two-day growth of beard on it, Colt said, "Yeah…okay…I can do that." After all, he owed Morgan big-time. Under any other circumstances, Colt would eagerly do anything for his boss. Right now, though, he was hurting so much that he wondered if he could keep himself glued together and focused enough to help anyone at all.

"Great. I'm appreciative. Take the car in the garage beneath the condo where you're staying over to Abbie Clemens's place. Here's the address...."

Colt found a pencil and paper and wrote it down. Philipsburg was a small town—less than 2,500 in population—and was like a second home to him when he came off missions. He knew the layout well.

Hanging up, he sighed. The condo, which was decorated in a Western motif, was silent—and lonely. Getting up stiffly, he padded on bare feet across the thick, dark blue carpet to the bathroom. First, he'd better shower and shave. Otherwise, this woman called Abbie would freak out over his rough appearance.

The heavy knock on Abbie's back door, off the kitchen, made her jump in reaction. It was an aggressive kind of knock, not a friendly one, that was for sure. Slipping off the chair and placing the half-finished pine swag on the table, Abbie hurried to answer it. Would that be Colt Hamlin already? It was nearly 9:00 a.m. Laura had called to say he would be coming by to help. Glancing through the window, which was wreathed in pale pink, Victorian style curtains with a swag of holly with bright red berries across the top, she could see a very tall, large man standing on the porch. Snowflakes twirled lazily from the gray sky behind him.

Abbie's heart beat a little harder as she opened the door. The man standing before her reminded her of an angry grizzly bear, a species that lived in this part of the Rocky Mountains. He stood about six foot one inch tall, and his shoulders were massively broad. His black hair was cut very short, with one rebellious curl dipping over his furrowed brow. He was built like a boxer, she decided as she quickly perused the unhappy set of his face. Everything about Colt Hamlin was square—his build, the shape of his jaw, his broad forehead. His nose looked like it had been broken many times. Her gaze ranged upward to his eyes. Though they were bloodshot, she could see they were a forest-green color, the pupils dark and huge. Intuitively, Abbie sensed that he was very tired and stressed out. Laura had warned her when she'd called that Colt was like a bear with his foot in a trap, and to take him in stride.

"Hi," she greeted him a little breathlessly, and stuck out her hand. "You must be Colt Hamlin? I'm Abbie Clemens. Thanks for dropping by to help me with this stuff. I really appreciate it."

Colt stared down at her proffered hand. He hadn't

known what to expect, but it wasn't this. Dressed in an apricot mohair sweater and cobalt-blue corduroy slacks, Abbie Clemens stood about five foot five inches in height, her medium-boned frame probably weighing in at about a hundred and thirty pounds. Her face was plain, but was set off by a riot of curly, carrot-red hair tied back from her heavily freckled, pale face by a pink-orange-and-white scarf. What drew him unexpectedly were her large blue eyes, which were soft and warm, and a wide, smiling mouth that sent a sheet of heat all the way through him to his toes. Her engaging smile was genuine. And the sparkle of welcome in her eyes appeared to be, too.

Jerkily, he lifted his hand and enclosed hers. Such a small, delicate hand covered with copper freckles, compared to his own bear paw. Clearing his throat, he growled, "Yeah, I'm Colt. Morgan Trayhern said you needed some help?"

A stream of tingles flew up Abbie's fingers into her arm as she released Colt's massive hand. For all of his masculine strength, she had to give him credit: he hadn't crushed her fingers. When she saw surprise flare in his narrowed eyes, she wondered why. Self-consciously touching her flyaway hair, which always looked uncombed because it was so curly, she stepped aside. Abbie knew she was not beautiful, not even pretty. She had accepted that her oval face, her straight nose with flared nostrils, and her polka-dotted skin slathered with hundreds of freckles she refused to hide with makeup, did not make her look glamorous.

"Come in," she invited, and gestured to the huge, white oak table where the pine swags lay. "Just take off your coat and have a seat here at the table while I finish off these last two decorations."

Abbie watched with compassion as he self-consciously jammed his hands into the pockets of his jeans and stepped hesitantly through the door. The dark brown leather bomber jacket he wore had obviously seen a lot of wear and tear. The white silk scarf beneath, spotted with melted snowflakes, gave him the look of an aviator. As he shrugged out of the jacket and placed it on the back of an oak chair, she smiled a little nervously.

Colt wore a maroon, fisherman's knit sweater, the wrinkled collar of a white shirt peeking out from beneath it. Everything about him shouted of stress. Laura had warned Abbie that he was suffering from PTSD. She knew what it was because some of the children she taught had suffered from it—especially Jason Trayhern, due to his kidnapping at an earlier age.

Treading gently, Abbie watched as Colt's gaze skittered around her bright pink kitchen, with its Victorian-style curtains. Going over to the sink, she put water into the copper teakettle. "Tea or coffee? You look like you could use one or the other." She kept her voice light and teasing. When his gaze whipped to her, she froze momentarily. He had the eyes of a hunter or predator—always shifting, always moving and restless. Abbie knew he worked for Morgan, but not in what capacity.

"Yeah. Hot tea sounds good." When he saw her jolt, then freeze, he realized he was snarling again. *Damn.* Clearing his throat, he added, "Thanks." It sounded lame.

Grabbing the chair, Colt pulled it out and sat down. The fragrant scent of pine surrounded him. There were at least a dozen thick ropes of woven evergreen branches on the large, rectangular table in front of him. Sniffing again, he said, "What's that smell? Cinnamon rolls?"

Grinning, Abbie put the teakettle on the gas stove and turned it on. "Sure is. Have you had breakfast?" Colt probably weighed around a hundred and eighty pounds, she judged. And his cheeks were hollow. He wasn't eating enough.

Shrugging, he muttered, "I'm not hungry." There was that snarl again, he thought with dismay. Every feeling was visible in her face. That shook him. In his trade, no one showed any expressions or emotions. Colt reminded himself that Abbie was a schoolteacher, not a spy or a mercenary. Her eyes were lustrous and so blue that they reminded him of the deep, breathtaking azure of a wide Montana sky in summertime. As he studied her, he saw her eyes grow tender. It was almost a physical sensation he received as she gave him that gentle, caring look.

"Are you sure? I can whip you up an omelette and some bacon real fast. I don't have to have these swags over to Laura's for an hour."

Rubbing his throat with his long, thick fingers, Colt muttered, "I got a cold comin' on or somethin'...."

"Ohh...well, in that case I'll put a little honey and lemon in your tea to soothe it." Reaching up on tiptoes, she grabbed a jar of honey from the cupboard and placed it on the counter. Her heart bounded as she turned and looked over at Colt. He was watching her with such intensity that Abbie wondered if the zipper on her slacks was open or something. Maybe he hadn't been around a woman for a long, long time.

Unused to such raw male scrutiny, she opened the fridge and pulled out a bottle of reconstituted lemon juice. In her job at the high school, she didn't meet many men who were single. Though Philipsburg was a tourist destination during the summer months, it mainly attracted families seeking an outdoor experience in nature. Abbie felt her skin prickle pleasantly. She was enjoying Colt's frowning inspection, but found it hard to believe he was attracted to her—Miss Plain Jane of Philipsburg, as she wryly referred to herself in moments of acute loneliness.

Taking the recently baked cinnamon rolls out of the oven, where she'd kept them warm, Abbie popped one onto a plate and set it before Colt. "I hear cinnamon rolls are cold killers."

Looking up at her, he saw a grin playing across her full lips. The twinkle in her eyes gave away the fact that she was teasing him. Warming to her, Colt picked up the fork and knife she'd placed beside the plate. "Yeah?"

"Absolutely."

"Better than vitamin C?" He cut into the warm roll, and the scent made his mouth water. The teakettle began to whistle shrilly and Abbie left his side. Colt felt the sunshine leave with her.

"Absolutely. My kids tell me candy and junk food are the best thing for colds and flu," she said with a laugh as she poured them each a cup of tea. Abbie turned for a moment to look at him. Colt was enjoying the huge cinnamon roll immensely. *Good.* He looked like he needed something positive in his life, even a small thing. Placing a teabag into each cup of hot water, she brought them over to the table and sat down opposite him. Moving a half-made pine swag to one side, she spooned a bit of sugar into her tea. When she lifted her head, she met his hooded gaze. Her heart pounded momentarily. The pupils of his eyes were large and black as he studied her. Now she knew what a bug felt like under a microscope. Being a biology teacher, she would have new compassion for them in her class.

"Cinnamon roll okay?" she asked lightly, holding his frank stare.

Blinking, Colt realized he was staring like a starving wolf. What *was* it about this petite woman with the wild, riotous hair? When she smiled at him, he felt that sunny warmth embrace him. She was so honest and unassuming in an emotional sense that it rocked him. "Oh…the roll. Yeah, its good. After where I just came from, food tastes damn—I mean darn—good." Colt had to remind himself he was back in the real world once more, not undercover, and not with military types where cursing was as much a part of daily life as breathing air.

Abbie's heart expanded with joy. Colt was trying so hard to be nice. "You're really tired, aren't you? Maybe if I made you a fortifying breakfast, you'd get some energy back?"

He shook his head and polished off the rest of the roll. "I just came off a rough mission," he muttered in apology, "and I'm sleep deprived. I'll catch up in the next few days and be okay. Thanks, though…" Taking the cup of tea, he dipped the bag up and down a few times and then put it on a saucer. After adding a spoonful of honey and a bit of lemon juice, he found himself thirstily drinking it down. Abbie was right. Within moments, his sore throat disappeared.

She fingered her cup and chose her words carefully. "When my husband was alive, he worked for Morgan as an operative."

Frowning, Colt lifted his head. He heard carefully concealed pain in Abbie's soft voice. She was frowning, too, her thin red brows bunched as she stared down at her cup of tea.

"I'm sorry…I didn't know…." he began. How stupid of him. He looked at her left hand. There was no wedding band on it. "So…you know what we go through…." He found himself giving an inner sigh of relief because Abbie understood.

She lifted her head and nodded slightly. "Yes, I do."

Shifting the cup in his large hands, Colt murmured, "How long ago?"

"Two years." She gave him a game smile. "Ted was in the Marine Corps. A Recon. He quit and came to work for Morgan. I'm a schoolteacher, and I loved moving here to the Rocky Mountains." Her eyes grew bleak. "I always worried about him when he went on a mission. You know how it is, I suppose?"

"My wife divorced me five years ago because of what I did," Colt told her bluntly. Not that he blamed Christine. He was gone nine months at a time, sometimes longer. No marriage could survive those conditions. The distress in Abbie's eyes touched him unexpectedly. "I know the person left behind worries a lot. It leaves you feeling pretty helpless," he added gruffly.

"It does," she agreed. "But Ted didn't get killed on a

mission, if that's what you're thinking." Abbie grimaced. "He died in a car accident during a blizzard. An eighteen-wheeler spun out of control and hit him head-on about ten miles from here."

Shaking his head, Colt said, "Damn, I'm sorry."

Taking in a deep breath, Abbie gave him a sad smile. "Yeah, isn't it a sick joke? All along, I thought Ted might die on a mission. Instead he gets killed this way. Go figure… Well, that was two years ago. Laura says I need to start living again."

Abbie gazed fondly around the small, cozy kitchen. "Laura persuades me every year to help her with the Five Days of Christmas celebration, and I love it. It's helped me a lot over the last couple of years." Running her fingers in a caressing motion across the swag of pine boughs and red and silver ribbons she was weaving among the branches, Abbie added, "Family means everything to me, and I know it does for Morgan and Laura, too. Have you ever attended this celebration? Or were you always on a mission when it happened?"

"I was always on a mission." Colt watched, almost mesmerized by Abbie's continued stroking of the thick green swag. For a crazy moment, he wondered what it would be like if she stroked him the same way. What would it feel like? Good. Damn good. Hungry for a woman's touch, he found himself lost in a haze of heat and desire for her. She was a complete stranger to him, yet somehow she'd gotten under his skin without trying. Stunned, Colt admitted he was tired and stressed out. He also told himself Abbie was guileless and open, unlike many of the women he'd met. So how could she become so much a part of him in such a short space of time? It had to be the PTSD, he warned himself. He was raw and hurting, and her natural warmth and vulnerability had opened up his heavily armored heart because right now he needed to be held, to be cared for and nurtured.

Abbie's lips parted as she saw the heated look in his hooded eyes. Her entire body responded violently to Colt's smoldering glance. She was old enough to know what that look meant. Yet she was shocked by it. In the last two years of grieving for her husband, Abbie had never given one thought to the possibility that another man might be interested in her. After all, she was no raving beauty.

"W-well…" Abbie stammered, breathless with the discovery of his attraction, "they throw a huge five-day party for all the Perseus employees who work here. Any mercs coming in off missions and who are staying at the condos outside of town to rest and recoup are invited, too. This year we have fifty people coming." She gulped and added, "It's fun because the whole family is invited. The children have a great time. Laura plans everything for the kids, and we adults magically turn into children ourselves during the process."

She smiled a little as she watched Colt's perennial scowl begin to ease and disappear. Did she have that much of an affect on him? Before, he'd been so dark and snarly. Maybe he was more cheerful because he had some food in his stomach now, or maybe the hot tea had soothed his sore throat. Or maybe it was *she* who had changed his demeanor.

Her conscience prickled her, reminding her smartly that she was only twenty-eight years old and in her prime as a young woman. Laughing to herself, Abbie realized suddenly that she had changed since he'd arrived, too. She'd been so mired in her grief for so long that hadn't realized how down she had been until just now.

For whatever reason, Colt was making her forget the past for a moment as he sat in her tiny kitchen, which was warmed with a wood-burning stove. Her rapid pulse suggested something was happening between them, that on some level at least he was drawn to her. Her of all people! She was not beautiful. She did not have a stick-straight model's body, but was all curves. Stymied as to why he was interested in her, Abbie gazed at him in puzzlement. As she sat there, however, it felt very good to be with such a ruggedly handsome man—a man she sensed was drawn to her, too.

"I told Morgan I'd work with you behind the scenes. I'm not going to the actual celebration," he said. Then he saw how crestfallen she looked.

"But," Abbie protested, "it might make you feel better...."

Shrugging, Colt set the empty cup aside. "I'm not good company, Abbie." Her name slipped off his tongue like hot, smooth honey. He liked the intimacy they shared right now; it was unexpected, and healing to his tangled emotions. "I nearly ripped your head off a little while ago at the door. Think what kind of damage I could do at a party." One corner of his thinned mouth hitched upward as he attempted to make a joke out of his present condition. He saw her eyes grow tender. His heart opened even more.

"I understand, Colt. I really do." Without thinking, Abbie reached out and touched his thick, hairy hand, which was resting on the table. "Its okay. You do what you can and don't apologize for the rest." Her fingertips tingled where she'd grazed his taut, hard flesh. There was such a dangerous quality to him. Yet Abbie felt protected and secure in his presence, not scared. Colt Hamlin, even if he was bleeding emotionally from his last mission, had a big enough heart to reach out to her, human to human. And in Abbie's book, that was something she needed and rarely received.

Picking up the swag, she began to weave the red ribbon through the boughs, which had been bound together with copper wire. "Whatever help you can give me, I'll be grateful for," she whispered. "Right now, you need to take care of you—first."

Colt studied another bough, on his side of the table. He laid it aside and then scooted the chair back and rose. Picking up the empty cups, he walked over to the drain board and set them down. Turning, he gazed back at Abbie as she worked effortlessly with the swag. There was high pink color in her cheeks. She looked beautiful to him, like a red-haired fairy princess, with nature all about her. And she was a biology teacher to boot. Moving back to the table, he sat down. As Abbie lifted her head, he said, "Why don't you show me how to weave this thing?"

"Oh, Colt, you don't have to! I just need some help moving the boxes filled with finished swags to the car."

He gave her a slight, one-cornered smile. Picking up a swag, he rasped, "I want to help you, Abbie. I'll let you know when I'm ready to cash in my chips and slink back to the condo."

Brightening, she grinned. "A glutton for punishment."

"Maybe…" But he didn't think so. No, for better or worse, Colt craved Abbie's sunny presence in his dark pit of a life. She made him feel hope when he'd believed he had nothing to hope for ever again.

2

December 21—Day 1

Abbie tried to still her fluttering heart as Colt Hamlin drove them expertly through the slushy, snow-covered streets, heading toward Morgan and Laura's huge cedar home outside of town. The snow was thickening, turning the sky a gunmetal-gray color. All around them rose the Rocky Mountains, silent and clothed in white, with dark evergreens at their base. It was a beautiful sight. Glancing distractedly out of the corner of her eye, she saw that Colt was paying strict attention to his driving. The roads had been salted earlier to melt the ice, but they were still messy.

Pushing her fingers through her unruly hair, Abbie said, "Laura said you fly for a living?"

Nodding, Colt glanced at Abbie for a moment, taking in her dark green wool coat, her hands in brown leather gloves, as she sat in the passenger seat of the van. "Yeah, I'm a chopper pilot."

Abbie didn't want to pry, yet her curiosity about this stalwart, silent warrior was eating away at her. They were leaving the town limits and heading down a small dirt road covered with slush. "You know Jason Trayhern, their firstborn son, is at the Naval Academy right now? Well, he wants to be a pilot in the worst way. A Marine Corps fighter pilot." She smiled fondly and settled her hands in her lap. "His grandfather, Chase Trayhern, was a pilot in the Korean War. I guess Jason got the flying genes from him."

"The Navy has set tough standards for jet fighter pilots," Colt warned heavily. "Marines go to naval flight schools to be trained. When I was in the Marine Corps, I went for the same thing." His mouth quirked as he slowed the van down. The road was now enclosed by huge Douglas firs that stood like silent sentinels around them. Colt had been to the Trayhern home before and knew the way. He noted that someone had dumped gravel on the well-traveled dirt road, improving driving conditions. "Only I didn't make the grade, so they gave me helicopter duty instead."

"You were disappointed?"

"Sure I was." He maneuvered the van deftly around a slight curve. "I hope young Trayhern doesn't have his sights set too high. I've seen a lot of guys ruin their lives because they didn't get jet fighters. Sometimes you have to adjust to what life gives you versus what you think life owes you." He grinned tightly and glanced over at Abbie. She was watching him raptly, her wide, trusting eyes luminous. There was something so incredibly gentle and nurturing about her. He found himself wanting to blather on to her about anything and everything that flitted through his mind and lay in his tightly guarded heart.

"Jason is a very troubled young man," Abbie admitted slowly. Her thin, arched brows fell momentarily. "That kidnapping wounded him in a way that Morgan and Laura just can't manage to heal."

"I heard from some of the other mercs coming through the office here that Jason was in trouble in high school. You were his teacher, right?"

"Yes, and Jason was very rebellious. His parents, of course, were hoping he would get A's in everything so he could make a run for the Naval Academy appointment. You know only two people from each state are chosen to go to the academy every year?"

"Yes. It's by Senate appointment, and your grades had better be 4.0 or better."

Opening her hands, Abbie said, "Jason started to rebel in his freshman year of high school. He was angry and he was a loner. He was always getting into fights with the bullies, always standing up for kids who had no one to defend them."

"Nothing wrong with that. Better than being a bully himself."

"Yes and no. Jason has a strong protective streak for the underdogs, but you can't go around punching bullies out...which is what he did with great regularity. And in today's schools, any kind of aggression hits a hot button, so he was in a lot of trouble."

"Did he get suspended?"

"Yes. It really hurt Morgan, who has so many hopes and expectations pinned on his son. You know, the Trayherns have a proud military tradition that goes back two hundred years or more. Every firstborn son goes to a military academy, if possible. And with Morgan being branded a traitor to the U.S. during the closing days of the Vietnam War, and not being able to defend himself for years after that, or clear his name, the public still remembers the stain on the family."

"That's enough of a dark cloud for any teenage kid to be carrying around," Colt muttered, "much less a parent's expectations that he make the Naval Academy. No wonder he's rebellious. I would be, too."

Sighing, Abbie said, "I love Jason so much. He's like the child I never had…." She lowered her lashes. "Ted and I wanted kids, but he was sterile. Maybe that's why I love my kids at school so much—I can mother *them,* instead." Abbie gave a strained laugh.

Her laugh sounded hollow to Colt, who divided his attention between driving along the serpentine road and absorbing the pain he saw banked in Abbie's turquoise eyes. His heart contracted, and that surprised him. In the last year, he'd deliberately hardened his heart and fought against feeling, because of his assignments over in the Kosovo region. The needless, ongoing killing over there had torn him up no matter how hard he tried to remain immune and disconnected from what he saw. Focusing on her soft, trembling lower lip as she admitted the painful secret to him, Colt took his hand off the steering wheel and reached out.

"I bet you'd be a great mother to any kid." His fingers closed momentarily on her shoulder and squeezed gently before he returned his hand to the steering wheel. "So, did you get hold of Jason and straighten him out?"

Beneath her heavy coat her flesh tingled where Colt had unexpectedly touched her, sending an ache through her breasts and a warm ribbon of heat down through her body. Surprised by his unexpected and tender touch, Abbie absorbed his craggy profile as he drove. "Yes. Even though I only taught the eleventh grade, I had a biology club for all kids at the high school. Jason has a great interest in anything to do with nature, so I had a parent conference with Morgan and Laura, and presented my ideas to them. They were relieved, really. They were at their wits' end about how to handle Jason. Morgan was so afraid he was going to blow any chance of getting into the academy. They knew his problems stemmed from the kidnapping. He'd gone through therapy—the whole nine yards—to resolve it, but nothing has helped him."

Colt's mouth twisted. "Men have a nasty habit of stowing all their dark crap very deep inside themselves and then sitting on it."

Up ahead he saw the huge cedar complex and slowed down. There were a number of SUVs, vans and pickups in the gravel parking lot outside the residence, and he swung the van in among them. Snow was falling thickly, and the gold-and-russet-colored log home of the Trayherns looked like a Christmas card, surrounded as it was by evergreens.

"No kidding." Abbie laughed. She melted beneath his intense, warm perusal for a moment after he parked the van. "I took him under my wing and gave him special projects. He blossomed, and he was able to talk to me about things he wouldn't to his parents."

Shutting off the engine, Colt sat back and gazed over at Abbie. She looked more like a wild child than a prim and proper schoolteacher. And he could see why Jason would have naturally gravitated to her; Abbie's warmth, openness and gentle nurturing qualities would draw anyone starved for those things. Hell, Colt was drawn to her for the same reasons! "And he settled down after that?"

"Mostly, yes. Oh, Jason had his moments. I mean, what teenager doesn't? I gave him an outlet and a reason to funnel all his energies into something he loved. By the time he graduated, he was carrying 4.0s and received the appointment."

Colt measured her with a warm look. "So, they owe you big time."

Abbie released her seat belt and opened the door. "If it hadn't been for them, I don't think I'd have survived, when Ted suddenly died two years ago, Colt. I was so devastated. They helped me pick up the pieces of my life and put it back together. No...the Trayherns, as you well know, love, care for and support their friends as well as those who work for them."

She saw Colt's dark, straight brows gather before she slid out of the van, the snow softly falling around them. Opening the sliding door, he picked up the first bulky box of pine bough swags. Colt thought about the devastation he had seen in Abbie's eyes over her husband's death.

As he trudged alongside her up the walk, when they reached the front door, which was decorated with a huge pine wreath covered in pinecones and gold lamé ribbon, he halted at her shoulder, looking down at her as she rang the bell.

"For whatever it's worth, Abbie, I'm sorry you lost your husband. I can see you had a great relationship. Those are the hardest to lose...."

Tucking her lower lip between her teeth, Abbie felt his warmth encircle her. For all his granitelike hardness, Colt was surprising her with his gentle side. "Thanks...

He was my best friend, too...." Rallying, she forced a slight smile she didn't feel as she drowned beneath Colt's hooded, smoldering gaze. "That's behind me now. Laura says I have to get on with my life. I have to start living again. That's why I'm going to go to this Christmas celebration. For two years I haven't. Oh, I've helped Laura with the decorating, but I just didn't have the heart to be there. I didn't feel like smiling or laughing...."

The door opened and Laura stood there in jeans, a red angora sweater with a cowl neck, and dark brown oxfords. Her face lit up with joy. Throwing her arms around Abbie, she looked up at Colt. "Merry Christmas! Welcome, Colt. I'm so glad you could make it. Come on in! We've been expecting you!"

Colt tried to remain immune to the festive, cheery atmosphere within the huge, eight-thousand-square-foot cedar home, but it was impossible. Soon he was on a ladder helping to hang the swags. Another merc by the name of Wolf Harding stood on the other ladder as they fastened and hung the pine garlands around the octagon-shaped living room. Christmas music was playing in the background as everyone helped ready the room for the festive kickoff event of the Five Days of Christmas celebration: dancing and a jazz band.

Colt knew everyone there. Maybe it was the fact that he knew the mercs and their wives that made him feel more at ease. The crew was pitching in to help make the living room into one huge dance floor. The butter-yellow leather furniture was moved near the walls, beneath the large windows. Swags graced the top of each window and dipped gracefully between them, really bringing out the Christmas atmosphere.

Colt had one helluva time keeping his mind on hanging swags. He wanted to watch Abbie; he was starved for her in ways that completely threw him off his guard. The wives—Shah Randolph, Sarah Harding and Susannah Killian—sat with Laura and Abbie in the middle of the room on the gleaming hardwood floor, making last-minute plans for the dance tonight. They looked like colorful, animated birds to Colt. More than once he keyed in on their low, conspiratorial whispers, little-girl giggles and outright raucous laughter as, cross-legged, they huddled in a circle.

When Abbie got up, went to the kitchen and brought back a tray of hot chocolate and freshly made chocolate chip cookies for him and Wolf, his heart melted. He got off the ladder along with Wolf and consumed a half dozen of the warm cookies as well as the thick, chocolaty drink piled high with whipping cream. Wolf grabbed a couple more cookies and went over to talk to the women.

Abbie held the tray in her hand as she stood next to Colt and surveyed the men's handiwork. "It looks beautiful, Colt. You guys did it up right."

An unwilling smile tugged at his mouth as he sipped the hot chocolate. "Thanks. Maybe we were inspired by the nice job you did making these swags. They're works of art."

Smiling up at him, Abbie saw that the hardness that had been in his expression earlier was dissolving. The fact that Colt knew the other mercs, Sean Killian, Jake Randolph and Wolf, probably helped. There was a tight bond, an obvious camaraderie between Perseus mercs. And that same rapport flowed to their wives and children, she knew. She was getting a firsthand reminder of it, and it felt fortifying to her newly healed heart.

Abbie was trying to find any excuse to be in Colt's company, she realized. That surprised her. Men had not interested her in the least since Ted died—until now. And the gleam in Laura's eyes when she had nudged her in the ribs to comment about how happy Colt looked for the first time since he'd come off his mission made Abbie assess that observation.

Somehow, she *was* having a positive effect on Colt, she decided. He'd arrived so uptight and withdrawn. Now she thought she could see a glimmer of happiness in his glacial gaze. She wasn't sure *what* was making him happy. Men often blossomed when around their own kind, and here in this warm, Christmassy environment, Colt was with three of his cohorts. Men always felt better in a group, especially when there was a bunch of women around. Yet Colt had given her many furtive looks throughout the last few hours as she sat with the women planning the myriad details. And every time he looked at her, Abbie felt his laserlike gaze moving over her like an incredibly warm, wonderful blanket. When Colt looked at her, she felt safe…and loved….

Loved? Abbie jolted inwardly at that realization. No. That was impossible. Automatically, she touched her cheek, which was heating up with a blush at that last spontaneous thought. Yet as Colt finished off his hot chocolate and handed her the white mug painted with colorful red-and-green plaid ribbons, and their fingers touched, Abbie saw his eyes darken like the sky before a coming storm. But it wasn't a scary storm…it was a storm of promise, and her heart fluttered wildly for a second.

"Thanks for feeding the animals," he teased, one corner of his mouth lifting.

Laughing softly, Abbie took the cup. She wanted to remain in contact with him, but decided it wouldn't be wise. "You are hardly animals."

"I think mercs see themselves as animals," Colt murmured philosophically, resting his hands on his hips, because if he didn't, he was going to reach out and touch Abbie's flyaway red hair. He itched to run his fingers across that coppery-gold mass of curls that framed her gentle face. He saw so much in Abbie's eyes: unsureness, joy, fear…. Fear of what? Him? Trying hard not to pressure her with his interest, Colt wondered what was going on.

When he looked up, he saw Laura Trayhern studying him with a maternal smile on her lips. She nodded, as if in approval, and then turned and walked to the kitchen with the rest of her planning team, a knowing look in her eyes. Knowing what? Colt wondered obliquely.

"Uh…" He cast around for the right words. "Are you going to the dance tonight?" Abbie probably had a boyfriend. How could she not have one? She was such a sunny beacon of light to anyone lost in the darkness. Simply being in her presence lifted his depressed spirit unaccountably, and he felt like a thief stealing her sunlight because he was so destitute of any within himself. His time in Kosovo had stolen his soul and left him feeling hopeless and emotionally eviscerated.

Abbie avoided his piercing gaze. "The dance?" Her skin prickled pleasantly beneath his intense inspection. They stood only inches apart. She found herself wanting to turn and move into his strong, supportive arms. Somehow, Abbie knew Colt would open his arms to her, pull her against him and hold her. Simply hold her. There was such a powerful protective energy around him; she automatically sensed he'd be a wonderful father to his children. And a wonderful husband to her. Egads! Where had *that* thought zinged out of? Suddenly panicked, Abbie didn't understand what was going on with her. She was having such an irrational, emotional reaction to Colt.

"Yes, the dance."

Stepping away, a little breathless, Abbie whispered, "Oh, no...I'm not going...."

"Why? You've probably got every single guy in Philipsburg standing in line to take you."

Touching her blazing cheek, Abbie jerked her gaze from his. "No…" She laughed, embarrassed. "The wall-flower of Philipsburg? I'm afraid you're wrong, Colt. No, I don't have anyone…." She grimaced, hating to admit it.

"But you said you were going to attend the celebration this year. Why aren't you going to the dance?" Colt found himself stunned that Abbie had no man in her life. Hope soared through him. He suddenly felt like a lobo wolf on the trail of finding someone who could ease his loneliness. Abbie. Beautiful, carefree, childlike Abbie, whose smile was sunshine pouring into his dev-astated soul.

Turning, Abbie forced herself to move a few feet away from Colt. He was too accessible and was opening up to her in a way she could barely say no to. "Well, uh, I just…it's the past, Colt. I know it's been two years, and Laura says its time to move on, but I don't know…."

He stood there, hearing her pain and indecision. "If someone asked you to the dance, would you go?" His heart stood still.

Abbie hung her head, her lower lip tucked between her teeth as she considered his question. Was *he* asking her? No, that was impossible. Did she want to go to the dance with Colt? Oh, yes! At the mere thought, her heart responded wildly. Casting him a confused look, Abbie whispered, "I know how plain I am. I don't have a model's body, my hips are wide and I'm slightly overweight."

In that moment, Colt felt the doors of his heart swing wide-open. She was so gut-wrenchingly honest. Stepping up to her, he settled his hands on her slumping shoulders. "You're not overweight. You're just right, Abbie. You have wide hips to carry a baby easily." He moved his fingers gently on her shoulders. "Babe, you aren't plain. I wish you'd quit thinking that about yourself. Any man would be crazy not to appreciate what you bring to his table." His heart thudded with fear, but Colt forced out the words he thought he'd never say to a woman. "Will you come to the dance with me tonight? Can I pick you up at nine?"

He saw the shock cross her face as she lifted hers to meet his eyes. "You...you want to take *me?*"

In that moment, Colt wanted to strangle whoever had ingrained in Abbie the belief that she was plain and overweight. Could it have been her husband? The kids at her school? Her parents? He didn't know, but he wanted to convince her otherwise. Giving her his best, charming smile, he rasped, "Yes, I want to take you to the dance tonight. I'll pick you up at nine. No arguments."

THE FIVE DAYS OF CHRISTMAS

★ ★ ★

The soft jazz music wafted across the crowded dance floor. Abbie sighed and moved slowly, deliciously, in Colt's arms. There were at least seventy-five people in attendance. The children were laughing and dancing with one another, and with various adults. The Trayhern home rang with happiness. The odors of baked cookies, cinnamon rolls and hot chocolate added to the festive atmosphere. Many people were dressed in red, green, gold or silver, and in Abbie's eyes, they looked like bright Christmas ornaments moving around the dance floor.

She felt Colt's arms tighten momentarily on her waist as he swung her around. How handsome he looked in a white cashmere sweater, burnt-sienna corduroy jacket and black wool slacks. She saw where he'd nicked himself shaving, a small cut along his rock-hard jaw. There was such a merry glint in his normally frosty eyes that she found herself drowning in them like a dry sponge in search of water. How long had it been since a man looked at her like that? Wanted her like that? *Too long,* a little voice whispered inside her heart. Sliding her fingertips along the shoulder of his jacket, she smiled up at him.

"I'm glad you asked me, Colt."

He preened. "Yeah?"

"Yes. Thank you…"

"You look beautiful in that emerald velvet dress you're wearing." And she did. In her hair was an orchid affixed with a bright, apple-green ribbon. The orchid, she had told him earlier, was a cattleya, one of her favorite species. It was a white blossom with a bright green lip and scarlet polka dots along the inside. She had gathered up her curly copper tresses and tamed them into a soft arrangement away from her face. The tiny gold-and-pearl earrings she wore, along with a similar pendant, set off her natural beauty.

"That orchid really makes you look like a wild child," he teased. The music was low and soft. Colt was having one helluva time keeping Abbie at arms length as they danced. He saw many of the mercs and their wives dancing, their bodies melded together. He wanted to meld his to Abbie's, but knew it wouldn't be right.

"Thanks…" Abbie whispered. The look Colt gave her was warm and filled with pride. "Tonight I really feel beautiful. Sort of like Cinderella." And she did.

Colt's smile was deep as he met and held her uplifted gaze. "You know how I see you? Like a red-haired fairy princess—maybe an Irish sprite—dancing from one orchid to another. That's quite a nice little greenhouse you have out back of your cabin. I don't know much about orchids, but walking in there tonight and seeing their beauty…well, I can understand why you love to raise them."

Sighing, she turned and eased a little closer to Colt. How badly Abbie wanted to lean her full weight against him and simply relinquish herself to his strong, caring arms. Colt's tenderness was surprising. She gloried in it. "There's one orchid I particularly love, but it's so expensive I'll never be able to afford it—ever—on my teacher's salary."

"Oh?" He saw her eyes light up with sudden enthusiasm. When she moved slightly closer to him, he picked up on her nonverbal signal and drew her more deeply into his arms. The emerald dress she wore was provocative and yet simple in its elegance. It had a scooped neckline, and from the empire waist, which outlined her small breasts, the skirt flared gracefully down to her ankles. The velvet material felt good beneath his hands. How badly he wanted to explore her more.

"You saw the framed print of the orchid in my living room earlier tonight? The one hanging on the wall behind my couch?"

Colt nodded. "Yeah, the white one with the hot pink and gold markings? I think you called it *Cattleya rex?*"

"That one. Yes." Abbie sighed languorously. "They call that orchid the 'treasure of the Incas.' It's found only in Peru, high up in the jungle near Machu Picchu, an archeological site that has wonderful Incan ruins. I would give my right arm to have one!" She laughed. "You saw how beautiful they are—the white petals of the orchid so huge and then that gorgeous central lip spilling out with those fuschia and gold colors. It reminds me of a Christmas tree, it's so breathtaking!"

Spinning her around, Colt absorbed her joy and excitement. The look in her eyes was something to behold, and it made his heart skitter—with happiness. As the music died away, he stopped and opened his arms reluctantly to allow Abbie to step back. To his surprise, she didn't move very far from him, or let go of his hand.

Morgan and Laura Trayhern walked up to the band podium. As Colt and Abbie turned expectantly, a hush came over the room. Colt saw young Jason Trayhern, dressed in his spit-and-polish, dark blue naval uniform with shiny brass buttons, following his parents rather reluctantly. Colt looked down at Abbie, whose attention was centered on the Trayherns.

"Jason is looking a little stiff and starchy."

"He *hates* being the center of attention. Really, he's very shy underneath it all." Abbie clasped her hands to her breast. "But doesn't he look handsome in his uniform! He's in his second year at the academy. I'm so glad he could get leave and come home! Look how proud Morgan and Laura appear...."

Colt followed his instincts. All around him, couples stood expectantly on the dance floor, their arms wrapped lovingly around one another. Well, he wanted to do the same thing. Mustering the last of his courage and hoping Abbie wouldn't step away from him, he slowly lifted his arm and placed it tentatively around her shoulders.

Instantly, her head jerked up. Her eyes flared as she stared up at him.

Fear shot through him. Colt almost pulled his arm away in that moment of panic as Abbie's guileless expression turned to one of shock. And then something crazy happened, something Colt never expected. Her eyes grew soft and he saw tears in them for just a moment, before she blinked them back. He thought she would step away, but instead she gave him a tremulous smile of uncertainty and took a step *toward* him. Her velvet-covered body met his as she slipped beneath his arm.

Colt couldn't believe his good luck. He had to be dreaming! As Abbie shyly slid her arm around his waist, his heart pounded. The courage it took her was enormous, he realized, as he drowned in her lambent gaze. Tightening his arm around her small shoulders, he smiled down at her. More than anything he wanted to kiss her parted lips.

Colt had to temper his desires. In a corner of his mind, he realized that this was the first time Abbie had had a "date" with a man since her husband's death. She was unsure. Maybe a little frightened. He couldn't blame her, and he wanted to do everything he could to make her feel comfortable. Another thought bolted through his spinning senses: Abbie liked him, or she would not have moved against him or slipped her slender arm around him.

Dizzied by what had just happened, Colt tried to listen as the Trayherns welcomed everyone to the party, then proudly introduced their son. Everyone clapped as Jason moved to the microphone to speak. Colt suspected the young man was uncomfortable, but he assumed a stiff military bearing, thanked them in a confident voice and was even able to smile slightly at his proud parents, who stood off to one side, their faces glowing with pleasure. And then Morgan turned and asked the jazz band to strike up another tune. Colt saw Jason quickly flee the podium, relief on his handsome, square face. How much Jason looked like Morgan! Colt thought. He was a younger version, almost a carbon copy, of his heroic father.

Turning, Colt smiled down at Abbie, who had a wistful look in her eyes. "Ready for another dance or am I tiring you out?"

Laughing, she said, "No, I *love* to dance! I haven't done it in so long." And she melted into his arms. How wonderful it was to slide up against Colt's hard form. With a sigh, she felt his arms go around her, intimate and claiming. This time, her breasts and hips grazed his solid form. "I'll probably be so sore and tired that when tomorrow's skiing venture takes place, I'll be glad to be manning the food shack and not moving around much."

Chuckling, Colt eased back a little to catch her gaze. "Do you need me to help you?" He suddenly found himself not wanting to be alone anymore. Basking in Abbie's sunlit warmth was somehow healing him.

"Sure, I'd love to have some help. Day two of our celebration includes skiing from noon until five. All the families gather at Brandy Hill, a great little slope just outside of town. All it has are rope tows to the top—nothing fancy. I always man the food booth for them."

"Do you ski?"

Wrinkling her nose, Abbie laughed. "Me? Barely. I fall more than I stand on my feet. How about you?" She was deliriously happy with the fact that Colt wanted to be with her tomorrow. Her heart did somersaults and she could scarcely believe all this was happening.

"Skiing isn't one of my strong points," Colt admitted in a droll tone. "If it's okay with you, I'll help you in the food shack. Keep you company."

She met and held his smoldering look, which sent heat flowing through her. His arms tightened around her briefly. "It's more than okay with me...."

Abbie could barely wait for tomorrow. The magic of Christmas had unexpectedly given her a beautiful gift to her...Colt Hamlin.

3

December 22—Day 2

The delighted screeches and shouts of the Perseus children filled the winter air as they ran through the twirling snowflakes toward the rope tow located at the base of Brandy Hill. Colt couldn't help but give Abbie a lopsided grin as they trundled boxes over to the small wooden structure that doubled as a makeshift buffet to feed the hungry families. It was noon, and everyone was starved.

Colt had driven over to Abbie's earlier to load the aluminum urns filled with coffee and hot, cinnamon-laced apple cider. They'd picked up sandwiches and bags of potato chips from the Trayherns as the hungry, excited crew boarded the bus leased for the occasion.

Last night, Colt had mustered up the courage to give Abbie a chaste, swift kiss on her flushed cheek at the door to her cabin after he'd brought her back from the dance. He'd wanted to do more...*much* more, but he didn't want to rush things with Abbie, either. The fact that her eyes grew lustrous after his impromptu kiss had made him feel like he was ten feet tall and walking on air.

Abbie opened the door to the shack. It creaked and groaned in protest. The building was constructed of Douglas fir, the wood grayed with age and from the harsh winters they had in this region of the Rockies. The weather was perfect for the afternoon ski party: the temperature was in the low thirties, and just a bit of snow was falling from a sky that was mostly gray with some spots of blue peeking out. It was a weekday, so the Perseus employees had the normally busy place all to themselves.

Setting the first cardboard box on a table inside the shack, Abbie smiled over at Colt as he brought in a heavier box. How handsome he was! The warmth banked in his eyes thrilled her. He gave her a bashful look, that strong mouth of his hitched in a slight smile for her alone.

Jason Trayhern, now in civilian clothes, jeans, hiking boots, a bright red sweater and a dark blue navy jacket, brought in another box.

"Hey, thanks," Abbie called to the young man. She saw the dark smudges beneath Jason's eyes. At nineteen, he stood six foot three inches tall, with his father's broad shoulders, wide chest and narrow hips. He was almost a carbon copy of Morgan with a square face, wide-set gray eyes and military short black hair. Abbie could see Laura's influence, however, in Jason's mouth; it wasn't as hard looking as Morgan's. Jason had Laura's sensitivity, too—a sensitivity that had caused him much angst over the years, Abbie suspected.

"You're welcome, Ms. Clemens." Jason stepped aside and helped Colt maneuver the largest, heaviest box onto the table—the one that contained sandwiches for the hungry crew hanging around outside the shack. Jason grinned a little. "I'll go get the apple cider dispenser for you now, ma'am."

"Great. Thanks, Jason. I wouldn't know what to do without your help." Abbie glanced at Colt, who worked at her side to unpack the boxes. She absorbed his nearness. He was dressed in a bomber jacket that had seen better days, an apple-green sweater, jeans that outlined his heavily muscled thighs to perfection, and hiking boots. A white silk scarf set off his outfit.

She smiled up at him as he met and held her glance. "I'm so glad you're helping me, too." Abbie glanced out the counter window, where at least twenty children of varying ages were laughing, playing and running around. The adults were helping them get their skis on so they could use the rope tow, now in operation. "This is a hungry crew we have to feed."

Nodding, Colt smiled at her and continued opening boxes. In the process, his hand accidentally brushed hers. Abbie had taken off her leather gloves to unpack and get everything set up, and so had he. Her flesh was warm. Inviting. How badly he wanted to continue touching her. "Yeah, those little rug rats out there definitely have a starved look on their faces. A bunch of hungry lookin' buzzards, if you ask me."

"Rug rats," Abbie sniffed. "What an awful name to call children."

"A loving military term," Colt assured her in a deep voice. He saw Jason coming with the huge aluminum urn containing the apple cider, and moved to the side door to swing it wide.

"Thanks, Mr. Hamlin," Jason huffed as he struggled with the huge urn.

Colt helped him place it on the counter where people could easily put a paper cup beneath the spigot to pour out a drink of the warm, fragrant cider.

"I'll fetch the hot chocolate now," Jason said, and left quickly.

"That boy is tense," Colt said quietly as he came back to the table to help Abbie spread wrapped sandwiches onto a large platter.

Abbie sighed. "I know. Poor Jase! I feel so sorry for him. He's trying so hard to do what his parents expect of him. See the circles under his eyes? I was talking to Laura earlier this morning, and she told me that Jason and Morgan had a big fight."

"The kid looks like death warmed over," Colt noted. "It musta been one hell—heck—of a fight." He took the first tray of sandwiches and placed them on the counter. Instantly, ten children rushed forward, their little hands eagerly grasping for the food.

"I guess his grades at the academy aren't good," Abbie murmured, low enough that no one could eavesdrop on their conversation. The last thing she wanted was to embarrass Jason; the youth had enough trouble right now. "He's doing the same thing he did in high school before I got hold of him—goofing off, partying, not being responsible. Another form of rebellion."

"Ouch. Not the place to flunk out of," Colt muttered. He gave her a wink. "Maybe what he needs is another Abbie Clemens at the academy to rescue him and set him straight, like you did here."

Giving Colt a wistful look, Abbie said softly, "My heart just bleeds for Jase. He's a complicated child—I mean, young man…. It's funny, I still think of him as a kid and I shouldn't. He's growing up so fast. They always do in their teenage years." She laughed softly.

The kid had probably not slept much after the argument, Colt guessed, because he had bloodshot eyes, too. Life was hard, Colt knew. And life was gigging Jason right now. Did he have what it took to pull himself up by his own bootstraps? Only Jason could answer that. Colt took a second tray of sandwiches and set them on the counter to replace the emptied one. Adults were ambling over now that the kids had their lunches in hand. The shack was being mobbed by hungry people, and Colt smiled a little as he watched the food disappear quickly from that tray, as well. Turning, he saw Abbie handing him a third tray piled high with sandwiches.

For the next half hour, they fed the hungry Perseus group. Jason excused himself and went out on the slope with his sister, Katy, who was now seventeen and a beautiful young woman, in Colt's eyes. She was the spitting image of Laura, except she had her father's height and stood nearly six feet tall, was medium boned and a super athlete. The twins, Peter and Kelly, now twelve years old, were holding on to the rope tow, their skis on, with their older siblings in front and behind them.

Colt was happy when he and Abbie were finally left alone. Everyone had gobbled up their lunch and flown off to the beckoning slopes. The shouts and laughter of the children was contagious. He saw a lot of the mercs becoming big kids themselves. Taking one of the rough-hewn stools, Colt brought it over to where Abbie had just sat down at the table. Neither of them had eaten yet, and he opened his turkey sandwich. Cups of steaming apple cider sat on the table before them.

"Are you going to ski pretty soon?" Colt asked. He watched her eyes widen—beautiful eyes he could fall into and lose his soul within. Colt knew that with Abbie, he was safe in a way he'd never experienced before with a woman. Her human touch, her ability to work well with both children and adults, was blatantly apparent. But he was a glutton; he wanted her all to himself.

Colt laughed harshly at himself. He couldn't believe all he was feeling—him, the loner. The guy who had planned to camp out in the condo for the holidays, drink himself into a stupor daily to numb the pain he felt. Somehow, Abbie's sunny smile, her dancing eyes and that heart that was a wide as the blue skies of Montana made him want to be with her, and with people. She was magical. And he wanted her—in all ways. Did she want him, however? Colt realized as never before that the loss of her husband had damaged her emotionally. She was just emerging from a long, dark tunnel of grief. Was she ready for a relationship?

What the hell could *he* bring to her? Give to her? A snarly, irritable, PTSD warrior who found it hard to stay in the mainstream of life and society—what a helluva prize catch he would make....

Picking up her cup of apple cider, Abbie sipped it, then smiled as she set it down on the peeled paint of the tabletop. "Me? Ski? Oh, gosh, Colt, I'm all thumbs and left feet! No, I just serve the food, I don't ski. I'd probably break my neck—or my leg—if I tried." She saw a smile lurking at the corners of his well-shaped mouth. Her heart pounded briefly as Colt gave her an intimate, smoldering look. She'd seen that same look last night as they'd stood on the front porch of her cabin just before he'd kissed her. Oh, it was a small kiss, Abbie chided herself. But it did big-time things to her, making her heart thud in her breast, her pulse leap wildly and a warm, throbbing heat settle deliciously in her lower body. She felt herself coming alive as a woman. Colt's one hesitant kiss last night, his lips caressing her cheek, had made her feel as if she were the mythical Persephone leaving the darkness of Hades and emerging back on the surface of the earth, to appreciate all its colors, textures and grandeur once again. Studying him through her lashes, Abbie wondered if he realized that his look was making her heart and body come alive. Did he? Probably not.

His grin widened. "I'm a so-so skier. But let me take you up later. I'll help you stay upright as we go down the hill, okay?" Colt chastised himself silently. If she skied that badly, he could keep his arms around her, hold her and remain close without anyone thinking anything of it. What a sneaky bastard he was. He didn't have the guts to just tell her how he felt about her. Colt was too frightened that Abbie would get scared and, like the clouds moving across the hill right now, snuffing out the sunlight, would run from him.

Easing off the stool, Abbie shrugged. "I'm a kid at heart. Sure, I'll try it." Her pulse throbbed momentarily as she saw his eyes grow hooded and that smoldering look grow more intense. A thrill moved through her. Abbie found herself feeling joyous in a way she'd never been before. As she puttered about, placing sandwiches wrappers into a plastic trash bag, she tried to sort out the myriad feelings Colt was effortlessly evoking within her. One chaste kiss! Just one, and Abbie felt like a teenager head-over-heels in love!

"You mentioned that your parents are in Florida?" she asked him.

Colt finished off the sandwich and picked up his apple cider. Just watching Abbie move around the shack and tidy it up sent a frisson of longing through him. She was so graceful. He wanted her hands ranging up his body with that same grace. Tearing his mind from that thought, he frowned and answered her question. "Dad's in a nursing home now. My mother died three years ago."

"Oh, I'm sorry." Abbie hesitated, then put the bag in the garbage can next to the table. There wasn't much room in the shack and she absorbed Colt's continued nearness. His brow was furrowed. "Were you going to go and visit your dad over the holidays?"

"No. He has Alzheimer's pretty bad. He doesn't recognize me anymore. He doesn't know where he's at mentally...." Colt's mouth flattened. "Usually I'm on a mission this time of year, but I fly in to see him at other times. He has to have twenty-four-hour nursing care."

Abbie sat down. "I'm so sorry...that must be so hard, Colt, to not have him recognize you, his son." She saw the damage it had done to him; it was clearly written in his features, even though he tried to avoid her gaze. She saw Colt try to shrug it off, but the anguish remained banked in his averted eyes.

Taking a huge risk, Abbie followed her intuition and said softly, "I understand that you've had some pretty awful missions over in the Kosovo-Bosnia region. I'm sure between your dad's deteriorating condition and the stresses on you over there, you must be exhausted." Tired all the way to his soul, Abbie guessed. She held her breath, knowing she had to tread lightly because of the PTSD symptoms he'd accrued after those missions. Abbie didn't know why she was broaching the topic with

Colt. It was a subject most men would refuse to speak about, especially with a woman.

Just the tender way Abbie gazed at him made the wall around his heart crack open. He actually felt physical pain and rubbed his chest where his heart lay beneath the sweater he wore. Staring down at the cup of apple cider he held, Colt rasped, "I thought I knew what hell on earth was, Abbie…but I didn't, not until these past three missions…."

She sat quietly and waited. Why was it so hard for a man to talk out his feelings? Colt's hard face was ravaged with emotions that were eating him alive. Abbie saw the way he worked his mouth into a brutal line to stop the avalanche she sensed behind it. As he moved the cup slowly around and around in his large, scarred hands, she felt her heart breaking for him. More than anything, Abbie wanted to slide her arms around his slumped shoulders and just hold him. That was what he needed right now: to be held. And she wanted to be the woman who did it.

The silence between them was strained and tenuous. Abbie knew from experience that if she sat quietly and let the pressure mount, then more than likely Colt would begin to talk. When he lifted his head, she saw dampness in his eyes. It tore at her.

"Three missions," Colt said gruffly. "Three horrible missions with no positive outcome. I'll tell you something, Abbie, that part of the world is a hellhole. There are no happy endings over there for either side. Not ever." He shook his head and took a quick gulp of the apple cider. Avoiding her look, he growled, "When I got off this last one...well, I was reeling from it. My partner, Carol, quit. She couldn't take it anymore. I don't blame her. It's rough over there...."

Abbie knew that mercs at Perseus worked in man-woman teams. And she knew from talking with Laura that Carol had been Colt's partner for a good five years. Abbie understood the camaraderie, the trust and teamwork that developed under dangerous mission conditions, and she was sure he was devastated by losing Carol, too. "And so you were going to hole up here and try to heal?" she murmured gently. When Colt lifted his head again, the dampness in his eyes was gone. He'd shoved all those raw feelings very deep within himself. His hands, however, gripped the paper cup hard.

He snorted. "I wasn't doing a very good job of it. Me and Jack Daniels..."

She flinched inwardly. He had been slugging down whiskey to numb what he was feeling. Getting up, Abbie followed her heart. She moved quietly and sat beside Colt, placing her fingers around his larger ones as they gripped the cup. She heard him take in a swift breath of air. His head snapped up. Heart pounding, Abbie sat quietly and looked at him, her hands wrapped around his.

"I understand a little of what you're feeling, Colt. When Ted died, I felt like someone had thrown me into a dark hole of hell that I didn't feel I could ever survive." Her mouth pulled upward slightly at the corners, and her voice was tremulous with feeling. "What helped me get through it were people who loved me—my friends...my family from North Dakota. The people I worked with at the high school were supportive, too. Laura Trayhern, bless her, became my strength. She, more than anyone, understood what I was going through, because of her own traumas, losing Morgan to the drug lords...."

Abbie's warmth and tenderness sent a hot sheet of longing through Colt. Easing his hands from hers, he placed the paper cup on the table and then picked up her hands again and held them. Drowning in her blue eyes, which were sparkling with unshed tears, he felt his heart rip wide-open from his brutally suppressed feelings. Abbie was so small and slender next to his bulk and masculine strength, yet he sensed with every fiber of his being that she was the stronger one here, not him. He felt as if a huge fist was jamming into his chest, causing very real pain, and he wanted to scream out in anguish.

Abbie watched as his mouth turned hard, his lips thinned. He avoided her eyes and stared down at their hands. She felt him quiver. Colt was wrestling to fight back the overwhelming emotions he'd stuffed away during those missions.

All her life, Abbie had been led by her heart, her passion, and the voice of intuition within her. That voice whispered to her to kiss him…now.…

Lifting her hands from his, she slid her fingertips up the rocky ridge of Colt's jaw and framed his face. Her gesture snapped him out of his suspended state. He lifted his head. His gaze narrowed intently on her, his black pupils dilating. She saw the tears banked in his eyes, and moved closer, till her body grazed his. Closing her eyes, Abbie felt her heart beating like a wild bird suddenly caged. Was she doing the right thing? Would Colt take her efforts the right way? Did he know she wanted to cry for him? To hold him? Lost as she was in the hungry need to make physical contact with him, Abbie knew, somewhere in her spinning mind, that it was right thing, even if she was scared to death.

"Colt…let me help…." she whispered. The line of his mouth softened as she grazed his lips with her own. He groaned, and the sound reverberated through her like the roll of a drum. Feeling bolder, she pressed closer and felt some of his tension dissolve beneath her tender ministrations. Repeatedly, she feathered her mouth across his, begging access, asking silently for him to give her the overwhelming pain he was barely holding at bay.

Then his arms came around her and captured her hard against him. The air rushed out of her lungs as he stood up, dragging her with him, her breasts and hips melding hotly against his own. His mouth opened and his lips crushed hers in a ravenous kiss. Fire erupted through Abbie as his arms wound around her back and he rocked her into his embrace. Automatically, her hands opened, and she found them sliding up around his thick shoulders and neck.

Colt smelled of evergreens and his own unique scent, making her respond to his questing mouth with equal ardor. Running her fingers through his short hair, Abbie moaned a little as his hand ranged down from her shoulder, across her rib cage toward her aching, taut breast.

Oh, how she wanted this man! Her heart spun with joy. Her pulse throbbed and her lower body melted against his narrow hips, on fire. She felt his desire for her, and more flames sizzled through her, making her knees go weak with need. Need for Colt.

His mouth was bruising and hungry against hers. Abbie felt him tremble savagely as she allowed him open access, his tongue laving her lower lip. As she pulled him tightly against her, his mouth commanding and needy, Abbie relaxed completely within his powerful embrace. She knew that her surrendering to him had triggered something else within him. Abbie felt it, lost as she was in a swirl of joy, hunger and need. She wanted to take his pain, transmute it in order to release it. Love had a way of doing that—of healing even the worst hemorrhaging wound within a person's heart and soul.

Willingly she offered herself—all of herself—to Colt in this magical moment outside of time. His skin was sandpapery against her softer flesh, his punctuated breath warm and moist against her face. She moved her lips against his mouth, and in that instant became aware of the taste of salt clinging to the corners. For a moment she was confused, and then she realized it was from Colt's tears. Tears of pain. Tears of agony. Tears he'd suffered and carried silently for so long by himself.

The salty tears met and mingled beneath their wet, searching mouths. She shifted her hands to his face, framing it as her tongue moved deep within him. Again he trembled, like a bull being shaken by an earthquake. Abbie held him with her womanly strength, guided by her heart, which told her this was healing him, helping him, and helping her, too. Never in all her life had she shared such a kiss with a man. Not ever. Euphoria enveloped her as she felt the last of Colt's tears ease. Drowsily opening her eyes, she burned beneath his stormy green gaze as he voraciously absorbed her into himself. She was small compared to his power and size. Yet as she caressed his cheek and smiled tremulously up at him, the taste of his tears still on her lips, she understood the healing power of one person's love and what it could do to unlock another's armored heart and soul.

Colt stood there, his senses screamingly alive, his lower body aching with a knot of fire and need. Gently, he eased his grip from around Abbie and set her carefully on her feet. He didn't want to let her go—not yet. *Not ever,* his heart whispered. There was such a thunderstorm of emotions raging through him right now that he found it impossible to find words to tell her. Hell, he couldn't even begin to define them himself. Part was rage and frustration over the missions. Another was grief over the people he'd seen die. And just as insistent were the new emotions exploding in his pounding heart—emotions about Abbie. Sweet, soft, strong Abbie. As he gazed wordlessly down into her lustrous eyes, Colt threaded his fingers through the silky, coppery hair that framed her blushing features.

"You're so sweet, Abbie. You're like a dream I've always had, but was afraid to believe in...."

4

Colt had cried—the first tears he'd ever shed over his life-altering missions. In fact, he never cried. The last time he recalled even getting close to it was when his ex-wife had walked out on him. Even more disturbing to him, he realized as he slowly got dressed the next morning, was the fact that he'd cried in Abbie's arms. It had been unexpected, the last thing on his mind.

He wondered now if she thought he was a wimp. Frowning, he shrugged into his bright red flannel shirt and tucked the tails into his jeans. Outside the picture window of the condo, the sky was a bright blue, the sun sparkling off the tops of the snow-covered evergreens that surrounded the small valley. The storm had passed.

"Yeah…right," he muttered, picking up his white silk scarf and, out of habit, throwing it around his neck. He'd worn the scarf while flying as a helicopter pilot, as the silk protected his neck from chafing as he rubbernecked around, while looking for the bad guys.

He was meeting Abbie at 9:00 a.m. to help her move her beautiful cattleya orchids, which were all in bloom in her greenhouse, to Laura and Morgan's home for the upcoming family dinner planned for the third day of Christmas.

Halting in the middle of the room, his leather bomber jacket in hand, he scowled, and his gut clenched. He was feeling such pain, such uncertainty, that he really didn't want to face Abbie, Colt realized. He was afraid. There, he'd admitted it. Afraid of what she might think of him crying during their heated, beautiful, healing kiss there in the shack yesterday. What must she think of him? Did she see him as weak? Probably.

Undecided, Colt slowly shrugged into his bomber jacket and straightened the collar. He'd never cried in front of a woman. Ever. But he had with her. What the hell was going down here? Rubbing his recently shaved jaw, Colt scowled darkly out the window. The world was beautiful here in the middle of winter. He didn't feel beautiful inside. Not at all.

Ruthlessly examining himself, which was not something Colt did often, he realized he had to get a grip on his escaping feelings when he was around Abbie. He didn't want to become a blubbering wuss in front of her again. Cringing over that possibility, Colt sensed that was why he was so damned scared and unsure this morning: Abbie just sort of unconsciously catalyzed his feelings—good and bad. He'd never met a woman who could do that. It was like magic, only it was dark magic and he had no interest in having his own private hell of a Pandora's box spontaneously opened without his permission or knowledge. Hell, he'd been kissing her, and enjoying it like an eagle on wing flying directly into the sun's warmth. Then, out of nowhere, Colt had felt warmth leaking out of the corners of his closed eyes and drifting down his cheeks to where their mouths clung wetly to one another.

At first, he'd been shocked by the taste of salt between their lips. And when he realized what it was, and where it was coming from, he'd torn his mouth from Abbie's and taken a step away from her, as if he'd been burned.

He couldn't bear remembering the hurt look on her face as she'd stood there, her lips wet and parted, her eyes huge with desire and, at the same time, shock over his unexpected action. What else was he to do? Cry some more? Weep his heart out in her slender but strong arms? What if someone had come up to the shack at that time and seen him crying? What would they think? Colt knew something like that would be bound to travel very fast in the tight circle of Perseus families. It was a closed community, and everyone knew everyone else's business. He didn't need it getting back to Morgan that he'd been crying like a hurt little boy in Abbie's arms. If anyone had come up and seen them kissing...well, that was acceptable to Colt. But not being discovered crying.

"Damn," he growled, his voice echoing around the living room as he dropped his hand from his chin. What was he going to do? The fact that he had been so vulnerable in front of her was making him feel like hell. And the fact that he'd abruptly turned on his heel and left Abbie alone in that shack, tore him up even more. He'd walked away. He'd run. Like a coward. He had hitched a ride home with another family and hadn't spoken to Abbie since.

"You're a damned coward," Colt muttered. He'd left

her in the lurch; left her to move all the stuff back to her van to transport to Morgan's home. Worse, after that life-giving kiss had seared his broken soul, he'd left her without explanation. She probably thought she'd done something wrong. But he was the one who had.

As he lifted his chin and glared out at the sunny morning, Colt knew he had to go over to Abbie's and talk to her. And if she was pissed off at him and his antics, so be it. He wouldn't blame her for her righteous anger over his immature, knee-jerk actions. The least he owed her was an explanation. And in his anguished heart, Colt hoped Abbie would not only understand, but would allow him back into her life. He was frightened by how easily she touched his emotions and freed them. Colt wanted her in every way, but he didn't want to pay the entry fee.

So where did that leave them? Leave Abbie? She didn't deserve this adolescent behavior of his. No, what he was proposing to do was steal the honey from the hive, but not feed the bees who made it. He was like an interloping bear, all he wanted to do was eat dessert and walk away, sated. Glowering as he moved slowly toward the door, keys to his car in hand, Colt didn't like himself at all. Abbie didn't deserve to be hurt like this. And yet he'd done a spectacular job of it. What would she think when she saw him on her porch? Scream? Curse at him? Tell him to get the hell out of her life? Worse? As Colt shut and locked the condo door, he had no hope that Abbie would allow him back in her life.

Abbie gulped as she opened the door. Colt stood there, hands shoved deeply into the pockets of his bomber jacket. He looked like hell warmed over—his skin pasty, dark shadows beneath his narrowed, bloodshot eyes, and his mouth twisted in a line of pain that sent a shaft of hurt through her heart.

"Come in," she invited softly, stepping aside. On her table were ten carefully wrapped pots of orchids, which she was about to carry out to her car and transport over to Laura's place for the dinner party tonight.

Abbie's heart beat hard in her chest as he gave her an anxious look. Then, with hesitation, Colt moved woodenly through the door. She shut it and looked up at him. The tension swirled between them.

"I guess…" Colt began awkwardly, his voice sounding like sandpaper, "I shouldn't have invited myself over here this morning, Abbie." Shrugging his drooping shoulders, he saw her eyes grow warm with compassion—for him. He couldn't help but absorb her beauty in that moment.

She was wearing a plum-colored angora shell with a white cotton blouse beneath it. Her hair was wild and free around her face and shoulders. A pang of longing shot through Colt. How badly he wanted to sift those red-gold strands through his fingers as he had yesterday afternoon. Her hair was so soft, and yet so strong and resilient...like her.

Wrapping her arms against her breasts, she clung to his every word. Feeling horribly vulnerable, she managed to answer in a strained tone, "I'm glad you did, Colt. I don't know what happened yesterday between us. You just left..."

Smarting despite her gentleness toward him, he pulled his hands out of his jacket pockets. "I, uh...damn, this is hard, Abbie." Opening his hands toward her, he muttered, "I'm sorry. It was me yesterday, not you. You did nothing wrong."

"I see...." Abbie's senses took over. She saw such vulnerability in Colt's face right now. His eyes were wide and pleading, his hands open in supplication. He was hurting so much even now that Abbie could almost taste his salty tears from yesterday. Her first instinct was to open her arms, step forward, throw them around Colt's neck and hold him. Hold him, rock him and let him know that he could find safe harbor with another human being.

The silence strung tautly between them.

"If I'm overstepping my bounds with you, Colt, let me know," Abbie whispered. She unlocked her arms and let them fall to her sides. Colt dropped his hands, too. They stood three feet apart, yet it seemed like the Grand Canyon stretched between them. "I feel you're more embarrassed over crying yesterday than anything else. Is that right?" Abbie searched his furtive gaze. At first Colt wouldn't look at her. He stared down at his boots for a long time, his mouth working. Finally, he lifted his head and tentatively met her eyes.

"I...well, I was...but it was more than that, Abbie." Colt nervously cleared his throat. "Well...men just don't cry. At least, I don't. And I enjoyed the hell out of our kiss." He closed his eyes momentarily and then reopened them, looking up at the rafters, which were hung with swags of fresh pine and red ribbons. "I didn't see it coming. One moment I was kissing you and enjoying every second of it. The next thing I realized, this stuff was running down my face."

Gently, Abbie said, "Do you know what the tears were

about?" She thought she knew, but wasn't going to say. Colt had to give voice to his trauma, not her.

Struggling mightily, Colt looked around. His mouth became a slash. Damn, it was happening again! He could feel that fist of pressure tightening around his heart, and he could feel the heated prick of tears at the back of his eyes. Just Abbie's voice was triggering all of this. Colt fought his feelings savagely. It seemed like he stood there an hour instead of just a minute grappling with the knot of emotions and tears that so badly wanted to vomit out of him. Finally, he got a handle on himself. Giving her a narrowed look, he rasped, "Yeah…it's about those missions over in Kosovo."

Abbie nodded, feeling as if she were walking on fragile eggs with Colt. He looked unhappy, his eyes burning with unexpressed emotions. How many times had Abbie seen this in Ted's eyes when he would come home after a traumatic mission? This was no different. Taking a huge risk, she walked up to Colt and placed her hand tentatively on his, which was balled into a tense fist at his side.

"Sometimes I hate our society, Colt. I see the damage it has done to men and women. Little boys are taught that it's not okay to cry, to show their feelings or talk about them. And so you go through life believing that if you do have feelings or tears, everyone will think you're weak and unmanly." She grimaced. "What a crock. If God hadn't given you tear ducts and a heart to feel with, that would be one thing. But he did."

She squeezed his hand. "I wasn't surprised at your tears, Colt. I can feel such pain and suffering around you. I figured it probably had to do with those missions you were on. All I could hope for was that you might trust me enough to let all that darkness spill out of you, let me be a shoulder to cry on…a set of ears to listen without judgment to what you went through and survived. That was all I wanted." Abbie gave him a slight smile and drowned in his stormy looking eyes. "I don't know about you, but when I cry, it feels so good to get it out of my system. I feel much better afterward. And there're so many things we should cry over. I felt honored that you'd share your tears with me, Colt. That kiss…those moments were very special to me. And I hoped they were to you, too…."

Had she said too much? Abbie cringed inwardly, then watched Colt's face in awe. Her words seemed to have had a profound physical effect on him. His brow, once scrunched, was easing. His eyes were losing that hurt and hardness. Most of all, his mouth was losing that tight look of silent, anguished suffering. She felt his fist relax and he enclosed her hand within his.

"I'm scared, Abbie." There. It was out. Colt braced himself. He saw her eyes flare with surprise and then… understanding. Her lips parted and she whispered his name like a prayer.

"Oh, Colt…you don't ever have to be afraid of me…."

Heartened, he rasped, "I figured you'd be royally pissed off at me, running out of there like the coward I was."

Shaking her head, Abbie forced back the tears that wanted to rush into her eyes. "I knew something had happened, Colt. I didn't know *what*. But I knew it wasn't me, either. It was something deep within you…and it had caught you off guard, judging by the look on your face." Taking a huge risk, Abbie leaned upward on tiptoe and placed a warm kiss on his cheek, then eased away from him. She saw pleasure replace his pain for a moment at her bold action. Her heart soared with elation.

"Colt, you were scared. And running from your fear. Well…" Abbie looked fondly around the warm kitchen, where sunlight poured through the Victorian lace curtains over the window above the sink. "I've been running for nearly two years, ever since Ted died. When I realized what I was doing, and that it wasn't healthy for me long-term, I stopped it. I faced the music. I faced the fact he was dead and not ever coming back." She touched her chest, above her heart. "The miracle was that when I did that, I started to heal, Colt." Giving him a look of pride, she said, "You came back here...to face me. You didn't have to—you could have hidden in that condo again. You're a lot braver than you give yourself credit for Colt."

Realizing her wisdom was based upon the harsh experience of losing someone she loved deeply, he nodded. "I hear you. I'm not proud of what I did to you, Abbie. I was scared. I still am. Right now, I feel like I'm in a helicopter that's tumbling out of my control." Giving her a long, intense look, he drowned in her shimmering blue eyes. "There's something about you that's triggering all this dark stuff in me. It wants to come out. I'm trying to sit on it, but it's alive, like a monster inside me, eating me up."

"I know, Colt. I know...." Abbie wanted to throw her arms around him. She saw his pain so clearly in his eyes. "I've been through that same gauntlet you're going through right now. My trauma wasn't over missions, but it was about death and loss, and that's something we share in common."

"The only difference," Colt said gruffly, releasing her hand, "is that you've survived your run through that gauntlet and I'm not sure I can or will…and I don't want to put you in the line of fire, either. You don't deserve to be hurt, Abbie. That's what really bothered me about all this—hurting you. You're innocent."

Whispering his name, Abbie risked everything and stepped up to him. She placed her hands on his cheeks and looked deeply into his distraught eyes. Right now, Colt was hurting so much that she couldn't stand there and not do something to try and help him. "You're innocent, too, Colt. Bad things happen to good people all the time, I've discovered." Her voice grew husky with unshed tears. "What matters is that you know I'm here for you in whatever way is comfortable for you. Okay? I don't expect anything from you, Colt. Let me be your friend? A shoulder to lean on…maybe cry on if you feel like it? I don't run when things get bad. I've weathered plenty of storms. I feel like I can help you with your storm—if you'll let me?" She held her breath.

Gently, Colt took her hands in his. Her face was open and incredibly trusting. "You're a brave woman, Abbie.

The way I feel right now, I don't know anyone who'd make the same offer to me that you have."

"I can stand the heat in the kitchen, Colt. Just try me." Abbie gave him an uneven smile that she didn't feel, because inwardly she was weeping for all the pain and grief he was carrying.

Shrugging back his shoulders, he gave her a warm look. "Okay...you're on, pardner. But if I get out of hand, just tell me. I'll slink back to the condo and nurse my wounds alone. Fair enough?" The last thing Colt wanted to do was hurt Abbie. She was putting herself out for him and he was going to try and keep her out of his line of fire.

"Great," Abbie whispered unsteadily. She eased her hands from his and stepped away. "I think I could use your help in getting my orchid girls over to Morgan and Laura's house. Care to help?" She forced her voice to become bright and cheery. It was not how she felt, but it was what Colt needed. Right now he was raw and unsure of himself, of the boiling emotions that seethed just below the surface.

She hurried to the table and placed one well-wrapped pot of orchids in his large, steady hands. Hands that she wanted to have touch her, love her and draw her tightly against his hard male body. Swallowing, Abbie tried not to pursue that desire. Right now, Colt was hurting. She was sure sex was the last thing on his mind, judging from the unaccustomed brightness she saw in his eyes as he stood there like an awkward little boy, holding the orchid so carefully in his big, pawlike hands.

Looking at the framed picture on the wall opposite the stove, he asked, "Is this the orchid in the photo?"

Abbie looked up as she carefully balanced a clay pot in her hands. "What? Oh, *that* orchid? No, that's another *Cattleya rex,* like the photo in the living room. Remember? I told you about it on the first night we were together?" She laughed gaily. "I wish I had one!"

Colt did remember now. All his memories were centered on Abbie and how good she'd looked and felt in his arms when they had danced together. "So why don't you have it in your collection?"

She smiled wistfully. "Colt, that particular orchid costs a thousand dollars for just one plant! I can't possibly afford it." She gently patted the newspaper wrapped around the orchid she held. "All these girls cost anywhere between twenty and fifty dollars apiece. I have an orchid budget—where I save my pennies for months on end, and then buy one that I want. No, I'm afraid *Cattleya rex,* my most favorite orchid in the universe, is not one I'll ever own."

"A thousand dollars?" Colt frowned. "They cost that much?"

Abbie grinned and opened the door. "Some orchid fanciers have specimens that cost upward of ten to fifty thousand dollars each."

"Wow," he muttered, following her out into the bright sunlight.

Hurrying to her heated van, Abbie took her girls and put them in the back in special boxes, where they would be protected during the short trip. She watched as Colt shut the door to keep the orchids warm. The plants could not survive cold temperatures for long. Anything below fifty-five degrees would kill an orchid.

As he walked back with her to retrieve more plants, his shoulder brushing hers as they trudged through the snow, he slanted a glance down at her. "Knowing the shape I'm in, would you like to go to the dinner with me tonight? Or do you want to put this snarly bear out to pasture so he won't bite you?"

Warmed, she laughed and said, "I'd love to, Colt." Her heart speeded up. The look he gave her was that of a predator hunting its next meal. She absorbed his hungry look and remembered that starved kiss he'd plundered her lips with yesterday. Maybe tonight would be healing to him, as it would be to her....

Colt couldn't keep his eyes off Abbie at the dinner table that evening. The Trayhern house rang with conversation, laughter and the giggling of children. A number of tables, draped with white linen cloths, had been placed in a U shape. Abbie's beautiful, colorful cattleyas were arranged among the silver and gold ribbons that flowed down the center of each table like a glittering creek.

Abbie sat opposite Colt at their table, looking delicious in a fuchsia silk, long-sleeved jacket and slacks. Around her throat she wore a strand of pearls, which she'd told him were a gift from her grandmother, and a set of small pearl earrings. Her eyes reminded him of blue sapphires. The softness of her mouth was permanently branded into his memory, on his lips and within his heart and aching body. She had pulled that wild, curly red hair into a girlish ponytail decorated with a large, pale green cattleya orchid with magenta spots on its lip. She looked exquisitely beautiful.

They sat next to Jake Randolph, his wife, Shah, and

their three children, ages three through ten. The children were like squirming puppies, their laughter and giggles filling Colt with an unexpected joy. To Abbie's right sat Wolf Harding and his blond-haired wife, Sarah, plus their two children, both girls. Part of what made this night so special to Colt was the fact that the mercs had all brought their families. The smiles, the joking and teasing among them was lifting his dark spirits.

On Abbie's left sat Jason Trayhern. Although he wasn't wearing his Annapolis uniform, he still looked all spit and polish in his casual clothes, and painfully correct in his bearing. Colt could see the young man idolized Abbie, and he also saw their special relationship, the doorway that she had to him. Abbie held Jason's heart… just as she did Colt's. That was her gift, Colt realized as he ate the beef Wellington. She knew how to create an opening to people like himself who were closed up and hurting. It was instructional for him to watch her work her natural magic on Jason. Within half an hour of sitting down, Jason was cracking jokes and laughing with her, and warming up to everyone else around him.

Abbie was so special. An ache built in Colt, so powerful and pulverizing that he wanted once more to feel Abbie's soft, smiling mouth against his. He wanted to

drink in, like the starving mongrel he was, her energy, her sunny disposition, her idealism and hope. On some level, Colt knew Abbie could heal him, just as she was helping to heal Jason of his wounds from the past.

Later, after coffee served with a dessert of fruitcake smothered with a white vanilla sauce, Colt mingled with the other families in the den, where brandy and Kahlúa and coffee topped with thick mounds of whipping cream were being served to the adults. Many of the children had gone down into the basement, where Morgan had set up a number of games for them to play. Abbie remained at Colt's side, and he'd taken the bold step of placing his arm around her waist as they moved among the groups and families. When he'd done that, she'd looked up at him, her cheeks flushed and her eyes sparkling with joy over his move. Colt felt like he was walking on air once more.

When the tinkling of a bell sounded, everyone stopped talking and the room grew hushed.

"Come on, everyone!" Laura called excitedly from the living room. "Time to trim the tree!"

Abbie clapped her hands. "I love decorating the tree!" she confided excitedly to Colt.

He grinned lopsidedly. "You're a child in a woman's

body, Abbie." He followed the rest of the merry crowd back to the living room. A number of mercs had helped Laura move the tables out of the center of the room, and they were now against the walls, the dishes and flatwear removed. Abbie's orchids remained, the silver and gold ribbons still on the tables to accent their color and beauty. Boxes of decorations, tinsel and lights had been set out for those who wanted to take part in the decorating.

Laughing liltingly, Abbie hurried ahead of him and went to a box of lights that would have to be strung first. How handsome Colt looked in his black slacks and pale pink shirt. He had shrugged off the charcoal jacket he wore, unbuttoned his cuffs and rolled up the sleeves to his elbows.

"Here," she said breathlessly as she looked over his shoulder at the huge, twenty-foot evergreen, "we need all you tall guys to get up on those ladders and string these lights."

Caught up in her infectious enthusiasm for the tree trimming, Colt took the box from her and headed over to one of three ladders that had been placed around the proud tree standing in the living room. Up on the other ladders were Mike Houston and Morgan. Colt climbed nimbly up as other men positioned themselves below

to help. Teamwork. Yes, that was what it was all about. As Colt sat perched on the ladder, he gazed across the cheerful crowd of onlookers. His gaze fell on Abbie, who stood near the back of the gathered crowd with Jason. Her eyes sparkled with such life that Colt found himself taking a deep breath. Happiness threaded through him, strong and clean. It helped wash away the darkness still inhabiting him.

Much later, after the tree had been trimmed and the children had put on the final touches of silver tinsel, Colt stood back with his arm around Abbie's shoulders to view their handiwork.

"What a beautiful tree!" Abbie sighed softly, giving him a warm look. The night had been magical for her… and him. Every hour that passed, Abbie saw Colt easing more and more out of his self-imposed shell. By the end of the evening, he was a different man. She absorbed his laughter, enjoyed his easy play with the kids, his joking with the other mercs. This was a side of Colt she had not known existed and she loved him fiercely for sharing it with her. This was the healthy side of him; the part that had not been wounded by those deadly missions. Abbie's heart still ached for him. Hope bounded through her for Colt, and for the two of them. All night, whenever possible, he'd had his arm around her waist or shoulders. Or he'd reached out to touch her in some small, but meaningful way. She appreciated his reaching out to her, and she knew Colt was entrusting himself to her…especially his raw emotions and his carefully guarded vulnerability. Abbie ached to love him, ached to be one with him and find herself waking up with him on some cold winter morning, warm and well-loved in his powerful arms.

Was she dreaming? Was it folly? How could she fall so hard for someone so quickly? It frightened her in some ways, but in others, being around Colt felt so natural, as if he were a simple extension of herself. Was this the magic of the five days of Christmas that Laura had always talked about? Christmas was such a healing time of year, anyway, to Abbie. For the last two years, she'd spent them alone, remembering the past. Now, this year, she was fully in the present and looking forward to a future—with Colt. Was she foolish? Crazy? Abbie wasn't sure, but she was going to take that risk and pursue whatever it was that they had. There was no guarantee of a happy outcome, she knew. Colt was wounded. And although he was showing her in so many small ways that he liked her, she knew it probably didn't match the power of her own emotions toward him. No, only time would tell, and she trusted herself enough to grant herself that gift.

"Come here," Colt whispered dangerously near her ear.

Abbie grinned and looked up at him as he gently grasped her arm and led her out of the living room, where everyone was singing Christmas carols. "Colt! Where are we going?" She laughed breathlessly as he led her into the den, now empty of people.

Giving her a wicked look, he placed her beneath the copper lamp that hung suspended in the center of the den. "Right here," he said, his smile widening.

Loving his unexpected spontaneity, Abbie looked up. There, suspended beneath the lamp on a bright crimson ribbon, was a huge sprig of mistletoe.

"Uh-oh," she murmured. "I'm in trouble."

"Are you ever, sweetheart. Come here…." Colt stepped up to her, slid his massive arms around her slender form and brought her fully against him. As he leaned down, he saw joy, like gold flecks of sunlight, in her eyes. She lifted her arms and slid them over his shoulders. Her lips parted. Groaning, he leaned down and captured them, a man starving for light instead of darkness.

The tune of "Oh Come All Ye Faithful" floated into

the room and surrounded them as Katy Trayhern, an accomplished musician, took to the piano. Abbie moaned softly as Colt's lips grazed hers. How glad she was that he had stolen her away! Had he read her mind? Known that she was desperately hungry and craving another kiss from him? Abbie sighed and fell against him, allowing Colt to take her full weight. With him, she was safe, and she knew it.

Colt quivered as she brazenly met and returned the fire of his aching kiss. Abbie was bold. She set him ablaze with her lips, caressing his with wantonness. Feeling the soft press of her breasts against his chest, he slid his hands downward across her small, strong spine and wide hips— hips roomy enough to carry a baby someday.

In those molten moments, with the Christmas music surrounding them and their bodies melting against one another, Colt could only feel desire, happiness and a deep, aching longing in his soul to make Abbie his forever. As he threaded his fingers through her ponytail and eased her away from him, her eyes were slumberous with desire—for him. Her lips were wet and well kissed. He saw her smile drowsily.

"Wow…" she whispered unsteadily.

With this woman in his arms who he considered more

magical than real, a woman who held his heart so tenderly that he didn't know what to do or say, Colt could only stand there, grinning. All he knew was that he was looking forward to the fourth day of Christmas with Abbie, tomorrow. His life, his heart, his soul were inexplicably tied to her. And although Colt still tasted the fear of his dark, wounded side, for at least this moment he wanted to pretend it wasn't there and that Abbie was all that existed in his miserable life. She was light to his eternal darkness. Light.

5

Christmas Eve, December 24

There was no way to gird himself for this Christmas Eve ahead of him. As Colt entered the second floor of the Veterans Hospital, which was located in Anaconda, Montana, his hands full of gifts for those who were bed-ridden, he was grateful for Abbie's nearness. She would help him get through this visit.

Every year, Morgan and Laura, along with the Perseus employees and spouses, took a bus to Anaconda, Montana, a large city southeast of Philipsburg, to visit the Veterans Hospital. The vets there came from all the U.S. military services. Anyone who had served could take advantage of VA hospitals for wounds gained in combat, or if they had no medical insurance of their own, to receive medical help during their civilian years. Veterans hospitals were spread across the states to care for those who had given so much to their country.

As members of Perseus split up to cover the five floors, Colt and Abbie took the second one, where most of the vets were from the Korean and Vietnam eras. Swallowing hard, he felt his gut tightening with a lot of suppressed emotions as they stepped onto the green-and-white tiled floor. On either side of the huge ward, white-haired men lay in white beds, their faces aged, but their expressions alert and expectant looking. Few of these vets had visitors, and he knew how much they looked forward to anyone who would spend a few minutes with them. Families could be hundreds, even thousands of miles away, so most vets languished alone, without support from loved ones or friends. That's why visits such as this were so important. It helped their morale and let them know that others appreciated their patriotic gift.

Colt carried two huge wicker baskets containing Christmas sacks for each vet. Abbie and the other women of Perseus had tucked many thoughtful and useful items into gaily decorated sacks to give to each patient in the ward. There was a slice of thick fruitcake in a plastic box, vanilla sauce in another, plus plastic flatware and a bright red napkin. A twenty-dollar phone card was included so that a veteran who was bed-bound could call his family over the Christmas holiday, along with a gold envelope that contained a hundred dollars in cash. Most vets earned meager government stipends and lived below the poverty level, so the money would come in handy.

His mouth growing dry as they walked past the swinging doors, Colt spotted a number of orderlies, men and women, dressed in white uniforms. One woman, a registered nurse with short black hair and dancing blue eyes, hurried over to them.

"Hey, we're glad you came! The guys here have been waiting for you." She smiled and gestured toward the ward. "The only one you can't give fruitcake to is down there at the end—Mr. Charles Langford. Charlie's blind and has diabetes, so he can't have sugar products." The nurse looked up at Colt. "Why don't you visit with him, sir? He just got a letter from his son, who's over in Kosovo serving in the army? I don't have time to read it to him. I'm sure he'd like you to do that for him. That's a Christmas gift in itself."

Nodding, Colt said, "Yeah, be happy to." *Liar.* He was scared. *Kosovo.* He glanced over at the old man named

Charlie, who was sitting up in bed, clothed in wrinkled blue pajamas that seemed too large for him. *Great.* Talking with a man who had a son in Kosovo was the *last* thing Colt wanted to do, but the nurse had already taken the wicker basket from him and set it on a nearby gurney. Then she gripped Colt by the arm and propelled him down the highly polished aisle to the last bed on the right.

"Hey, Charlie! You've got a visitor…." She looked up at Colt as she steered him to the man's bedside and drew out a chair for him to sit on. "Your name, sir?"

"Colt," he told her uncomfortably as he sat down.

"Charlie, meet Colt." The nurse leaned over and patted the sixty-year-old vet's stooped shoulders.

Charlie gave her a slight smile. He lifted his long, thin arm, his large-knuckled fingers extended outward. "Hey, Colt…where are you, son? Nurse Jones here was promising me that someone would read my boy's letter to me." He gripped the badly wrinkled letter in his other hand. "I'd be mighty appreciative if you could do that."

"Of course," he murmured. Charlie had obviously hung on to that letter like life itself; it was wrinkled and worn from the old vet handling it so much. Colt felt panicked when Nurse Jones hurried away. Turning his full attention to the vet, he saw that Charlie's eyes were a milky, opaque color. He was totally blind, Colt realized. Mouth tightening, he lifted his hand and met Charlie's outstretched one. The old man's fingers wrapped strongly around his.

"Good to meet you, Colt. They said Morgan Trayhern's people were comin' in this morning. We've been pretty excited all week. We don't get many visitors, you know? I've been here for five years now." He grimaced. "This diabetes is killin' me inches at a time." He managed a sour smile, trying to make a joke despite the serious nature of his illness.

Squeezing Charlie's hand, Colt released it as if it was a hot poker burning him. He looked up to see Abbie chatting excitedly with vets on the other side of the ward. Each man lit up like a lightbulb beneath her effusive warmth and care. Uneasily, he returned his attention to Charlie. "I'm sorry to hear that," he murmured. When he realized that Charlie had one leg missing up to his knee beneath the mass of blankets, Colt winced. When diabetes was serious, gangrene would set in, and then that part of the body had to be amputated or the person would die. The man's skin was washed out and he was gaunt looking. His hair hung in a semicircle, like a halo, around his bald, shining head. Silvery hairs stuck out like a hen's nest, in need of a combing. Despite the old soldier's medical condition, Colt couldn't resist the smile on his nearly toothless mouth. It was clear the man had been through hell, and yet he was still in good spirits.

"What war did you serve in, sir?" Colt asked.

Charlie sobered. "I was in Korea with the marines at the Frozen Chosin."

"Helluva place."

"Helluva place," Charlie agreed grimly. "Got my legs shot up there. Nearly froze to death. One of my buddies paid with his life to get me help." His smile dissolved. "I've been in and out of VA hospitals since then. About twenty years ago, I got diabetes. My son, who's serving in the Army M.P.s—military police—over in Kosovo, is real worried about me. My wife, Wanda, died five years ago, and now—" he sighed "—I'm a full-time resident here." He brightened and held up the badly worn white envelope. "This is from Stephen, my son. It would be a heck of a Christmas gift if you could read it to me. I'd be forever grateful. Nurse Jones usually reads his mail to me, but they've had emergencies going on for the last two days and no one has had time to spend with me to read it. Maybe you could?"

He held out the envelope to Colt. His hand was trembling badly.

Colt hesitantly took the crinkled letter. It was still sealed. He saw hope burning in Charlie's heavily lined face. "Sure," he rasped, "I'll do that for you…." And he slowly opened it as if it were going to bite him. He didn't want to know what was inside that envelope. A frisson of fear ran through him.

"I'm so proud of my son," Charlie said. "He's an officer, you know. A captain. A chip off the old block here." He managed a strained laugh. "Well, I wasn't too happy at first that he chose the Army over the Marine Corps. I'd have liked him to have been a marine, but it was his choice." Opening his hands, he added, "I worry atrociously about him. He's up there on the front lines tryin' to keep peace between the Serbs and the Kosovars. The people hate each other over there. And over what? Religion, of all things! Whatever happened to 'love thy neighbor'? Where is tolerance? They're a crazy bunch over there, if you ask me."

His conscience eating at him, Colt felt his mouth drying up. He longed for a glass of water, anything to ease the pain forming like a fist in his chest region as he slowly opened the typed letter. "It's bad over there," he managed to say in a strained tone.

Charlie sat forward, attentive, his face glowing with expectation at having the letter read.

Taking a deep, ragged breath, Colt began to read out loud to him.

"Hi Dad...I hope this reaches you by Christmas. I'm sorry I can't be there. I know Frannie is sending you a box of goodies, so let me know if it arrives in time? She said she was making you some sugar-free cookies that you could eat a little of once a day. Just be sure and clear it with your doc first, okay?"

"Frannie is his wife," Charlie said excitedly. He rubbed his hand together in anticipation. "Ain't got the box yet. Bet it will arrive today...I hope...."

Colt heard the excitement in his voice. There were tears glimmering in Charlie's eyes. Shutting his own eyes tightly, Colt dragged in another breath of air. He felt like he was suffocating. Forcing his eyes open once more, he went on.

"I don't know what to do, Dad. This place is hell on earth. The people hate one another. I never knew what hate was till me and my company came over here. They keep telling us to keep the peace, but Dad, it's worse than any nightmare I could concoct. I survived the Gulf War and felt lucky, but this place is worse...."

Colt hesitated. His voice became choked. Glancing up, he saw Charlie's face go slack and heavy with concern. Colt's heart began to pound in earnest as he forced himself to go on.

"Yesterday, we found the body of a dead Kosovar girl. She'd wandered into a Serb part of town, chasing her little puppy, which had gotten loose. They'd stoned her to death before we could reach her because she was on their property. She was just fourteen, so pretty...what a waste of life."

"My poor son," Charlie whispered. He ran his hands across his face and sniffed. "Oh, my poor boy...how awful. And that little girl... I just can't believe it...I just can't. An innocent child..."

Colt fought his own reaction. The words blurred on the paper. The letter trembled in his hand. Flashes of what he'd seen—the blood, the screams, the terror—avalanched through him. Sweat popped out on his deeply furrowed brow as he sat there trying to get a handle on his escaping emotions. In an effort to avoid feeling, he looked up at old Charlie. The man was sitting there, his hands tightly clasped in his lap, tears streaming down his face.

"Finish it," he told Colt in an unsteady tone. "I need to hear the rest. My son...he's hurting, and I know that hurt. Damn war..."

Colt stood up and sat down on the side of Charlie's bed, his back to the rest of the ward. He didn't want anyone to see his face or the tears glittering dangerously in his own eyes. His hip grazed Charlie's. The old man reached out, found his hand and squeezed it—hard. He continued to hold on to Colt's hand with a clinging grip.

"Please...read the rest?" he quavered.

Shaking his head, Colt forced himself to read the rest of the letter in a low, ragged tone that only Charlie could hear. Colt wasn't sure he could finish it; each word ripped more scar tissue off that bleeding wound within him from his own experiences in Kosovo.

"Dad, I'm sorry to send this letter to you so close to Christmas. You don't need to hear this, but I have to talk to someone about it before it eats me up alive. My men can't see me cry…and I don't ever want to tell Frannie about this. You're my only outlet, and I know you understand because of all that you went through in Korea. I got out of the Humvee and ran over to where the little girl was lying in the middle of that cobblestone street. I hoped she was still alive. Her puppy was sitting next to her, howling. It just tore me up, Dad. I leaned down and felt for a pulse. She was gone. All I could do was pick her up in my arms. She was so pretty. I just stood there with her in my arms, holding her and thinking of our own daughter, Tracey, who is almost the same age. I kept thinking about this poor dead girl's parents and what they would do when they found out she died like this. I wanted to cry so bad, but I knew my men were watching me.

"The street was deserted. The Serbs were hiding inside their homes, but I could feel them watching me…watching us from behind the curtains over the windows. I could feel their hatred and I could feel that they weren't sorry they'd taken this child's life. I mean…my God, she was only fourteen and *innocent*. She had her whole life ahead of her. I took her back to the Humvee and we wrapped her in a blanket. I didn't want to let her go, so I sat in the passenger side and held her in my arms. I didn't want her to be left alone. I wanted her to know someone cared. Some of the guys started to cry, Dad. I tried to stay firm and brave for them. I tried to tell them it was all right, when nothing was, really. I felt so damned helpless and useless to them—to myself.

"And then the puppy started toward us. I ordered my sergeant to grab the little guy. He was about the size of a cantaloupe, and my sergeant stuffed him inside his parka because it was so cold. I figured the Serbs would kill him, too, because he belonged to a Kosovar. I couldn't save the little girl, but we could save her puppy. And then we left and went back to H.Q.

"Back at our bivouac of tents, the puppy has become our mascot of sorts. One of the guys named him Toto, because the little girl reminded all of them of Dorothy from Oz. She'd been wearing a rainbow-colored skirt and a white blouse. In some ways, the puppy has helped us. But he reminds me daily of what I saw. All I can remember is holding her…her face so clean, so unlined and innocent. I go to sleep seeing her. I dream about her, and it's driving me crazy. I don't know what to do. I was hoping you could help me...let me know what will get rid of her face in my nightmares.

"I'm sorry to burden you with this. I wish I could be there with Frannie and Tracey to celebrate Christmas with you, but I can't. Maybe next year, if the army sends me stateside, we can make it. Just know I love you. I wish you were here so we could visit. I always liked the times when we'd sit down and just talk. I know you'd have something to say that could help me through this. Merry Christmas, Dad.

Your loving son,
Stephen."

Colt heard the old man sob. He looked up, and found Charlie blurred before him. The old vet had covered his face with his hand, and was sobbing loudly. Shocked that he would cry so openly in such a public place, Colt sat there frozen for a moment. The words from the letter ripped him apart. He'd seen similar travesties over in Kosovo.

Setting the letter on the bed stand, Colt released Charlie's hand and awkwardly patted the old man's shaking shoulder as he wept unashamedly. Then, driven by something deep within him, Colt opened his arms, drew the thin old man forward and held him while he cried for his son's painful experience. As Charlie laid his head on Colt's shoulder, his weeping grew harsher and deeper. He gripped Colt with his thin arms. Colt closed his eyes and tried to breathe, but it was impossible. The world skidded to a halt for him as he sat there holding a man crying for his son's pain.

Tears jammed into Colt's own eyes. It took everything he had to stop them. Bending his head foreword, he held the old man gently in his embrace and let him weep.

Abbie remained near Colt after they'd left the VA hospital. Their second stop was at the main shelter in Anaconda, St. Mary's Shelter for the Poor, which helped street people and the homeless. Morgan donated a hefty check every holiday in support of the organization's efforts, and the Perseus team always came to help serve the Christmas Eve meal. This was the kind of thing Abbie loved the most—helping those who were not as well off as she was. But now, as she stood behind the counter with Colt, helping him serve the turkey he'd been slicing to those who were standing in line, she saw his face fill with silent suffering.

She knew it had to do with what had happened at the VA hospital. She'd seen Colt holding old Charlie. Even the men on the ward had known that something important and touching was going on between them. Charlie's weeping could be heard throughout the room. The men had remained quiet out of respect. Abbie had watched their faces and saw that before long there wasn't a dry eye in the place. She knew it had to do with the letter, but wisely did not ask Colt for details, even after they'd finished giving out the gift sacks to each veteran.

As she spooned mashed potatoes and savory gravy onto a young woman's tray, Abbie smiled gently at her. The girl was barely fourteen, her black hair matted and uncombed. As she responded with a slight, wobbly smile of her own, Abbie noticed that her clothes were threadbare. Abbie couldn't help crying inwardly for the child. She saw Colt looking at the girl, too, as if she were a nightmare staring back at him. His eyes seemed bloodshot, his mouth a hard line against the suffering he was holding at bay.

Maybe when he took Abbie back to her log cabin tonight, they might be able to talk. She hoped so, because right now, Colt was looking shell-shocked. Abbie knew that whatever transpired in the VA hospital had stirred up Colt's own PTSD symptoms, and he was wrestling with them by the minute. She could feel his ongoing anguish, his pain. And all she wanted to do was provide a safe harbor tonight.... Could she reach out to him? Would he trust her in his vulnerable, raw state?

"Coffee or tea?" Abbie asked as Colt moved tiredly to her kitchen table and sat down. Outside, it was snowing once again. Darkness had long since fallen, and the temperature with it. The scents of cinnamon and orange peel drifting around the warm kitchen from the saucepan on the stove made her feel a tad better. On the bus ride home, Colt had been silent and withdrawn. He'd barely spoken to anyone. She'd seen the worried looks on Morgan and Laura's faces, too.

Colt sat down and wrapped his hands together on the table. "Whiskey," he said abruptly. "I need some. Do you have any?"

Abbie hesitated. The anguish in his tone was harsh and alive. "No...I'm sorry." He refused to look at her, staring at his hands intently. His mouth was tight and it was obvious he was trying hard to hold back his own raging emotions. Moving quietly around the table, she held out her hand to him. "Come here?"

Colt twisted his head at the sound of her gentle voice. He stared at her outstretched hand as if it would bite him. Yet despite the storm roiling unchecked within his heart and gut, he reached out for that slender, strong hand of hers. Right now, he needed Abbie. Desperately.

"Follow me," she whispered as he eased out of the chair and stood up. Leading Colt to her living room, to the overstuffed couch in front of the fireplace, where a wood fire snapped and crackled, Abbie guided him to sit down. When he did, she moved to his side after easing the shoes off her feet. Snuggling next to his bulk, she placed her arms around him and drew him close. At first he resisted. Then she saw his eyes gleam like silver fire, and he capitulated.

Abbie felt diminutive against Colt, but she sighed softly as he slid his arms around her and laid his head against her neck and shoulder.

"There…" she sighed, kissing his hair. "This is better. Much better…" And it was. Christmas music floated unobtrusively around them. The peaceful crackling of the fire reached their ears. Abbie felt Colt begin to relax. In her heart, she knew he needed to be held. Held and kept safe from all that he had experienced today. Her heart soared with the knowledge that she could at least give him this small gift.

"It was a hard day for you," Abbie began gently, and moved her hand up the sleeve of his apricot-colored sweater. "The gift you gave Charlie…well, that was special. You helped him so much, Colt…." Abbie waited. She knew she was treading on thin ice as she broached the subject of Charlie breaking down and weeping unashamedly in his arms. Yet intuitively Abbie understood that this was where the storm within Colt was centered, and it had to be addressed. By providing an opening, she was giving him the opportunity to talk it out if he would. And Abbie knew he needed to talk. She saw his ravaged emotions in his eyes.

Colt nuzzled against Abbie's soft, slender neck. She smelled of a spicy orchid fragrance and her own special scent as a woman. Her arms were strong and caring around him. He desperately absorbed her form, the sound of her husky voice edged with tears. "How did you know?" he managed to ask in a cracked voice.

"Know what, darling?"

"This. That I need this. You."

Abbie laughed gently and rocked him in her arms.

"We all need this, Colt. We all need to be held safe against a world gone mad at times. This is the gift of Christmas. Knowing that other people can reach out and help you, heal you and hold you. We're a big family at Perseus. Morgan and Laura know the hell that everyone goes through, what you might have seen or experienced on a mission…the awful things…. But they also know what helps to heal you—family, care, love and helping others less fortunate than us."

Nodding, Colt closed his eyes tightly and continued to absorb her soft, tremulous voice. Abbie's lips were so close to his cheek. He could feel her moist breath feathering across his flesh.

Her heart was beating in time with his own, her small breasts pressed against his chest. "Yeah," he began brokenly, "I needed this…."

To hell with it, he thought suddenly. He was going to tell her exactly how he felt. Tightening his grip around her for a moment, he rasped, "I need you, Abbie. You're like a bulwark of strength to me right now. I feel so damned weak. I feel like I'm hurtling out of control…."

She rocked him gently back and forth. Tears squeezed from her tightly shut eyes. "We all feel like that, Colt. Life doesn't always deal fair hands to everyone."

He knew she was referring to her husband's death. Yet Abbie had survived it and was flourishing. "I wish I had whatever it is you have…." he said gruffly.

"What?" Abbie choked back a sob as she felt Colt reaching out to her.

"You've survived the hell of losing your husband, and yet you're whole and can move on. Me? I'm nailed by what I saw during those missions over in Kosovo. Today…that letter… Damn it, Abbie, Charlie has a son, an Army M.P. over there…. The letter…" Colt couldn't go on. All he could do was hold her tightly and bury his face against her neck. Violently, his feeling surged upward. Tears leaked from his eyes no matter how hard he tried to force them back.

Abbie opened her eyes and saw the streaks glistening down his hard, taut cheek. Opening her hand, she caught them on her fingertips. "Its all right, Colt. Let it out…all of it. I'll just sit here and hold you…. Please… you're safe with me, darling…."

Abbie knew her words were healing to him. She felt a powerful shudder work through Colt. His arms held her like steel bands and the air rushed out of her lungs from his sudden, hard embrace. The first sob worked up and out of his tormented mouth, and then another. Her entire body shook as he buried his head against her and sobbed again. Oh, why did men fight so hard to run away from their feelings? She closed her eyes, rocked him and held him with her womanly strength for a long, long time.

Finally, the storm within Colt passed. It seemed like a miracle to him as he eased away from Abbie at long last. He had no idea what time it was and he didn't care. Feeling cleaner and more steady than he had in weeks, Colt gave her a burning look of silent thanks. Abbie's expression remained tender and caring. Her lips were parted, and he could see the remnants of tears drying on her own flushed cheeks. How beautiful she looked to him. Raising his hand, Colt grazed her tear-stained flesh with his fingers. "You are so incredible, so strong, Abbie…and I feel like a limp dishrag emotionally in comparison." He forced a one-cornered smile.

She caught his hand, kissed the top of it and held it in her lap. "Part of caring for another person is being there for them, Colt. I knew you needed this—to be held… to be listened to. I saw how much you were hurting."

Nodding, he sagged back against the couch, eased his arm around her shoulders and brought Abbie against him. She came without resistance, her hand resting in the center of his chest, over his heart. "Thank you…"

he murmured gruffly. Leaning over, he pressed a kiss to her unruly red hair. "You're strong, Abbie. I'm so in awe of you. You're small, yet mighty."

She laughed a little and closed her eyes, reveling in his tenderness toward her. This is what *she* needed, whether he realized it or not. Now that Colt was unafraid to show his emotions to her, he was completely vulnerable with her, too. It was a Christmas gift she thought she'd never share with another man. Ever. Not even in her wildest dreams had Abbie thought there could be another man with Ted's sensitivity or ability to share with her. But there was: Colt Hamlin. "You're such a gift to me, Colt...in all ways...."

"Yeah," he griped good-naturedly, "a crybaby."

She looked up at him. Although his eyes were bloodshot, his gaze was clear now. No longer did Abbie see the murky storm of emotions that had been there before. "I happen to like men who can cry. Crying doesn't make you weak, it makes you look strong to me, Colt. Look how much crying helped Charlie...."

Lifting his hand, Colt cupped her small face and studied her shining blue eyes. "I wanted to cry with him, Abbie, in the worst way. But I fought it like hell itself. That letter…well, it was enough to rip the hardest-hearted man apart. It did me."

"It helped to heal you," Abbie said gently. "Like cures like sometimes." She turned her cheek and pressed a kiss into his open palm.

"You're healing to me," Colt rasped unsteadily as he guided her face upward for a kiss. "You look at me, and I feel my heart opening. Your laughter makes me feel hope again, Abbie." He hesitated before he kissed her parting lips. Drowning in her slumberous blue eyes, he whispered roughly, "It's you…all of you, the way you are, that's helping me, supporting me in a way I've never experienced before. I can't explain it…. And whatever it is, sweetheart, I want more of it. I want more of you…."

His words fell around her like a warm blanket of love. Abbie leaned forward, her lips grazing the hard set of his mouth. Colt's eyes were alive once more with tears, and she understood how open and raw he was feeling right now. Lifting her arms, she eased them around his neck and deepened her kiss, her lips sliding tenderly across his until his mouth melted and opened to receive all that she could give him with her heart and soul.

As Abbie swirled in a golden haze of light and de-sire, wrapped in Colt's arms, she knew that somehow, through the fires of his anguish and pain, she was falling in love with this modern-day warrior who'd been so deeply wounded by what he'd seen and experienced. Abbie hadn't expected to be able to love again. She drank headily of his kisses, moving her lips tenderly against his.

Colt finally eased away. He didn't want to, but knew he had to or else. He saw Abbie's brows knit momentarily, saw the question in her eyes as he slid his hands across her shoulders.

"If I don't stop, sweetheart, I'm going to lift you into my arms, carry you off into your bedroom and never let you go." He gave her a humorous look. "And I need your okay to do that, first. It has to be mutual."

Her heart pounding with joy, Abbie caressed his cheek. Colt's eyes were alive with raw, burning desire—for her. "I feel like I'm coming back to life, Colt. I never thought...well, I never thought I'd ever feel again after Ted's death, but I am. Its a miracle...." And it was, Abbie thought as she gazed wonderingly up into his eyes. Just the way his mouth crooked, that confidence and strength in his smile, sent a flash of longing coursing through her.

"You're my miracle," he whispered roughly, not wanting to let her go. "And it's all happening so fast that I'm spinning from it. I really didn't want to help you. Morgan persuaded me, and now I'm glad he did." Brushing his fingers across her unruly hair, he smiled lopsidedly. "I'm scared, Abbie. I need to know how you feel about me…us…if there is an us or not…."

Sighing, Abbie gave him a tender look and snuggled back into his arms, her head in the crook of his shoulder. "There is an us as far as I'm concerned, Colt. And like you, I'm bowled over by our attraction to each other. What you do to me, how you make me feel—it's…wonderful, unexpected."

Was it love? Colt wondered, sinking back against the couch with her in his arms. It had to be, yet he was unwilling to speak those words yet. He was afraid Abbie might run or turn him down. "It is for me, too," he confided in a gravelly tone as he ran his fingers slowly across her upper arm. "This is turning into a Christmas I'll never forget," he murmured, kissing the top of her head.

Abbie opened her eyes and stared off through the living room. She felt the solid, heavy beat of Colt's heart beneath her palm. "Do dreams come true, Colt? Or am I a dyed-in-the-wool romantic who doesn't have a prayer?"

Chuckling, he rasped, "We have a chance, Abbie. Wanting a relationship is the first step."

Her heart thudded. "Do you?"

He felt her grow still in his arms. Fear sizzled through him. He forced the truth out. "Yes." And even more fear shot through him. "Do you?"

Abbie whispered, "Yes…but I'm afraid, Colt. I don't know of *what,* I just am."

"Maybe because things have been happening so fast. Maybe because of your loss of Ted…"

She sat up and eased away just enough to look deeply into his hooded eyes, which still regarded her with desire. "Do we have the time? Are you going back on the merc schedule soon?" Inwardly, Abbie was fearful. Would she lose Colt, too? Oh, she knew Ted had died in a stupid automobile accident, not on a mission. But every time he'd gone on a mission, there was a chance he'd never return. Abbie knew she couldn't put herself through that emotional gauntlet again and survive. Did she have the right to tell Colt that? Anguished, Abbie searched his vulnerable face. Her heart, her body, responded wildly to his look. How badly she wanted to make love to Colt. But to do that, there had to be something of substance, something lasting, between them. She waited painfully for his answer.

Searching her eyes, Colt sensed her trepidation about the possibility of his returning to mission status. "Right now, the way I'm stoved up from the last one, I'm not going back on the roster, Abbie. I have to leave after Christmas to go visit my dad in Florida, to make sure he's okay and see if he needs anything. Then—" he shrugged, "—I was going to come back here in hopes that we could pick up where we left off."

Relief flooded through her. Wetting her lips, Abbie whispered, "Yes…I'd like that, Colt. I really would…."

His grin was boyish. "Yeah?"

She giggled a little. "Oh, yes."

He touched an errant curl near her cheek and twisted it gently around his index finger. "I gotta get going now…got some stuff that needs taking care of…."

Abbie tried to hide her disappointment. She wanted Colt to stay, but lacked the courage to ask him. Okay…"

"Tomorrow we have brunch over at the Trayherns, and then the kids get to open up their Christmas presents. May I escort you?"

Sometimes he was so achingly formal. Abbie gave him a tender smile and grazed his stubbled cheek, which felt like sandpaper beneath her sensitive fingers. "Of course you can. It's my favorite day, Colt. The kids—" she laughed excitedly "—oh, the kids love it! Morgan and Laura buy everyone a gift, including the adults. They're such generous people—almost to a fault. But the children just go crazy. I love to watch them digging for their own gift in the pile under the Christmas tree."

Colt absorbed the shining quality in Abbie's eyes. "You were made to be a mother," he told her quietly. And she was. The unexpected thought that he could give her the greatest gift of love—a baby—filled him with a sense of power that set his heart pounding. There was no question that he was falling helplessly in love with this sunny woman with red hair and an incredibly giving heart.

"I'll see you tomorrow morning," he promised with a growl. There was something very, very special he had to do first....

6

December 25, Christmas Day

Abbie sat on one end of the couch with Colt's arm around her shoulders as they waited for Morgan and Laura to begin passing out the gifts from beneath the huge, sparkling Christmas tree. Sighing happily, Abbie felt a contentment that she'd never thought she'd feel again. With snowflakes twirling lazily outside the huge picture windows of the Trayherns' massive living room, Christmas was as beautiful as a picture postcard.

It had snowed all night, so the evergreens surrounding the cedar home, the rounded hills embracing it and the massive Rocky Mountains in the distance all had a new layer of glistening powdered sugar. The sky was a leaden gray and hung low, promising more snow throughout the day. That was all right with Abbie.

Her heart, her thoughts, were centered on Colt, and she was enjoying his nearness. She hadn't slept much last night because her feelings churned from giddy joy to abject terror. Colt's ability to shed his hard warrior mask and be incredibly human with her had forced her to look at what she really wanted out of life.

Giving Colt a tender look, she watched one corner of his mouth crook in a grin as he met and held her gaze. Abbie felt him squeeze her shoulders gently. All around them, the volume of noise was rising as the children sat in a semicircle around the tree, squirming eagerly as they waited for the gifts to be handed out. The adults had cameras or videocams ready to record the exciting event.

"You think these kids are going to make it?" Colt asked her, his lips near her ear.

Abbie giggled. "They look like they're going to burst with excitement, don't they?" The littlest children, beaming with barely contained anticipation, had scooted up to within inches of where Morgan and Laura stood in front of the tree. The older children sat back with more decorum and patience. It was the littlest tykes, the ones who believed fervently in the spirit of Santa Claus, who kept crowding right up to the gift givers' feet.

"Yeah, they do. It's nice to see that kind of innocence," Colt replied, gazing down at Abbie. She looked beautiful this morning. He had learned that she loved velvet, and today she wore a violet-colored velvet turtleneck along with some very sensual looking black satin jeans that were driving him crazy. A spray of white Dendrobium orchids with red lips, which hailed from Australia, was fastened expertly into her gleaming, curly hair, which she'd tamed and clipped up at the back of her head. The resulting cascade of curls shone gold and copper in the light of the chandeliers above them.

Abbie absorbed his words and saw the happiness in his eyes. Colt looked so handsome this morning. He wore a white cowboy shirt with pearl snaps, a tan-colored corduroy sport coat, dark brown slacks and his black cowboy boots. She had the maddening urge to tame that slight, rebellious curl that dipped over his brow back into place, but she stopped herself. When she was around Colt, Abbie found herself wanting to touch him all the time. From the moment they'd arrived this morning for brunch, Colt had kept his arm either around her waist or around her shoulders, and it had raised some eyebrows.

Abbie had seen many of Colt's friends nod and smile at them, as if approving of their newfound closeness. Especially Laura, who practically beamed like the rising sun.

"May I have your attention for just a second?" Morgan called out in his deep baritone voice. He held up his hands, a grin on his face. Dressed in a bright red sweater, comfortable Levi's and cowboy boots, he looked down at his wife.

Laura laughed. Gazing down fondly at the eager three-, four- and five-year-olds gathered anxiously around their feet, she said, "You'd better hurry, darling, or these kids are going to overwhelm your position, tactically speaking." Today Laura had chosen a gold lamé long-sleeved top with a glittering red-green-and-white scarf around her neck. Since satin jeans were the rage, she wore a pair of wine-colored ones with her sensible black loafers. Smiling down at the excited, squirming children, she said, "Better hurry, Morgan, they're going to overrun us any moment now!"

Everyone laughed.

Morgan chuckled and gave the children at his feet a warm look. Off to his right was his son, once again in his dark blue uniform with shining brass buttons down the front.

"Well, I guess if I don't want to get swarmed, I'll make my thirty-minute speech very, very short."

There was a collective groan from the crowd. No one wanted a long speech at this point, particularly the antsy, eager children.

"How about a two-minute speech?" he asked, grinning.

Everyone clapped and cheered.

Laughing, Morgan slid his arm around his wife and drew her near. "Everyone, we're glad you were here to celebrate Christmas with us." He gave Laura a look of love and pride. "This was her idea, not mine, but over the years I've come to see that it's a great one."

Again there were claps and cheers.

Laura laughed. "We want to thank all the hard workers behind the scenes who helped bring this off. You know who you are. And we hope that you have a wonderful Christmas Day. Morgan? Should we start handing out the presents?"

The children leaped to their feet, screeching and clapping loudly. The adults broke into laughter.

Morgan raised his thick, black eyebrows. "I think we'd better, Laura, or they're going to charge us."

Abbie watched as Laura and Morgan went to the massive tree and began pulling out the bright, colorfully wrapped presents. She knew that Laura had gone to great lengths to contact the mothers to find out what each child would like to have for Christmas. Because Perseus was top-heavy with money, the Trayherns spared no expense on the many charities they funded around the globe, nor did they stint on holiday gifts for the kids.

Colt sat there, Abbie beneath his arm, her warm body leaning against him while he watched the children's faces light up with anticipation as the gifts were quickly distributed. Giving her a glance, Colt saw that her cheeks were suffused with pink. Her hands clasped on her knees, she was raptly watching the children, a soft smile playing across her lips.

How badly he wanted her. All of her. Colt had done a lot of thinking last night, and he'd had a long talk with Morgan earlier this morning before everyone had come to brunch. Would Abbie approve of his new plan?

He noticed that when they'd strolled into the living room earlier, before everyone settled around the U-shaped table for brunch, she'd spotted the three-foot-tall, gold-foil-wrapped gift with a huge, bright red ribbon on top, at the rear of the Christmas tree. She'd commented that some lucky little kid was going to get a really big gift. Colt had smiled and said nothing. Little did she know that gift was for her!

Although the Trayherns gave everyone a present, parents included, no one else was exchanging gifts at this party. However, Laura had enthusiastically endorsed Colt's idea that he give his gift to Abbie after all the others had been distributed. His heart hammered briefly with anxiety. Would Abbie like it? Would she see the symbolism behind it? Realize what he hoped for them? Or would she be horribly embarrassed? Angry at him? Colt wasn't sure. However, when he'd talked to Laura about it, she'd been over-the-moon enthusiastic. Her blatant approval had convinced Colt to go ahead with his wild plan. Now, if only Abbie would approve of what he'd done....

Morgan stood amid the torn Christmas paper, bows and ribbon. Laura stood with him, a satisfied expression on her face. The children were already raptly playing with their new toys, lost in their own happy world.

"Morgan, dear..."

"Yes?" He smiled down at her and then lifted his chin and held up his hands. Everyone began to quiet except the little ones.

"I think..." Laura said dramatically, "that there's one

gift still left under our Christmas tree. Did you not hand it out for a reason, dear? Hmm?"

Grinning mischievously, Morgan gave his wife a teasing look. "You can really ham it up, can't you?"

Everyone tittered at their obvious dramatics.

"I'm not the one who is gulping down Krispy Kreme doughnuts, darling. The only ham around here is standing next to me...."

The crowd erupted with laughter and giggling.

Morgan frowned good-naturedly and patted his waistline. "Well, it's true I've got a little more 'ham' than I should...." He chuckled. Waving his hand toward his audience, he said, "We have a very special occasion for a very special person. Colt? Would you like to come up and tell us more?"

Abbie looked up at him as his name was called. She saw trepidation in his expression as he looked down at her. Giving her a slight smile, he stood up. What was going on? Morgan and Laura were beaming at him like proud parents.

The crowd quieted as Colt carefully wove his way through the scattered gift wrap, children and toys. Sitting up, Abbie saw Laura smiling widely at her from across the room. Something was going to happen, she sensed. Colt went to the back of the tree to carefully pick up the gold-wrapped gift with the huge red bow. As he brought it forward and held it in his hands, the Trayherns moved off to one side, arm in arm, waiting expectantly for him to speak.

The room grew very quiet.

Colt looked around. He nervously cleared his throat. "I want to thank Morgan and Laura for letting me do this," he said, nodding in their direction. Colt's heart hammered with anxiety. He saw the quizzical look on Abbie's face. She didn't have a clue; that was good. Managing a boyish, shy smile, Colt said, "I'm not much good at speeches. In fact, standing up here is like getting put in front of a firing squad."

Everyone tittered.

Swaying from one foot to the other, Colt held Abbie's gaze. Swallowing hard, he forced himself to speak. "Sometimes life has a funny, quirky way of handing out gifts that we never expect to receive. Five days ago, I met Abbie. I was just going to help her behind the scenes here, and that was all. But she has a way of making a person feel good about himself, making him feel that he's a part of her world and life." Colt saw Abbie's expression grow soft.

"And with the Trayherns' approval—" he lifted the package "—I wanted to give Abbie something that comes from my heart to hers. I've seen her give so much to everyone else that I felt this special gift was deserved. Abbie? You want to come up and open it? Please?" He held his breath as she sat there with a stunned look on her face.

And then she stood.

Everyone cheered loudly, calling her name and urging her to go up there.

Winding her way among the children, toys and scattered gift wrap that littered the room from one end to another, Abbie came forward amid the clapping.

Her cheeks had high color as she approached. Colt handed her the gift and then pulled up a chair so that she could sit down and open it in front of everyone.

"Colt?" she whispered. "What is this all about?"

His mouth stretched in a smile. "It's for you, Abbie. Go ahead and open it. Don't tip it, though. It has to stay upright. Okay?"

Abbie sat and smiled at the crowd. "I don't know what this is all about," she said with a laugh.

"She will!" Laura called out gaily.

Laughter circled the room.

With trembling fingers, Abbie carefully removed the exquisite wrap and ribbon, keeping the box upright on her lap. Colt was at her side, his expression one of pride and, if she wasn't mistaken, of love—for her. Heart pounding as she set the box on the floor next to the chair to open the top, she felt Colt's large hand on her shoulder.

As Abbie opened it, she gasped. She jerked her head up and twisted to look up at Colt, who was grinning unevenly. His eyes were alive with warmth and anxiety.

"Colt!" she gasped. "You didn't!"

He became terribly bashful and avoided her widening eyes. "It's for you, Abbie...."

Disbelievingly, Abbie quickly pulled the huge, vibrant orchid out of the box. It had been swathed in bubble wrap to protect it. Colt knelt down on one knee next to her and held the clay pot while she removed the packing material from around the lush bloom.

"Oh!" Abbie whispered as Colt held the exotic plant toward her. "It's a *Cattleya rex!* Oh!" She reached out with trembling fingers to touch one of the six stunning blossoms.

Everyone clapped and cheered.

Abbie was speechless. Colt smiled up at her as he

placed the pot in her hands. He saw the tears swimming in her eyes.

"How…" she began brokenly as she looked down at the healthy green plant in her hands.

Feeling good at her reaction, Colt leaned forward and kissed her on her flaming cheek. The crowd erupted with lusty cheers.

"I called up an orchid warehouse in California. The guy had one plant and I had him ship it here overnight." He gazed into her wide blue eyes, which sparkled with gold in their depths. He saw how happy the gift made Abbie, and his heart swelled with pride and joy. Colt knew now that he'd made the right decision to get the orchid.

Tears slipped down Abbie's cheeks as she stood and held up the gorgeous white blooms, with their yellow and fuschia lips, for all to see. After the applause and whistles subsided, she said, "What you don't know is how rare and expensive this particular orchid is. It's called the Christmas orchid." She gave Colt, who was now standing self-consciously at her side, his hands clasped in front of him, a tender look. "And this guy…well, I'm stunned at his gift. It costs so much…and I've always dreamed of owning one someday." She smiled brokenly. "Of course, on a teacher's salary, that would never happen."

Everyone laughed.

Colt placed his arm around her. "What Abbie doesn't know is that, to me, she's like this orchid—rare and special. I found out orchids can live to be over fifty years old." Giving her a fond look, he rasped, "And this is my way of hoping that what we have will last as long...or even longer. But like an orchid, friendship takes a lot of care, feeding and watering. I'm willing to do that if she is...."

"Colt, this is such a surprise...the orchid is so beautiful," Abbie sighed as she looked at it one more time. It sat in the center of her kitchen table as she and Colt enjoyed a cup of eggnog in the late afternoon. Her hands around the bright red ceramic cup, Abbie gave him a smile and shook her head. "I'm still in shock. This orchid cost you a lot of money."

Shrugging, he said, "What's money, Abbie? Look at the Trayherns. They're worth multimillions. They give a lot of it away." He gazed at one of the huge blossoms, nearly the size of his fist, and then held her teary gaze. "I wanted in some way to tell you how much you've come to mean to me. When you told me that it was your favorite orchid, and that you'd never be able to have one… well, I wanted to make that dream come true for you. It was the least I could do for all you've done for me."

Abbie gave him a wry look. "All the care, watering and feeding?" she teased gently. Her heart opened as he flashed her that shy, boyish look again. How easily touched Colt was.

"Yeah…you could say that, Abbie. I feel like you rescued my soul from a dark, dark place." He pushed his empty cup aside and turned to her. "It's you. Your heart. Your love…" And he grazed her hair with his hand. Her gaze turned lambent with desire—for him.

"I'm so afraid, Colt," Abbie whispered unsteadily, her scalp tingling deliciously at his touch.

"I know you are. And I think I know why…."

She could barely hold Colt's gaze as he quickly wiped her tears away with his thumbs. When he placed his hand on her shoulder, she sniffed. "I'm such a coward, Colt. I—I lost one man…and I'm afraid to lose you, too. You're a merc…."

"I understand," he told her in a deep, quiet tone. Sliding his other hand over hers, which was clenched in her lap, he whispered, "Abbie, I've made some decisions. And you need to hear them." He bowed his head for a moment, worked his mouth and then looked up at her shining blue eyes, which were soft with invitation. He felt her love, her need of him in every fiber of his being. How badly he wanted to return that love, but some things had to be said first. And depending upon how Abbie received the news, Colt knew they'd either move forward with their relationship or it would dissolve. Never in his whole life had he felt as frightened as he did now, because he realized that he loved her with a burning fierceness that would never die.

Abbie sat very still as she watched Colt wrestle with unspoken emotions. His hand curling protectively around her shoulders made her feel a bit better. "W-what do you want to say?"

"That I'm scared to death, Abbie. Scared of how you might take what I say…what I feel…." He shook his craggy head. "Well, here goes. Life's a risk, anyway. Right now, I'm putting my heart in your hands…." He took a deep breath. "Five days ago, when you crashed into my life, I never thought it possible to fall in love with someone so quickly. You just kind of walked in with your sunshine smile and that wide-open heart of yours, Abbie, and took me by storm."

Colt grazed her hair and forced a lopsided smile. Her expression was tender and it gave him the courage to go on. "That's what I feel for you—love. And respect. And I want to keep exploring what I've discovered about us. I know we need time to continue to get to know one another, and I'm more than willing to give us that if you are. This morning, I went over and talked to Morgan. I told him I wanted a desk job here, at the main headquarters of Perseus. I want off the merc mission list for good."

"I—I see…." Abbie gulped. She clung to Colt's gaze, absorbed his hesitant, grazing touches. Hope warred with fear in his eyes. "You wouldn't miss being on missions?" Abbie knew that Ted had lived for that kind of life and would never have left it even if she'd begged him to. Searching Colt's serious expression, she waited.

"Abbie, no matter what you say, what you decide, I'm not going back in the field. I'm done with that part of my life." His mouth quirked. "My last missions over in Kosovo showed me that." Shaking his head, Colt murmured, "No, I want to settle down. You've shown me what I've been longing for deep inside, but it was something I was afraid to even dream about."

"What was that?" Her voice was off-key.

"A family." He shrugged heavily. "Kids… Just being

a part of the last five days, celebrating Christmas, has made me want to settle down and have a family. I think I can be a good father, or at least I'll try to be." Lifting his head, Colt smiled gently at Abbie. "And I know I've found the woman I want as my life partner, who will be the best mother to our children I could ever find."

Shaken, Abbie closed her eyes. She pressed her hand against her eyes, tears spilling down her face. "Oh, Colt..."

"Come here," he urged in a husky voice, and he pulled her chair out and took her in his arms. "I love you, Abbie. Will you give me a chance to prove to you my love is real?"

Slipping into his embrace, Abbie whispered, "Yes... yes, I will, Colt..." After embracing him fervently, she eased away, took his hand in hers and said, "Follow me?"

Wordlessly, he followed her though the living room, past the snapping, crackling fire that warmed the cabin, to her bedroom. Christmas music played softly in the background. The room featured old Victorian lace, a brass bed, a plum-colored velvet quilt that looked very old and well-loved, and dainty white curtains framing the window.

Turning, Abbie looked up at him, her hands resting

on his massive chest. "I don't know how it happened either, darling. I love you...." There, the words were out. The truth hung suspended between them as she saw his green eyes flare with surprise, and then burn with joy. Abbie saw all the tension bleed out of Colt with her softly spoken vow. She began to unsnap each pearl button on his cowboy shirt, one by one. "Like you, I was scared at how powerfully I was drawn to you. And over the last five days I knew...I knew in my heart, Colt, that you were the man I wanted in my life...." Her hands stilled as she met and held his burning gaze. "I know we haven't had the time to really be together...and I want that with you."

Abbie eased the shirt off his massive shoulders, revealing his darkly haired chest. He helped her by placing the shirt over a chair near the wall. As his fingers brushed the hem of her sweater, she whispered, "Now that you're not going to be out in the field anymore, I know we'll have that time...." She smiled tremulously up at him. "Love me? I want to lie with you, love you and be a part of you...."

Her words cascaded like molten heat over Colt. Nodding wordlessly, he eased the sweater off Abbie. She wore an ivory silk camisole beneath it, but no bra. Colt removed the spray of orchids from her hair and unclipped her unruly hair. It fell in silky abandon around her shoulders like a living waterfall.

"Come here...." he rasped as he pulled her onto the bed.

Time slowed until each moment was a thing of beauty to Abbie. As they continued to undress one another, then lay naked and warm on the velvet coverlet, she saw a predatory look come to Colt's eyes. Moving into his arms, her slender form pressed against his hard masculine body, she closed her eyes and lifted her head. Colt's mouth closed over hers with such hunger that a bolt of jagged heat flashed through her. Abbie's lower body exploded with need of him.

She inhaled the sweet pine scent that clung to Colt, and tasted the strength and cajoling power of his mouth as he rocked her lips open. Sliding her hands up his muscled arms to his bunched shoulders, Abbie felt herself being eased onto her back. His fingers trailing fire, he cupped her breast with a gentle but possessive grip. A sigh, a moan of need, escaped her parted, well-kissed lips. As she arched upward, so that her hips met his, his lips settled on one hardened peak. Abbie gave a little cry as he began to suckle strongly.

Her world exploded. Behind her closed eyes, fireworks shimmered in vivid color, sending sparks through her being. Never had Abbie felt so cherished as in this moment. Every touch of Colt's hand as he slid it down her rib cage, across her hip to her thighs, told her how much he loved her. A fierce ache sprang to life as he stroked her moistness, a ragged sigh escaped her. She tried to please Colt in return, but he seemed bent on pleasuring her completely, instead. Abbie felt like a prisoner, captured within his arms, surrounded by his massive body. All she could do was surrender to the white-hot pleasure now throbbing up through her as he continued to stroke her in slow, delicious exploration. How badly she wanted him!

As if sensing that, Colt moved carefully on top of her. Abbie opened her eyes as she felt his knee settle heavily between her thighs. The glint of a hunter who had captured his quarry burned in his eyes as he held her gaze. She smiled tremulously and eased her arms around his damp neck. Without speaking, she moved her hips upward and drew him deeply into herself, and the action freed her soul to fly on wings of joy.

Colt's world shattered. A groan ripped from him as her slender legs wrapped strongly around his and brought him fully into her hot, liquid depths. His mind exploded. No longer did he think; he could only feel. The spicy fragrance of Abbie reached his flared nostrils, her little cries of pleasure rippling through him like fiery caresses. He gripped her hard in his arms, never wanting to let her go. As she arched provocatively, her hips melding with his, he thrust into her. Somewhere in the haze and fire of his being, he knew they were making love without any protection. Yet his heart whispered that even if Abbie became pregnant from their coupling, it was something they both wanted. Above all, Colt wanted to give Abbie the child she'd always wanted, but had been denied.

Time throbbed to a halt as he brought her into heated rhythm with himself. They fit together like two lost puzzle pieces. Each brush of her lips upon his, each movement of her hands, ranging teasingly across his damp, tense body, told him of her love for him. Their primal need for one another culminated rapidly, and within seconds, Colt felt her tense in his arms. He could feel the fiery liquid of her body surround him, and he surged forward, hoping to prolong her pleasure. And then he felt a massive explosion occur, and all he could do was cling to her, their heads resting against one another.

Golden seconds spun between them in the aftermath.

Abbie was breathing in gasps as Colt continued to hold her. Slowly, very slowly, she felt him ease out of her, then gather up the velvet quilt and pull it over them. Sighing happily, she lay her head in the crook of his shoulder, her arm around his rib cage. Her breasts were pressed against his heart, which was pounding in unison with hers. Smiling softly, she nuzzled against him and felt his lips caress her temple and then her hair.

"I love you," she whispered unsteadily.

"I know you do," Colt rasped. Leaning down, he watched her open lustrous blue eyes that glowed with gold in their depths. Abbie was happy.

His heart soared. Colt had desperately wanted to please her, to give her joy to replace the tragedy and loss of the last two years of her life. "I love you, sweetheart. And I want to spend the rest of my life showing you how much you mean to me."

Abbie closed her eyes as Colt caressed her cheek, her neck and shoulder beneath the coverlet. "You're such a gift to me, darling."

He chuckled indulgently. "I hope I'll be like that orchid of yours out there on the table—around for a long, long time."

Laughing softly, Abbie opened her eyes and drowned

in his forest-green ones. How young Colt looked now, with the stress of the days before erased. In some part of her fluttering, joyful heart, she sensed it was because he was no longer going out on missions that could rip him apart inwardly. Everyone had a limit to the amount of trauma they could endure. She knew Colt had reached his. And because he had, he was looking for a new life— a better one…with her.

"And like that orchid, my beloved, you are strong, enduring, and so easy on my eyes…." she whispered.

Colt ran his hand across her slender yet strong, womanly body. "Can you put up with me? Or when I get irritable and cranky, are you going to put me in your greenhouse to cool my heels?"

Giving him a wicked, teasing look, Abbie teethed his earlobe gently. "Not a chance! We'll talk it out. Communication is the key."

Laughing freely, Colt dodged her lips, his ear tingling. "You're going to teach me how to talk to you, Abbie. I admit I'm not good at it…." His smile slipped as he leaned down and captured her soft mouth in a kiss. Eventually, he eased back and whispered, "And I want to learn, because I want to make you happy…forever…."

★ ★ ★ ★ ★